Crimes of Hate

An Anthology

Curated by Bret McCormick

A HellBound Books LLC Publication
Copyright © 2023 by HellBound Books Publishing
LLC
All Rights Reserved

Cover and art design by Timmy Art for
HellBound Books Publishing LLC

No part of this book may be reproduced, stored in a
retrieval system, or transmitted by any means, electronic,
mechanical, photocopying, recording or otherwise without
written permission from the author
This book is a work of fiction. Names, characters,
places and incidents are entirely fictitious or are used
fictitiously and any resemblance to actual persons, living
or dead, events or locales is purely coincidental.

www.hellboundbookspublishing.com

Printed in the United States of America

Crimes of Hate

Contents

Introduction   1
Bret McCormick

The Casque of Amontillado   5
Edgar Allan Poe

I Hate You   13
Jennifer Trumbull

Don't Be Stupid   35
Randall Smith

Psychopaths, Grieving, and Timeslips   71
P.K. Kleypas

SF   197
Steven Purselley

The Last Ray of Summer   247
Anthony Ferguson

Cherry Boy   277
Che Trujillo

Crepuscular   295
Bret McCormick

The Interlopers 329
Saki (H.H. Munro)

Other HellBound Books 340

INTRODUCTION

What do we know about hate?

Most of us recognize hate as one of the most powerful and deadly emotions. As humans we seem to be hardwired for (among other things) hate. Many of the milestones of human history arise from expressions of hate. One of the earliest stories in the Bible concerns a man murdering his brother. Chapter four of Genesis is familiar to everyone, religious or not, because the story of Cain killing Abel is one of the most frequently cited fables in the world. Is our capacity to hate the reason why humans ultimately found themselves at the top of the food chain? And are the most hateful among us the masters of us all?

Everyone admits to hating *something* but cultural influences have civilized the savage breast and the word hate hardly means what it once did. People say, "I hate waiting in line" or "I hate annoying TV ads" or "I hate quiche." But how many of us resort to violence because of these types of hate?

When I was a child it was common for me to hear conversations that went something like this: "I love ice cream!" "You do?" "Yep, I sure do." "Well, if you love it so much why don't you marry it." This banter was considered the height of wit around second or third grade in elementary school. I was amused, years later, to find Pee Wee Herman resurrecting this old chestnut on his Saturday morning kids show.

I also have memories of a lot of kids saying things like "I hate school!" But I don't recall anyone every replying, "If you hate it so much, why don't you murder it?"

We generally believe that murder is the ultimate expression of hate. Of course, people commit murder for all sorts of cold-blooded profit motives as well. But the savagery enacted in the name of hate is rarely carefully planned, more likely it erupts out of a consciousness blinded and overcome by rage. *Blind rage* has been a literary cliché for the better part of recorded history. These murders are the strange fruition of that powerful and destructive emotion we call hate. Why do some of us give in to these murderous impulses while others never even raise a fist?

In compiling this anthology, it was my intention to focus on stories of crime motivated by hate. Not racially, politically, or religiously motivated violence, even though these are labeled 'hate crimes' in contemporary media. Originally I wanted stories in which any 'horror' arose solely from the human psyche. I did not intend to include any stories with supernatural elements. However, as the months rolled by, I found I was receiving few straight tales of hate. Almost all the submissions had some supernatural angle. This may be because the publisher, Hellbound Books, is known for its exceptional catalog of mostly paranormal horror tales. Finally, I relaxed my requirements and accepted some very good supernatural stories about hate.

As I mentioned before, the concept of the crime of hate has been with us since the beginning of man's ability to write of such things. Consequently, it seemed only fitting to include a couple of classic tales dealing with the strange fruition of human hatred. Edgar Allan Poe's ***The Casque of Amontillado*** opens the anthology and ***The Interlopers*** by Saki (H.H. Munro) provides an appropriately hateful bookend as the final tale presented herein. In between these two classic stories you will find seven very imaginative and original creations by some very talented contemporary authors.

Jennifer Trumbull gives us her take on what happens when a privileged young woman with everything going for her decides to kill someone in the aptly titled ***I Hate You***. Randall Smith cautions ***Don't Be Stupid*** in his disturbing tale of an eleven-year-old boy who's not quite right. ***Psychopaths, Grieving and Timeslips*** is a most unusual novella from P.K. Kleypas dealing with hate and the ensuing guilt it can arouse in 'normal' people forced to deal with psychopathic family members. ***SF*** by Steven Purselley is a coming-of-age tale of profound darkness. ***The Last Ray of Summer*** by Anthony Ferguson is another tale of family drama and the extreme measures required to end the acts of a sociopathic father. Che Trujillo offers an inside look at the initiatory practices of an urban gang and a glimpse into the mind of a victim turned killer in ***Cherry Boy. Crepuscular***, my own contribution to this collection, tells of the lingering consequences crimes of hate can generate even decades after the fact.

Immerse yourself in the strange situations and states of consciousness these authors have conjured for your amusement. And be cautioned against unleashing your own crimes of hate on the unsuspecting world.

Bret McCormick 2023

The Casque of Amontillado
Edgar Allan Poe

The thousand injuries of Fortunato I had borne as I best could, but when he ventured upon insult, I vowed revenge. You, who so well know the nature of my soul, will not suppose, however, that I gave utterance to a threat. At length I would be avenged; this was a point definitely settled—but the very definitiveness with which it was resolved, precluded the idea of risk. I must not only punish but punish with impunity. A wrong is unredressed when retribution overtakes its redresser. It is equally unredressed when the avenger fails to make himself felt as such to him who has done the wrong. It must be understood that neither by word nor deed had I given Fortunato cause to doubt my good will. I continued, as was my wont, to smile in his face, and he did not perceive that my smile now was at the thought of his immolation.

He had a weak point—this Fortunato—although in other regards he was a man to be respected and even feared. He prided himself on his connoisseurship in wine. Few Italians have the true virtuoso spirit. For the most part their enthusiasm is adopted to suit the time and opportunity—to practice imposture upon the British and Austrian millionaires. In painting and gemmary, Fortunato, like his countrymen, was a quack—but in the matter of old wines he was sincere. In this respect I did not differ from him materially: I was skillful in the Italian vintages myself and bought largely whenever I could.

It was about dusk, one evening during the supreme madness of the carnival season, that I encountered my friend. He accosted me with excessive warmth, for he had been drinking much. The man wore motley. He had on a tight-fitting parti-striped dress, and his head was surmounted by the conical cap and bells. I was so pleased to see him, that I thought I should never have done wringing his hand. I said to him— "My dear Fortunato, you are luckily met. How remarkably well you are looking today! But I have received a pipe of what passes for Amontillado, and I have my doubts."

"How?" said he. "Amontillado? A pipe? Impossible! And in the middle of the carnival!"

"I have my doubts," I replied, "and I was silly enough to pay the full Amontillado price without consulting you in the matter. You were not to be found, and I was fearful of losing a bargain."

"Amontillado!"

"I have my doubts."

"Amontillado!"

"And I must satisfy them."

"Amontillado!"

"As you are engaged, I am on my way to Luchesi. If anyone has a critical turn, it is he. He will tell me—"

"Luchesi cannot tell Amontillado from Sherry."

"And yet some fools will have it that his taste is a match for your own."

"Come, let us go."

"Whither?"

"To your vaults."

"My friend, no; I will not impose upon your good nature. I perceive you have an engagement. Luchesi—"

"I have no engagement — come."

"My friend, no. It is not the engagement, but the severe cold with which I perceive you are afflicted. The vaults are insufferably damp. They are encrusted with nitre."

"Let us go, nevertheless. The cold is merely nothing. Amontillado! You have been imposed upon. And as for Luchesi, he cannot distinguish Sherry from Amontillado." Thus speaking, Fortunato possessed himself of my arm. Putting on a mask of black silk, and drawing a roquelaire closely about my person, I suffered him to hurry me to my palazzo.

There were no attendants at home; they had absconded to make merry in honour of the time. I had told them that I should not return until the morning and had given them explicit orders not to stir from the house. These orders were sufficient, I well knew, to insure their immediate disappearance, one and all, as soon as my back was turned. I took from their sconces two flambeaux, and giving one to Fortunato, bowed him through several suites of rooms to the archway that led into the vaults.

I passed down a long and winding staircase, requesting him to be cautious as he followed. We came at length to the foot of the descent and stood together on the damp ground of the catacombs of the Montresors.

The gait of my friend was unsteady, and the bells upon his cap jingled as he strode. "The pipe," said he.

"It is farther on," said I, "but observe the white web-work which gleams from these cavern walls."

He turned towards me, and looked into my eyes with two filmy orbs that distilled the rheum of intoxication. "Nitre?" he asked, at length.

"Nitre," I replied. "How long have you had that cough?"

"Ugh! ugh! ugh! — ugh! ugh! ugh!—ugh! ugh! ugh!— ugh! ugh! ugh!—ugh! ugh! ugh!" My poor friend found it impossible to reply for many minutes. "It is nothing," he said, at last.

"Come," I said, with decision, "we will go back; your health is precious. You are rich, respected, admired, beloved; you are happy, as once I was. You are a man to be missed. For me it is no matter. We will go back; you will be ill, and I cannot be responsible. Besides, there is Luchesi—"

"Enough," he said; "the cough is a mere nothing; it will not kill me. I shall not die of a cough."

"True—true," I replied, "and, indeed, I had no intention of alarming you unnecessarily—but you should use all proper caution. A draught of this Medoc will defend us from the damps." Here I knocked off the neck of a bottle which I drew from a long row of its fellows that lay upon the mould. "Drink," I said, presenting him the wine.

He raised it to his lips with a leer. He paused and nodded to me familiarly, while his bells jingled. "I drink," he said, "to the buried that repose around us."

"And I to your long life."

He again took my arm, and we proceeded. "These vaults," he said, "are extensive."

"The Montresors," I replied, "were a great and numerous family."

"I forget your arms."

"A huge human foot d'or, in a field azure; the foot crushes a serpent rampant whose fangs are imbedded in the heel."

"And the motto?"

"Nemo me impune lacessit." (No one provokes me with impunity).

"Good!" he said. The wine sparkled in his eyes and the bells jingled.

My own fancy grew warm with the Medoc. We had passed through walls of piled bones, with casks and puncheons intermingling, into the inmost recesses of catacombs. I paused again, and this time I made bold to seize Fortunato by an arm above the elbow.

"The nitre!" I said, "see, it increases. It hangs like moss upon the vaults. We are below the river's bed. The drops of moisture trickle among the bones. Come, we will go back ere it is too late. Your cough—"

"It is nothing," he said; "let us go on. But first, another draught of the Medoc."

I broke and reached him a flagon of De Grave. He emptied it at a breath. His eyes flashed with a fierce light. He laughed and threw the bottle upwards with a gesticulation I did not understand. I looked at him in surprise. He repeated the movement—a grotesque one.

"You do not comprehend?" he said.

"Not I," I replied.

"Then you are not of the brotherhood."

"How?"

"You are not of the masons."

"Yes, yes," I said; "yes, yes."

"You? Impossible! A mason?"

"A mason," I replied.

"A sign," he said, "a sign."

"It is this," I answered, producing a trowel from beneath the folds of my roquelaire.

"You jest," he exclaimed, recoiling a few paces. "But let us proceed to the Amontillado."

"Be it so," I said, replacing the tool beneath the cloak and again offering him my arm. He leaned upon it heavily.

We continued our route in search of the Amontillado. We passed through a range of low arches, descended, passed on, and descending again, arrived at a deep crypt, in which the foulness of the air caused our flambeaux rather to glow than flame. At the most remote end of the crypt there appeared another less spacious. Its walls had been lined with human remains, piled to the vault overhead, in the fashion of the great catacombs of Paris.

Three sides of this interior crypt were still ornamented in this manner. From the fourth side the bones had been thrown down, and lay promiscuously upon the earth, forming at one point a mound of some size. Within the wall thus exposed by the displacing of the bones, we perceived a still interior recess, in depth about four feet in width three, in height six or seven. It seemed to have been constructed for no especial use within itself but formed merely the interval between two of the colossal supports of the roof of the catacombs and was backed by one of their circumscribing walls of solid granite.

It was in vain that Fortunato, uplifting his dull torch, endeavoured to pry into the depth of the recess. Its termination the feeble light did not enable us to see.

"Proceed," I said; "herein is the Amontillado. As for Luchesi—"

"He is an ignoramus," interrupted my friend, as he stepped unsteadily forward, while I followed immediately at his heels.

In an instant he had reached the extremity of the niche, and finding his progress arrested by the rock, stood stupidly bewildered. A moment more and I had fettered him to the granite. In its surface were two iron staples, distant from each other about two feet, horizontally. From one of these depended a short chain, from the other a padlock. Throwing the links about his waist, it was but the work of a few seconds to secure it. He was too much astounded to resist.

Withdrawing the key I stepped back from the recess. "Pass your hand," I said, "over the wall; you cannot help feeling the nitre. Indeed, it is very damp. Once more let me implore you to return. No? Then I must positively leave you.

But I must first render you all the little attentions in my power."

"The Amontillado!" ejaculated my friend, not yet recovered from his astonishment.

"True," I replied, "the Amontillado." As I said these words I busied myself among the pile of bones of which I have before spoken. Throwing them aside, I soon uncovered a quantity of building stone and mortar. With these materials and with the aid of my trowel, I began vigorously to wall up the entrance of the niche. I had scarcely laid the first tier of the masonry when I discovered that the intoxication of Fortunato had in a great measure worn off. The earliest indication I had of this was a low moaning cry from the depth of the recess. It was not the cry of a drunken man. There was then a long and obstinate silence. I laid the second tier, and the third, and the fourth; and then I heard the furious vibrations of the chain. The noise lasted for several minutes, during which, that I might hearken to it with the more satisfaction, I ceased my labours and sat down upon the bones.

When at last the clanking subsided, I resumed the trowel, and finished without interruption the fifth, the sixth, and the seventh tier. The wall was now nearly upon a level with my breast. I again paused, and holding the flambeaux over the mason-work, threw a few feeble rays upon the figure within.

A succession of loud and shrill screams, bursting suddenly from the throat of the chained form, seemed to thrust me violently back. For a brief moment I hesitated—I trembled. Unsheathing my rapier, I began to grope with it about the recess; but the thought of an instant reassured me. I placed my hand upon the solid fabric of the catacombs and felt satisfied. I reapproached the wall; I replied to the yells of him who clamoured. I re-echoed—I aided—I surpassed them in volume and in strength. I did this, and the clamourer grew still.

It was now midnight, and my task was drawing to a close. I had completed the eighth, the ninth, and the tenth tier. I had finished a portion of the last and the eleventh; there remained but a single stone to be fitted and plastered in. I struggled with its weight; I placed it partially in its destined position. But now there came from out the niche a low laugh that erected the hairs upon my head. It was succeeded by a sad voice, which I had difficulty in recognizing as that of the noble Fortunato.

The voice said— "Ha! ha! ha!—he! he! he!—a very good joke indeed—an excellent jest. We shall have many a rich laugh about it at the palazzo—he! he! he!—over our wine— he! he! he!"

"The Amontillado!" I said.

"He! he! he!—he! he! he!—yes, the Amontillado. But is it not getting late? Will not they be awaiting us at the palazzo, the Lady Fortunato and the rest? Let us be gone."

"Yes," I said, "let us be gone."

"For the love of God, Montresor!"

"Yes," I said, "for the love of God!" But to these words I hearkened in vain for a reply. I grew impatient. I called aloud— "Fortunato!" No answer. I called again— "Fortunato—"

No answer still. I thrust a torch through the remaining aperture and let it fall within. There came forth in reply only a jingling of the bells. My heart grew sick on account of the dampness of the catacombs. I hastened to make an end of my labour. I forced the last stone into its position; I plastered it up.

Against the new masonry I re-erected the old rampart of bones. For the half of a century no mortal has disturbed them. In pace requiescat!

I Hate You
Jennifer Trumbull

"I hate you," Julie said. She wasn't smiling but her words carried no more emotion than if she had said she hated disco music, Greek food, or sitcoms. Her lazy eyes, half-closed, focused on Marcus but carried none of the usual indicators of animus. These were not the eyes of a raging woman. They were the eyes of a casual, disinterested individual, a bystander with no skin in the game.

"Hate's a very strong word," Marcus said.

Marcus was still trying to figure out exactly what was happening here. He had only become conscious a few moments earlier. His perfect mouth full of expensive dental work flashed his signature grin. That grin had served him well through all his 34 years and had usually gained him instant favor, especially with females.

Julie said nothing, just stared at him with those lazy eyes. She was not buying the grin.

"You don't mean that." In fact, Marcus had no idea at all of what the young woman meant. Marcus released a well-practiced laugh, one he had used with unfailingly positive results in boardrooms, bedrooms and on the golf course. Marcus was accustomed to getting his way. He had not yet conceded that things were not falling into line under the direction of his personal will.

This despite the fact that he had awakened to find himself sheathed in plastic wrap, bound to an uncomfortable wooden chair in what appeared to be an abandoned warehouse.

He tried to remember. How had he gotten here? Had he been with her last night? Sex? His mind was a foggy landscape of ill-defined images. There had been drinks…at the country club…or was it Herschel's downtown? Was Fred Bernard there? Maybe.

This was some sort of practical joke. It had to be. No other explanation seemed possible. At some point the jokester would appear like a hidden guest at a surprise birthday party. Surprise! Everyone would have a hearty laugh. Afterwards, long afterwards when it was least expected, Marcus would get revenge. For now he would play along.

Julie lit a cigarette. A menthol Marcus noted when she exhaled toward his face.

"Hey, uh, mind giving me a hit off that? I normally smoke Marlboro reds but I'm dying for some nicotine. Can you do a brother a favor?" He broadcast the grin as a sign that he was at ease, rolling with the situation, as able to take a joke as anybody.

Julie pursed her lips, weighing his request. She shrugged and rose from the thrift store easy chair Marcus could not help noticing must be infinitely more comfortable than the one to which his butt was attached. Julie stepped right up to him and placed the cigarette to his lips. Marcus inhaled deeply, then exhaled with eyes closed. That helped. The nicotine.

"Thanks."

Julie returned to her chair, falling into it with one leg draped over an armrest. Her less than ladylike pose reminded Marcus of Patti Smith for some reason. An old clip from the Mike Douglas show maybe? Tilting her head back, Julie inhaled deeply from her cigarette and stared up at the gridwork of iron supporting the metal roof, then blew a silvery cone of smoke toward the skylight some forty feet directly overhead.

"Where are we?" Marcus asked, careful to remain smiling.

"Jefferson County. Northwest of Beaumont. The old insulation factory."

"Never heard of it."

"Most people haven't." Julie turned from the skylight to stare directly into Marcus's eyes. Her serious gaze intensified the simple statement. "The place shut down in 1993."

Marcus laughed. This time the laugh was a bit more difficult to muster, harder to make it sound real. "Who's behind this? I bet Dempsey's in on this. Or Bernard. Yeah, this is exactly the kind of trick those two would love to play on me."

Marcus looked around the vast expanse of the derelict facility. There were no signs of other people. The nearest wall was at least 100 feet from his position. The concrete floor was filthy with years of accumulated grime but mostly empty. A few random items of unidentifiable machinery were scattered here and there. Through gaps in the outer wall Marcus could see rampant vegetation, a jungle of weeds and trees that had not moved inside simply because the concrete floor was too inhospitable for seeds to get a foothold.

"Come on, who put you up to this?"

Julie took a final drag from her smoke and flicked the butt directly at his face. Bound as he was, Marcus was unable to dodge the glowing projectile. It struck him on the left cheek.

"Ow! What the fuck?"

"There's nobody else. Just me. Just us."

"I don't get it. What's this all about? This makes no fucking sense!"

Julie smiled. It was not a happy smile but one of grim satisfaction, a recognition of her commanding position in this confusing situation. "It's harder to flash that smile when you're out of your element, isn't it?"

"What the fuck is going on here?" Marcus strained at the cocoon of plastic wrap and found it did not give.

"You're good-looking, Marcus, but I'm starting to think you're not so smart. Not as smart as people think. Not as smart as *you* think."

"What's the point? What are you trying to prove here?"

Marcus knew Julie in a casual sense. She was the younger sister of one of his fraternity brothers, Matt Josephsen. He had not seen Matt for over a year. It had been twice that long since he had seen Julie. At a Christmas party, was it? No, at that New Year's Eve bash the Josephson's always threw at their beach house in Port A. That's right. He had seen Julie there. Two years ago. They had all been pretty wasted. But Marcus could remember sitting across from her at the dinner table. Before he had gotten totally smashed. Julie had seemed a lot happier then. Had he slept with her? For God's sake, he could not remember.

"Did I do something to you? Have I offended you somehow? You're Julie, right? Matt's little sister?"

"Ooh, you remember. Lucky me. Marcus Tanner remembers me. To what do I owe this coveted place in your memory, Marcus?"

"What?"

"Why do you remember me?"

Marcus drew in an unsteady breath of humid air. "Did we…? I mean, did I take advantage of you in some way? Julie?"

"You're asking if we had sex?"

"That…or anything. If I've offended you…"

"No, Marcus, we didn't screw. Have you offended me? Probably not in the way you mean. You've committed no single act, uttered no single comment that caused me to hate you. No, I just hate you for who you are. *What* you are."

"Exactly what am I?" There was no disguising the anger in Marcus's voice. Immediately he regretted expressing defiance in this delicate situation.

"You're an arrogant user, a narcissist, a man who uses the talents of others to enrich himself while making sure others are never recognized. You steal, you lie, you live a luxuriously parasitic life. You take everything and give nothing. You're a tapeworm, Marcus. Better looking than most tapeworms but still…just a tapeworm."

Julie stood, walked toward him, suddenly spun and kicked him solidly in the left side of his face.

Marcus screamed in pain. And anger. Again, he regretted losing his composure. He had screamed like a little girl for god's sake. He had never done *that* before. After the pain in his face had subsided to a dull throb, after he had spit a mouthful of blood onto the dusty floor, he shouted, "What the hell was that for?"

By this time Julie had settled back into the comfortable chair. "Spin kick. I learned it in kickboxing class last spring. This is the first time I got to use it outside the studio."

"What the fuck do you think you're doing here?"

"I'm ridding the world of a pest, an organism that provides nothing of value. I'm killing you, Marcus. How do you feel about that?"

His face went blank. His wheels were turning. The truth was too dark to face so Marcus went back to thinking this was all a big joke. He laughed loudly, spit some more blood, then said, "Is this about money? Kidnapping? Ransom? That sort of thing?"

"See, Marcus, you're really *not* very bright. I come from money. You know that. Sure, I could extort some money from you but how could I possibly hope to get away with it? You know me. You're a longtime friend of my brother. As unpleasant as it may be, the fact is I am going to kill you. I'll enjoy doing it and I'll get away with it." Julie stared into his eyes, examining him like a bug under a microscope, taking pleasure from his emotional distress.

When he spoke again, his voice was raspy, dry. "Why? Why are you doing this?"

"Other than the reasons I've already stated? That's a good question. Not sure I can fully answer it. I suppose what you really mean is why you. Why not some other person? Right? You want to know why I picked you?"

"Yes. Why?"

"The truth is I've wondered what it would be like to kill someone for a long, long time. I read a lot of true crime books, learned about serial killers, listened to podcasts and watched documentaries. There's an incredible wealth of information available on the subject of murder, Marcus. Why do you think that is?"

Julie paused. She withdrew the green cigarette pack from her pocket and lit another one. Marcus could not help but wonder if she intended to burn him with it. She had asked a question but he offered no response. Instead he stared at her warily the way a mouse watches a snake coiled and ready to strike.

Julie released a cloud of smoke. "No ideas on that? Well, I think it's because everybody is fascinated with killing. Deep down everybody wants to kill. It's in our nature, part of our programming. Haven't you ever wanted to kill somebody?"

"No!" Marcus shook his head vigorously then regretted it as the throbbing pain from her kick returned. "You're sick. You need help, Julie. We can get you help."

"Nice try, Marcus. It took me a while to settle on you. See, I was struggling with the idea of killing an absolute stranger. I decided it had to be someone I hated. Someone I really hated. Someone I despised so much that it would seem perfectly natural to eliminate them."

"How could you hate me so much? We hardly know each other." His face twisted with confusion, Marcus stared imploringly at Julie. "I had no idea you hated me."

"That's what decided it for me. You in your narcissistic arrogance were clueless. You didn't know how repugnant I found you. I never discussed it with anyone else so that made you the ideal target. If you didn't know, if no one else knew I despised you, well the cops would never even put my name on a list would they? They work on assumptions of motive and opportunity, right? Opportunity won't enter into it because we've never spent any real time together. You won the murder lottery, Marcus."

Julie smoked and waited to see how Marcus would respond. Several moments passed.

Finally, Marcus began to scream. He screamed for help at the top of his lungs.

Julie watched from her chair, a slight smile on her face.

After a minute or so Marcus stopped screaming.

"I figured we'd have to go through that bit of realization," Julie said. "You could scream twenty-four seven and no one would ever come. The nearest business is miles away. The nearest residential property is over five miles away. This entire compound is fenced. No easy access. Not likely that hunters would break in. I imagine you and I are the first humans on the property in, I don't know, probably years."

They sat in silence for five minutes or more.

His mouth was dry, his throat raw from screaming.

"Can I have some water?" Marcus asked.

"No. I don't think so."

Julie stood and walked away toward a doorway in the prefab wall.

Marcus started to shout but then remained silent. What was there to say? If this crazy bitch was serious about murdering him there was nothing he could say that would be of any help. Instead he needed to try to free himself.

That night Julie went out to dinner with Rosa Stanford and Dana Chapel, old friends from her university days. The trio gathered at Delaney's Restaurant in the Montrose district. Rosa was crazy about the pasta there and always tried to sell the others on Delaney's. Neither Julie nor Dana had the same passion for pasta but there were plenty of other items on the menu making Delaney's as good a choice as any.

"There she is," Rosa said, waving, when Julie entered the dining room.

Julie smiled and dispensed the obligatory gentle hugs and cheek kisses before seating herself.

"Here, try these stuffed oysters," Rosa said, sliding the appetizer dish toward Julie. "They're to die for."

Dana nodded an agreement.

"No, thanks," Julie said with a wave of her hand. "I'm in the mood for a fresh salad."

"Your loss," Rosa said cheerfully, glad to have another oyster for herself.

"You must live on salad," Dana said. "I don't think you've gained a pound since we were in school together."

"I may not have gained a pound but my weight has an unpleasant way of redistributing itself," Julie said. "I feel vigilance is called for."

"I can't believe you're not married yet," Rosa said, popping an oyster into her mouth.

"She could be if she wanted to," Dana added. "Half the eligible men in town would love to date Julie."

"You two are very sweet. I'm not ready for marriage yet."

"The consummate career woman." Dana said.

"Not just that. I'll know when it's time. Until then I'm enjoying life."

"What have you been doing with yourself lately?" Rosa asked.

"Lately I'm doing a bit of research."

"Anything you can tell us about?" Dana asked.

"I won't bore you with the details but I'm studying murder."

Rosa laughed. "Murder! Studying murder. That figures." To Dana she said, "This one has a morbid streak."

"I know," Dana said. "I remember all the books about serial killers she had stacked around her apartment."

"Don't tell me you two aren't the least bit interested in murder," Julie said, sipping her water.

"Not the way you are, girl," Rosa said. "You've got an obsession."

"Maybe you're right," Julie smiled.

"Is there any particular aspect of murder that you're researching?" Dana asked, waving at a waiter.

"I'm especially interested in the gratification the killer gets from the act of killing."

"Gratification?" Rosa's eyes widened. "Would you listen to yourself? This is not masturbation we're talking about. It's murder, Julie!"

Julie laughed, then took a roll from the basket on the table. "Don't tell me you've never wondered what it would be like to kill someone. Never? Not once in your life?" She tore a small piece from the dinner roll and placed it in her mouth.

"Literally? No. I mean I've wanted to kill Raymond a number of times." Raymond was Rosa's husband.

The waiter appeared at the table. "Are you ladies ready to order?" he asked.

In the warehouse, bound to his chair, Marcus noted the numbness in his feet and hands. After hours of struggling he had given up on any hope of freeing himself from the chair. His hands and feet had been secured with zip ties or maybe wire. His entire body was wrapped in several layers of the same heavy duty clear plastic that dock workers use to secure merchandise onto wooden pallets for shipping. The chair he sat on was securely bound to a metal post making it impossible for him to even try to stand or hop away.

Outside the wind was rising. It smelled fresh. Under other circumstances, Marcus would have enjoyed this cool evening breeze. Now it only reminded him that he was *not* on the golf course, not aboard his 32-foot cabin cruiser, *not* on the balcony of his high rise condo overlooking the Houston skyline. Not free.

He was extremely thirsty. Hours before he had let his bladder release. There wasn't much shame in pissing himself even though he hadn't done that for over thirty years. Shame required an observer, The presence of someone other than oneself. He was alone.

Maybe not entirely alone.

In the darkness, he heard unseen creatures moving about. Rats maybe? Marcus told himself, no, it would not be rats. This place had been empty for years. It had been an insulation factory. There was nothing here that rats would want to eat. No food source, no reason for rats to come around.

Still, something was skittering about, making the occasional thump or ping against the discarded scraps of metal that littered the warehouse floor.

He was thirsty. Very thirsty.

Marcus woke from a vivid dream in which he had been kayaking on the Colorado River. The colors were brilliant, otherworldly. But now he was tied to the chair. Julie's heels clacked on the concrete as she approached him. She was wearing dark clothes, dark glasses and big dangly earrings.

"Wakey, wakey," she called half-heartedly.

In one hand was a white paper bag. In the other a bottle of water. Marcus's eyes locked on the bottle of water. He wanted that water more than he had ever wanted anything.

Julie stopped at the comfortable chair and set the bag down. She twisted the cap off the bottle of water and walked toward Marcus. She held the open bottle under his nose. He tried to move his mouth toward the bottle but she kept it out of reach.

"I've heard deprivation heightens awareness. I bet that water smells good to you right now." Julie took a gulp from the bottle.

"Please…" The word was raspy, quiet. How could he be so dehydrated after just one day in captivity?

"Deprivation activates olfactory awareness. You can smell the water, even from a great distance. One of those nice survival mechanisms mother nature built into us."

"Please…" Marcus repeated. He coughed. A dry painful cough.

"I don't suppose a little sip will hurt anything." Julie put the bottle of water to his lips and let an ounce or so pour into his mouth.

It was heaven. The taste of that water was the most remarkable sensation Marcus could recall ever experiencing.

Julie went to the chair, lifted the white bag and plopped down in her Patti Smith pose. She opened the bag with a rattling flourish. "Fresh kolache. Can you smell it?"

Marcus said nothing. He stared as she took a bite.

"Not bad," she said. "Not as good as Koepke's, but not bad."

Marcus said nothing. He stared at the water bottle.

"Did you know that a third of the murders in the U.S. go unsolved? That's an important bit of information to know. See, law enforcement agencies don't like to admit a thing like that. The information is available but you have to dig for it. Not exactly the sort of statistic your local police want to publicize. They want people to feel safe, to have faith in the authorities to punish evil doers. But the stats say a full third of murders go unsolved. Then, when you figure in the number of accidental or deliberate wrongful convictions that number hovers pretty close to fifty per cent. Fifty per cent!"

Julie leaned forward, took a bite of the kolache, and rested her elbows on her knees. There was a smile on her face. This was the most extravagant display of emotion

Marcus had ever witnessed in her. But his mind did not linger on that observation. He was thinking of water.

"Fifty per cent," Julie said again. "That's as good as a flip of a coin. Nothing like the image the cop shows on TV have painted all these years. Propaganda. Imagine how many more murders there would be if people realized how good their odds were of getting away with it!"

Julie noticed the fact that Marcus's eyes were fixed on the water bottle.

"You probably want another drink, don't you?"

His Adam's apple bobbed and he nodded.

Julie stood and approached him. She gave him a second swallow of the precious water.

"Want the last bite of my kolache?"

He knew food would only make him even thirstier. Marcus had read somewhere that adult humans could survive anywhere from a month to two months without food. What the body absolutely required was water.

"Please. More water." Marcus coughed involuntarily as the water moistened his paper dry throat.

"Sure you don't want this last bite?"

Marcus fixed his dull eyes on her. He shook his head.

"Your loss."

Using one finger Julie pushed the kolache into her mouth.

"Please…"

"No more water for you. Don't want to spoil you!"

Julie tousled his hair playfully like a doting mom. She returned to her chair.

Marcus wanted to say something. He wanted to stumble onto some magic combination of words that would cause his captor to reconsider, to release him. But already he knew that was never going to happen. He wanted water. If he spoke, it would just dry his mouth out more quickly. He stared at her and remained silent.

"You're not giving up already, are you?"

Julie eyed him critically.

"Where's the signature Marcus bravado? The brash proclamations? The overweening ego? One day without water and you've caved? I'm disappointed, Marcus. You'll never know how truly disappointed I am."

Julie stared at the high ceiling.

"Bet you wish you were hanging from one of those support beams, eh? I mean, hanging is not an especially pleasant way to die but it's a lot quicker isn't it?"

Marcus felt weak and pathetic. It was a feeling he could not remember having experienced in all his years. He tried to suppress the swell of emotion. He thought for a moment he might succeed but soon he was screaming. Not words, just sheer animal frustration, anger, rage. This was worse than talking. Already his mouth was dry again. There was no reasoning with himself. The civilized, intellectual part of his mind, a part he had never actually cultivated to any large degree, was overwhelmingly dwarfed by the animal mind lurking in his amygdala. He screamed until something within him snapped.

Then Marcus began to cry.

Through his tears he could see Julie examining him with her clinical gaze. Then a smile appeared on her face.

"Not trying to play on my sympathies are you? That's a wasted effort. And those tears are a real waste of body fluids."

Marcus barked a savage cry of defiance. It was the sort of sound he never would have imagined himself making. Not in a million years. It was the sort of sound helpless patients bound in straitjackets in mental institutions might direct at their attendants.

"It's hard for me to hate you now, Marcus. You're so weak. You're pathetic. I almost pity you. But I'll hold onto my hatred. I want you to get the full experience of what it's like to die because someone despises you."

Marcus could not look at her. He wanted to withdraw into some secret place inside his own mind. He wanted to be back in that dream of kayaking. Anywhere but here. Seeing anything but Matt's kid sister Julie.

The wind picked up outside the derelict warehouse and a gust rushed over the two of them. Julie crinkled her nose.

"Ooh, something's stinky. Did you go poop in your pants, Marcus?"

He had. Sometime in the night, when he could hold it no longer, his bowels had evacuated. The smell would have been much worse if not for the plastic wrap in which he was cocooned.

"Amazing what a difference a couple of days can make in a person's outlook. Eh, Marcus? Two days ago you never would have dreamed of crapping on yourself. Your sense of arrogant superiority was still unchallenged. A vacant property, a hateful woman, a chair, some plastic wrap, all of these have conspired to strip you of your narcissism. It was actually much easier than I imagined it would be."

Julie stared at him. She jiggled the water bottle in a taunting gesture.

He had to ask. "How?" After that one word, Marcus felt he had betrayed himself. He should have just stayed silent, said nothing, stoically embraced his fate without interacting with his tormentor.

"How did I get you out here?"

Marcus hesitated, then nodded.

"After the country club you went to Herschel's. You never knew when enough was enough, did you, Marcus? One more drink. That was all I needed. I was there, in the club. I have been following you. You were oblivious. When you stumbled out into the parking lot I saw my perfect chance. A simple cab ride and you could have avoided all this. Just the two of us there in the parking lot. It was perfect. When you unlocked your car I just walked up behind you and zapped you with my stun gun. You dropped like a bag of laundry. I sort of shoved you as you went down so you fell mostly into your car. I pushed you the rest of the way in and drove you out here. Your car's in the swamp now. Getting you wrapped up in that chair was the hardest part. I could have definitely used some help. But then there would have been a witness. So I toughed it out. It was pretty satisfying actually. You know that little boost of pride you get when you've successfully met a challenge? Have you ever felt that?"

Marcus said nothing. It took all his willpower just to look into Julie's eyes. But he couldn't hold his gaze there.

"Have you ever accomplished anything on your own? Or was it always someone else getting you through the drill? Matt told me you never would've passed your math classes without his help. What did he get out of helping you, Marcus? Friendship? Loyalty? No, I don't think so. You just always felt it was your right to coast on the efforts of others."

Marcus did not want to think about that. It was true. Yes, it was true. But he didn't want to think about it.

Julie left a few minutes later without saying anything more.

Sometime in the afternoon he got a strange surge of energy. Like a glimmer of hope. Irrational but there it was. For a while, probably only moments, he felt it was possible to escape. Once more he went through all the possible movements allowed by his confinement. There was nothing useful in the exercise. His hands and feet were numb. He feared the lack of circulation was doing irreversible damage. Then he laughed. He was dying. So his feet and hands would die first. So what? Then the surge of adrenaline or endorphins or whatever it was that had given him a brief hope of survival vanished and he was left again in despair. Thirsty despair.

The next thing he knew it was dark. The middle of the night. Something was moving on him. Maybe more than one something. Then he felt the bite. Of what? Rodent teeth? In his cheek.

Marcus screamed but it was more of a husky ill-defined sound, dry and unrecognizable as a scream. Just a sound of desperation emitted by one animal as another animal tried to make a meal of it. The unseen thing squealed. Marcus shook his head as vigorously as his failing strength allowed. Finally the thing dropped to the floor and skittered away. It would be back. He knew that. And soon he would be unable to shake the hungry rat or whatever it was off his face. When it returned it might bring friends. What would he do then?

Nothing.

He would do nothing he was not already doing.

Marcus was dying. Slowly. He had no choice in the matter. He could neither slow nor accelerate the process.

When he inhaled he felt air passing into his mouth through a hole in his cheek.

How long had that little bastard been gnawing on him?

Marcus screamed with impotent rage. He hated himself for not being able to scream a real scream. Despite his rage the cry was just a pathetic wheezing expulsion of air from a powerless numb human body. He laughed. He didn't want to but he laughed. And he could not stop. It was some other thing, some other personality using his wrecked body to laugh that sick hissing sound.

Marcus hated himself.

"Ooh, that looks nasty."

Julie was leaning in close, examining his wounded cheek. There was sunlight outside the warehouse. He could not focus his eyes on her. But it was Julie. It smelled like her. Who else would it be?

"Some varmint practically burrowed into your mouth."

Marcus imagined she wore a disgusted expression but her face held no details for his dying eyes.

"News reporters have been talking about you, Marcus."

He heard her shoes tapping on the concrete as she went to her chair.

"Lots of speculation about what may have become of you. The police are sparing no expense, they are following up every lead. Not that they have any real leads."

Marcus coughed a feeble cough. His face ached. His entire body ached.

"Do you know how long you've been here?" she asked.

Three days, Marcus thought, but he could not make his mouth speak the words.

"Five days, Marcus. And I've got to say you look like shit. This whole murder thing is new to me. I never imagined animals would be eating your face. I thought it would take longer. I thought your will to survive would be stronger. I was wrong."

Marcus was aware of the woman seated in the chair a few steps away. But it seemed he was also floating on a raft with his cousin, Daniel. It was summer vacation and they were splashing around in the lake down the hill from his uncle's cabin. Daniel was telling him about kissing Carly Richter after school last Friday.

"I've been wondering if I should bury you," Julie said. "After you die. Or should I just let you rest here until someone discovers you. No telling how long that will be."

Cousin Daniel laughed. "She wants to bury you! Silly bitch." Marcus joined in the laughter.

"I have a gun in the car. Do you want me to end it now?"

Marcus laughed.

"Think that's funny?" Julie cocked her head and stared at the mess wrapped in plastic. She wondered what thoughts were going through his failing brain. "I think I've got what I wanted from this experience, Marcus. After I leave today, I don't think I'll be coming back. Shall I put a bullet in your head before I go? Can you nod or show some sign that you understand the question?"

The boys on the raft giggled. "She wants to shoot you in the head!" Daniel laughed uncontrollably. Marcus laughed so hard he thought he'd pee on himself. He nodded like a bobble head toy.

"Should I take that as a yes?"

Julie rose from her chair and leaned down in front of him.

"Do you even see me?"

Marcus laughed. On the raft with Daniel he laughed. In the warehouse with Julie he just sort of coughed. His stinking failing body disconnected from anything that might be described as reality.

Julie went to the car and returned with a nickel-plated revolver.

"I'm going to set you free now, Marcus. Funny but I don't hate you anymore. Isn't that weird? I guess you could say I still hate the Marcus I knew. The one who relied on my brother to pass his math exams. But where's he now? He's not here."

Julie put the barrel of the gun to Marcus's temple. She squeezed the trigger.

There was a brilliant flash of light. Like a supernova.

"Wow! Did you see that?" Marcus wanted to say to Daniel. But he realized Daniel was not there.

Then Marcus wasn't there either.

Julie walked back to the car, deciding along the way that she would toss the gun into the gulf when she visited her parents in Port A the following weekend.

That night, when the rodent returned, drawn again to the smell of blood. It dined without interruption.

Marcus was not there to notice.

Don't Be Stupid
Randall Smith

Adults think kids are stupid.

I think adults are stupid.

If adults weren't so damn stupid all the time maybe my mama would still be alive.

A little over a week ago on a Saturday afternoon me and Billy came running into the kitchen from the back porch. We'd been down on Sycamore Creek and we saw a tall skinny man kill two other men. If Mama and her boyfriend Chet had just listened, if they'd only believed us and right away, then maybe things would've worked out different.

We were just edging along the creek trying to sneak up on a big buffalo carp in the shallows when we heard a man say, "Hold on a minute, Franklin."

The way he said it was kind of scary. Like his voice went squeaky and stuck in his throat. I didn't know the man but I didn't have to know him to understand his voice didn't normally sound that way. He was scared. I turned around and shushed Billy. He's just eight and not as smart as me. He was pushing up behind me on the trail and I didn't want him to say something that would let the three men on the other side of the creek know we were there.

The reason I knew we needed to be quiet was because the tall skinny one, the one the other man called Franklin, was holding a big black pistol in his hand. He was pointing it at the other two. Franklin was talking but he wasn't talking loud. His eyes were squinting the way some people's eyes do when they're angry.

"I told you it wasn't me!" The guy that was talking was a fat man, shorter than Franklin. He was wearing a faded green Army surplus jacket. Under the jacket was a T-shirt that was too small for his big belly. On his head was a floppy hat like maybe a fisherman could wear to keep the sun off his face. Our granny wears a hat like that when she works in her flowerbeds. The other guy, the one standing next to the fat guy was just sort of in-between. He had long red hair and was wearing a Batman T-shirt. His arms were real white and his teeth were real big. Made me think of a beaver or a woodchuck or something.

Now Franklin spoke loud enough that me and Billy could hear him. "Wasn't you? Who else could it be?"

The red-headed guy looked like he was about to piss in his pants. His eyes were big and he was jerking around like a nervous dog. I knew he was going to try and run. I could see it in my mind before he ever made the move.

"This is bad," Billy whispered.

I shushed him again, but super quiet so no one could hear us. They were on the other side of the creek. It *was* bad enough. I knew that but I didn't have to say it out loud. Billy's just eight and he's not as smart as me. Not yet anyway.

The one called Franklin shoved the gun right up in the fat man's face. I guess that just about did it for the red-haired guy. He started flailing and stumbling and tried to run away. Franklin smacked the fat guy in the face with his gun. Hard enough that I could hear the smack over the sound of the creek and the traffic going over the Rosedale Street bridge just beyond the trees. Then he swung his gun and fired into the redhead's back. The gun wasn't too loud. Not like in the movies. It was just a pop. Then another pop. The redheaded guy's arms just went all spastic like he was a spider and somebody was putting a cigarette out on his back. He fell.

Billy jerked when the redhead went down. But he was smart enough not to say anything. He didn't make a sound. He was barely breathing. Me too.

The fat guy fell to his knees and started crying. Big man about the same age as my mama, bawling like a baby. He choked as he talked. I couldn't make out the words but I knew he was begging for his life. The sunlight through the sycamore trees sparkled on the spit that was drooling out of his fat face. I felt sorry for the guy. I'm sure he knew just like I did that he was about to die. But even though I felt sorry for him, I hated him, too. I mean he was a grown man on his knees crying. I didn't think I'd do that, even if someone had a gun on me, and I'm just an eleven-year-old kid. Then I felt a little guilty for hating the fat man. I felt a lump in my throat and my mouth was super dry.

"What was you thinking?" Franklin shouted. "Think we'd just roll over and let you screw us?"

"Please!" Fat guy wailed.

Then Franklin pulled the trigger. Just a pop. Not a scary sound. Could've been a car backfiring or bottle breaking or a car door slamming pretty hard. Not a scary sound at all. But the floppy hat flew off in a red mist that reminded me of the steam from Granny's vaporizer when I had a chest cold and they kept me in a room at her house with Vick's VapoRub all over my chest. There was a red nightlight in the room and it made the steam from the vaporizer look a lot like what had just come out of the fat man's head.

Franklin stepped up alongside where the fat guy was lying on the ground. He knelt down and said something real quiet. I guess the man wasn't dead yet, cause Franklin held the gun to his head and fired again. Fat guy's body jerked. Then Franklin went through the man's pockets. He got the guy's wallet and took some cash out of it. I guess he didn't think it was enough money, cause he said "shit" before throwing the wallet on the ground.

He stood back up and walked to where the redheaded guy had fallen. He leaned down and fired another shot into Red. Then he went through Red's pockets. He got some green money out of that guy's wallet, too. Still he wasn't happy. He did a sort of little dance around the body, the way some folks do sometimes when they're so damn mad they don't know which way is up, like the anger inside him was trying to bust its way out.

Franklin looked up at the sky and said, "Motherfucker!" Real loud. I couldn't help but think he was calling God a motherfucker, the way he looked up and all. And then I felt bad about even thinking that. My granny would've beat my ass with a belt if she knew I'd even had that thought. She took us to Eastland Street Baptist Church whenever she could talk our mama into it. But Mama wasn't any crazier about church than me or Billy. We went every Easter for sure. And I think that bothered Mama because she had to make sure we had nice clothes to wear on Easter Sunday. Mama didn't have money to throw away on new clothes when we weren't going to wear them enough to get the value out of them.

Anyhow, Franklin was so damn angry he hauled off and kicked the dead man in the face. He stomped around a while then he went over and kicked fat guy a couple times. Then he jumped up and down on him with both feet. He lost his balance on account of the guy was so fat and I'm sure it was hard to stand on top of his roly-poly body. Well, he fell down on his ass and when he hit the ground he squeezed the trigger on his gun without really meaning to.

That's when our real trouble started.

That bullet Franklin fired came right toward us. Snapped a sapling off right in front of us. That bullet came so close you could hear the whiz of it as it came through the air, through the sapling and snapped into the limestone bank behind us.

We weren't ready for something like that to happen. Both me and Billy sort of shouted out from the scare. No words, just fear noises that came up out of our throats without us wanting that to happen. The word for that, something I heard before is … involuntary. That's what it was. Involuntary.

Franklin sat up straight and took aim on us with that black pistol. He squeezed the trigger but nothing happened. Just a click I could barely hear.

"Run, Billy!" I shouted.

You should've seen us scrambling up the creek bank like a couple of mountain goats. When we got to the top I looked back over my shoulder and saw Franklin jump off the far bank and splash down into Sycamore Creek. He was moving as fast as he could but the water was slowing him down. Between him having to cross the creek and climb up that steep ledge on our side I knew me and Billy had time to make it to our backdoor. We could see it from where we stood. All we had to do was run across the vacant lot behind the Minit Mart.

We ran for all we was worth. Billy did a damn good job of keeping up. He was only a couple of steps behind when we reached the screen door that opens into our screened in porch. The door leading into the kitchen was open. I could hear Mama talking in the kitchen.

"Mama!" I yelled. "Call the cops right now!"

I slammed the screen door and latched it and me and Billy ran into the kitchen.

Mama was surprised but smiling. She had a cup of coffee held up in front of her face and she was sitting at the kitchen table across from Chet. Chet was her latest boyfriend. He worked in a warehouse somewhere and he was big and muscly so I guess Mama thought he was good looking. His face was nothing special. In fact I would've said he was homely. And I would've only said 'homely' because Granny beat my ass once for calling a girl ugly. When I pointed out that the girl truly was ugly, Granny told me to say homely instead.

"Call the cops!"

Mama sort of half laughed and Chet picked up his coffee for a sip. I could see in his eyes he was disappointed that we'd interrupted his private time with Mama. "What's all this?"

"There's a man shooting at us with a gun! He's coming across the vacant lot right now."

I looked out through the screen door. Franklin was walking fast toward our back door and I could see him sliding one of those bullet-holders into the handle on his gun. Clip. That's what you call it. He put a fresh clip in his gun and I can't explain it but that little thing he did sent chills up my spine. I knew if he even had a second clip all loaded up with bullets that this Franklin was a very bad man to be messing with.

"There he is!" Billy said, edging backward toward the dining room. He was scared. I don't mind saying I was scared. But Billy was the only one being smart in that moment. I was watching Franklin and Mama was asking a lot of questions instead of just calling the police like I told her to. Chet looked all concerned but instead of bolting the door like a smart person, he stepped out onto the screened in porch. Like I said he was big and full of muscles. I guess he figured he could whip Franklin's skinny ass any day of the week. In a fair fight he would've. But was Chet so stupid he didn't realize his muscles couldn't stop a bullet?

See what I mean about adults being stupid? They were so caught up in their grown-up thoughts, thinking me and Billy were over acting or telling tall tales. Mama didn't call the cops, she just stared out the back while Chet strutted out to prove he was the big dog. What Mama and her friends call the alpha male.

"What the fuck you think you're doing?" Chet hollered at Franklin.

By this time Franklin was just maybe ten steps away from the stairs that lead up on the screened porch. He raised his gun and pop! Chet fell on the porch with a hole in his chest. I saw blood spread out like a cartoon map of some island on his shirt. His eyes were blank. I knew he was already gone.

Mama screamed and started doing what she should've done before. Before she could dial 911 Franklin fired again through the screen door and Mama's head just slammed backward. Billy cried out and I saw a splash of blood hit his face.

"Hiding place!" I said real quick. He knew what I meant and he beat feet out of there.

Franklin was in the act of tearing the screen door out of its frame. I slammed the kitchen door closed and locked it. A bullet hole tore through the door. Splinters hit me in the face, then I ran to join Billy in our hiding spot.

In the middle of our house is a sunken cellar. It's got a concrete floor that's about four feet lower than the rest of the floors in our house. Mama always called it our pantry and it was full of shelves with laundry detergent and canned goods and trash bags and stuff. Down low in one corner there was a place where some bricks had fallen away over the years. The hole there was big enough for kids like me and Billy to slip through and get underneath the house in what Mama called the crawlspace. She'd told us not to go under there, threatened to whip us, but we went down there all the time. We liked it. It was like a cave.

I could hear Franklin beating on the kitchen door and I knew he'd get through it pretty quick. I looked down and saw Billy's head peeking out of our cave. "Hide!" I whispered, waving him on deeper into our cave.

Now I don't know how I came up with my plan but it just jumped right into my mind and I didn't have no time to think it through. Maybe it was something I'd seen on TV or maybe God was giving me ideas to save my life. I know that's what my Granny would say. Anyhow, I picked up two bricks from the stack of loose ones near the cave hole. I climbed up on the top shelf by the door. It creaked under my weight, but it held. I heard wood splintering and I knew the kitchen door was no more than kindling wood now. Then I heard Franklin walking around quiet like, leaving the kitchen and moving into the dining room. That's when it popped into my mind to take out the light bulb. I reached out to the overhead fixture and unscrewed the light bulb. It burned my fingers. Still I kept on with it till I screwed the bulb out enough that the pantry went dark.

Franklin's feet moved around and came to the pantry door. He turned the doorknob. The door opened and he poked his head in. I held my breath and raised one of the brinks. I knew I wouldn't get any second chance. When I put that brick to Franklin's head I needed to really connect. I needed him to go down hard.

Franklin tried the light switch. Nothing happened but he flicked it a couple more times. That's when I knew I was smarter than he was, even if he was a full-grown killer. If he'd just looked up he could've seen me perched on that top shelf. There was enough light coming through the door that he could've seen me plain as day. But he didn't look up. He turned and went off to explore the rest of the house.

I sat there on my shelf just waiting. I hoped Billy had the good sense to stay put.

I could hear Franklin moving around the house, looking here then there, first the living room, then me and Billy's room, the bathroom and finally Mama's bedroom. All along the way he was flinging doors open, tossing things out of his way. From the sound of it he ripped the shower curtain down. I heard him open Mama's closet door. He even poked at the attic access panel but he was smart enough to see there's no way me and Billy could've crawled up there, not with all the things Mama had stacked on the shelf just under it. He was mad. I heard him cuss then he broke a few things. Maybe some of Mama's decorations or her perfume bottles. It sounded like glass, whatever it was.

By this time I needed to pee. Real bad I needed to go. Still I swore to myself I'd hold it until Franklin left or I got the drop on him. I didn't care if I had to piss in my pants sitting on that pantry shelf. I wasn't budging until I knew me and Billy were safe.

After a while, I heard Franklin come back into the dining room. He pulled out a chair from the table and sat down. I heard that chair creak under his skinny ass. Mama always said the joints in that chair had wallered out. She kept saying she was going to glue the chair good and solid but she never had. Neither had Chet, even though I'd heard him tell her he would.

Franklin tapped around on the table with his fingers and with the barrel of his gun. He was thinking. Or trying to think. He may have been scared or maybe just pissed off. One thing's for sure, he didn't like the idea of us two kids getting away from him. Minutes passed and he took out his phone and punched some numbers. He must've had the speaker on cause I could hear the sounds of the phone like it was right there in front of my face. I heard the call ringing and I heard a voice, deep and gravelly come out of the phone.

"Where you at?"

"I'm in Poly. Heading back soon."

"Get what you went for?"

"Hell no!"

"What about Rance and Tony?"

"They dead."

"You been busy."

"Real busy. Got some collateral here too."

"Somebody saw you?"

"Yeah. But they ain't talking."

"Scared or dead?"

"Dead."

"You better get out of there and cover your tracks."

"Yeah."

Franklin punched his phone off and began tapping the table again. I heard him get up then I saw his shadow fall into the pantry. He swung the door wide to let in as much light as possible. He knew we hadn't run off. He knew we had to be hiding somewhere in the house. He stood there a second.

"What's this?"

I knew that meant he had spotted our cave. He stepped one foot onto the wooden pantry stairs. I don't know why he paused. But I did know that was my one and only best moment to hit Franklin on the head with those bricks. I raised them both high above my head and brought them down with all the strength I had. Those bricks connected right sharp with his skull. I heard a crack. Franklin groaned and squeezed the trigger of his gun. A bullet bounced around in the pantry. I'd thrown so much of my weight into hitting him that I came right off the shelf on top of him. Now all of this happened a lot faster than the time it takes to tell the story.

Franklin slammed into a shelf on his way down and when we hit the concrete floor a couple of jars of pickles smashed right beside us. He'd taken a good long fall and when his body hit it was at an angle that must've really messed him up, maybe snapped his neck even. I was lucky because it hurt, but he'd broken most of my fall. And I still had hold of those bricks even though my fingers got all smashed and bloody. He tried to push himself up but not fast enough. I was sitting on him, straddling him like a pony, and I just laid into his head with those bricks. I hit him till I was tired of hitting. After that Franklin wasn't moving.

When I caught my breath, I climbed back up the shelves, reached out and screwed the lightbulb back in. As I was climbing down I saw Billy poke his head out of the cave.

"Did you kill him?" he asked me.

"I don't know. But it's safe for you to come out." Billy crawled out and stood up next to Franklin. "Watch out for the broken glass." I said.

Billy squatted down and looked at Franklin's bloody head.

"What're we gonna do with him?"

"I'm thinking about that."

"Mama's dead ain't she?"

"Yeah. Her and Chet too."

Billy started to cry. I went over to him and put my arm around his shoulders. "It's sad," I said, "but we're alright now. Are you hungry?"

Billy dried his tears on his sleeve and nodded.

"Grab some of those potato chips and we'll go in the dining room, have a snack, and figure out what we're gonna do."

Billy grabbed some barbecue flavored potato chips. On a shelf higher up I saw the cheese puffs and I reached those down to him because I knew they were his favorite.

"Go on in the dining room," I told him. I thought those chips were gonna make him thirsty. "Don't go in the kitchen," I said. I didn't want him to see Mama the way she was. "I'll bring you a soda in a minute."

I never saw a sadder sight in my life than my own little brother carrying those two big bags of snack chips up the pantry stairs. He looked over his shoulder at me, real solemn like, then he went on to the dining room table. I heard him bust a bag open and then he was munching away.

I looked down at Franklin. "Why'd you have to do all this?" I said.

"Huh?" Billy hollered from the table.

"I wasn't talking to you," I said.

I looked again at Franklin. Could be he wasn't dead. Then it came to me how to make sure he didn't surprise us by waking up and coming after us again. There was two rolls of duct tape on the shelf next to the garbage bags and the little wooden tray where Mama kept a couple screw drivers and some pliers and a hammer. I tore into a fresh roll of duct tape.

Billy showed up in the pantry door holding the cheese puffs and stuffing them into his mouth quicker than he could chew and swallow. "Who were you talking to?" he asked me.

"Him," I pointed at Franklin with the toe of my shoe.

"Can he hear you?"

"Quiet, Billy! You can watch, just don't talk to me."

I started by taping Franklin's ankles together. Not just a little bit. I taped and taped. Then I swung his legs around so his feet were under the bottom shelf and I taped his feet to the four by four support beam that the shelves were attached to. I pulled his arms out and taped his wrists to another support beam so he was stretched out catty corner across the pantry floor. I just kept on taping until the roll was finished.

I looked up at Billy. He was nodding at me like he thought I'd done good. He didn't say anything cause his mouth was so full of cheese puffs.

Right then Franklin moaned and coughed. I jumped and Billy's eyes got huge but he didn't spit out his cheese puffs. He just stared, wondering what was going to happen next.

About then I remembered how bad I'd needed to pee. Funny how when you get in a fight your need to pee can just vanish. Now the urge was back and I felt like my bladder was gonna explode. I started to go up to the bathroom but then I got a real nasty idea. I turned back around, unzipped my pants, and peed all over Franklin's face.

"Omm!" Billy said and then he started giggling, blowing orange crumbs all over the place.

Franklin moaned.

"He didn't even wake up," Billy said. "I think I'd wake up if somebody peed on my face."

"Not if they'd whipped your noggin with a couple of bricks, you wouldn't."

Then I thought about the time when Franklin might wake up. I thought how he might start hollering. I took my shoe off, wadded up my sock and shoved it into his mouth.

"He might choke on that," Billy said.

"So what if he does?"

"Watch out for the broken glass," Billy said.

I slipped my shoe on over my bare foot and went to the bathroom to wash my hands. My knuckles were raw and sore from the bricks and hitting on Franklin.

"Stay where you are," I said to Billy. "I'll bring you a soda."

I went in the kitchen. The back door was torn all to hell and back. I could see Chet's body out there on the screened in porch. I could hear the sounds of traffic over there on Rosedale. It struck me as odd that with all the shooting and shouting nobody had called the police. Probably none of the neighbors even noticed. I guess people reporting gunshots to the police only happens in the movies.

Mama was a mess. I only looked for a second because I didn't like to see her that way, didn't want to remember her that way. I stepped over her body and got a couple of sodas from the fridge. Right then, her phone started ringing. I looked down and saw the thing chirping and vibrating on the kitchen floor. It was Granny calling. I took the meat tenderizing hammer from the holder on the stove and smashed Mama's phone until it was trash. Then I went back to the dining room.

"What was you hitting in there?" Billy said.

I opened a can of soda for him and set it in front of him. Then I sat down, opened my own soda and grabbed a handful of cheese puffs.

"Those are mine," Billy whined. "You eat these." He pushed the bag of potato chips toward me. I dropped my handful of cheese puffs on the table in front of him. He grinned. "Thanks."

I tore into the potato chips. Till that first chip was in my mouth I didn't know how hungry I was.

"What were you smashing? In the kitchen?"

"Mama's phone."

That didn't make sense to Billy. His eyes showed it. Truthfully, it wouldn't have made sense to me on another day, before all this had happened. But my mind was buzzing, just whirring away, with ideas that didn't quite seem my own.

"Why?"

"A little while from now, after the police find out what's happened, after Granny knows, when the whole world knows cause it'll be on TV and in the newspaper, people are gonna ask us why we didn't call the police right away. Understand?"

Billy nodded but I don't think he really understood. Not totally.

"Why didn't you call the police?" he asked after a while.

"Because I'm not through with that bastard Franklin."

"What are you gonna do to him?"

"I haven't decided."

Billy laughed.

"Are you gonna poop on his face?"

His question was so unexpected and simple minded I couldn't help but laugh. I spewed chewed up chips out of my mouth and soda came out of my nose. That burned like hell but still I was laughing and Billy laughed too.

I started thinking about the long term on all of this and another idea came to me. We could be put away for a long time for torturing Franklin. At least I thought we could. And I was dead set on making him suffer for what he'd done.

"This is all real serious, Billy," I said. "More serious than anything ever. They can lock us up, take us away from Granny."

He looked surprised. "We gonna have to live with Granny now?"

"I'm pretty sure."

"Have to go to church every Sunday?"

"Yep."

He made a miserable face.

"But that's better than prison."

I needed a way to impress on Billy's mind how serious all this was. Then it came to me. I went to Mama's room and got one of her scented candles and a box of matches. I put the candle on the table in front of Billy and lit it.

"You and me are gonna make a solemn oath," I said.

"What's that?"

"Just watch. Now, I'm gonna do it first so you know I'm not asking you to do anything I wouldn't do." I held my hand over the flame. It hurt like hell but I grabbed my wrist with my other hand and held my palm over the flame until I had a nice round burned spot. "Goddammit!" I shouted. I couldn't help that. But right away I felt guilty and I said, "Sorry, God."

Billy's eyes were real big. "Why'd you do that?"

"To help you remember."

"Remember what?"

"That prison is a lot worse than getting burned. Your turn."

"No! I don't want to."

But I grabbed his hand with both of mine and held his palm over the flame. I held it there till his burn was as good as mine. He screamed and cried. Then I let him go.

"Why'd you do that?" He was sobbing.

"So you'll remember. It hurt. It hurt bad. It hurt me bad, too. We're like blood brothers now. Not just brothers but blood brothers sworn together with a promise. Sworn with fire. We promise not to tell a soul about any of this. If we spill the beans, they'll lock us away, Billy. Prison's a bad place. Almost as bad as hell. In prison you get hurt every day and there's no way you can get away from it. You're locked in. Just imagine getting hurt worse than that burn every day for the rest of your life."

Billy stopped crying and wiped his tears away. "I don't want to go to prison."

"I know you don't. That's why I burned you so bad. So you'll always remember and you won't say nothing." I knew Billy wasn't as smart as me. I knew there was still a chance that he could say something that would land us in prison.

"I won't say nothing," he said.

"Yes, you will."

"No, I won't," he just about screamed. I could see he was about to start crying again.

"Yes, you will, because I'm gonna tell you exactly what to say. From now on for the rest of your life, if anyone asks you about today, you say 'I don't remember.' Say it."

"I don't remember."

"That's right. Now, on account of you being young, grownups will think you truly don't remember. I watched a show on TV about people who forget bad things. They don't try to forget them; they just forget because it hurts to remember. Just think of that candle flame on your hand and say 'I don't remember.' No matter how many times people ask just keep telling them that. If you do that, we'll both be safe. We'll have to live with Granny but that won't be so bad. You'll see. Okay?"

Billy nodded.

"Tell me what happened today, Billy!" I said real sudden like.

"I don't remember," he said, then he looked at the blister on his hand. "Is this gonna get infected?"

"I don't think so. I'd put some ointment on it for you but that would mess up my plan."

"What plan?"

"You'll see. Come on."

We went back into the pantry. Franklin was still all taped up. No way was he gonna get out of that. A whole roll of duct tape? I remembered Chet saying, 'When all else fails, use duct tape.' Mama and him used to laugh about that. He said it a lot. He was right. Without that duct tape we could not have been certain old Franklin would stay put.

I saw the big black gun laying on the floor with the pickles and the broken glass. I went down and picked it up. I dried it off a bit on my shirt. Billy was watching from the doorway.

"Are you gonna shoot him?"

"I think I will," I said. I aimed the gun at his face but then I remembered I wanted him to suffer. I didn't want to kill him right off. I pointed at his knee and squeezed the trigger. Franklin's body jerked, his eyes flew open and he started screaming. Well, he would've been screaming if my sock wasn't in his mouth.

"Let me!" Billy said, coming down the steps. "I wanna shoot him, too."

"Okay," I said. "But be careful. I don't want you shooting me. Just point at his leg and pull the trigger." I placed the gun carefully in his hands.

Franklin was freaking out. He was trying to thrash but I'd taped him up too good for him to move much. A lot of blood was coming out of his leg, spurting, and mixing with the pickle juice on the floor.

Billy leaned over him and took aim.

Franklin shook real wild like, shaking his head. He was begging like the fat man had begged him down by Sycamore Creek. He wasn't crying, though. So I didn't hate him the way I'd hated Fat guy.

Billy squeezed the trigger.

But the gun just clicked.

"No fair!" Billy whined.

"Guess he's out of bullets," I said. "Let's check his pockets. Maybe he's got some more."

I kneeled down and started going into his pockets. He tried to thrash around to keep me from doing it. I pickled up one of the bricks and held it over his face. "Be still or I'm gonna bust your teeth out," I said. Franklin's eyes got super big and he went into a coughing spasm. Maybe he was choking on my sock. I didn't know. Didn't care.

I emptied out his pockets. He had a couple wads of folding money. I remembered him taking cash out of the dead guys' wallets down by Sycamore Creek. I counted the money. It was two hundred and thirty-seven dollars.

"Ooh! I want some!" Billy said.

"Listen, Billy, I'd give all of it to you, but how's that gonna look after the cops show up. Eight-year-old boys don't usually have that kind of money."

"Dammit!" Billy said.

That may have been the first time I ever heard him cuss. He always tried harder than I did to be a good boy. He'd heard about hell at Granny's church and he didn't want to go there.

"What happened here, today, Billy?" I asked him, real quick.

"Huh? Oh … I don't remember."

"Good boy! Keep saying that and only that for the rest of your life and everything will be okay."

When I looked back down at Franklin he looked like he was scared shitless, like he couldn't believe what he was hearing. He'd just figured out that he had picked the wrong kids to mess with. Weird noises came up out of his throat, muffled by the sock, but pathetic and scary all the same.

"It's not fair. I don't get no money and I don't get to shoot him, either."

"Okay," I said, "you can hide the money in the cave until it's safe for us to take it out and spend it."

"Goody!" Billy rushed down the steps and snatched the money out of my hands and crawled off into the cave.

"Hide it good!" I hollered.

"I will."

I looked down at Franklin. He shook and tried to fight against the duct tape. His leg was bleeding a lot and must've hurt like hell. Just for pure meanness, I kicked him where I'd shot him. He screamed. Good thing for that sock.

"I'll be right back," I called to Billy. "Stay away from Franklin till I get back. I don't want him to hurt you."

I climbed the steps and went to the kitchen. I kept my eyes pointed away from Mama. I would've closed the back door but there wasn't enough of it left to close. Chet was too big for me to budge. I just crossed my fingers and hoped nobody walking across the vacant lot saw him lying there dead on our screened in porch. That idea troubled me, so I went to the linen closet and got an old sheet and spread it over Chet's body. Maybe he'd just look like a pile of laundry if anybody walked past.

Then I went for what I set out to get in the first place. Under the kitchen sink there was some plumbing tools Chet had left there a few days before when he'd fixed up a leaky pipe. He'd used a little blue propane canister to heat the pipes. He called it 'sweating the joints.' I looked in the pile of tools and found the spark igniter right where he'd left it. I grabbed the igniter and the propane and went back to the pantry.

I wasn't expecting what I saw. Billy was standing over Franklin, peeing in his face. I couldn't help but laugh.

"You got to," he said, like he thought I was complaining.

"Go right ahead," I said. "Be my guest."

Billy finished up and put his little pecker back in his pants.

"What's that?"

"Propane. It's even better than shooting him."

Franklin saw what was about to happen and he tried his best to break out of the tape but all he did was wear himself out and make his leg bleed worse.

I turned on the propane and used the igniter to get the flame going just like I'd seen Chet do. Once it was going good, I handed it to Billy. "Here you go."

Billy took the thing with both hands and squatted down next to Franklin.

"Don't get to close," I warned him. "I don't think he'll bust loose but he might."

"Okay," Billy said. Then he started burning Franklin's eyes.

Franklin thrashed and thrashed but that duct tape held.

The smell of burning skin and urine overtook me and before I knew it I was throwing up.

Billy laughed. "What's the matter? Too stinky for you?"

We thought it stunk up till then but all of a sudden it got worse. Franklin must've crapped in his pants. He was moaning and twitching. He couldn't see a thing because Billy had burned his eyes to a crisp, the same way Granny cooks her bacon. She says we'll get worms if she doesn't burn the bacon but I always liked the way Mama cooked it a lot better.

"Is he gonna die now?" Billy asked.

"We have to make sure he does," I said. "We can't let him live to talk about it."

"I don't remember," Billy said, like he was practicing.

I rubbed his head. "Good boy. You want to finish him off?"

Billy shrugged and nodded.

"How do you want to do it?"

He looked around. "Hammer?"

"Good idea." I got the claw hammer down from Mama's little toolbox and handed it to him. "Here you go. Finish him up good." I took the propane and started thinking about how best to place things so the cops wouldn't imagine a couple of kids had done all this to Franklin. I remembered about fingerprints. "I'll be right back," I said.

I went to Mama's bathroom and got a washcloth and started wiping down anything I thought I wouldn't want me and Billy's fingerprints on. I could hear Billy whacking away at Franklin's skull.

When I got back to the pantry Franklin's head, Mama's hammer and my little brother were all just covered in red. It was a hell of a mess.

"Looks like you killed him good, Billy," I said.

Billy stood up. "Still wish I could've shot him. Can we keep his gun?"

"Naw. The cops'll be looking for that right away. If there's no gun they'll start asking questions we don't want them asking. Pull your bloody clothes off right now."

"Why? What're you gonna do?"

"I'm gonna burn them."

"Why?"

"So the police won't have reason to think you smashed Franklin's head with a hammer. Come on, right now. Go get in the tub and wash every bit of yourself. With soap."

Billy didn't like taking baths, I knew that, but he didn't argue. He stripped down naked as a jaybird and went off to the bathroom. I started rethinking my plan of burning the clothes. A fire was more likely to draw attention than just bagging them up and putting them in a trash can somewhere. I could hear Billy drawing his tub of water. I went to the kitchen sink and washed up a bit. I took my clothes off and put them in a plastic garbage bag along with Billy's. I went to our room and put some fresh clothes on.

"What are you doing?" Billy called from the bathroom.

"Just take your bath. I'll be back in a minute."

I went out the backdoor and ran fast as I could across the vacant lot to the Minit Mart. They have a big dumpster out back. I was glad to see it was full of all kinds of stinky trash. I threw our bag of bloody clothes down in there where it wouldn't be noticed even if somebody looked in the dumpster. Then I ran back home.

On the back porch Chet still had that sheet over him. I wondered if that was a bad thing. I thought maybe any old killer would've done the same thing to make him less noticeable. But maybe not. Maybe the cops would think a killer wouldn't waste any time. But then they were gonna see somebody took some time in killing Franklin. And while I was thinking all this through I remembered my sock in Franklin's mouth. I felt pretty sure I needed to get rid of that.

Pulling that thing out of Franklin's mouth wasn't easy. All of a sudden I was feeling pretty sick about what me and Billy had done. And Billy had hit him so many times with the hammer that his face didn't really look like a face anymore. It reminded me of a dog I saw once that had been hit by cars and was just a red mess up on Vaughn Boulevard. I thought I might throw up again but I didn't.

I was holding the sock with just two fingers like it was a dead rat or something when Billy came out of the bathroom all wrapped up in one of the big towels.

"What's that?"

"The sock that was in Franklin's mouth."

"Gonna burn it?"

"No." I told him what I'd done with the clothes.

"So what you gonna do with it?"

"I don't want to run all the way to Minit Mart again. I don't think anybody saw me the first time but I don't want to risk it again."

Billy shrugged.

"I guess I'll bury it in the backyard. It won't take much of a hole. Go get some clean clothes on and wait in the bedroom for me. Don't go in the kitchen, okay?"

Billy nodded and went off to our room.

I took one of Mama's big spoons out in the backyard and dug a little hole in the flower bed back there. Granny was always telling Mama she needed to take better care of her flower beds but Mama didn't like planting flowers and things the way Granny did. Once I had the sock in the hole and all the dirt back in place I took some of the dead leaves and scattered them on top of it so it wouldn't look like somebody had been digging.

I went back inside. Billy had left his water in the tub and I figured I might as well use it for my own bath even though it was a little pink from blood. It was a good thing that most of Franklin's blood had gone on Billy's clothes. I washed myself up pretty good then drained the tub. I even cleaned the tub with Comet cleanser and the scrub brush. I looked around real careful and it seemed pretty clean to me. No drops of blood or anything that might look strange to a policeman. I dried off, got dressed again and went to our bedroom.

Billy was sitting on the floor playing with his toy truck. I took the big towel he'd been wrapped in and threw it in the dirty clothes hamper in the bathroom. When I came back, Billy said, "What are we gonna do now?"

"What happened here today Billy?"

He looked puzzled for a second then grinned and said, "I don't remember."

I reached over and slapped him pretty hard. He started crying, asking me why I'd hit him.

"I did it to make you remember you can't ever smile when you say those words. Now what happened?"

"I don't remember."

I asked him again a little louder. He answered me a little louder. We kept on like that a minute until we were shouting at each other.

"Yeah," I said, "I think that'll work. Don't ever smile and every time they ask you what happened just keep saying you don't remember and each time just say it louder. They'll think you don't want to remember because it's so bad."

"It is real bad, isn't it?" He started crying again but this time it was because our mama was dead and we weren't gonna be with her anymore. I put my arm around him and told him things were gonna be okay, even though in my heart I wasn't sure at all that things were gonna be okay. We'd just tortured and killed a man. Yeah, he'd killed our mama, but I knew for sure the law doesn't allow for folks, especially kids, making up their own justice. I felt like what we'd done *was* justice. But where the law or God would stand on it I couldn't say.

When he was settled down a bit I explained the rest of my plan. I told him the cops needed to think we'd been tied up so we couldn't go for help. I asked him if he understood and he nodded. I told him I was gonna tape us both to the legs of our bed and that I'd need his help to do it.

"How long do we have to stay that way?"

"Granny always stops by after church on Sunday. So she'll be along by one o'clock tomorrow or so. Since Mama didn't answer her phone today she may stop over before church. Anyway, Granny will be the one that finds us. She'll think we were tied up the whole time and didn't see anything real bad. But you gotta remember when she asks you what happened …"

Billy frowned and shouted, "I don't remember."

"Good boy."

"When do we need to get taped up?"

"Pretty soon," I said, "we want it to look like we been taped up since close to the beginning of all this mess."

"What if we have to go to the bathroom?"

"We'll just have to go in our pants. That'll look real to the police. They'll think we wouldn't ever piss in our pants if we didn't have to."

Billy nodded. "What if we gotta do number two?"

"Well, that'll be even better." I rubbed his head and went downstairs to get another roll of duct tape.

The sight of Franklin made me want to vomit. I gagged and looked away. I noticed where I'd thrown up before. Would that seem strange to the police? I decided it would. I got a roll of toilet paper and cleaned up my vomit then flushed it all down the toilet.

I needed to think of a way that we could both be taped up with our hands behind us. I knew I could tape my hands in front of me and then slip my legs through my arms so they'd end up behind me but once I did that how was I gonna get my hands on the other side of the bed leg? I finally decided we could lift the leg of the bed up on a big book like Mama's dictionary and I could back up to the bed leg and push on the dictionary until the bed fell and I'd just have to slip my hands back so they ended up in the right position. Might get my fingers smashed but I had to make this look real enough that folks would believe it.

I fetched Mama's dictionary and told Billy what I needed him to do. Our bed is not one of those lightweight things most people have. It's a big bed made of mostly iron. Mama found it at some auction house over on Vickery. She said it was an antique and we should be proud of it but I always thought it was ugly. It took some strength to lift up the corner by myself high enough that Billy could slip the dictionary under it. Took us a couple of tries before we got it just right where the bed leg was sitting right at the edge of the book.

Then I taped Billy's feet together, taped his hands around the other bed leg and behind his back. I put a piece of tape over his mouth. He didn't like that but I told him I was gonna do the same to myself and that was the only way it would look real enough, so he went along with it. I put tape on my mouth, taped my ankles and wrists, slipped my hands behind my back and scooted on my butt till I was in position. That old bed is heavy. But that was good in terms of the way it would look to the police. I pushed and pushed at that dictionary and finally the bed fell and my hands were just where they were supposed to be. I imagined we looked just like a couple of kids that had been tied up by some bad men.

That was the longest night of my life. Billy cried off and on all night. I could tell he wanted to whine about our situation but he couldn't say a thing with that tape on his mouth. That night lasted forever. A few times I heard Franklin's phone ringing down in the pantry. I guess whoever he'd been talking to before was wondering what had happened to him. Funny thing is I did finally fall asleep though I wouldn't have figured it was possible.

I woke up to the sound of somebody beating on the front door real loud. There was sunlight coming through the curtains at a low angle. Then I heard Granny calling out Mama's name. She got louder and louder but of course nobody came to the door. I could tell by the sunlight that it was still pretty early in the day. I was glad that Granny had come early. If I'd had to wait until after she went to church I would've been hurting even worse than I already was. There was cramps in my shoulders and upper back and not a thing I could do to relieve them. I needed to pee real bad. I wanted to sell our situation so I just let loose and peed in my pants. I could see Billy had already wet himself during the night.

Granny went to the back door and that's when the screaming started. She shouted Mama's name and just kept shouting, "Oh, dear God!" I heard her knocking things around as she rushed inside the house. She must've stopped at the pantry door cause she let out a scream that sent shivers down my spine. "No! Sweet Jesus!" She banged around some more going from room to room shouting for me and Billy. Billy woke up then and looked over at me. I stared at him hard and nodded. He nodded back at me and I knew he was ready to not remember.

Our door swung open and Granny looked like a mad woman. Her face was all twisted and her arms were just not behaving the way they normally did. When she laid eyes on us she screamed like someone had smashed her toes with a hammer, then she bawled and blubbered thanking God over and over that we were alive. When she saw how we were tied up she went to the kitchen and got a knife then came back and cut us loose. She was afraid of hurting us so she just picked at the tape on our faces. I pulled mine off quicklike and it did hurt like hell but I was glad to be free of it. She took a lot longer to get the tape off Billy. When she did she sobbed, "What happened?"

I just stared at her trying to look like I was in shock or something. Billy saw me and he got that same blank look on his face. I was real proud of him when he said, "I don't remember."

"Oh, dear God! You poor child." Granny hugged him tight to her and reached one hand over and rested it on my shoulder.

Of course, Granny called the police. Pretty soon there was half a dozen cop cars outside in the street. Some of the neighbors were gathered along the sidewalks watching like it was a carnival or something. Lots of cops came and went through the house. A lot of them said things that let me know they thought this was a big deal and they were glad to be a part of it. Lots of them said things to us like they were sorry for our loss and that me and Billy were brave and stuff like that. A Detective called Joe Malloy came in and asked us lots of questions. Billy said he didn't remember a few times. I tried to make it sound like I didn't know much. Finally, after a while, Granny threw a fit. She told that Detective he could put his investigation where the sun don't shine. Now, that ain't exactly cussing but it was the raunchiest thing I'd ever heard come out of Granny's mouth. I was kind of proud of her. She said she was taking us home with her and they could ask questions some other time.

Driving away in her car, Granny asked what we wanted for dinner. I told her chicken fried steak if it wasn't too much trouble. "Dear God, child," she said, "of course you can have some chicken fried steak. That's the least I can do for you." At her house, she set us down in front of her TV set and started cooking. I whispered in Billy's ear that he was doing a good job of not remembering. "Keep looking all blank like you've been doing." He looked at me real serious like and nodded. Then we watched a cartoon show he picked but I didn't pay much attention to it.

Later that evening a plump lady with a satchel and a clipboard knocked on Granny's door. She was from a group that protects children. Said she needed to do a quick assessment of us. Granny told her she could come in but not for long. We all sat in the living room. Granny's living room always smells like mothballs. It's just her way I guess.

The woman, who said her name was Candice, asked us some gentle questions. Not like Detective Malloy's questions. Billy just kept saying he didn't remember. It was clear to me she felt sorry for him. She asked me if I could identify any of the people who had been in our house, the one's who'd done the bad things. I nodded and gave her a description of Franklin. After a while she packed up her satchel, gave my Granny a card and said she'd be in touch. She said Billy's reaction was pretty normal for a kid who'd been traumatized. She said he might need some therapy and she'd tell Granny how to get in touch with the right people. I took that as a win. My idea of having him not remember seemed to be doing exactly what I'd hoped it would.

Later one of Granny's church friends called to ask why she wasn't there for the Sunday sermon. Granny went on for a long time all about it. Then others called and I imagined everyone she knew at her church wanted a piece of the excitement. For the next few days people kept coming and bringing food. They'd look at the two of us and whisper things amongst themselves. A lot of them wanted to hug us. A lot of them smelled like mothballs or medicine. Me and Billy got to eat a lot more cake and ice cream and fudge than Mama would've ever allowed. Billy gets kind of rowdy when he's full of sugar but Granny didn't complain. I think she took it as a sign that he was gonna be alright. I liked all the easy treatment and the sweets but I dreaded next Sunday rolling around. We'd be in church and they'd be laying hands on us, praying over us, asking us if we were right with the Lord and stuff like that. I'd already had a taste of that at Granny's church but I knew after what had happened it was gonna be even worse. And it was.

Before that first Sunday came around, though, on Thursday I think it was, Detective Malloy came to the house. I could tell Granny didn't like him but she let him in. He said he needed to follow up with a final interview to finalize his paperwork or something along those lines. We sat in the living room. Like a polite Christian lady, she offered him coffee and a piece of cake. We had more cake in the house than the grocery store bakery. He didn't look much like a cake eater but he smiled and accepted her offer. When she went in the kitchen to fix coffee and cake, he studied me and Billy.

"You know," he said softly, "there's a few things that bother me about what happened at your house. We found some dead men across the creek and we think they were killed by the man we found in your cellar."

"Pantry," I said.

"Right. But that makes me wonder why he'd come from the creek up to your house and kill your mama and her boyfriend. Why would he need to do that?"

Billy started looking real worried, like he might cry.

"I know you don't remember anything," the detective said, pointing at Billy. "But you," he pointed at me, "might have a recollection of why he'd climb that creek bank and come across the lot to the backdoor. Like maybe he was chasing somebody that saw him kill those two fellows."

I said nothing. Billy whimpered a little. I guess he figured he needed to provide a little diversion. He started saying, "I don't remember, I don't remember, I don't remember."

Granny came out of the kitchen and said, "Can you leave Billy alone? He doesn't remember a blessed thing."

"Yes, ma'am," the detective said. "Maybe you could take him in another room so we don't upset him."

Granny thought it over and I guess it seemed to her like the right thing to do. She took Billy's hand and led him off into the spare bedroom where we'd been sleeping. After we heard her close the door, Detective Malloy started talking again, real quiet like.

"Candice with Child Protective Services says you only remember seeing the one man. The dead man from your pantry. That right?"

I nodded.

"You didn't see any other men in your house?"

"I heard sounds but I didn't see anyone. I did hear him talk on the phone to somebody."

"This was after he tied you and your brother up?"

"Yes, sir."

"Remember what he said?"

"Something about he didn't get the money he was expecting. He said he killed some people and he said there was collateral."

"Collateral damage?"

I shrugged. "I guess."

"I don't think the uniformed officers let you into the pantry. They try to protect kids from seeing things like that. You know what happened to that man in there?"

"I heard Granny telling her friend about it over the phone." Truth was I'd heard her tell it several times to several friends. If she wanted to shelter us from knowledge about the way Franklin died she should have been more careful.

"What do you think about what happened to that man?"

I thought that over for a few seconds. "I think, since he killed my mama, he got what he deserved."

Malloy made an odd face and said, "I think I agree with you. So you didn't hear anything that might help us find the ones who killed him? You overhear any names?"

I shook my head.

"It took whoever it was a long time to do what they did to him. All that time you didn't hear anything? He must've been screaming. He might have shouted out a name?"

"I heard a lot of bumping around. I didn't hear him screaming. Maybe they covered his mouth with something?"

"That's highly likely." Malloy nodded.

I thought for a minute. "Finding the ones who did this ought to be pretty easy for you. Can't you just go find the people he called? Get the number off his cell phone?"

Malloy stared at me long and hard then he grinned. "You're a real smart kid aren't you?"

I started to smile but then I felt like I might be playing into his plan if I did that. I felt like he was 'buttering me up.' That's what Granny calls it. Mama used to say it, too. It's when somebody says nice things about you to get you to do something they want. I think the detective wanted me to drop my guard, to trust him. Instead of smiling, I said, "Mostly Bs and Cs."

That surprised him. He looked like maybe he was thinking I wasn't so smart after all. "I'm not talking about schoolwork. Most of that's crap. I can tell you that right now. No, I'm talking about the real world. I'm talking about being smart in a way that matters, smart in a way that helps you get through life."

I shrugged. "I'm a kid, mister. What is it you want from me?"

Maybe I shouldn't have said that. Malloy got a look like I'd just made a stupid move in a game of checkers. "Those burns you and Billy got on your hands. Who did that to you?"

"Franklin."

"So you know his name."

"Yeah. He told us. He wanted us to be afraid of him. He told us he'd do a lot worse if we told anybody about him."

Malloy nodded. He was thinking but I don't know what.

"But Franklin got killed. So I don't have to worry about him coming back."

"The men who killed him are worse than Franklin. Could be they'll come back for you and your brother."

"We were tied up in the bedroom. Wouldn't they just have killed us then if they wanted to?"

"Maybe."

"You're gonna catch those men aren't you? Won't you protect me and Billy? Keep them away from us?"

"I'll do my best."

I nodded like I had faith in him.

"You read the dictionary a lot?"

At first his question took me off guard but then I knew why he was asking. "When I read books sometimes I don't know the words. Mama tells me to look them up."

"That why the dictionary was under your bed?"

"Mama wouldn't want me to keep it there but I get tired of always fetching it from her bookshelf."

"Do a lot of reading?"

"Not as much as my friend, Kevin. He's real smart. But I like scary stories."

"Scary stories? Like what?"

"I have a book of stories by Edgar Allan Poe and another one by H.P. Lovecraft."

"Poe? You reading Poe at the age of eleven? I couldn't understand that guy when I was a senior in high school."

"I have to use the dictionary a lot. Sometimes I even have to look up the words in the definition. It's slow-going but I think I get the gist of his stories. Most the time."

"Gist?" Malloy shook his head. "Maybe that was my problem back in high school. Maybe I didn't use the dictionary enough."

"Maybe," I said, after he stared at me a while. I could tell Malloy was a smart man, not stupid like a lot of adults. I was uneasy, though. I felt like his smartness and my smartness might end up butting heads, if you get what I mean.

Right then Granny came back into the living room. "That poor child. I just pray someday he's able to get over all this."

"Yes, ma'am," Detective Malloy said. "I hope he adjusts. In time he probably will. I'm pretty sure this one will make out all right. He's a smart boy."

Granny grinned with pride and touched my head. "He *is* smart. No reason why he shouldn't be making straight As. Teacher says he could but he just doesn't apply himself. I'm sure the coffee's ready. Let's have some coffee and cake."

I felt like the detective had said and heard what he came to say and hear. I expected him to stand up and say he had to go. But he didn't. Instead, he said, "That sounds wonderful."

Granny smiled real big and went off into the kitchen.

"Don't worry about getting those straight A's," Malloy whispered.. "That's all bullshit. You're a smart kid. I know it and you know it. What you don't know is that I sometimes have need for a smart kid like you. I think I'll stay in touch with you. Would that be alright? Maybe have you do some work for me once in a while. What do you think of that?"

"Paying work?" I asked him.

He nodded.

"I think that would be fine. Does Granny have to know about it?"

He shook his head.

"Sounds like a deal," I said.

Granny came in with cake and coffee for her and Detective Malloy. She gave me a glass of milk to wash my cake down. The cake was from Mary Beth Stevens, Granny's best friend from church. Everybody says Mrs. Stevens is the best cook in the church when it comes to baked goods.

It *was* some damn good cake. I could tell the detective liked it.

Psychopaths, Grieving, and Timeslips
P.K. Kleypas

Leah hated her mother. She had good reason to despise the woman. But what kind of person hates her own mother? Leah didn't like the way her hatred made her feel about herself. She never really came to grips with her feelings until after her mother's death.

People said Leah was bright but introverted and aloof. She had always been annoyed by her more touchy-feely acquaintances, the ones who insisted on embracing at every meeting, who always complimented any minor change in appearance.

Oooh, I love what you've done with your hair!

Are those new earrings? They're so becoming.

Fostering a sense of connection through hastily constructed compliments at best seemed to Leah the grasping of insecurity and at worst a confidence game of emotional manipulation. When wrapped in socially mandated hugs she usually felt violated, like something was being taken from her, something she needed to protect.

Her suspicion and discomfort was not without reason. These were rooted in her own mother's effusive insincerity. Somewhere along the way Mom had read some self-help book about winning friends and influencing people. Taking the author's message to heart landed her a second husband with lots of money. As her social circle expanded to include the city's richest and most prominent citizens, friends with little to offer were discarded one by one.

"When I turn a page, I really turn a page," Leah's mother, Katherine, was fond of saying.

By the time she was 34 and Leah was 17, Katherine seemed to have forgotten that she had once been a teen mother, that her nine-month-old daughter had attended her high school graduation. Though she had no higher education, Katherine was a conquering hero, resting at the top of her own personal food chain, queen of all she surveyed. She had no patience for losers, which Katherine continually reminded Leah she was.

Leah realized that she had benefited from her mother's ambitions. It was her stepfather's money that had purchased her first car and paid her tuition at a well-respected though not Ivy-League university. It was her stepfather's circle of friends who practically fell over themselves offering her attractive entry-level positions in Fortune 500 companies. What did Leah have to complain about?

If material gain was the metric, nothing.

A few seemingly insignificant events had driven home the final wedge between Leah and Katherine. The first happened during Leah's freshman year at university. Her mom was on a tirade about some overblown injustice committed by an acquaintance whom Leah knew to have been very helpful and devoted to her mother. Katherine had ranted on about the many poor qualities of the person in question.

Finally, Leah asked, "Mom, is there *anyone* in the world you *do* respect?"

After only a moment's hesitation Katherine had responded, "No. But everyone has their use."

In earlier times Leah might have dismissed her mother's words as the sort of flippant remark people make when they are upset, a defense mechanism, an oral flourish devoid of any real meaning. But this time Leah realized Katherine was speaking the truth. She respected no one. No one was worthy of her respect. No one. Including Leah.

There had always been an underlying friction between Leah and her mother, but Katherine was well thought of and successful so Leah had usually felt obligated to hold her mom in high regard. Everyone held Katherine in high regard. Many put her on a pedestal. How often had Leah heard comments like, 'What a fortunate girl you are to have a mother like Katherine.' After this latest offhand but sincere declaration from her mother, Leah began to suspect Katherine might just be a teeny bit of a psychopath.

The second incident, drove the wedge even further into place and happened at the time of her stepfather's death. Not once did Katherine shed a tear for the loss of her husband. Nothing resembling a grieving process ever took place, even though Charles had given her everything she had ever aspired to and worshipped her in the process. She busied herself with all the necessary financial arrangements. When friends and family gathered around her, thinking they were consoling the distraught widow, Katherine would say things like, "I'm so sick and tired of crying. I'm all cried out." In fact she'd never had a tear to offer for the loss of her husband. That emotional well was dry.

What a strong woman Katherine is.

That's what all her friends said and thought.

Leah was repulsed. And worse, she feared that she might become increasingly like her mother as time progressed. Already she had noticed the qualities she most despised in herself were traits she had inherited from Katherine.

A couple of years after Charles' death, Katherine began dating Rick Tindall, one of the wealthiest men in the city. Rick wanted to marry her but made it clear that there would be a prenup in which his children would be favored. Katherine dropped the old guy like a hot potato. Leah had not heard news of the breakup and when she came home to visit for the holidays she asked her mother how Rick was doing.

Katherine was busy putting away groceries. "Who dear?"

"I said, how's Rick?"

"Rick?" A look of confusion clouded Katherine's face.

"Rick Tindall," Leah prompted, incredulously. The last she had heard her mother and Rick were planning a trip to Europe.

"Oh, him. We broke up a couple of months ago."

"Why? You were planning a trip to Rome."

Katherine gave a silly, insincere laugh. "I suppose I came to my senses. I don't want to take care of an old man. I could see the writing on the wall. I'm well out of that."

"I can't believe you didn't know who I meant when I asked about Rick. Someone you were intimate with just a short time ago." Leah said.

"When I turn a page, I really turn a page," Katherine replied, placing a head of lettuce on the cutting board. "Hand me a couple of tomatoes from the crisper, would you dear?"

Leah's lifelong discomfort with her mother, the uneasy maneuvering of a child naturally desiring love and approval from a parent, the effort directed at trying to salvage something of value from her relationship with Katherine came to an abrupt halt. She despised the woman who had given birth to her. It was a harsh and disturbing, but heartfelt realization. Leah hated Katherine. Daughters weren't supposed to hate their mothers, especially such a wonderful, accomplished mother, one whom everyone adored. Leah stopped visiting her mother at holidays or any other time. She screened her calls and never answered when the display on her smartphone read 'Mom cell.'

When Katherine finally managed to get her on the phone a few months later, she said, "If I didn't know better, I'd think you were avoiding me."

"Really?" Leah responded, her voice like ice water. "What, besides an overweening ego, makes you think you know better, mother?"

There was a long pause, followed by, "What? I don't understand."

"Goodbye, mother. When I turn a page, I really turn a page."

Leah ended the call. That was the last time Leah and Katherine ever spoke.

How many times had Leah seen and heard her mother put people in their place, cut them down to size the way Leah had just done to Katherine? Many. Katherine had gloried in her power over others. Leah knew she had just scored a victory against her mother, but the win was hollow, cold and joyless. It left a bad taste in her mouth. She despised her mother completely but she dreaded becoming just like Katherine. The disdain she had demonstrated with her mother proved to Leah she could be every bit as cruel as Katherine and that knowledge left her hollow and full of self-loathing.

The next morning, sipping coffee at her desk, feeling a bit less hollow, not nearly so self-loathing, Leah wondered if she would ever regret severing ties with her beautiful, aggressive, egotistical, manipulative, ambitious, vicious mother. A smile formed on her lips as she realized the answer was no.

She had often wondered why her mother had named her Leah, a Hebrew word meaning 'weary.'

"Oh, is that what it means?" Katherine had said, feigning surprise. "I just thought it was a pretty name."

Bullshit.

Just like everything that came out of her mother's mouth.

Bullshit, bullshit and more bullshit!

Leah *had* been weary. Weary from the weight of her mother's machinations, insults and betrayals.

Now she felt buoyant, alive and renewed. Hopeful.

It was a wonderful thing to be free of Katherine.

Then Leah's mother died unexpectedly in an automobile accident.

Quantum entanglement. Spooky action at a distance. An invisible link between distant objects allowing them to instantly affect one another.

"Let me help you think about it in another way," Ramona said. She waited, then added, "Is that all right?"

"I'm sorry," Leah answered. "I didn't realize you were waiting for approval. Of course. I'm always open to anything you have to say, my trusted advisor." The 'trusted advisor' was the sort of conversational embellishment to which Leah was prone when imbibing. Tonight she'd had three large glasses of cabernet sauvignon. That amount of wine poured into her 115 pound body within little over an hour was certain to induce flowery verbiage, insincerity and a distinct lack of concentration.

"I hope you're going to remember this conversation," Ramona said. "I think it's important at this juncture for you to be as thoughtful as possible. Want a cup of coffee?"

"I'd love a cup of coffee!" Leah exclaimed. Ramona rose from her seat and started toward the kitchen to brew a pot. Then Leah added, "First thing tomorrow morning!"

She giggled but Ramona was not amused.

"Maybe we had better continue this some other time." Ramona was wearing her no-nonsense mask, her disappointed, wounded friend expression. She stood staring at Leah with her fists resting on her earthmother hips.

"Don't be upset with me," Leah said with drunken sincerity.

Ramona went back to her seat on the colorful sofa and eyed Leah with benign authority. A painting of the Holy

Mother peered over Ramona's shoulder, doubling the sense of matriarchal scrutiny.

"Don't be angry. I'm the injured party here, right? The grieving sister? I'm the one whose mother just died. I think that entitles me to a couple of glasses of wine. So what if I get a little loopy? We all grieve in our own way. You've said so yourself."

"Is this grief? Really? You despised your mother. Your words, not mine. Is this grief? Or a self-indulgent avoidance of your true feelings?"

"Touché! I'll grant you that, my observant, insightful counselor."

"Are you aware that you become annoyingly precious with your words when you've been drinking?"

"Only because you are forever reminding me of that fact." Leah hiccupped. "Excuse me."

Ramona brought the palms of her patchouli scented hands together in front of her face. "Alright, we're done here."

"What? What did I do?"

"Like all drunks, you are incapable of focusing and comprehending serious discussion. We'll pick this back up after you have that cup of coffee in the morning. It's too important to tackle while you are drunk and much too frustrating for me."

Her phone rang and her head hurt.

"Uhnh," was the closest approximation to 'hello' her mouth, throat and brain in collaboration could accomplish at that moment. The previous evening's eloquence and air of frivolity had evaporated during the night leaving Leah only the most rudimentary communication skills and no enthusiasm whatsoever.

"Sounds like you haven't had that cup of coffee yet."

"Oh, Ramona." Leah smacked her lips together in an effort to kickstart her salivary glands. She knew a little moisture would improve her enunciation dramatically. Her tongue sandpapered the roof of her mouth. She headed for the kitchen and a bottle of water.

"Want me to call back later?"

"Hold on." Leah twisted the top from a bottle and gulped water. "Okay. Better. I needed water."

"Want to talk now or later?"

"Now's okay." Leah began heating water for coffee and lowered her near naked body into a chair at the kitchen table. The vinyl of the 1950s vintage chair was amazingly chilly. "Ooh."

"Something wrong?"

"Vinyl on my butt. Cold. Nothing serious."

"I don't know if talking to you when you've got a hangover is much of an improvement over talking to you when you're drunk."

"Try me."

"Sure?"

"Yep. The pain in my head will help me focus."

"Do you remember anything I said last night?"

"Sure. Before you kicked me out you were getting into quantum entanglement."

Ramona laughed. "You never cease to amaze me. You *were* listening. Good. You can be truly annoying but you have a first-class mind like a steel trap."

"I take that as a compliment. Okay. Continuing on down the trail of quantum entanglement."

"Right. As above, so below."

"As you so often tell me."

"There are some ideas we can never overstate. That's one of them. We think of quantum entanglement as a purely subatomic phenomenon. It's not. The same action at a spooky distance is happening at every level in the material world. The effects become increasingly complex and more difficult to predict or even describe at the level we consider everyday reality."

"Chaos magick. That's where you're headed with this, right?"

"You're much more fun to talk to when you're not drinking. But, no, not exactly. Just listen without trying to be the brightest kid in class."

Leah gently massaged her aching forehead. "I'll try."

"I did a reading for you after you left last night."

"Yeah?"

"Yeah. First, you need to go see your grandmother right away."

"For real? Why?"

"You told me she's still alive. That's been a while. She is still alive, right?"

"Right. I mean I haven't spoken to her in years. We haven't been close since I was a little girl. Grammie and Mom never got along."

"She lives in that little town with the dinosaur tracks, right?"

"Glenrose."

"That's it. The next step of your journey lies in Glenrose."

"Why?"

"That's for you to find out."

"Why Grammie? I barely know the woman. She was one of the pages my mother turned."

"Well she's a page you need to revisit."

"What about work? Roger will not be happy if I just take off."

"I looked into that, too. According to last night's reading, Roger will be completely on board with it."

"We'll see."

The water was hot. Cradling the phone between her ear and shoulder, Leah poured a mug full of the boiling liquid and emptied a packet of micro-particle coffee into it. She gave it a quick swirl with a teaspoon and sipped it. Heaven. Or a cheap substitute for heaven, one that was good enough to help her rise out of the local hell of her hangover.

"Trust me."

"This is me trusting. What about the quantum thing?"

"Entanglement."

"Mmmhmm."

"The only reason we humans have created a mental model of it as *entanglement* is because we think in terms of discrete objects. The way we *think* of things has a profound effect on how we experience everything."

"Thoughts held in mind produce after their kind. Another of your oft quoted aphorisms."

"Another way of saying it is 'thoughts are things.' But don't sidetrack me. We were talking about entanglement."

"Discrete objects?"

"You. me, an oak tree, a cat, a dog, the planet, a bolt of lightning. Objects. That's how we think of them but that's all wrong."

"The right way is?"

"No nouns, just verbs. Nouns are a mental trap. A prison of words. There are no 'things' per se, only *processes*. You are a process within a larger process. You and I are both sub processes within a larger process. The bacterium in your gut are just another aspect of your process. Ultimately there is only one process – the universe, god, goddess, collective consciousness, the Om, whatever you want to call it."

Leah sipped her black coffee.

"You there?" Ramona asked.

"Yeah. I was just processing caffeine into my body process."

"Are you going to seriously consider what I've told you or try to score smart-ass points?"

"No offense. What's the big deal?"

"This one shift in thinking will change everything for you. Entanglement implies a messy, unwanted attachment between separate things or entities. There are no separate things or entities. It's all just one big process. The word entanglement is inappropriate. There is nothing here to fear. It's all one process, by extension it's all you."

"I'll keep that in mind."

"Do. Call me after you see your grandmother."

"Sure. No problem," Roger said.

Figuratively, not literally, Leah's jaw dropped. Was this the same guy who had given her grief over taking a week off last Christmas?

"Wow!" Leah said. "That was easier than I expected."

"This is important," Roger said. "Your mother died. You need time to grieve. Without it you'll be setting yourself up for an ugly fall. Later down the road." Leah's mouth popped open but before she could say anything, Roger aimed a finger at her and said, "No clever talk, okay. Emotions are real and really powerful. Even for people like you who want to keep their emotions buried. Go. Grieve your mother. Take as long as you like. Ink City will be here when you get back. Whenever that is. How are you fixed for money?"

"What have you done with Roger? You're one of those pod people, right?"

Roger smiled with one half of his face. "I'll go back to being a petty tyrant later. Right now I want you to take care of yourself. Now, what about money?"

"I'm set. Plenty in the bank and undeclared cash in the safe in my closet."

"Good girl. Don't hesitate to ask if you need anything. Not just money. Anything."

"Okay." Leah felt uncomfortable with Roger's prolonged eye contact.

"I know you don't like it when people are touchy-feely. I respect that. But I want you to know I care about you. You're one of the most important people in my life. I don't want your mom's death to mess you up in any way."

A lump? In her throat? WTF? This was not right. She did not like hugs. But now she wanted to give Roger one. Tentatively, she stepped forward, arms outstretched. Instantly he wrapped her in his muscular and heavily tattooed arms. Oddly, she did not feel violated. This did not feel like something was being taken from her. Her life force was not being sucked away by some energy vampire in human disguise. Quite the contrary, she felt like she was receiving something, something of value. Even better she realized she was giving something of value. These thoughts surprised Leah.

"Everything will be okay, but it *is* a process. You've got to let it work itself out," Roger said.

There was that word. Process.

"I hated my stepfather. I thought I was glad when he died. Maybe I was. Maybe the world *was* a better place without his sorry ass. Still, I went through an emotional meat grinder for months after we buried him. I'm not saying it's the same for you. But you *will* have things come up. Things that you have not anticipated. Let it happen. Don't resist. That which we…"

"That which we resist, persists. I know, I know. You've only said that about a million times."

"Right. Sorry."

Roger released the embrace and looked at Leah with an expression she found difficult to look at. She let her eyes drift away from his.

"Go out and grow," he said. "You'll be a different person when you get back."

Moments later, Leah walked away from Ink City, the tattoo parlor where she had worked ever since she chucked her career in marketing.

Turning points.

Turning pages.

The first had been a major one, when she walked away from her mother's malevolent influence. Another followed when she bailed on a very lucrative career in corporate

America, a career she had carefully navigated toward beginning in seventh grade and continuing through college. After that, a quick left turn had landed her in the fringe world of skin art among the dark-clad souls Roger called the 'night gaunts.' There was nothing pejorative about the term. Roger considered himself a night gaunt in good standing.

Her mascara ran and she used the sleeve of her black shirt to dry her tears. When she saw her reflection in the rearview mirror of her car her face was a mess.

Why am I crying?

Who are these tears for?

Certainly not for Katherine. I hated that bitch.

Process.

Grammie Dale lived in a tiny house fashioned from petrified wood in the oldest section of Glenrose. Leah tried to remember all she had ever known about her grandmother. It seemed there wasn't much to recall. Katherine had seldom spoken of her mother. Grammie was never part of the gatherings at Charles and Katherine's home. Grammie was one of those embarrassing little details Katherine swept under the rug.

Like Leah's biological father. Vince, the man Katherine had divorced when Leah was ten. A man Leah had barely known, who had died in some military incursion in the middle east when she was twelve. Had she felt a sense of loss? Hard to say. She did have a pleasant memory of her dad teaching her to swim when she was five, Vince supporting her tiny body in his arms and moving her around on the surface of the water while she giggled. A lake? Where had that been? The suntanned man with dark hair and a mustache, the man with her mother's name tattooed on his right shoulder. Had she loved him? Had he loved her? Questions to which there might be no legitimate answers, only forced ideas and wishful thinking. Default mental postures, social norms generated by scriptures, books, movies and songs.

It was just about sunset when she pulled her VW into the steep driveway in front of Grammie's place. The golden glow of the setting sun brought out millions of tiny sparkles from crystals embedded in the petrified wood.

A memory.

The house.

The petrified wood.

As a little girl Leah had equated Grammie's house of petrified wood with the gingerbread house of the witch in the story of Hansel and Gretel. From wherever that memory had been stored it came rushing forward filling the mental screen of her here/now mind. The memory delighted her. For the first time in years, Leah laughed with joy. She had told Grammie that the house reminded her of the gingerbread house.

"I may be a witch," Leah remembered Grammie saying, "but I wouldn't try to eat that gingerbread. It's old and hard. You might break a tooth."

Leah hadn't brought much with her; a backpack with a few changes of clothes and some toiletries and, in a separate case, her laptop. Shouldering both, she approached the front door. The screen door was closed but the door behind it was standing open. Leah could hear kitchen noises, water running, the clink of utensils on ceramic. She glanced over her shoulder at the setting sun. The amber light through the dense foliage was dreamlike, familiar. For a moment she believed she was in a dream.

What a strange thought.

She knocked lightly on the doorframe.

"Is that you, hon? Come on in." There was no mistaking Grammie's voice even though Leah had not heard it for years.

She opened the screen and stepped inside.

"Grammie?"

"In the kitchen, come on back."

The house was the same. She hadn't thought of this living room for years but now here it was exactly as it had been when she was a child; the crocheted blanket draped over the sofa, the old photos on the mantle, some of which seemed to be from the 19th century, a photo of Grammie with her husband Vernon taken at their wedding occupying the central position, a painting of a waterfall on the wall near the door leading into the kitchen.

This is a dream. I don't belong here.

For God's sake! Where are these thoughts coming from?

"Do you still like spaghetti?"

Leah entered the kitchen and there was Grammie in a pale blue dress and a yellow apron that said, 'Kiss the Cook." Same Grammie. A little more wrinkled, a little heavier, but still vibrant, smiling, with sparkling eyes.

"I was expecting you," Grammie said.

"How? How could you be expecting me?" Leah had tried three times to call her grandmother on the landline. There had been no answer. No voicemail. She certainly didn't have an email address or a computer.

Grammie shrugged. "I just felt you. Do you still like spaghetti?"

"Of course!" Leah lowered her bags onto the floor near the little kitchen table. She was bewildered to find she actually *wanted* a hug. Which seemed alien, felt foreign, like trying to eat with chopsticks for the first time but being really excited by the prospect. What was going on here? The embrace no longer seemed a formality, a social convention to be endured. She felt a positive attraction to this little gray-haired lady, an energy flowing from those pale blue eyes. She wanted a piece of that. Arms spread, she approached Grammie and hugged her for the first time since she was ten years old.

Maybe I'm one of the pod people. This feels good. What is up with me?

"I am so glad you're here." Grammie whispered.

They sat at the little table. A gentle breeze stirred the curtains in the window above the kitchen sink. The last vestiges of that dreamy golden sunset were bouncing off the trees outside, playing tag with the soothing blues and grays of the advancing night.

"Tell me. How did you know I was coming?"

"We all just know things sometimes. You know. Ice cream?"

"No thanks, Grammie. I'm stuffed."

"Sure? This is a special occasion."

"Maybe tomorrow."

"Okay."

"So you didn't get a call from Roger or Ramona?"

"No, dear. No one called me. Sometimes we just know what we need to know. You understand. You used to understand when you were small."

"I did?"

"Don't you remember?"

"Now that I'm here I think I'll remember more and more. Your living room looks the same."

Grammie laughed. "Yes, I'm a creature of habit. More so all the time. The more the world changes the more we cling to the familiar."

Leah looked at Grammie, sitting silently for a long moment.

"So you knew about Mom passing?"

Grammie nodded.

"You didn't want to come to the funeral?"

"Why would I? She didn't want me to be part of her life. Why should I be part of her death?"

"I understand." Leah shifted in her seat. "You know, Mom and I were sort of … estranged."

"I know dear. Don't let that trouble you. Katherine was not an easy person to love."

"You know I was on the outs with Mom. You knew I was coming to visit. You treat me like we've been together all this time but I haven't seen you since I was ten, Grammie."

"We're bound by love, Leah. That doesn't change."

"You never came to visit. You never wrote letters."

"Visit? No. Your mother didn't want that. She would've been embarrassed by my presence in her new world. But I wrote. Lots of times. I don't suppose she told you."

Leah felt her cheeks burning with anger. "No. She didn't." Just another example of Katherine's insistence on dominating every situation.

Control freak bitch!

Leah felt her hands clenching into fists under the table. She wanted to strangle…

Grammie slowly stood from her place at the table and gathered her dishes into a single stack. "Don't hold it against her, sweetheart. I imagine she's in the midst of a turbulent crossing."

Leah unclenched her hands and let the blood flow freely into them again. Her aggression no longer found expression in her hands but it lingered in the flesh of her cheeks, a burning anger she was not yet willing to release entirely. "Turbulent crossing. Like the journey to heaven or hell? I don't believe in all that stuff Grammie."

Leah recognized the fact that her voice carried a tone of disdain. Immediately, she regretted having spoken to her grandmother using that tone.

"The crossing happens whether you believe it or not, hon. Your beliefs can flavor the experience, shift it slightly this way or that, but we all reap what we've sown." Grammie turned and stared at her, with authority but a calm authority. "Katherine's in troubled water. Forgiveness is in order. If we hang onto the hurts of the past, cling to all the nasty things she did, we won't help her. Or ourselves."

"Frankly, I don't give a shit about helping her, Grammie."

"I know, Leah. But you do want to help yourself. That's why you're here."

Grammie took her dishes to the sink and ran water over them.

When Leah woke in the middle of the night she saw by the old-fashioned alarm clock on the nightstand in Grammie's guest bedroom that it was 2:59 am.

She had been dreaming of flying reptiles. Dinosaurs. No, pterodactyls. They weren't called dinosaurs, were they? They were of a different order. Flying reptiles. Ancient birds of the prehistoric skies.

In the dream the sunlight was gold and mystical just as it had been when Leah arrived at Grammie's. Many dark forms darted about in the humid air, supported on leathery wings. At one point Leah suddenly felt she *was* one of the flying reptiles. There was a sense of exhilaration as she navigated the sky of that time before humans walked the earth. Still, as she flew about shooting this way then that, loving the sensation of riding the wind, her self-image, her internal identification was very much as it had always been. She felt herself to be a human mind in a reptile body. Leah was not thinking like a reptile, she noted with a sense of awe, though she was not really certain what sorts of thoughts a reptile would have. Other than hunger and the desire to satisfy that craving.

She hovered over a rocky ledge and saw another winged reptile landing in a nest composed of branches and all sorts of wilting foliage. Katherine? The reptile was her mother. She just knew with that certainty one sometimes experiences in dreams. The Katherine reptile stabbed a powerful beak into an egg in the nest. A thick yellowish substance erupted from the shell and the Katherine bird greedily devoured the disgusting food source. Thrusting the enormous beak into the ruptured egg, sucking up the gooey contents, then tilting its head skyward so the food could slide down the long reptilian throat to its distended stomach. From inside her bird body, Leah felt a shudder of revulsion. Another reptile slammed into her in mid-flight.

For an instant Leah was human again, a high school girl carrying an armload of books in the school hallway when a bulky, pimply-faced member of the football team slammed into her causing her to scatter her books on the floor amid the many feet rushing to the next class.

Now, the reptile Leah tumbled down out of the dreamy sky onto the jagged rocks below.

That's when she had awakened.

2:59 am.

Her bladder was full. She eased herself out of the bed and went to Grammie's bathroom as quietly as possible, not wanting to wake her grandmother. From behind the closed door of the other bedroom Leah could hear soft snoring, gentle, barely audible. The bathroom smelled like Listerine. She peed then debated whether or not to flush. She chose to wait until the morning. She would flush in the morning. Surely Grammie wouldn't mind.

Leah returned to her room.

Her heart jumped up into her throat as she passed through the doorway into the bedroom.

There was a little girl in a plaid dress kneeling in the center of the floor. The girl was playing with two dolls, one in each hand.

"You were very bad," the little girl said, bashing one of the dolls with the other. "You were so bad I have to kill you."

"No! Don't kill me!" the little girl said, affecting another voice, playing out the character of the doomed doll victim.

"You were bad. Now you must die!" The girl giggled, taking a great deal of pleasure from the beating one doll was giving the other. "Time to turn the page," she said in a sing-songy little voice which might have seemed cute under other circumstances.

The girl dropped the 'dead' doll on the floor and looked down on it, gloating with satisfaction.

Turn the page?

Only now did Leah realize the identity of the little girl. Katherine. It was her mother. As this thought occurred to her, the little Katherine on the floor slowly raised her malevolent face. The hatred in those young eyes was deeply troubling to Leah. She wanted to look away but found herself hopelessly entangled with the child's hate-filled eyes.

"Who said you could come in my room?"

"Grammie told me to…" Leah stammered.

"You shouldn't snoop," the little Katherine chided, clucking her tongue against the roof of her mouth. "You know what happens to snoopers."

Now, the child was impossibly tall, a vapor of shadows trailing from her scarecrow body, leaning into Leah's face, her breath foul with the smell of dead things, her teeth chipped, jagged and sharp. She belched and a viscous yellow fluid erupted onto her chin.

The egg? From the dream?

"Don't let her frighten you," Grammie said softly.

Leah looked over her shoulder and saw Grammie, younger, stronger, standing in the doorway.

"Don't let her trouble you."

The giant girl with the jagged teeth roared, bellowing with rage. The room exploded into movement as if a tornado had hit the house. Drawers flew from the dresser, arced around the room smashing photos and framed prints from the walls. The scarecrow mouth opened impossibly large and closed over Leah's head. The smell. It was horrendous, like dead animals decaying in a hot, nasty sunbaked porta-potty. Leah gagged.

She jerked awake, gasping for air, afraid she was vomiting in the bed.

The clock on the nightstand said 2:59 am.

"What the fuck?" Leah gasped, gulping in air. Oxygen. Delicious oxygen. It was fresh, good, invigorating. "What the hell is going on?" she whispered.

Her bladder felt ready to burst.

Quietly Leah crept into the bathroom. The smell of Listerine, though mildly annoying, was a vast improvement over the stench of the monster girl's mouth, a dream stench that still clung to her nostrils.

How could that be?

"Get a grip, Leah," she told herself.

She checked the toilet for her previous urination. Nothing but clear water.

So that was just a dream? A dream of using the toilet? What the…? She would have sworn that had really happened, that she had been awake.

The clock. 2:59am.

Leah peed and, once again, opted not to flush.

Climbing back into bed she noted her grandmother's gentle snoring. The clock still displayed 2:59 am.

Leah pulled the cover up around her neck and stared at the ceiling.

When she turned over on her side the little girl was kneeling on the floor again. Behind the girl a younger, smaller child, a boy was also kneeling. As Leah watched the boy slowly vanish from sight, just like the effect she'd seen many times in movies. The little girl looked up at her. First her expression was neutral, empty, void of emotion. Then the malevolence she had displayed earlier bubbled up from within the little body. Like oatmeal cooking on a stovetop, the girl's face became coarse, her skin dry like an Egyptian mummy, bubbles burst on the surface of the child's face, casting foul-smelling wisps of smoke into the air.

A chilling voice eased out of the child's throat. "This is my room. You can't stop me from playing here."

In a flash, the enormous monstrous face with the broken, rotten teeth was gaping over Leah.

She woke with a scream, cut short halfway out of her throat.

Sunlight was shining through the window.

Her bladder ached. Leah threw herself out of the bed. In Grammie's bathroom she peed. She gave no thought to flushing, she just did it. She rinsed her face with water and looked at herself in the mirror.

"What the hell is wrong with you?" she said breathlessly.

"Good morning, dear," Grammie called from the kitchen. "Ready for some breakfast?"

When Grammie received no response from her granddaughter, she went to the guest bedroom and found Leah perched on the edge of the bed crying. The old woman said nothing but took a place on the bed beside Leah and placed an arm gently over her heaving shoulders. Between sobs, Leah related her experiences in the night, gasping, choking on the words, telling of the terror, the malevolent little girl, then the towering demon her mother had become.

"I know. I know dear," Grammie would say softly each time Leah paused.

Leah cried until she was exhausted.

All cried out.

That's what Katherine had said to her friends when they gathered around her at Charles' funeral. That circle of fools thinking they were comforting a brave and stoic woman in shock from the loss of her husband.

It had taken a while but now Leah was all cried out. At least for the moment. Something told her there were still untapped depths of sorrow hiding deep within her, all the more volatile for having been neglected for years. An icy subterranean cavern full of frozen atrocities sleeping and dreaming of a spring thaw.

Leah's sorrow was real. She was all cried out. But why? Why was she shedding tears for a woman she hated?

"Grammie, I think I'm losing my mind," she said, the words catching in her throat.

"No, honey, you're not losing your mind. You're just rediscovering it."

What an odd concept. Why did she say that?

Leah stared at Grammie.

"Come on. Let's go have some breakfast."

Leah slipped into some sweats and joined Grammie in the kitchen.

Waffles.

"Grammie, I love waffles," she said, sitting down and staring at the stack of golden-brown goodness her grandmother had prepared for her.

"Butter?"

"Of course!"

Grammie handed her the butter dish. The butter was perfectly soft. Grammie must have left it out on the stovetop while she was cooking allowing it to soften. Leah carved large chunks of butter from the stick and spread it as evenly as possible all over her waffles. There were three waffles stacked on her plate and each was generously buttered by the time she had finished.

"Butter just adds a lot of unnecessary calories," Grammie said as she applied a much more conservative amount of the stuff to her single waffle. "But it's certainly delicious."

"True dat," Leah eagerly agreed. "Syrup?"

Grammie slid a small bottle of pure maple syrup toward her. Not a big plastic bottle of artificially colored corn syrup claiming to have been made with 'real' maple syrup, but a glass bottle of 100 percent pure maple syrup. The genuine article. Leah felt the sandy grit of crystallized sugar as she unscrewed the cap.

"Grammie this is so perfect!" She cut a triple thick bite of syrup drenched waffles from the disks on her plate and shoved it into her mouth.

"I remembered you liked waffles," Grammie said, negotiating her own modest bite of waffle.

"Real maple syrup. I don't think I've had maple syrup since the last time you made me waffles."

"Some things are best done right or not at all. I wouldn't let that genetically modified corn syrup pass my lips."

Leah laughed. "I remember you telling me the way I ate my waffles was unladylike."

"Yes. It still is. Unladylike, but it's allowed in my kitchen."

Leah laughed again. The laughter naturally dissipated under its own weight and Leah found herself staring across the table at the beautiful soul encased in the aging body of her grandmother.

"Thank you," she said.

"You could not be more welcome, dear. I have longed for this time to come."

Between bites of waffle washed down with orange juice, Leah continued the conversation with her Grammie.

"You know so much. Things you're not supposed to be able to know. How?"

"Whether or not I'm supposed to be able to know things depends on who's doing the supposing."

"Okay. But how? How do you do it?"

"I start by believing I have a right to know things, by realizing I am connected through…I guess you can call it love…connected with anything I care to know about."

"You sound like Ramona."

"Your hippie earth mother psychic friend. I like her. I just love those colorful throws she has over her sofas. It brings back memories of the early 1970s when your grandfather and I fancied ourselves freaks."

Bewildered, Leah stabbed her fork into the hard surface of her plate. "There you go again! How the hell do you know about Ramona? You've never been to her house. Have you?"

"Yes. And no. Not in the usual sense. Ramona and I are old friends. Astral acquaintances. Even before you met her. She's a dear soul and we visit in dream time fairly often."

"That, too, sounds like Ramona. You've been friends since before I met her? How's that?"

"I was the one who asked her to strike up a friendship with you at that street fair. Remember that?"

Leah hadn't thought of her first meeting with Ramona in a very long time. "That's right. She was giving those readings at the Urban Health Expo on Sixth Street."

"I knew you two would hit it off. Having Ramona watching over you was one of the ways I dealt with not having you here with me. Not having you as a part of my life."

The lump in Leah's throat was not unswallowed waffles. "Careful. You're going to make me cry again."

"Rule number one: during this visit you cry whenever you feel like it. The old days of pent-up emotions are over and done with. Your mother may not have wanted to deal with the inconvenience of your deeper feelings but I do. I will. I insist upon it."

"Fair enough," Leah said, swallowing the lump despite her agreement to let it remain. She gulped orange juice. "So you arranged for Ramona to be my friend?"

"I encouraged it. It probably would've happened anyway. If not with Ramona specifically, then with someone like her."

Leah tried to imagine someone else like Ramona. That was difficult to picture. As far as she knew Ramona was one of a kind.

"Have you ever been in a room full of tuning forks?" Grammie asked.

"No. Can't say that I have."

"But you do know what a tuning fork is?"

"Of course."

"Once, years ago I visited the Association for Research and Enlightenment in Virginia Beach. They had a demonstration in a room full of tuning forks. The teacher whacked one of the forks on the edge of the table causing it to vibrate. Every other tuning fork of the same key in that room began to vibrate. That stuck with me. It helped me to understand things that had been happening all my life. Things I'd been taught not to believe were possible."

"Yeah." Leah stared, both at her grandmother and at some as yet ill-defined image that was forming in her psyche.

"Like attracts like. You were never like your mother, even though she did try to mold you in her own image. That's why it's so important for you to take the time to grieve, to discover, to assimilate and to let go of everything that doesn't belong to you. You've carried the weight of your mother's sins for far too long."

"Sins? I don't believe in that church stuff, Grammie."

"I'm not talking about churches or religion. I see why you make that association. Sin is a word you hear a lot from the pulpit. It's become emotionally charged and filled with erroneous, dark connotations. The word sin simply means to miss the mark. That's all it means. It has nothing to do with being a good or bad person or anything in between. Life is for learning. Mistakes, missing the mark, are part of that learning process. What I was saying was that in addition to dealing with your own mistakes in this life you were also struggling with your mother's. Because she tried to dominate you. Tried to make you an extension of herself."

Leah's mind floated in the coalescing truth of what her grandmother said. "Yeah. You're right. That's exactly what she did. And I hated her for it. But at the same time I felt I wasn't entitled to hate her for that. Everyone thought she was so perfect. Everyone wanted to be like her. They thought I should be like her."

"And you tried to be like her. You failed because you're *not* like her. You were never supposed to be like her. Your mother was a psychopath. May her soul find peace."

"Psychopath?"

Grammie held Leah in her gaze but said nothing.

"I mean, yeah, I've had that thought. I suspected she might be a psychopath."

"But then you'd feel guilty for even suspecting such a thing."

"Right! Right on. Exactly."

"You're feeling a little bit of guilt right now, even though you're relieved to have found someone else who knows Katherine was a psychopath."

"Yes. Yeah, Grammie."

"So let's take some time to talk about your mother. There are things I need to tell you. Things that may help break you free of her domination."

"All right."

Grammie sighed and looked out the window above the kitchen sink. "Where do I start? She was always a troubled child."

"Troubled?"

"I probably don't mean that in the way most people use it. She didn't act out, at least not at first, not openly. She was always very smart. Your grandfather loved her dearly. When she was young they spent a great deal of time together. Because he loved her he couldn't see…the dark side of Katherine. I saw but I never shared what I saw with Vernon. He loved his daughter with all his heart. He deserved that. I wasn't about to take that away from him."

"I'm not sure I follow exactly."

"Vernon was a devout Christian, a Baptist. He was a wonderful man. But incapable of seeing or believing anything outside the fundamentalist Christian views he'd been raised with. If I'd shared what I knew about Katherine, Vernon would not have believed me. If he had believed he would have labeled Katherine evil. He would have had no choice. His mind had been tightly bound to a very specific belief system at an early age. For him there was no breaking free. I can't fault him for that."

"But you were always different. You were never that churchy kind of person."

Grammie laughed. "You're right. I was never churchy. I went to church, of course. In a town like Glenrose back in those days especially, going to church was just something you did. Like putting on clothes before you left the house. If you didn't you could be severely stigmatized, shunned. I went to church. That's where I met Vernon. But I always knew there was more. More than what old brother Dave Philpot was shouting from the pulpit."

"Dave Philpot? That was the preacher's name?"

"Yeah. And he, too, was a good man. Just misguided. Trapped in a limiting belief system, even though one of the basic tenets of his church was that the truth will set you free. He wasn't free but he was incapable of seeing that he was not free. It was the same with Vernon, the same with just about all the folks in this town. It's less like that now."

"You were always different, you thought differently. How did that happen for you and not for the others? And why did you stay here in Glenrose all these years?"

"I resonated with a different belief system. I probably inherited that from my mother. And her mother. People could see I was loving. I was kind. So they tolerated me. They just thought I was a good Christian."

"But you weren't."

"I was. I was as much a Christian as I was any other thing you could label. Who we really are transcends all that, you know. Some people can convince themselves that they are nothing more than the label that's been slapped on them since birth. I never could believe that. Vernon's mother saw I was different. She didn't like it. She wanted him to marry Sue Ann Blevins. But I got Vernon. He was a good man. He never tried to force me to see things his way."

"You loved him."

Grammie nodded.

"What became of Sue Ann Blevins?"

"She married Dan Howard. Her grandson is the mayor here."

"Hurray for Sue Ann."

"Yeah." Grammie laughed and finished her last bite of waffle.

Leah resumed her assault on her own plateful of food. Already she was feeling full but there was still half left, a half-moon shaped stack of waffles swimming in a small pond of syrup. Leah was determined to finish it if only to display appreciation for her grandmother's kind effort.

Grammie took her plate to the sink, ran water over it and returned to the table, cradling her cup of coffee in both hands. "We've gone pretty far afield. And that's okay but we need to talk about Katherine. Right away so it has time to sink in."

"Okay, Grammie."

"The first time I really knew about Katherine was when she killed her little brother."

The fork fell from Leah's fingers and clattered on her plate. She stared at Grammie, her cheeks bulging with waffles she had not finished chewing. "I don't understand. Killed? What brother?"

"Vernon junior. He was three years younger than Katherine."

"I never heard of him. Are there pictures of him in the house?"

Grammie shook her head. "No pictures. We didn't talk about little Vernon. It was just too painful. Especially for your grandfather."

"What happened?"

"Little Vernon was just three. I didn't know it but he had taken a gallon pickle jar I used for watering my plants and he was filling it with sand from the sandbox Vernon had made for the kids. An ice cream truck came along the street with that loud music blaring. Little Vernon ran down the driveway with that glass jar in his hand. He fell. He fell on the broken jar. His poor little heart…he bled out before the ambulance arrived."

Leah's eyes welled with tears. She felt her grandmother's grief as Grammie related that distant tragedy brought painfully near by the retelling.

"Katherine had been out there in the yard. I was here in the kitchen. I heard the ruckus outside and one of the neighbor kids pounded on the front door. They were all gathered around little Vernon on the sidewalk. Oh, the blood. So much blood. I began screaming for Katherine. Where was she?

"Later, Mrs. Henderson across the way said her niece had told her that Katherine had shoved Vernon junior. Pushed him while he was running down that driveway with that big glass jar in hands. I couldn't believe it. Didn't want to believe it. Katherine came home later that day and said she'd been at her friend Haley's house.

"It was a bitter blow, losing little Vernon. Vernon senior was crushed. He just couldn't understand why God would let something like that happen. I told you he'd always been very close with Katherine. He took her everywhere with him in that old pickup truck of his. After Vernon junior was born I'm sure Katherine noticed a shift. Her daddy had a son. And of course that was very important to Vernon. Every man wants a son just like, I suppose, every woman wants a daughter.

"Katherine didn't like sharing her father's attention with her little brother. She didn't like the fact that this little interloper had her daddy's name. She felt her status in the group had been threatened and like a dog she wanted to fight for her place in the pack. Did she mean to kill him? Maybe not. But after he died, after she got away with eliminating her little brother, things just got worse. Imagine what happens to the mind of a little girl who kills her brother, gets away with it, never faces any consequences for her actions, never has any sense of remorse.

"Now she knew no one suspected her of anything. How could such a pretty little thing be guilty of anything wrong? She saw that, understood that advantage, and she began to use it. Naturally, after little Vernon died, her daddy went back to lavishing all his attention on her. That's what she wanted. Deep down I guess I knew she'd made her brother fall, caused his death. But that was a truth I wasn't willing to face. Not for a long time. It was a truth Vernon never would've owned up to."

"Grammie. I'm so sorry. I never knew. Mom never even mentioned having a brother. Not that I can remember."

"She'd erased him. Why would she ever talk about him?"
Katherine had turned a page, perhaps her first.

After they had done the breakfast dishes, Grammie made a pot of tea and suggested they go out into the backyard for a while. Stepping out the back door Leah took in the surroundings.

"This is different," Leah said. "Isn't it?"

"Yes. It is. The stone circle I put in several years ago. The last time you were here there was another flower bed in that spot."

"Right. And there was a swing hanging from that tree."

"You loved that swing." Grammie seated herself in one of the lawn chairs at the edge of the unusual stone circle in the center of the backyard.

"I sure did." Leah took the chair next to Grammie, noticing that the thing was covered in a fine dust of yellow green pollen.

"We're going to be covered in pollen," Grammie noted. "That's okay. A little pollen never hurt anyone. Unless they had allergies."

"What made you decide to install this stone circle?" Leah tucked her feet up under her and nestled into the chair, sipping at her tea.

"Just a focal point. A peaceful place to relax. Something like a meditation garden."

"It's a good idea. I like it."

"Me too." Grammie smiled.

"So I guess there's more about Mom that you want to tell me."

"Mmmhmm." Grammie set her cup down on a little glass-topped table with folding legs. "Vernon was never the same after little Vernon died. He made a show of being cheerful for Katherine. And for me. But his heart was broken. He died of cancer when Katherine was thirteen.

"Life goes on. A year or so later, a man from the church, Jimmy Pritchard, started showing interest in me. It was nothing serious. I had no intention of marrying the man but I liked having him as a friend. I'd invite him over for dinner once in a while. He never did more than kiss me. On the cheek. Not even on the mouth." Grammie laughed.

"Not exactly Romeo. Is that what you're saying, Grammie?"

"He was no Romeo and I was no Juliet. I certainly wasn't interested in getting married. But Katherine threw a fit. Many fits. She was convinced that I was going to marry Jimmy. No matter what I said I couldn't convince her otherwise. She grew more and more out of control. Said a lot of hateful things and became impossible to live with. The next thing I knew she'd run away to Oklahoma and married your father. Back in those days, you could pretty much marry anytime after the age of fourteen in that state."

"And she was sixteen."

"No, dear. This was the first time. She was fourteen. They married in Oklahoma and rented a place in Fort Worth. He worked in a big bakery there. Right away she had a baby. A baby boy. Vince's mother showed up at the hospital the day he was born and found Katherine trying to trade her baby for a baby girl that another woman had given birth to. They chalked it up to postpartum depression. I wondered. They named the child Jason. Shortly after they took the baby home he died in his sleep. That's what they said. Crib death. I wasn't so sure."

"Oh, Grammie."

"I'm sorry I have to tell you all this but I think it's essential to your well-being that you know. Once you know, you can move on."

Leah nodded.

"The baby was dead. Vince was underage so his parents had the marriage annulled. They took him home and Katherine came back to stay with me. She was more unbearable than ever. She had deliberately gotten pregnant so Vince would marry her. So she could have her own home, her own place where she could be the authority. All because she thought I might marry Jimmy Pritchard, which I had no intention of ever doing. Maybe she didn't really think that at all. She just wanted to be the queen of the house. I started to think she wasn't above trying to arrange an accident for me. I watched her like a hawk during those days. The whole thing was a mess."

Leah nibbled on her lower lip. "Mom always said the reason she married so early was that my father was head over heels in love with her and chased her relentlessly until she gave in."

"Well, she would say that wouldn't she? It sounds a lot better than the truth. Fits her self image better. Katherine wanted everyone to believe she was incapable of error. A lot of people gave her the benefit of the doubt. Many were willing to believe that about her. Sadly, she may have believed her own propaganda. I don't think she was ever capable of admitting being wrong about anything."

"So at fifteen she had already been married, birthed and lost a child?"

Grammie nodded.

"So many secrets."

"Psychopaths are very fond of secrets. Katherine was no exception. Right away she started chasing after Vince again. She had caught him once and she knew it was just a matter of time before she could snag him again. Don't get me wrong. I loved Vince. He was a good young man and he was very pleased that a pretty girl like Katherine seemed smitten with him. But she wasn't smitten. She could see Vince was the sort of boy she could wrap around her little finger. I'd guess a lot like your stepfather, Charles, though not nearly so wealthy."

"Mom did dominate Charles. No doubt about that."

"And she dominated Vince. Soon she was pregnant again. With you. They married a second time and this time Vince's parents just bit the bullet and went along with it. Your parents moved back to Fort Worth again. I made every effort to be a part of your life. It was important to me. I wanted to be a buffer between you and the monster Katherine had become."

"Do you really think she was a monster?"

"Maybe that's a little harsh. But she was definitely swimming in murky water. On more than one occasion, when she was living with me again after the first marriage to your daddy, I heard her screaming in her bed. I'd go in and find her terrified, saying a dark man was holding her down on the bed, trying to get inside her. I knew she really meant a sort of demon, not a man at all."

"Was that her fault? The demon thing?"

"They don't own you unless you let them, Leah."

"And you think Mom let something in?"

"Yes."

"Last night she said I was in her room. She tried to dominate me. Loomed over me like a monster with nasty teeth."

"Like minds attract. If she can make you think your only hope of peace is to become like her, then you'll begin to resonate at her frequency. Right now you're sort of on the fence, you could fall either way. She's determined to make sure you fall on her side. That's how that order of being propagates in this world. Through fear. By clouding the minds of fearful humans."

"What should I do, Grammie?"

"Refuse to be afraid. And remember, these bodies are just garments we wear for a while. That dark thing is not really your mother. Not in the sense that we're inclined to think. That thing is an illness. And you get to choose whether or not it will infect you."

"I do? How?"

"Absolutely. By resonating with a different frequency."

"What frequency?"

"One of your choosing."

"You make it sound simple. Easy."

"It is simple. But it's not easy. You'll be challenged. Your mother spent a great deal of energy dominating you throughout your childhood. She wanted the seeds she planted to bear the same dark fruit that grew in her. Katherine's at a crossroads in her journey. She will have to divert your progress otherwise the parasite she carried will have no host, no way to stay in this world. That will be hard after building up a lifetime of momentum toward dark places."

After a while, Grammie went inside to compose a shopping list for the grocery store. She encouraged Leah to linger at the stone circle. Leah leaned back in her chair with her eyes closed, soaking up the warm sunlight, breathing in the fragrant scents from Grammie's garden.

A shadow fell across her face.

"Hey there," a pleasant, youthful voice said.

When Leah opened her eyes she found a teen girl with long blond hair standing over here.

"Hey."

"You must be Leah. Ila said you'd be coming soon."

It was an instant before Leah remembered Ila was her grandmother's name.

"She did? When did she say that?"

"A couple weeks ago I guess. I'm Rose." The young woman extended her hand. On her wrist was a handmade bracelet made from mimosa seeds that had been carefully sewn together in a moderately complex and appealing pattern. The bracelet seemed familiar.

Leah took her hand. "Good to meet you. Nice bracelet."

"Thanks. Ila taught me how to make these."

Right. Leah had made one just like it long ago. What had become of her bracelet? "I remember now. Grammie taught me, too, when I was eight or nine."

"Grammie. I love the sound of that. Lots better than what we call my grandmother."

"Really? What do you call her?"

"Meemaw!"

Leah could not suppress a laugh. "Really?"

"Yep. Isn't that about as downhome redneck as you can get? Meemaw!" Rose said the word this time with an exaggerated Texan twang.

They both laughed.

"I'm sure your grandmother is a very nice woman."

"She's okay. Nothing like Ila, though. You're lucky to have a grandmother like her."

"You know, you're right. The sad thing is it's taken me a long time to realize that."

Rose nodded. "Yeah. She kind of told me a little bit about how you haven't been able to spend time with her. But hey, you're here now, right? Are you a goth?"

Leah was thrown off guard by the sudden shift in direction Rose had taken with the conversation. After a moment she remembered that was just something teen girls did. Sometimes. Some girls.

"I don't know that I'd call myself a goth. Why do you ask?"

"I think goths are cool. When Ila told me about you, the way you dressed, the clothes you wear, lots of black, you know, the tattoos and everything. The eye make-up. Kind of sounded goth to me. You don't like goths?"

"I have nothing against goths. I think it's labels I have a problem with."

"Hmmm." Rose gave that some thought.

The back door banged.

"Oh, good, you girls have met."

"Hi, Ila," Rose stood and went to Leah's grandmother for a hug.

Leah watched the two of them. A sense of resentment rising inside her, nothing big, just an awareness of emotional discomfort, resistance to the way things were. This girl from the neighborhood was more familiar with her Grammie than she was. That wasn't Rose's fault. She seemed like a nice girl. It wasn't Grammie's fault either. Still Leah felt cheated, like something of value had been stolen from her, kept out of her reach but all the time made freely available to others. There was no one to blame. Katherine, of course, but she was dead.

Wasn't she?

"How's your mama, Rosie?" Grammie asked, withdrawing from their hug.

"Oh, you know, same as ever."

"Rosie comes over and helps me out with the house cleaning," Grammie said to Leah.

"That's really nice," Leah said, pushing her incipient resentment into the dark hole where all her unpleasant feelings and memories were stored. The subterranean ice cave. The cave that never thawed.

"Will you two be okay just hanging out together for a while?" Grammie asked.

"Sure," Rose said, nodding as if it was an excellent idea.

"Yeah, but what's up?" Leah asked.

"Nothing's up really. I need to go to the grocery store and check on a shut-in friend of mine. I won't be gone that long. You girls might enjoy getting to know one another."

"I know I would," Rose said unabashedly.

Rose's happy face, her eager enthusiasm were contagious. Leah couldn't help smiling. "Yeah, me too. It's okay, Grammie. We'll try not to destroy the house while you're gone."

"You little heathens better behave yourselves."

Grammie went back inside the house and a moment later Leah heard her old Ford Escort start and pull away, the sound of its engine receding in the distance.

"Let's go inside. I gotta dust and stuff," Rose said, starting for the back door.

Leah followed her into the house.

Right away Rose gathered a dust cloth and some spray polish and began touching up all the surfaces in the living room. Leah watched her from the kitchen doorway.

"It's really nice of you to help Grammie like this," she said.

"Help Ila? You kidding? She's helping *me* out. She lets me do this to earn a little money. I'm saving for band camp this summer."

"Really?"

"Yeah. I tried getting a job at some of the fast-food places around town. I'm too young. They want you to be at least sixteen. Federal law or something."

"How old are you, Rose?"

"Fourteen."

Rose was fourteen. At the age of fourteen, Katherine had been getting pregnant and leaving the state to get married, rebelling against her mother and seducing a poor local boy who had no idea what he was getting into. Rose was a totally different kind of fourteen-year-old, the kind who cleaned houses to save for summer band camp, the kind who thought goths were really cool. Probably not a manipulative thought in her head. Ever.

"How's the summer camp fund looking? You going to have enough money?"

Rose stopped dusting and gave the matter some thought. "With the birthday money I got from Meemaw…" once again Rose exaggerated the pronunciation of the word. Leah joined her in laughter, effortlessly, like it was the most natural thing in the world. "With that money and a little bit more I make from babysitting I think I can swing it."

As if to illustrate the certainty of her claim she whacked a bookshelf with the dust cloth sending a small cloud of dust billowing out into the room. She fanned the dust away from her face.

"I guess that wasn't the slickest move," she said.

Once more Leah laughed, a pure joyful laugh. It felt so good she just let it continue until the laughter exhausted itself.

"Was it that funny?" Rose asked, looking a bit surprised.

"Maybe not. I just like you. You're so natural, so honest. I feel good being here with you." Leah said, plopping down on the sofa.

"Thanks. I like you, too. Ila said I'd like you. She's always right about pretty much everything."

"Why do you think that is?" Leah asked.

Rose continued dusting but slowed the movement of the dust cloth as she contemplated her answer. "I think it's because Ila is of a different order."

"Interesting. Explain."

"Well, I mean what do I know? I'm just a kid. Straight C student. Not the sharpest tool in the shed. But from what I've seen I think Ila is a cut above the average citizen."

"Really?"

Clearly this guileless fourteen-year-old girl had spent some time considering why Grammie was such a unique person.

"Yeah. Don't you think so? I mean she thinks for herself. All the time. About everything. I mean everything. Most people don't do that. They let the preacher or mama and daddy or the schoolteacher or the law do the thinking for them. Not Ila. She thinks. And when she does, she connects with a larger mind. You could call it God. I don't but others might. And she's so open to it she just always gets the answers she needs. And she's so kind and generous, with everyone, like me for instance. She makes it seem simple, like anyone can do it. And she's so convincing that I believe her when she says there's nothing she does that I can't do. She gives me confidence. Who else does that? Nobody, really. Even my own family members want to be better at something than me. Hear what I'm saying? I mean Mama wants to be a better cook than me. Dad thinks he's better than me just because, well, I'm a girl. He's not mean to me but maybe you understand that sort of chauvinistic attitude. My Meemaw, she wants to be a better Christian than me. That's okay. She can have that. Am I making any sense?"

"Yes," Leah said, her admiration for this gentle soul growing. "You just covered a lot of ground, Rose. And everything you said made perfect sense. I think you may just be a cut above the average citizen yourself."

"Really?" Rose was clearly delighted with Leah's assessment.

"Really." Leah recalled the resentment she had felt earlier when she watched Grammie and Rose hugging one another. Now she felt like Rose was welcome to as many hugs from Grammie as she could get. Not only was Grammie an exceptional woman but she was helping this insecure girl realize she too could be exceptional. And wasn't that exactly what Grammie had been doing for Leah?

"Well, if I'm a cut above anything I owe it to Ila. I see everything in a different light now thanks to her."

When Grammie came into the house loaded down with groceries, she was sweating.

"Need help carrying things in?" Rose asked, hopping up from her seat next to Leah on the sofa.

"Much appreciated," Grammie grunted, moving into the kitchen and easing the tangle of bags down onto the table.

Leah followed Rose outside and between the two of them they collected the remaining bags of food. The sun had warmed the day considerably. Leah hadn't noticed the change sitting in Grammie's cool living room. And earlier in the day, in the backyard, the temperature had been cool, pleasant. The afternoon had become just plain hot.

Rose helped Grammie sort through the bags of groceries, automatically putting items in their proper place, dancing a graceful duet with Grammie in which they efficiently situated all the purchased items without running into one another in the small kitchen. Leah watched. She didn't try to help. Rose knew where everything belonged and could anticipate Grammie's movements. Leah would have just been in the way had she tried to help. So she didn't.

Grammie dried her face with a paper towel.

"It's gotten downright hot out there today," she said. "I guess summer's arrived early this year."

"It's hot," Leah agreed.

"Maybe we could go swimming," Rose suggested with enthusiasm. "I love to swim. Do You?"

"Swimming? Where?"

"Dinosaur Valley State Park. There's a nice deep spot just upstream from the dinosaur tracks. Want to go? It'll be fun."

It seemed that Rose was not prepared to take no for an answer.

"I don't know," Leah said, looking at Grammie.

Her grandmother twisted the top off a bottle of water, swigged, then nodded quickly, "I think that's an excellent idea. I've had my exercise for the day. Why don't you girls go burn some of your youthful energy?"

"Sure?" Leah asked.

"Of course I'm sure. Get out and have some fun. I'll make us a nice dinner."

"Okay." Leah was warming to the idea of an outing.

"Alright!" Rose stretched, raising her arms in a triumphant gesture. "I'm gonna run home and get my swimming suit. I'll be right back." Like a whirlwind the eager fourteen-year-old was gone through the back door.

"She's a trip," Leah said.

"Yes, she is." Grammie smiled. "You like her don't you?"

"I do."

"I'm so glad. I hoped you would."

"She's so humble. She presents herself as maybe not being so bright but I think there's a good deal of depth to Rose."

"You're right. She's just shaking off the mistaken notions of a less than perfect upbringing. The same thing you're doing."

"We're both fortunate to have your guidance," Leah said.

"And I'm fortunate to have two young, bright lights so close to me at my age."

Leah thought about going to her grandmother and hugging her but then it seemed fine just the way things were, the two of them embracing through eye contact, radiating affection.

"Did you bring a swimsuit with you?" Grammie asked.

"No. I wasn't planning on swimming. But I have some shorts and a T-shirt that will serve the purpose."

"Remember Dinosaur Valley? You used to love going there."

"I remember. Sort of. Don't they have some giant dinosaur statues somewhere in the park?"

"They do. You always wanted us to take your picture with those dinosaurs."

"I did?"

"Yep. I'll have to get those photos out later and show them to you." Grammie thought for a moment, then started out of the kitchen. "I just remembered. I have something for you."

Leah went to the guest bedroom and changed into her shorts and T-shirt. She felt a chill as she was pulling her shirt over her head. Recalling her dreams of the night before Leah looked around the room, halfway expecting to see the little girl in the checkered dress. There was nothing unusual about the appearance of the bedroom. As she turned to leave, she heard an echo of the little girl's words. It was in her mind but more powerful than a typical memory, like an actual echo, welling up out of the ice cave.

This is my room. You can't stop me from playing here.

When Leah returned to the kitchen she found Grammie seated. On the table was a plastic dinosaur about seven inches long, a pale purple colored toy, a stegosaurus. With a puzzled expression, Leah lifted the toy dinosaur and examined it. "This is it? The thing you had for me?"

Grammie nodded. "Don't you remember him?"

Leah searched her memory. "Hmmm."

"You took that dinosaur everywhere with you. You called him Jason."

Leah jerked. The name was like a slap bringing her mind to attention. A torrent of memories poured into her consciousness. The dinosaur. Her dinosaur brother. More than a toy, her brother, her constant companion. Jason. The little dino brother who talked to her when they were alone. Jason.

"Jason?" Leah said aloud.

Grammie nodded.

"Like the other Jason? Mom's first child?"

Again, her grandmother nodded.

Leah started to say something to Grammie, to try to explain the flood of memories and their attendant emotions, but she did not get the chance.

The blond tornado, Rose, blew through the back door. "I'm back! Are you ready to go? You're going to absolutely love it. I just know you will. They uncovered some new tracks last spring. Dinosaurs are just the coolest. Don't you think so?"

Leah looked up at her new friend, the plastic stegosaur still in her hands.

"What's this?" Rose asked, reaching for the toy.

Leah let her take it. "It's my dinosaur brother, Jason."

"For real? That's cool. You like dinosaurs as much as I do, don't you?" Rose held the purple stegosaur up at eye level.

"I suppose I do."

"You two girls run on and have fun. Want to take my car?" Grammie offered.

"No. Of course not. We'll take the bug," Leah said.

"I love VW beetles," Rose said. "They're sort of modern and retro at the same time, you know?"

As they moved toward the front door, Grammie called out, "Leah, be sure to be home by sunset."

Leah drove through the old town square of Glenrose, past the Somervell County Courthouse, meandering through the town, then out into the countryside, following the signs toward Dinosaur Valley State Park.

"You've been to Dinosaur Valley before haven't you?" Rose asked.

"Yeah. My memories aren't so clear. That was a long time ago. Grammie tells me I used to make her take pictures of me with the big dinosaur statues."

"Those are so cool. I've taken my picture there lots of times, too. You know, we're a lot alike, Leah."

"Yes. I think we are."

As they neared the entrance to the park, rounding a curve in the road, a brown pre-fab building came into sight in a meadow on the right side of the road. There was a large, freshly painted wooden sign which read, Creationist Museum.

"I think that's new," Leah said, pointing at the building.

"Really? It's been there as long as I can remember," Rose said. "The Creationist Museum. It's kind of cool."

"So you've been inside?"

"Yeah. It's interesting. I think it's the fundamentalist Christians' response to all this dinosaur enthusiasm."

"Really? I've got to say, Rose, sometimes you don't sound like the straight C student you claim to be."

Rose grinned. "I have my moments."

"Yes, you do. Now tell me about that museum."

"It's got some cool stuff inside."

"Such as?"

"Such as an iron tool, something called a star-awl embedded in a piece of limestone that is supposed to be millions of years old. It's a tool, you know. A man-made tool. Inside a piece of rock that's millions of years old."

"Really? I never heard about that."

"Also, they have a display showing some human footprints that were found in the same strata as dinosaur tracks."

"For real?"

"Yep. Human footprints but really big human footprints. They say it proves the validity of the Bible because there's a part in there somewhere about giants on the earth a long time ago. And I think they believe that the age of the earth is in the thousands of years, not millions. So some giant human, a fallen angel or something, was hunting down dinosaurs a few thousand years ago. Something like that."

"Hmm. What do you think of all that?"

Rose pursed her lips a moment. "I think both the scientists and the Christians are right. And they're both wrong, too. I think they're both operating under what my dad calls unexamined assumptions. Maybe the earth's not as old as the scientists assume it is. Maybe there were giant humans at some point in history. That tool embedded in stone proves either stones form a lot quicker than scientists think or there were people on earth making tools a lot earlier than they believe. I think they're both a little right and a little wrong. Ila's always saying this is just a big dream we're living in anyway."

"Really. She says that?" Leah asked.

"Yeah. You never heard her say that? She says it a lot. I tend to believe her. Sometimes things happen in real life that just have the feeling of a dream. Kind of crazy things that some people would say are impossible, you know? Impossible or not. They happen."

"Yes," Leah said, "they certainly do."

"I've done some thinking about that. Ever heard of Electrical Universe theory?"

"I don't think so."

"You should check it out sometime. You can find a lot of lectures on the subject on YouTube. Basically there's a growing number of physicists who believe the universe, the entire universe, is basically an electrical phenomenon. I'm no scientist but what I like about these guys is they tell you in detail why they believe the things they do. Because their speculations are borne out by lab experiments, the things they say make a lot more sense than the theoretical stuff astrophysicists have been dreaming up for such a long time. You know, like the Big Bang theory and dark matter which is just a fairy tale to explain why gravity cannot account for all the things astronomers are witnessing now that we have better telescopes. Anyway in electrical universe theory Earth could be a lot younger than we thought. The geological processes that we thought were caused by millions of years of erosion and glaciers and all that could have been created overnight by massive electrical discharges. A lot of skeptics say the EU guys are talking nonsense but the debunkers seldom state their reasons for saying that. But the EU theorists always document their reasons for their ideas. So who would you trust, you know?

Anyway I was thinking, the whole idea of where consciousness comes from could be explained if it was just data carried on electrical currents just like in computers and smartphones. We all know electromagnetic processes happen in the brain. Did you know there were a lot of reports of dead people contacting their relatives through telephones in the early 20th century? This guy named D. Scott Rogo wrote a whole book about it. Documented cases. Suppose consciousness is just the accumulation of all experiences everywhere in the universe since the beginning of time. Or maybe this supermind riding on the electrical energy is what people have called God. Or like that line in the song and in the Epic of Gilgamesh about riders on the storm. So it could be gods as in plural. That's just my own personal theory. The EU guys don't say that but I think my idea fits in with their observations. Kind of mind-blowing don't you think? It gives credence to the old idea that everything, even rocks and trees, it's all conscious. Like all this matter in the universe arises out of consciousness not the other way around. There are a lot of people, smarter people than me, who believe that's true."

When Rose stopped talking, Leah just stared at her a moment.

Rose stared back. "What?"

"Rose, I don't feel qualified to comment on your ideas. I'll try to remember to check out this Electric Universe thing."

"Electrical Universe theory. EU for short. Not to be confused with the EU that stands for European Union."

"I'll be sure not to confuse those things. Right now I think I need a short breather. I need to let my mind have a little time to mull over what you've said."

"Yeah. It's a lot to wrap your head around for sure."

Leah slowed her car at the entrance to the Dinosaur Valley State Park.

A female park ranger came out of the headquarters and leaned down toward Leah's window. "Hello," she said, "welcome to Dinosaur Valley. Are you wanting a day pass or planning on camping?"

"We're just here for the afternoon," Leah answered.

"Okay. That'll be ten dollars."

"Hi, Josephine," Rose called.

The ranger stooped even lower to get a view of the passenger seat.

"Oh, hi, Rose! Back again so soon?"

"Yeah. It's hot so we're gonna swim. This is my new friend Leah."

"Pleased to meet you, Leah," the ranger said before straightening up.

"Likewise," Leah said, handing the woman a ten-dollar bill.

"You two have fun." Josephine handed a slip of paper with a number and a map on it through the window to Leah. "Keep this on your dashboard during your visit. Day pass holders are expected to be out of the park by sunset."

"We will be," Leah answered.

"Be safe."

The ranger returned to the small headquarters building.

Leah drove on into the park.

"Do we need to use this map?" she asked, gesturing toward the paper on her dash.

"Naw. I'll show you where to go. There's only one good spot for swimming and there's parking just up the hill from there. Should be lots of good shady places to park on a weekday like this."

Leah followed Rose's instructions and in a short time they parked and were descending stone stairs down to the river. It was pretty. The shores were lined with all manner of green vegetation and the slow-moving water of the Paluxy River reflected the blue of the sky.

"Beautiful," Leah said.

"Yeah. This is the time of year to come. Later in the summer everything turns brown and the river sometimes dries up completely."

Rose led Leah across a stone walkway to the far side of the river. A moveable sign indicated tracks in a pool of water against the far shore.

"See here," Rose said, pointing, "two different types of dinosaur tracks. The rangers say this looks like a smaller dinosaur was being chased by a big one." Rose drew her hands up close to her shoulders and stomped around, chomping her teeth, offering Leah her impression of a tyrannosaur.

Leah laughed. "Rose, you are not right girl!"

"I know. That's what everyone says. Come on, the best swimming spot's over here."

Leah followed her friend along a trail and up over some large boulders to a place where the river was deeper and large trees, hundreds of years old, shaded the water.

"We call this the blue hole," Rose explained. Then, dropping her towel on a rock, she jumped into the water.

Leah put her own towel next to Rose's and after a moment's deliberation, decided to just put her car keys in the pocket of her shorts. It didn't seem like the best idea to leave them wrapped in her towel where some passerby might find them, though there weren't many people around. The older lady with the picnic basket was not likely to be a thief. Neither was the little girl holding her hand. A little water wouldn't hurt her keys. At least she hoped it wouldn't.

"How's the water?" Leah called, edging toward the river.

"It's a little cold at first. But just jump right in. That's the best way. You get used to it pretty quick."

Leah followed Rose's advice, dropping rapidly into the water, submerging, then breaking the surface with a shriek of both shock and delight. "My god, it's cold!"

"You'll adjust." Rose was skimming the surface of the river, doing the backstroke in and out of the shady patches thrown by the overhanging trees.

Leah drew a deep breath and swam through the water, allowing her body to find a peaceful agreement between the ambient air temperature and the river's chill. The sound of a guide drifted upriver to her ears as she swam. The guide explained how prehistoric creatures of the early Cretaceous Epoch had deposited footprints in this muddy river bottom 113 million years ago. The monotonous drone of the guide's narration mingled with the drones of a variety of insect species crawling and flying through the valley in the rich ecosystem the river provided. There were occasional excited vocalizations from the throats of the boy scouts the guide was addressing. These, too, had a faraway, dreamy quality as if the air was too thick, heavy like the water, providing resistance to the sound waves as they emerged from their point of transmission in the movements of creatures and humans and traveled to their termination in Leah's eardrums and brain. Interpretation of the sounds was hazy, losing meaning, dropping off into a symphony of natural music with no intentional information, just a lullaby for the listener. The world seemed tired, weary of its constant interspecies attempts to capture attention and to assign meaning.

Weary.

Leah.

She sank beneath the water, letting the molecules of combined oxygen and hydrogen caress her in a manner no other earthly substance could. This was the womb, the cradle of life. Here all living forms, no matter how diverse, simple or complex were created. This was the workshop of the gods. Leah lingered as long as she could, embraced by the liquid gathered like a silver blue ribbon in this lowest level of the limestone terrain. When her lungs began to ache for oxygen, air, the breathable atmosphere to which she was accustomed, she broke the surface and rose on her feet, flinging her wet hair from her face. Some of the water clung by force of gravity to her hair and body but most returned like a homesick child to the body of the river.

There was a hum, an alien drone filling the air, a vibration striving to bring all movement into resonance with it.

Where were the people?

Where was Rose?

The guide and boy scouts had vanished. The old woman carrying a picnic basket in one hand and holding a little girl's hand in the other whom Leah had glimpsed just before immersing herself in the river was gone. The world as Leah knew it was gone. A sensation of dread tried to fight its way up through the many layers of her consciousness and express itself as a full-blown emotion but it was powerless to do so against the sedative influence of the drone. The drone ruled this world and everything within it, including Leah.

The drone was Leah.

Or maybe it just wanted her to believe that.

How had she been sucked out of the place she called reality and deposited in this other echo world? The process had been relatively unobtrusive. No claps of thunder, no bone-jarring jolts. Just a wave of realization dawning in her heavy consciousness like the onset of the effects from a shot of morphine. The pervasive drone was drugging her, lulling her, drawing her into its mysterious all-consuming process.

Process.

The process called Leah was being dissolved by a larger process for which she had no name.

This alien state of being was not immediately identifiable as a threat, it was in fact soothing, lulling and all the more frightening to Leah by virtue of its insidious appeal. Her mind cast about, searching the landscape for anything solid to hold onto.

In the dense azure sky above her, reptilian birds soared on cosmic updrafts, making no sound, no more threatening than a swarm of mayflies. The vegetation surrounding the river grew but in an ill-defined way, nothing more than swirls of greens, blues and yellows, an experimental abstract watercolor by an inexperienced artist. The world was here but distinctions were muted to the point of insanity.

Is this what it's like to be crazy?

There was only the drone.

Then Leah saw the form across the river. It was dark, amorphous, perhaps scaly? Reptilian? It shifted like a seal basking on a sunny beach. A head emerged from the bulk of the thing and eyes caught the light of the sun, sending a wordless signal to Leah. This was something. Something on which to focus her attention. Something that might stop her mind, her identity from being absorbed completely in the drone.

Sensing her scrutiny, the thing sharpened itself, rendering its features in a more focused form. It was dark. It was reptilian. It breathed. Presumably air, but what it wanted most to breathe was Leah. It wanted to inhale her, to take her into itself, digest her and pass her on to the master of this realm. The drone. That oppressive vibration.

It seemed familiar. She moved slowly through the sluggish primeval water toward the thing. She knew it. It clearly knew her. Perhaps the beast on the rock was her home? The place she belonged? Sensing her thoughts, the thing fashioned a face for itself. A face capable of smiling. That smile beckoned, the eyes encouraged Leah's progress. She knew the eyes and smile. Those features belonged to…

Katherine.

Her mother? Here? That seemed unlikely. That was an idea Leah knew she needed to fight. She would not believe that. She refused to accept the idea as a building block of reality.

The thing knew her thoughts. Felt her resistance. It raised an appendage. A leg? An arm? Was it a tentacle? It beckoned.

But the spell was at least partially broken.

Leah stopped, planting her feet firmly on the solid stone bottom of the stream.

That thing was angry. Its anger was not revealed by abrupt movement or angry noises. It didn't bellow or make any movement to come toward her. It could not. It was planted on the rock, on the far shore of the river. It had no power to force her to approach. Its only power lay in the deception that it was a worthy destination, something Leah herself might desire. Once Leah knew that the thing had no hold on her. It was powerless.

In response to Leah's thoughts the thing's anger dissipated and transformed into a sort of hopeless sorrow. It didn't moan but the emanation of its energy had the same mournful quality that a moan would have signified. It was not a monster. No, that was not quite right. It *was* a monster but not something to be feared. Pity was a more appropriate response. The thing on the rock shifted listlessly, losing its detail, becoming little more than a pulpy pile of biological debris, perhaps not even alive, but heaving with some unidentified influence. An internal chemical reaction?

"Would you care to join us?"

The voice came faintly, but clear and sparkling in its quality, like the tinkling of silverware in a distant dining room.

Leah turned and looked back toward the other shore of the river, the rocky bank from which she had entered the water.

A woman sat on a large stone with a tablecloth set out in front of her. She was taking items of food from the open picnic basket beside her. A little girl waited patiently, watching the woman's methodical handling of each item extracted from the basket.

"We have some lovely sandwiches," the woman called, this time a little louder, a little clearer, a bit more substantial. Her words still had the appeal of silver bells.

The little girl looked at Leah.

It was only then that Leah recognized the woman. It was Grammie. The little girl was…not Katherine. The little girl was Leah.

I must swim toward myself.

Leah laughed at the seeming absurdity of the thought.

"Join us," the woman beckoned. And when she did the drone diminished almost to the point of silence. She raised a white triangle. It was a sandwich. "I think you'll like these."

Leah moved toward the shore. She heard nothing but felt the clinging sorrow of the amorphous beast sucking at her back, trying to regain a grip on her consciousness.

"What is that thing?" Leah heard the little girl ask her grandmother. "It's ugly."

"Nothing to fear, dear," the woman said. "It's a pitiful mistake. That's all."

Leah dove under the surface of the water and swam with all her strength toward the woman, the girl and the sandwiches. Near the shore, she broke the surface.

"Isn't this the best?" Rose said, swimming toward her.

The woman who was not her grandmother and the little girl who was not Leah quietly munched their sandwiches and made picnic conversation about butterflies, trees and sunlight. They were seemingly unaware of Leah and Rose. The boy scouts down the way applauded their guide for his excellent presentation, then marched off single file toward the next point of interest on their itinerary.

"You okay?" Rose asked.

Leah stared. At the world. Her world. A world that seemed amazingly strange and rare due to its recent absence from her perception.

This is reality. Right?

"Hey, Leah," Rose said a bit louder. "You're acting kind of weird. Are you okay?"

"Yeah," Leah said, wiping river water from her eyes. "I'm fine."

"Good. I thought maybe you'd gone off to la la land for a minute. You know, like heat stroke or some kind of mental seizure. You're not epileptic are you?"

"You're kind of talking a lot," Leah said, hoping Rose would shut up, but not wanting to hurt her feelings.

"Yeah, I get that a lot. I'll zip it."

Rose went back to swimming laps around the blue hole. Leah just moved about randomly in the water questioning the validity of the inexplicable experiences she had encountered since her return to Glenrose. This was not a puzzle to be solved by logic. In terms of the reality she had been taught to believe and advised not to stray from, there was little doubt that Leah was having what most would call a psychotic break.

This distressed her, terrified her actually.

What if these episodes just continued to occur for the rest of her life? What if she was in the middle of applying a tattoo to some unsuspecting customer's back? Would she just zone out? Or might she begin drawing images of the strange things she was seeing in her mind's eye or alternate dimension or bardo or wherever it was these things were happening?

Am I in hell?

After a while the picnickers gathered their belongings and left. Leah waded up out of the water onto the large rock where they had been. She spread her towel and laid down on it to let the sun dry her. After a minute or two she was joined by Rose. Rose spread her towel alongside Leah's and eased herself down onto it, throwing one arm over her eyes as she allowed the sun to cast its penetrating rays into her body.

Soon Rose said, "I hope you still like me. I know I talk too much sometimes."

This simple pair of statements brought Leah out of her self-absorbed reverie.

"Oh, Rose…"

"Yeah?"

"Of course, I still like you. I apologize for being short with you earlier. I'm just going through a lot of strange things in my head. And…well, part of the time I'm not sure it's just in my head. It's scary. I'm sorry that I became annoyed with you. I like you. I like you a lot."

"I like you a lot, too, Leah. And I do talk too much. I know that. Just the way my brain is wired, I guess. But I know how to listen, too. If you want to talk about your mom or anything. I want to hear what you're thinking."

Leah's lifelong tendency to withdraw into her impervious shell of introversion was being challenged. Her norm would have been to withdraw, to walk away without explaining anything or, at most, to say, 'I don't feel like talking about it.' But what had that strategy gotten her?

Ever? A great deal of distance and misunderstanding between herself and her friends, potential friends and coworkers. It had channeled her into a college degree and career she absolutely hated.

Things had been better since she had thrown the past out like yesterday's garbage and had become a tattoo artist. Roger could be prickly at times but he was also a really good influence on her, a solid friend. Ramona was an angel; the best friend Leah had ever known. Grammie. Reacquainting with Grammie was something like a dream come true. But also like a nightmare come true. It was only since Leah had arrived in Glenrose that her breaks with reality had started. She was frightened but, even so, she realized all of the good things she experienced were the result of opening up and reaching out. Her years of lonely isolation, keeping her thoughts to herself, had given her nothing worth holding onto.

As Leah considered all this, Rose became restless.

"If you don't want to talk, that's okay too," she offered tentatively.

"Okay," Leah said. "I'll talk, you listen. But let's get something straight right now at the start, okay? No matter what I say, no matter how I seem, I am your friend. So don't second guess me alright? I am your friend. I like you. Don't be insecure around me because I'm pretty insecure myself and we'll just end up misunderstanding one another and weakening our friendship. Okay?"

When Leah looked over at Rose there was an almost ecstatic expression on the girl's face.

"Right on. Of course. We are friends from now on. I like the sound of that!" Rose looked up at the sun and shouted, "Wahoo!"

Leah's confused expression precipitated an explanation from Rose.

"Sorry, but I just feel so good I had to let it out. Express it, you know? I've never had a friend like you and I'm just really happy about it."

Leah smiled. "Okay. I'm happy, too, Rose." The smile left her face. "Now, what I'm going to talk about is…well, parts of it are painful. And it's kind of a big deal that I'm even able to talk about it now. So you're going to have to just bite your tongue and not say anything unless I tell you it's okay to speak."

"Alright. That makes sense," Rose agreed.

"Okay." Leah laid flat on her back and addressed her comments to the sun and the blue sky, softly, so any passing strangers would not overhear. "My mother was a very aggressive, rebellious teenager. By the time she was your age she had already been married and had a baby. The baby died."

Leah paused, expecting that her young friend might not be able to resist a spontaneous exclamation. There *was* a sharp inhalation from Rose, indicating surprise perhaps, but she was true to her word and did not speak.

"There's a lot I could say about that but really I just found out about it so I'm not really qualified to speak on the subject. I have feelings about it but I'm still processing those feelings. I guess everything I've learned from Grammie since I've been here just sort of validates what I already felt about my mother. But it's still kind of…shocking, bewildering, troubling…heartbreaking."

Leah drew in a couple of deep breaths, trying to make each one prolonged and controlled. The deliberate introduction of oxygen into her system might help her maintain a grip on her emotions. She did not want to call attention to herself or derail her explanation by bursting into tears.

"So I think I'll just talk a little bit about things I remember from my childhood, my own direct experience of my mother.

"First, she was always beautiful. Men and women were both drawn to her because she seemed so together, so poised and in charge of everything. She was always volunteering for everything, president of different clubs, things like that. I always felt like I was just in the way, keeping her from being who she really was and doing the things she wanted to do. I was born when she was just sixteen. There's a picture somewhere of Mom at her high school graduation, dressed in her robe and mortar board, and right there beside her is me in a baby carriage.

"My dad adored her. But he was in the military because he didn't have a lot of other options. He was gone a lot. Sometimes when Dad was overseas Mom would receive flowers from men I didn't know. That bothered me. I asked Mom about it and she laughed and said it was some kind of mistake, that the florist must have had the wrong address. That was something she did back then, that nervous laugh. I came to realize it as a tell. It meant she was lying. Later she must've figured it out herself because she stopped doing it. About the flowers, I thought about writing to my father and telling him but I never did. Partly because I didn't want to hurt him and partly because I wasn't sure it was not the sort of thing all adults did. Maybe they married but were not monogamous when they were apart. Lots of things adults did were very confusing to me. I had a hard time making sense out of the way adults said one thing but did another. How they attacked others for doing the very things they themselves were doing. It was a maze to me and I couldn't find my way out of it.

"When we were at church or out in public anywhere, my mom made a big show of saying and doing all the right things, the things she believed others expected of her. People thought she was just perfect. When we were alone she could be very brutal. I knew she would not have been that way if my father was there. But he wasn't there. He was half a world away. And there was no one to run interference between me and my mom. Grammie tried to be there for me but Mom didn't let her come around that much. Grammie was here and we were in Fort Worth. I wanted to see her more. She was always the best part of my life. I guess she still is. Except for my friend Ramona. And you.

"Sometimes Mom would go into a rage and say things like they had never wanted me to be born. She would beat me with her belt for little things like accidentally breaking a plate. When I was four I learned a bad habit from a neighbor girl. Her name was Donna Bess. When she was annoyed with someone she would stick her tongue out at them. I'd heard her mother telling her not to do it, I knew it wasn't polite behavior but, at the same time, I thought it was funny. It made me giggle.

"One night at dinner I stuck my tongue out at Mom. She reached over and slapped my chin with such force that I nearly bit my tongue off. Blood went everywhere. We both freaked out. She took me to a doctor but there really wasn't much he could do. I don't know how she explained the injury to the doctor. I don't know if he suspected abuse.

"I do know that months later she had a visitor. Some old woman I don't remember seeing before or after that day. They were drinking tea and at one point they talked about disciplining children. Mom sort of bragged about not being afraid to use the belt. She said something about sparing the rod and spoiling the child. I was little and still trying to figure things out. Hell, I'm still trying to figure things out. But anyway…I believed I had deserved any beatings or other punishment my mother had given me. I jumped into the conversation and said something like, 'When I was bad and stuck my tongue out at Mama, she slapped me and made me bite my tongue. Didn't you, Mama?' I thought I was being a good kid by condoning my mother's behavior, by admitting I deserved to be punished. The old woman just stared at me blankly. My mother said, 'No, honey, I wouldn't do something like that to you. You're misremembering. You were playing with one of your friends and fell on the sidewalk.' That was the first time I remember her gaslighting me. Over the years it became a regular habit for her.

"Anytime we were out in public and another adult commented on how polite I was or how smart I was or how mature I was…it was like Mom couldn't stand to hear anyone complimenting me. She would immediately say something to undermine the compliment, something that would invalidate it. Every time she spoke about me it seemed to discourage me from anything remotely resembling a positive self-image.

"I could never discuss anything with her. Emotional stuff I mean. She didn't have time or patience for it. Everything she did led me to believe that I was pretty much worthless. A waste of her time. Sometimes images would arise in my mind, things that I felt like were memories but I couldn't be sure. Like being locked in a closet for a long time. Like being left with babysitters who sexually abused me. But I couldn't be certain about any of that because Mom just gaslighted me so many times I doubted my own judgment, my own memories. I couldn't trust her and she'd made damn sure I didn't trust my own memory. I pretty much ended up not trusting anything or anyone.

"After she divorced my dad she went on the hunt for a man with some money, a new husband who could give her the lifestyle she craved. She found Charles, poor dumb schmuck. That's not right. He wasn't poor and he wasn't dumb. I hate to call him a schmuck but that's the way I think of him because he was so incapable of seeing through my mother's manipulations. Charles was a good man. He was educated and successful. What he was not is good looking. He was thrilled that a pretty woman like my mom wanted to be with him. He fell head over heels.

"Once at a cocktail party at our house, I heard one of his friends ask him how he'd met Mom. He said at a Christmas party she'd walked up to him and said, 'Do you believe in sex at first sight?' They all had a big laugh over that. I was in the next room and they didn't know I'd heard it. It might not have made any difference if they had known. The people at those parties all had money, they all liked to drink and they had a certain sense of entitlement. Every one of them thought they were special somehow and deserving of more than what the inferior people of the world had a right to expect. And Mom was the spider at the center of the web of all this greed and self-importance. She knew these people were by far the easiest to manipulate. Just appeal to their egos, flirt with the men and lavish empty compliments on the women. She was in her element.

"Charles was very good to me. He never mistreated me in any way. He encouraged me to apply at good universities and he paid for my education. Sometimes he intervened when Mom was out of control. But as smart and successful as Charles was, he was still just putty in Mom's hands. She could throw a temper tantrum that reduced him to a submissive, insecure, child. So many times I saw him buy her flowers and do other things to get back in her good graces, even though she was the one who'd been out of line, unreasonable, just…psychotic. She knew where his buttons were and she pushed them every chance she got.

"Finally, after Charles died, I don't know, a light just sort of turned on in my head. I guess I realized that I was actually an okay person and mom was never going to be anything more than the greedy, manipulative bitch that she was. I just quit having anything to do with her. As soon as I made that decision I realized the only reason I'd gotten the degree I earned at the university was because it was what *she* had wanted. Well, Charles wanted it too. But still I was living a life that I did not want. So I quit.

"I'd always wanted to be an artist. When I was little, I'd show Mom a picture I'd drawn with my crayons. She'd point out everything that was wrong with my drawings. Once in a while she'd put one on the refrigerator but I think that was just because she'd seen that other mothers did that. She was incapable of feeling the normal emotions women have but she was savvy enough to imitate their behavior.

"I did want to be an artist but I didn't want to starve to death for the sake of art. I'd gotten accustomed to having a decent apartment and plenty of food in the refrigerator, you know? So I did some research and realized that being a tattoo artist is the best entry level position into the field of art. If you're any good, you make decent money from year one and it just goes up from there. You make your own hours, you dress and behave in a manner that reflects who you really are, not some corporate bullshit image an old white guy in a boardroom came up with. So that's what I did.

"I work with a guy named Roger. I started to say I work *for* a guy named Roger but he's made it clear he considers me an associate not an employee, though he does own the place, Ink City. He can be tough. His standards are high, both in the quality of the tatts and in the sense of customer service we provide. He knows it's important for our customers to feel comfortable in our space. So we do what we can to provide a positive experience short of being phony and working too hard to get them to like us. People with tattoos always have more than one. Well, my dad had only one. It was my mother's name on his left shoulder. Poor Dad. After she divorced him he had that tatt covered up by a larger one of a scorpion. His zodiac sign was Scorpio. But most people these days get multiple tatts. And if they like your work, they come back. People don't usually flit around experimenting with different artists they don't know.

"So I make good money. Things are going great really. I have time to do other things besides work and I experiment with other forms of art, you know, take classes in sculpting and painting. It wasn't until Mom died that I began to realize what a box my head was in even though I'd broken free of my mother. I wasn't getting those regular doses of emotional abuse from her but deep inside I was still hurting from the pains she'd inflicted on me when I was too young to defend myself. People tried to talk to me about it but I was in denial. Everyone could see what I was unable to see; that my mother had done a number on me and I needed to heal.

"I have this great friend, Ramona. She's a sort of psychic medium. She does tarot readings and Reiki healing and stuff like that. She's kind of a throwback to the hippie women of the sixties and seventies. You know, you see them in old magazines and in documentaries about Woodstock or Haight Ashbury. Those long-haired, free-wheeling women with their amazing colorful clothes and their unshaved armpits.

"Ramona's the one who talked me into coming here to see Grammie. She's helped me all along in the process of getting out from under Mom's thumb and taking responsibility for my health, both physical and mental. She applauded my decision to just cut Mom completely out of my life. She said I had broken the spell. She said once the spell was broken I needed to start using my own magic to build the world I wanted to live in. She makes it seem like a fairy tale but it's a fairy tale you can believe in, you know? There's nothing phony about Ramona at all. She's the best friend I could hope for. You'd really like Ramona. And I know she'd love you."

Leah drew a deep breath. Her body was dry except for a bit of dampness on her underside. The sun was beginning to feel uncomfortably warm.

"I think I've had enough sun for one day," Leah said. "Ready to leave?"

"Sure."

They stood up, folded their towels and climbed up the stone stairs, under the cover of ancient oaks, to the parking lot above. The changing position of the sun meant the VW was no longer in shade.

"Car's going to be like an oven," Leah said.

"It'll be okay. We can sit on our towels, can't we?"

"Sure."

Leah rolled the windows down and let the hot air escape from the car's interior.

"I don't get out much," Leah said. "I have covered parking at my apartment complex and I forget how hot a car can get in the Texas sun."

"Yep. It's hot alright."

Leah started the car, cranked up the AC but left the windows down.

On their way out of the park they drove past the gift shop and the field where the two gigantic dinosaurs stood.

"Want to stop and take our picture with the dinos?" Leah asked.

"Only if you do."

Leah wondered if she had told her young friend too much. She did not want their outing together to end on a somber note.

"I'd like it. It'll give me something to remember this day by."

Leah pulled to the roadside. Grabbing her phone, she and Rose took a series of selfies including the obligatory fearful pose in which they acted as if they were about to be eaten by the tyrannosaur. The mood was considerably lighter and they both were laughing as they returned to the car.

"You know this is the first time in the last 24 hours I've even thought about my phone," Leah marveled. "That's got to be a first."

They climbed into the VW.

"Yeah, I know what you mean. Most of my friends are completely obsessed with their phones."

"You're not?"

"Can't be obsessed with something you don't have. Well, I mean you can, but that's a different sort of obsession I suppose."

"You don't have a phone?" A tone of incredulity crept into Leah's voice. A fourteen-year-old girl with no smartphone? In this day and age?

"Nope. Mom and Dad have done a lot of research on the negative effects of smartphones on young teens especially. They say I can have one on my sixteenth birthday. I don't mind. I have a computer and internet access. I don't feel like I'm missing out on much. Besides, I like real life a lot more than most kids my age. I'm not into all the social media and gaming, you know?"

Leah could see the validity of Rose's parents' concerns but she also knew how cruel kids Rose's age could be about material possessions and the status they supposedly bestowed on their owners. Leah had been down that road but

Charles had always been willing to buy her anything she asked for. At the time she'd considered herself one of the lucky ones and had not been above flaunting her possessions in front of kids who had less.

"I think you are probably mentally and physically healthier than most of your friends. If today is any indication. How many laps did you do in the blue hole?"

Rose smiled. "I didn't count. I usually just swim until I'm tired."

"Listen. Rose, I'm feeling a little weird about the way I dumped on you back at the river. That was a lot of dark stuff to lay on a girl your age. I hope I didn't upset you."

"I asked you to tell me. I wanted you to. It is a lot to think about. It made me realize how good I have it. I've had my complaints about my family but nothing anywhere near what you've been through."

"Still want to be friends?"

"Of course I do!"

"Do me a favor, Rose. Please don't talk about the things I told you with anyone else. Not everyone would understand or accept that stuff."

"I won't tell anyone."

"Thanks."

"I think I know what you're talking about, though. People not understanding. There was this kid Tommy in middle school. His parents got arrested for sexually abusing him. Everyone knew about it. It was in the news and lots of teachers and kids at school talked about it. They treated Tommy like *he* was the criminal. Nobody would have anything to do with him."

"Did you try to be friends with him?"

"A little. I didn't really know what to say, you know?"

Leah did know. When she was fourteen, talking to boys seemed an impossible task. She still struggled with social poise when it came to guys. Unless she had been drinking, in which case she was, if not poised, uninhibited.

"Swimming always makes me a little hungry. I'm wanting a milkshake. How about you?"

"Depends. If you're offering to buy, then yes. If not, I need to save my money for band camp. Sorry to be a mooch."

"Rose, you are not a mooch! Of course I'm buying!"

"In that case, bring it on!"

They pulled into an old-fashioned burger joint on the highway at the edge of town, the kind with the menu and speakers at each parking space, where you order from your car and they bring your food out to you.

Leah opted for a plain vanilla shake. Rose selected mint chocolate chip. When the carhop delivered their order, Leah paid and tipped generously.

"You sure?" the bespectacled girl asked, clearly unaccustomed to receiving a five-dollar tip, especially on such a small order.

"You bet. That's all for you, Tanya," Leah said, reading the girl's name tag.

"Thanks, ma'am."

"Do you know that girl, Tanya?" Leah asked before taking a sip of her shake.

"I know who she is but I've never really talked to her. She's a couple of years older than me. Her parents are Seventh Day Adventists. They make even my Meemaw seem liberal minded."

Leah laughed. "Yeah, you sort of indicated that your grandmother was pretty religious."

"That's an understatement. Her whole life centers around the church. That's fine for her but I'm not interested in going to church every Wednesday night and twice on Sunday. It's just too much."

"Does she try to get you to go with her?"

"Relentlessly. I don't like it. And the boys my age who go to that church all the time…"

"Yeah? What about them?"

"Well, they make the guys in the band seem like studs."

Now Leah really laughed.

"That sounded like a left-handed compliment."

"It was."

"Tell me about the guys in band."

"They're okay. What should I expect after all, right? They're geeks like me."

"As one geek to another, I have to say there are worse things a girl could be."

"I know. I kind of like being a geek. But I don't think I'd mind being a little more popular."

"Trust me, Rose, a lot of the issues that seem very important now will just vanish into thin air soon and you'll wonder why you gave them a second thought."

"You sound like my mom, now."

"Well, you're mom's right."

"Do you think there really is a hell?" Rose asked.

"Why are you asking me?" Leah felt herself extremely unqualified to offer an opinion about anything even remotely theological.

"My Meemaw is always on me about attending church. It bugs the crap out of me. My mom says Meemaw is just trying to save me from going to hell. Like her motives are good."

"Does your mom think you're in danger of hell?"

"No. Of course not. I don't even have a smartphone for god's sake! I'm a geek band girl. What could I possibly have done that would send me to hell? If there is one, I mean. Hypothetically."

"I'm not the best person to ask about these things. I never really believed in heaven or hell but since I've been here in Glenrose I've experienced some things I would've thought were impossible. I just don't know, Rose."

"If Meemaw knew about some of the things Ila has told me, she'd probably say Ila was a witch."

Leah laughed again, enjoying this view into her young friend's concerns.

"I guess Grammie is pretty much a witch when you get right down to it."

"Yeah. But she's about the kindest person I've ever known. My Meemaw would say she was probably going to hell because of what the Bible says about witches and stuff like that."

"Think of whatever Grammie is as just another religion. Like that girl Tanya. She's in a fringe denomination of Christianity. Different. But you don't think she's going to hell do you?"

"No. Of course not. Anyway, I wasn't really thinking about Ila or Meemaw or Tanya."

"Explain."

"I was thinking about…your mother."

"Oh." The light went on in Leah's head and it made perfect sense. The things Leah had told Rose about Katherine were probably the worst things the girl ever heard about someone to whom she had such a direct connection, as opposed to foreign dictators and serial killers and such.

"I feel uneasy saying this but the things your mom did to you were awful. I can't even imagine a parent doing those things or what I would be like if I had been through that. I mean, I whine about being pressured into going to church. It's annoying but it's not..."

"What?"

"Evil."

There it was.

"Do you think there is any payback for people like your mom after they die?"

"I don't have an answer, Rose. I could speculate but I can't say anything that would carry any sort of conviction. I guess that's part of what I came here to figure out. I think Grammie will help me sort through it."

Rose nodded. "Ila can help you with that if anybody can."

Leah was determined to veer away from any further discussion of such serious topics. When she dropped Rose off at her house, she wanted to part company with a light heart and a smile on her face, for Rose's sake.

"How's that mint chocolate chip shake?" she asked.

"Great. Thanks for buying it. The chips can clog up the straw sometimes. It's a little more challenging than just a regular shake with no chunks in it. But I kind of like that."

"Yeah. I figured you for a girl who likes a challenge."

When Leah dropped Rose off at her house the sun was low in the sky, near the horizon.

"Can I come visit again tomorrow?" Rose asked hopefully as she stepped out of the car.

"Sure," Leah answered. "But don't come until after lunch okay? I'm pretty sure Grammie and I have a lot to talk about. Some of it's private, just between her and me."

"I understand," Rose said. "See you around one then?"

"See you then."

Leah watched Rose go inside. She wondered if Meemaw was in there somewhere, peeking out through the curtains to get a glimpse of her. She circled back to Grammie's neighborhood and parked in front of the little storybook house made of petrified wood.

What a perfect house for Grammie.

Leah got out of the car, threw her towel over her shoulder and went up onto the porch. To the west, the sunlight through the trees was every bit as beautiful as it had been the evening before. A breeze stirred the branches, creating a kaleidoscopic play of golden light over the yard, the stone house and Leah. The sunlight seemed nourishing. Full of life.

As before, the screen door was closed but the wooden door was open. Leah slipped inside and was about to call out to Grammie when she heard what sounded like an argument in progress.

"I hate you! You stupid bitch! You're always trying to control me!"

"Grammie?" Leah called out, rushing toward the sound.

She heard a door slam.

When she entered the living room she found Grammie seated on the sofa, her head bowed, her face full of sorrow.

"Grammie, what's wrong?" Leah said, stepping up to within a foot or two of her grandmother.

Grammie said nothing.

"Grammie?" Leah had a rising feeling of nausea in her stomach. Her throat constricted and there was a bitter taste in the back of her mouth. What was happening? She knew it had nothing to do with the milk shake.

Then, Leah noticed. Grammie on the sofa was at least twenty years younger than the Grammie she had left behind when she and Rose took off for Dinosaur Valley. Her hair was darker, she had fewer wrinkles, she weighed less. What's more, Leah was certain the Grammie on the sofa was completely unaware of her presence.

"Oh, Grammie," Leah whispered, "What's going on?"

The door to the spare bedroom, the room where Leah had been sleeping, flew open, its doorknob banging against the wall.

"Who the fuck has been in my room?" a young girl screamed. The girl stood in the doorway, a teen girl about Rose's age. But very different by most every measure from Rose. Leah knew it was Katherine.

This youthful specter of her mother was slender and emanated a wave of strange energy. Leah noticed a halo of distortion around her like the effect of summer heat rising off a paved road. With savage gusto Katherine threw two items into the living room.

Leah recognized them as her laptop and her backpack.

"What the fuck?"

She struggled to understand. It was tough enough accepting that she had a window into a time long before she was born. But if that was the case, how the hell was it that her backpack and laptop were here to be flung about by an out-of-control teenaged version of Katherine?

"I said who the fuck has been in my room?" Katherine screamed.

Now, the ambient sound in the room underwent a dramatic shift. The change was so abrupt it made Leah's ears pop. After the pop Leah could hear the drone. The same drone she'd heard during her nightmarish experience on the river earlier that day.

Grammie raised her head and looked at her daughter with weary, exhausted patience.

"No one. No one has been in your room, Katherine. Why do you say that?" Grammie's voice sounded distant, muffled somehow. As if the drone was trying to bury her words, eradicate her ability to communicate.

"Because of this stuff!" Katherine shouted, pointing at Leah's belongings which were now on the floor in the middle of the living room.

"What stuff?" It became apparent that this apparitional version of Grammie could not see the laptop or the backpack, just as she was unable to detect Leah's presence.

Instinctively, Leah gathered up her things and placed them on one of the chairs opposite Grammie's sofa. When she did this she felt a tangle of tumbling energy, something like a cloud of very humid air or a fog, enveloping her body. Something attaching itself to her.

She looked at Katherine standing in the doorway and beyond her, in the bedroom behind her, Leah saw fantastic dark shapes shifting, glistening faintly. They gave the impression of plants bursting into form like timelapse images of growing flowers or vegetables that Leah had seen in documentary films. These things were nothing so lovely as flowers nor benign as vegetables. These were ugly things, hungry, vicious and aggressively seeking entrance into this world.

The drone grew more insistent, more pervasive.

Leah's chest experienced a sharp pain. She was terrified. These things…Leah saw they had extended branches, or maybe tentacles, and had attached themselves to Katherine. Katherine's complexion grew dark, grayish blue like a body discovered by police in some murder investigation. But she wasn't dead. No, she was bristling with life, but that life was not human.

The discolored apparition stared at Leah, its eyes squinting.

She's starting to see me.

The specter of Katherine stumbled out of the bedroom dragging the rootlike attachments behind her. The root tentacles oozed a nasty viscous fluid. The fluid stained everything with which it came in contact, the door frame, the Persian rug on the floor of the living room. It was vile looking, and smelling, Leah noted as the odor of the thing or things that had now mostly overgrown the entire bedroom, obscuring the walls, the furniture, the bed, assailed her nostrils.

"Who are you?" the dark Katherine demanded. The air around this repugnant entity was now swirling with that puzzling distortion like a heatwave, making it impossible to see anything clearly except for Katherine and her demonic face.

She's trying to make me see only her.

She's trying to suck me in.

"Katherine, you're not making sense," Grammie said, rising from the sofa.

Then Katherine pounced. She flew forward, moving faster than anything Leah had ever witnessed in her life. Her feet didn't move. She was shoved forward by the dark tendrils wrapped around her feet. This evil crop of hell spawn was using Katherine like a fucking chess piece.

Katherine slammed her fist into Grammie's face. Leah's grandmother cried out in pain and fell back on the sofa holding her hands over her eye. Then Katherine turned and faced Leah. When she spoke a thick clump of ooze dribbled down her chin and fell on Grammie's rug.

"Who are you? Why are you here?" The blue-gray apparition demanded.

Katherine could obviously see her. She was staring directly into Leah's eyes through eyes of her own which increasingly resembled day-old oysters.

Leah said nothing. She had a faint hope, a half-formed idea, that if she did not engage with this disgusting, terrifying apparition she would be better off, possibly even undetectable.

"How can I help you?" Grammie asked, still holding her bruised eye.

Katherine whipped away from Leah and hovered over Grammie.

"Help me?" Katherine howled with laughter. A laughter that turned Leah's blood to ice water. "Have you lost your mind, mother? You can't help me! You can't even help yourself, you pathetic old cunt!"

The drone redoubled its intensity.

From somewhere deep in the recesses of her mind, at least that's where she supposed it came from, Leah heard the tinkling silver bell intonations of another Grammie, a different Grammie, one who was not a victim. The voice said, "Remember to be home by sunset," calling from ages away.

Leah turned and grabbed her laptop and backpack. When she did her movement attracted the attention of the Katherine puppet monster thing. It turned and swayed, trying to ascertain Leah's exact position. Like a mouse under the gaze of a cat, Leah froze.

"Katherine!" Grammie shouted.

The hideous thing whipped around and began beating Grammie with both fists. Leah's grandmother curled into a ball and did her best to shield herself from Katherine's attack.

"Go back. Start over," the tinkling voice said, faint but urgent. "Before the sun is gone."

Leah shouldered her backpack and laptop and dashed for the front door. She dared not look back. Behind her she could hear the angry apparition flinging furniture from its vengeful path, desperately trying to get its hands on her. She felt the pressure of the thing's demonic energy against her back.

The front door!

Leah slammed into the screen door and tumbled out onto the front porch.

The drone fell silent.

An inexplicable shift occurred. A folding of time, a rearrangement of her perceptions.

Leah was not sprawled on the porch but standing in front of the door admiring the dreamy setting sun. Her heart was not pounding, her breathing was not jagged and frantic. Her eardrums popped the way eardrums will when airline passengers undergo a change of altitude. The pop of her ears was like a bubble of probability bursting within a bundle of possibilities. An odd sense of waking passed through Leah's mind. What could that possibly mean? Was she hungrier than she realized? Was this a result of low blood sugar?

A profound forgetfulness swept over her.

Where am I?

Oh, yeah.

Here she was at Grammie's house. Her bags were slung on her shoulders. Leah could hear noises from the kitchen. She knocked on the door.

"Is that you?" Grammie called. "Come on in, hon."

Leah wandered into the house, noticing that everything looked very much as she remembered it from when she was a girl. She found her Grammie in the kitchen.

"Why'd you knock, dear?"

Leah stared at her grandmother in bewilderment. Grammie smiled at her and tilted her head as if to convey curiosity.

"And what are you doing with your bags? I thought you left those in the guest room. Did you have a good time with Rose?"

Again, Leah's ears popped. Louder this time.

It was only then that Leah remembered she had already spent a day at Grammie's. She had arrived yesterday. At sunset.

Why had she thought she was only now arriving for the first time?

Leah groaned when the memory of the blue-gray demonic Katherine caught up with her. She dropped her bags and collapsed into one of the chairs at the kitchen table.

It took some doing but Grammie was persistent and patient, careful with her prodding. After half an hour had passed, when the sun was well below the horizon, Leah finished her report of the nightmare breaks in her reality that had occurred that day.

"I know this is very trying for you," Grammie said, placing her bony hand on Leah's hand. "But I think it's a good idea to eat something. Don't you?"

Leah hesitated, then nodded.

"Good." Grammie got up and prepared a couple of plates of food.

Leah looked down at the plate Grammie set on the table in front of her. Stir-fried vegetables with shrimp. Grammie was amazing. After all these years she still remembered Leah's favorite foods. If only she had an appetite. "Thank you, Grammie. This looks wonderful."

"You still like stir-fried veggies with shrimp?" Grammie asked, seating herself at the opposite end of the small table with her own plateful of food.

"Yes, I love it. Normally, I do. My stomach feels constricted. I'm afraid I'm going insane, Grammie."

"You're not going crazy," Grammie said, taking a small bite of food from her own plate. "You're just facing your demons. It's a necessary step in reclaiming power over your life. Eat a little bit. You'll probably find it makes you feel better."

Leah selected a shrimp from among the colorful veggies on her plate and ate it. She washed it down with iced tea.

"Grammie, I feel like I'm going insane. I don't know how much more of this I can stand."

"You're up to the challenge," Grammie said, reassuringly. "It's just part of growing up."

"Why is this happening? You say it's a part of growing up but I don't think many people face the sorts of things I have since I came here. I came back to Glenrose thinking I'd see you, we'd exchange stories, maybe cry a little, sort of lay Mom to rest and then I'd go home feeling better. I had no idea I was going to slip off into the twilight zone."

"When has anything in your life ever been as simple as you hoped?"

"Never," Leah admitted.

"Just canceling an automatic payment is like taking on a Federal case these days," Grammie noted. "No customer service. Not like we used to have."

Leah shrugged and nodded in agreement.

"All of us, even the most well-adjusted among us, carry a reservoir of darkness in our subconscious. The quality of our conscious lives, our waking hours on this planet, depends on where we choose to focus our attention. It *is* a choice. Right now you are casting off the mental chains your mother placed on you before you were old enough to make your own choices."

"Is Mom dead? I mean really? It doesn't seem that way. It seems like she's tormenting me now worse than she ever did when she was alive." Leah stared down at her plate.

"Eat. It's important. Crazy thoughts get a stronger foothold in the minds of people who are not properly nourished."

An involuntary little jerk of a laugh escaped from Leah's mouth. It seemed to the older generation eating was a panacea for all life's challenges. She looked up at Grammie, fearfully hoping her grandmother knew how to fix this problem, whatever the hell it really was.

"Inappropriate laughter is a sign of an overwrought, undernourished mind. These bodies we find ourselves in can be cumbersome, they demand a certain amount of maintenance. Eat, so you'll have the necessary strength of mind and body to properly address this challenge," Grammie said.

Leah took a bite from her plate, chewed, swallowed, then repeated the process. Her stomach made an involuntary rumbling sound. "I guess I *was* hungrier than I realized. This is delicious, Grammie. Thank you for remembering my favorite foods and serving them to me after all these years. I feel like such a shit for just turning my back on you all these years."

"You did not turn your back on me. It was your mother's manipulations that made you believe I was not trying to stay in touch. She manipulated your mind the same way she tried to manipulate anyone who ever crossed her path. Don't blame yourself for the psychotic behavior of your mother. This is your time for healing. Self-condemnation is not allowed."

"Okay." Leah said. She moved the vegetables on her plate around with her fork like a recalcitrant child before selecting a snow pea, spearing it with her fork and inserting it into her mouth. She chewed, then said, "Grammie, what's the end game here? What's the best we can hope for?"

"We free you of any unwanted influences and make you the captain of your ship, the master of your soul." Grammie sipped iced tea from her glass, maintaining eye contact with Leah.

"Sounds good. Theoretically. Before I came here, as Ramona pointed out, I was wallowing in confusion, drinking way too much, sort of sweeping the problem under the rug, I guess. I came here expecting to lay everything to rest. Make peace with you, bless Mom on her journey to wherever she's headed and return to my life. Then go back to inking pictures on people's skin. I was not expecting the kind of crazy shit that's happened since I got here."

One of Grammie's eyebrows arched at the sound of the word 'shit' coming from her granddaughter's mouth.

"Sorry, Grammie. Pardon my French."

"No problem. I just want you to realize words have power. All words. Words are tools, not to be spewed indiscriminately. When you meet a person who randomly uses profanity, you find they have only rudimentary control of their circumstances. Sometimes they have no control at all. Intent rules the universe. Words are the instruments of intent. If you remember nothing else I teach you, remember this."

"Okay. I'll keep that in mind."

"Be focused on what you wish to achieve in your life. If you remain focused on your true intentions, you will find they unerringly manifest."

"Does that work for you? I mean really? It sounds nice but…"

"Of course it does. I never stopped holding the intention that you would return and be a part of my life. Here you are."

Leah smiled. Her grandmother's sincere affection kindled a fire within her. A surge of well-being swept through her and as it did, her appetite returned. She ate the delicious and colorful food her grandmother had lovingly prepared.

"Now, I suppose the real question in your mind is how to fight this attack on your consciousness."

"Right."

"I think it's important to realize that the entity that is attacking you is *not* your mother. Not really. It's just using her as a disguise. Ultimately, it's a complex of appetites buried deep in the collective consciousness of the human race."

"Grammie, you just said a mouthful. Sounds like psychobabble. Why don't you break that down for me? I want to understand."

"The streams of consciousness we think of as demons, poltergeists, maybe even fairies for some, these are all just forgotten aspects of ourselves. Most of us didn't know that until Freud and Jung came along and published their ideas in the field of psychology. At the lowest level of consciousness, the oldest part of ourselves, is the will to survive. In the material world, survival at any cost is the prime directive. This brutal approach to existence has been in place for millions of years. The ideas we consider the higher human values, things like charity, forgiveness, cooperation, these are relatively recent developments in the human mind. That's why so few of us are able to make productive use of these concepts. We're infants just learning to walk in the realm of higher consciousness."

Grammie watched Leah, searching for some sign that what she had said was making sense to her granddaughter.

Leah nodded. "I think I understand everything you're saying. You say the entity attacking me is not my mother. What does that really mean?"

"Something much older, darker and relentless than your mother, than any human being for that matter, is trying to reassert itself in our world. Humans are trying to bring light into what has often been a very savage world. We've been here, what? A hundred thousand years? Maybe. The creatures that left those footprints in the Paluxy riverbed were here for millions of years. By comparison, we're barely even the new kids on the block. The key to understanding and securing a pattern of collective well-being into the future is to realize that savagery is our old operating system. Humans are using an upgrade called tolerance and cooperation now. It's a relatively new concept for this planet. Consequently, most of us aren't very good at it yet."

"What's all that got to do with Mom exactly?"

"Every one of us makes choices. Every day of our lives we make one decision after another. If you plotted these choices in a visual form, it would look something like the famous 'tree of life' illustration. You know the one I mean?"

"Yeah. Ramona's got a painting of the tree of life hanging in her living room. It's a celtic thing isn't it?"

"Yes. It's an attempt to create order in our thoughts about a larger reality. In the symbol you've probably noted that the tree's roots are just as extensive as its branches."

"Right. It's kind of symmetrical."

"It's an illustration of an ideal. That ideal is balance. We humans are masters of the planet by virtue of our advanced intelligence compared to other lifeforms. But as a race we are still in our infancy. That's why, despite our intelligence, we continue to engage in self-destructive behaviors. War, pollution, overpopulation, greed, failure to see ourselves as a collective, these are the mistakes that could potentially destroy us, erase us from the planet just as the dinosaurs were once erased. There is an indwelling consciousness to nature. That consciousness changes its mind when it reaches what it perceives to be a dead end. That's why the dinosaurs are gone now."

Leah drew a deep breath. This talk of a consciousness in nature reminded her of Rose's rambling thoughts about Electrical Universe theory. She ate another shrimp before commenting on her grandmother's statements. "I do not disagree with anything you've said. I think I get it. You're describing humanity in terms of a really big picture. I think I get it, truly I do. But how does all that relate to what's going on here and now? What's it got to do with Mom? Why am I seeing – more than just seeing – *experiencing* the things I've seen and felt since I came back here?"

"Good questions. I think this space on the planet, this location, this house here in Glenrose, Texas, is where the switch got flipped in your mother. She was here when she deviated from the higher pattern and reverted to an older but ultimately more deeply rooted pattern. Katherine may have entered this world as a soul with very little chance of achieving the human ideal in the first place. I don't know. Anything I might say about that would be pure speculation. For whatever reason, at some point in her childhood, early on, before the death of little Vernon, she began to identify with that subconscious darkness in which we are all rooted. One thing leads to another. Each decision we make in life takes us higher or lower on the stairway of consciousness. It can be a stairway to heaven or a plummet to hell. Somewhere along the way, Katherine turned over control of her vehicle to a consciousness much older than her individual identity, she took a backseat to powerful subconscious forces and let that mechanism seize control. Once a human being relinquishes control of the higher mental processes, the parasite takes over and convinces the host it *is* them. That identity shift gives forces which really no longer belong in our world an avenue of expression. All the greatest tragedies of human history can be traced back to the unbridled greed and aggression of those prehistoric forces finding expression in the here and now."

"Grammie, what can we do? What can I do? This is big. Much bigger than me. How do I fight it?"

"Realize your own connection with everything, including the darkness. Acknowledge that darkness is an aspect of your being but remember you are moving toward the light. If you're always looking back at the darkness you will halt your progression toward the light. The light represents your highest goal. The darkness represents the past, including its many mistakes."

"The process. Ramona tried to impress upon me that I am an aspect of a process, not a separate thing unto myself."

"Right. That's exactly right," said Grammie.

"I feel like I've enrolled in some metaphysical seminar. All this stuff you've told me, I don't reject any of it, it's just that it seems so…what's the word I'm looking for? Churchy? Religious? New Agey? All of the above. Just not the way I think about things. Until now."

"I'm trying to plant some seeds in your mind, give you some ideas to apply to your journey in life. Believe me I would've much preferred to share all this with you a little piece at a time during the years we've been apart. Now I feel like every minute counts. We don't have much time."

That last phrase snagged Leah's attention. It had an ominous ring to it. "What do you mean, we don't have much time?"

Grammie smiled. "No cause for alarm, Leah. But neither one of us will live forever. And as the song says, 'Life is for learning.'"

After dinner they washed the dishes and went into the living room to talk.

"Do you ever sit outside at night, Grammie? Out by the stone circle?"

"Sometimes. Especially when the moon is full. Why do you ask? Would you like to do that?"

"Yeah. I think I would."

"Alright then." Grammie stood and went to a drawer in the end table. She retrieved a small bottle and sprayed her arms with it. "Here," she said, offering the bottle to Leah.

"What's this?"

"Peppermint oil. Keeps mosquitoes away."

Leah followed Grammie's example, then followed her out into the back yard. A wonderful breeze was blowing out of the south, caressing the skin and causing the leaves in the trees to sing a song of transition from one season to another. The air was fresh. Leah felt wonderful, especially compared to the way she had felt an hour or so before. A bright half-moon lit the night sky.

"The moon is beautiful, isn't it Grammie?" Leah said, taking her seat in one of the lawn chairs. The white stones of the circle appeared almost luminous in the moonlight.

"The half-moon," Grammie said, "the symbol of balance. More powerful than either light or darkness during the sojourn in this world."

"How so?" Leah asked, staring up at the moon, enjoying the breeze on her face and in her hair.

"Planet Earth, the classroom where we learn to negotiate duality. At one end of the spectrum, darkness. Everything we consider evil, everything that's wrong with the world. At the other end, light. Representing everything good and everything we dare to aspire to in this world and beyond. The full moon happens once a month. The dark of the moon happens once a month. The half-moon happens twice every month as the moon goes through its phases. This is a reminder that balance is essential to the soul who would master the lessons of Earth."

"I don't think Rose's Meemaw would like to hear you say such things."

"Rose says her grandmother would consider you a witch. Are you a witch Grammie?"

"If you need to label me I suppose that's as good a label as any."

"I get what you're saying about labels. I think people like Rose's Meemaw can't accept people who live outside the label they've chosen for themselves."

"They reject what they can't understand."

"Grammie, I'm having trouble understanding, too. The stuff I've seen since I've been here is like stuff from a horror movie, you know? Stuff I never thought I'd see *except* in a movie. Now I know I saw what I saw. I know it has a sense of reality, that it's valid, but it represents a reality I am not familiar with. It's scary. I always thought when you encountered a poltergeist or a demon you just called a priest, he performed an exorcism and everything turned out okay."

"That's fine for Catholics but you're not one of those are you?"

"What are you saying?"

"I'm saying what you believe has everything to do with what you experience and how you deal with what you experience."

Leah frowned and stared up at the moon. Transparent clouds swept over the half-moon, riding on the high level late spring wind.

"Since I'm not a Catholic, I can't rely on a priest."

"But you can rely on me. You clearly believe I can help you with this problem. And I am committed to doing just that. That's why I'm here."

"I don't want to sleep in the guest bedroom again tonight. That's where that thing seems the strongest."

"You called it a thing."

"I don't know exactly what it is. What should I call it?"

"You remember talking with Ramona before you came here? The conversation about processes?"

"Yeah. I remember."

"Apply what she told you to this situation."

"This is all just a big process."

"You are both *all of it* and every seeming piece of that process. When you say that thing is strongest in the bedroom, you are saying *you* are most fearful in the bedroom, closest to your own darkness in that bedroom. The part that you consider *real* and *normal* is weakest in the bedroom."

Leah's brow tensed with thought and resistance to this perspective.

"Am I wrong?" Grammie asked.

"No, Grammie, you're not wrong. I'm just trying to get my head around it, you know?"

"And I'm here to help you with that."

"So, what should I do?"

"For now we'll start with discovering why that room is a dark spot for you."

"I guess that's obvious. It was Mom's room wasn't it?"

"It was. Do you remember anything unusual that happened to you there? Not since you've come back but long ago when you were a child."

Leah considered the question. She had memories of playing in the room, being tucked into bed at night by her Grammie. She remembered her mother on one occasion staring at her from the doorway. In the memory Katherine's expression was haughty, disdainful. Then her mother turned and left. Leah remembered nothing more about the incident, what was said, anything that had happened, but she did remember the sense that her mother did not love her. A lonely, hopeless realization that she was not good enough to deserve Katherine's love.

"Do you remember reading any adult books in that room?" Grammie asked.

"What do you mean by adult books? Like pornography?"

Grammie waved a dismissive hand. "Nothing like that. Just books that we wouldn't expect a ten-year-old girl to read."

Leah shook her head. "No. None I can think of. Why do you ask?"

"One day I came into the guest bedroom and found you reading *Ultimate Evil*. Does that ring a bell?"

"No. *Ultimate Evil*? What's that?"

"It was a true crime book. Nonfiction about the Son of Sam killer."

"I don't know what that is. Son of Sam killer?"

"It happened in New York in the middle 70s. Long before you were born. A series of murders. The police arrested a man named David Berkowitz. They believed he was a lone wolf serial killer. An investigative journalist named Maury Terry said the case involved an extensive network of Satan worshippers, a cult, and that some of the murders were committed by other members of the cult."

"How bizarre. I was reading that?"

"You don't remember?"

"No."

"Naturally, I felt like it was inappropriate reading for a girl your age. I took it away from you and you became quite upset with me."

"I did?"

"Yes. You threw a fit. You acted like Katherine, the way she had acted during her most troubled years."

"Really? Did I hit you? Is that what you mean?"

"No. But you screamed and threw things."

"Gosh, Grammie. I would expect to remember something dramatic like that." Leah searched her memory but found nothing remotely like the scenario her grandmother had just described. "Where would I even get a book like that?"

"That's what I wondered. I asked your mother about it and she suggested that Alan Danforth might have left it behind. Alan was a friend of your father's who stayed here a few days before he shipped out with the Navy. Katherine said Alan liked to read that sort of thing. I didn't really believe her. I thought Katherine had left the book in that room, that she wanted you to find it."

"That's creepy, Grammie. Mom was a bitch but…I don't know."

"That was just the first time."

"What do you mean?"

"The second time, I found you reading a book called *The Exorcist*. Ever heard of that?"

"Of course. It's a famous horror movie about a possessed little girl. Everyone's heard of *The Exorcist*. I was reading that book? The one by…what was his name?"

"William Peter Blatty."

"Right. When I was ten I read that book?"

"I don't think you read all of it. I was appalled when I saw what was on the page I found you reading."

"What was it?"

"It doesn't bear repeating. It was vile, vulgar, evil. I asked you where you'd gotten the book and you said it was wedged between the wall and the headboard of the bed. Once again, you threw an absolute fit when I refused to let you keep it."

"Grammie, I can't believe I don't remember any of this."

"Compartmentalization. The mind divides itself into separate compartments for a variety of reasons. Usually when one set of ideas conflicts with another."

"What did you do with those books?"

"I burned them."

"Grammie! I can understand you wanting to shield a child from the stuff in those books but burning? That's a little extreme, don't you think?"

"Both of those books dealt with demonic entities. I saw no benefit to passing them on. Especially since the people most likely to read those books are the least likely to be able to defend themselves against unwanted influences."

"Really?"

"Most readers of that sort of thing are just thrill seekers, looking to have their notion of reality challenged."

"And?"

"Well what do *you* think a demon is, Leah?"

"A dark spirit?"

"And what is spirit?"

"You got me there."

"Consciousness. An aspect of consciousness. Therefore how does it propagate?"

Leah shrugged.

"Through information. There are no devil worshiping cults until such a thing is presented as an option through books like those or through conversation with cult members. If the idea is presented as a desirable thing, a path to power, boom! All of a sudden you have humans acting out the dreams of the dark collective subconscious."

"I never thought of it that way."

"Most people don't. The mind is a very rich, fertile garden. Anything you plant in it reproduces. No matter what seeds you plant. *Any* idea planted into human consciousness reproduces. It cannot be otherwise. That's why children should not be allowed to read books like the ones I found you reading."

"Wow."

"I felt like that Blatty fellow did everyone a disservice by publishing a book that contained the name of a Sumerian demon. He introduced that name, that concept, he planted that seed in the minds of millions of people. For what? Money?"

"I feel like there's a lot of stuff inside me that I know nothing about. This thing with the books, I don't remember that. Me throwing a fit when you took the books away from me? That's news to me. And these – visions, for want of a better word – I never imagined I was the kind of person who could even have such experiences."

"I don't think you ever would have without your mother's influence. I don't know what Katherine's inception point was. I don't know what book she read or what information she was given by another person. All I know is that very early on, long before I suspected it, she had surrendered herself to dark influences. I knew that was true and I was determined not to let the same thing happen to you."

"Did you confront Mom about the second book? *The Exorcist?*"

"Yes." Grammie said quietly.

"What happened?"

"That's an episode of which I am more than a little ashamed."

"Grammie. Why?"

"I told Katherine I believed she was leaving those books for you to find. She was dismissive. She laughed in my face. Then I told her if I ever found you reading another book like that I'd kill her."

"Grammie! I don't believe it."

"It's true. When I said that to your mother I saw fear in her eyes. For the first time ever your mother was afraid of me. The consciousness controlling her certainly didn't want to lose its puppet, its vehicle here in the material world."

"What happened after that?"

"Katherine severed all ties with me. After that I never saw you again. Until now."

"So you just let her take me away?"

"I've been watching over you ever since. Guarding you. Helping you stay out of harm's way."

"And that's made a difference?"

Grammie's face brightened. "It has. Soon you'll see just how seriously I took my role as guardian."

"I believe you but tell me more."

"Later. That's a conversation for another time. I'm tired. Let's just sleep on it for now."

Leah put a comforter and a pillow on the sofa in the living room and laid down wondering how soon, or even if, she would be able to fall asleep. She looked at the door to the guest bedroom.

From the opposite end of the house Leah could hear Grammie brushing her teeth and getting ready for bed.

"All comfy?" Grammie called.

"Yeah. I'm good." Leah said.

A moment later Grammie appeared in the doorway near the bathroom. She wore a white cotton nightgown with thin blue stripes and a little pink floral embellishment near the collar. To Leah she looked cute, quaint, old fashioned, not the sort of woman to take on demonic influences.

"Call me if you have any issues during the night."

"Issues?"

"You know what I mean. Issues is a good catch-all label. It could cover anything from needing an extra pillow to seeing dark visions. Everything in between." Grammie smiled. Her freshly brushed teeth glistened in her sweet face.

"I think I'll be fine here." Leah said.

"Good. I hope so. But don't hesitate to wake me. For any reason. Even if you just want someone to talk to."

"Okay. Goodnight, Grammie."

"Goodnight, dear."

Grammie switched off the hallway light and disappeared into her bedroom.

The light from the bright half-moon filtered in through the sheer curtains in the living room windows. Leah heard the sounds of tree branches tossed by the gusty nocturnal breezes. From somewhere in the distance she heard the sound of a train horn, lonely and mournful in the vague darkness outside. Soon she could hear the soft snoring of her grandmother. Like pretty much everything about Grammie, even her snoring was cute, inoffensive, almost friendly sounding. Leah smiled at her own musing. What exactly was a 'friendly snore' anyway? She reasoned with herself that a friendly snore was any snore that issued from an especially friendly person. Someone like Grammie.

When Leah woke, the moon was much lower in the night sky. She could see it through the thin curtains behind the sofa.

"I think it's over here," someone said. It was the voice of a little girl.

She looked at the door to the guest bedroom. It was standing open. Leah was certain it had been closed before she fell asleep. There was a loud bump like a piece of furniture pushed against a wall.

"Shhh!" the voice said. "You're being too loud."

Whose voice was that? Two thoughts occurred simultaneously in Leah's mind. The voice she was hearing could be that of Katherine as a girl or it could be her own voice, the voice she had back when she was ten years old.

Could be both.

Leah looked toward her grandmother's bedroom. The door was closed but Leah made out the distinctive sound of Grammie's purring snore. Should she wake her?

The noises in the guest bedroom continued. Leah looked at the open doorway. The room was dark. Not entirely dark. Just as with the living room, moonlight was spilling in through the windows.

She was curious. And she was not frightened. Not really. Noticing this, she was emboldened to investigate. Leah threw the comforter off and went to the guest bedroom. She stuck her head in the room, seeing nothing unusual at first.

"Shhh!" the girl said. The shushing was followed by a giggle.

When Leah looked toward the far side of the bed she caught the slightest glimpse of a child's head disappearing behind the bed. Another giggle and the soft sound of someone crawling along the floor toward the headboard.

Leah cautiously walked around the bed to the far side. Again, she saw a fleeting image of a child's feet hurriedly crawling behind the headboard. Pursuit seemed the only option. Leah went to the head of the bed and saw right away that the bed was entirely too close to the wall for any child, no matter how small, to have crawled behind it.

Curiouser and curiouser.

Leah returned to the other side of the bed and switched on the lamp on the nightstand. The alarm clock's digital face said 2:59 am. A chill tickled the back of her neck.

A child's laugh sounded from far away somewhere under the bed.

"Uh oh," the child said softly, then giggled.

Leah asked herself what she should do next. She looked around the room. There were no visible specters, no fantastic shapes or toothy giants. She drew a deep breath and convinced herself to take a closer look. Seizing the headboard with both hands she pulled it away from the way. The sound associated with the bed's movement seemed completely inappropriate. Instead of the sound of a bed sliding across the floor it was more like the sound of rusty hinges creaking, like the sound a vampire's coffin lid might make in an old black and white horror movie.

The child laughed.

What was so funny? The sound or Leah's reaction to it? She felt cold, suddenly very cold. Like stepping into a walk-in freezer.

Behind the bed she saw something. There. Leaning against the baseboard. It was green. A book? Leah squeezed into the space between the headboard and the wall and retrieved the paperback book from among the dust bunnies and dead insects. Clearly Grammie had not swept back here for some time.

Raising it into the light she read the words on the book's spine. It said *The Family*. She turned the book and looked at the front cover. The background was all green. The words *The Family* took up a fourth of the book's front. Above the title was an illustration of a man with a lot of black hair, a beard and mustache. The man's eyes were crazy looking, insane. The author's name was Ed Sanders.

Leah heard the giggle again. This time from the foot of the bed.

When she looked, she saw the little girl in the checkered dress, both hands gripping the footboard of the bed. Katherine smiled at her. It was not a pleasant smile.

"Uh oh," she said, laughing.

An immense dark form rose from behind Katherine and placed its gnarly hands with fingers like the twisted roots of a tree on the footboard. Together the thing and Katherine shoved the bed, compressing Leah into a tiny dark space.

She fell.

Somewhere.

She crawled on her belly in musty smelling earth, the book tightly clenched in one hand.

I must be in the crawlspace under Grammie's house!

It never occurred to Leah to ask how she had ended up in the crawlspace. A dim light shone in the distance ahead of her. Leah focused on that light. The space was tight. Just barely big enough for her to drag herself along. Above her she could hear footsteps on the floor inside the house.

"I think we may have rats," a voice said.

"Better call the exterminator," another voice answered.

Leah finally reached the source of the light. It was a small grating near Grammie's back porch. With desperate energy Leah maneuvered her body around in the tight space until she could kick at the grating. After three sturdy kicks the thing gave way, falling outward.

"Those rodents are damn noisy tonight," a voice said somewhere above her.

"Did you call the exterminator?"

Leah pushed herself through the narrow opening, scratching her arms and legs in the process. Still, she clung tenaciously to the paperback book in her hand. Now she was in the backyard. The moonlight clearly illuminated everything. The breeze swayed the trees.

Then another sound. A sound similar to the sighing of leaves disturbed by the wind. But somehow different. Leah saw movement. All along the ground in the distance. Like a high tide rising on a beach. A black tide.

Rats!

Thousands of rats rushed toward her from every direction.

She had to get inside the house! Back to Grammie!

Grabbing the knob on the back door she twisted but the thing did not yield. Had Grammie locked the door before going to bed? She must have. She looked over her shoulder and saw the ocean of rats sweeping over the stone circle, flowing like turbulent water around the lawn furniture.

I've got to get inside!

Leah grabbed the heavy planter on the step beside her and flung it through the glass in the back door. The planter and broken glass fell noisily onto the floor inside. Leah thrust her body through the opening, paying no attention to the cuts inflicted on her arms and legs, failing to notice the glass cutting her feet as she rushed into the house.

The rats were right behind her.

"Grammie!" she screamed.

She ran for her grandmother's bedroom as the swarm of black rodents poured in through the broken glass. Leah flung open the door to her grandmother's room and rushed to the bed. She heard the gentle snoring.

How could Grammie sleep through this?

"Grammie!" she screamed, throwing aside the covers on her grandmother's bed. The snoring continued.

But Grammie wasn't there.

Leah felt the surge of rats arriving at her feet and starting up her legs.

She screamed.

With every ounce of energy available to her, Leah screamed.

She woke up on the sofa. Drenched in sweat. Her temples throbbed. Her heart pounded. Before she realized she was awake, she started to scream again.

But she was awake. The rats were just a dream.

Just a dream?

Leah breathed deeply and made a concerted effort to regain control of her body, mind, and emotions. When she felt a little better, she looked toward the guest bedroom. The door was open. Unsteadily, on shaky legs, she got up, crossed the living room and closed the door. It made more noise than she had intended.

Had she woken Grammie?

Looking toward Grammie's room she heard the snoring.

While she'd been fleeing for her life from a sea of rats Grammie had been peacefully snoozing. And why not? It was Leah's nightmare, not Grammie's.

Leah went to the kitchen and got herself a glass of water. Her mouth was terribly dry and the water felt heavenly on her tongue and in her throat. She drank about half the water and returned to the sofa.

Would she be able to fall asleep again?

If she did fall asleep would she experience another nightmare?

Leah looked at the back door. No broken glass, no heavy planter spilling dirt onto Grammie's carpet.

A dream.

Just a dream.

But Rose had told her Grammie said everything, everywhere, all of reality was just a dream.

She set her glass of water on the coaster on the end table nearest her pillow.

That's when she saw it.

The green paperback book.

The Family.

The bearded man with the crazy eyes leered at her from the cover of the book.

She was almost afraid to touch it. Then, with a surge of determination, she snatched up the book and headed for Grammie's bedroom. After all, Grammie had said to wake her if, for any reason, she was needed.

Any reason?

Holding the book, Leah paused at the door. Grammie was snoring. Soft, cute snores. She rapped on the door with her knuckles.

"Grammie," she called.

No answer.

Leah twisted the knob and opened the door. The snoring continued. Grammie was one heavy sleeper. Leah moved toward the bed. Standing right beside it, she said again, "Grammie."

Nothing but snoring.

"Wake up, Grammie," Leah said, reaching for the blanket. "Wake up!"

When she pulled the blanket back there was nothing there but an empty bed.

The snoring continued.

Leah screamed.

"Wake up! Wake up, child!" Grammie said, shaking her by the shoulders.

Groggy, thick-headed, Leah opened her eyes to the morning light. The windows in the living room revealed the fact that the sun was already well above the horizon.

"Wha...?" Leah rubbed her eyes.

"You screamed in your sleep," Grammie said, peering down with concern at her granddaughter.

"That was a dream? Am I really awake now?"

"All we see and all we seem is but a dream within a dream," Grammie said before sipping her coffee. "Edgar Allan Poe wrote that. Poor tormented man. But he knew the truth."

This was after Leah had told her grandmother about her latest nocturnal adventures, after Leah drank her first cup of coffee and ate a bowl of oatmeal.

"More coffee?" Grammie asked.

"Yes. But I'll get it." Leah rose from the kitchen table and refilled her coffee mug from the half-full pitcher resting on the coffee maker warmer.

She returned to her seat.

"I'd say last night's dream shows a marked improvement over your previous encounters."

Leah did not understand that. At all.

"What do you mean? I was terrified."

"Yes. I'm sure you were. But take note – you fought your way through those strange events with your own ideas and abilities. You faced what was happening in the bedroom. You weren't afraid to investigate. When things got worse you moved toward the light. When the rats came you broke into the house."

"But you weren't there! Your bed was empty."

"That's a good sign, too."

"How so?"

"Think about it."

"You weren't there. I was alone. The rats were swarming."

"The rats were swarming but you were realizing you had to face this thing alone. I was no longer there. It was up to you."

"I'm glad that part was just a dream. I'm glad you're here Grammie."

"I'm glad too, hon. Still, you get the significance of the message."

"Yeah. My circus, my monkeys."

Grammie laughed. "One way of putting it."

"But you're the one who's shown me how to look at all this. Without you I'd be clueless."

"All we see and all we seem are but a dream within a dream," Grammie said.

Leah and Grammie stayed indoors through the first part of the day. After lunch, Leah told Grammie to expect a visit from Rose.

"Let's get out the Scrabble board, shall we?" Grammie suggested. "You like Scrabble don't you?"

"I haven't played in a long time but I used to love it." Leah said.

"Rose likes it, too. When she shows up, we can all play."

So they set up the Scrabble board on the coffee table in the living room. It was fun. More fun than Leah had anticipated. She found Grammie was a keen Scrabble strategist, often making huge scores on short words by maximizing tile values and board positions. They laughed a lot and improvised an additional rule in which you earned double points for adjectives.

At three o'clock Leah noticed that Rose had not yet arrived.

"Don't you think that's odd?" Leah asked.

"Odd that a teenage girl isn't exactly where she's supposed to be at any given time?" Grammie said, her tone obviously one of sarcasm. "Unheard of."

"Should I call her?"

"You can, if you like. Her number's on the note board beside the phone in the kitchen."

"Note boards? Phone in the kitchen? Why haven't you ever gotten a smartphone, Grammie? They do away with the need for landlines and note boards." Leah rose and went to the kitchen.

"I'm getting along fine without a smartphone. I don't need another recurring expense, especially at my age."

"You're not that old Grammie. You'll be around for a long time yet."

"Maybe not as long as you think. But long enough."

"What's that?"

"Never mind. Make your call."

With little effort, Leah found the number and called it on Grammie's antiquated Harvest Gold telephone. It rang and rang but no one answered.

Leah returned to the living room.

"There's no answer," she said.

"Rose's grandmother spends a good deal of time on the phone. She only leaves the house to attend church. The telephone's the way she socializes these days."

"You mean Meemaw?" When Leah said 'Meemaw' she pronounced the word with the exaggerated redneck twang Rose had used. She laughed and Grammie joined in the laughter.

"Rose will be here exactly when she's supposed to be. Want to play another game of Scrabble?"

"Sure. Why not?"

The afternoon passed quickly. Leah and Grammie enjoyed their time together.

"It's about dinner time," Grammie said. "Why don't I fix something up?"

"You sure? I could certainly afford to take you out for dinner."

"Nonsense. I love to cook. And anything I make will be better than what they serve at the local restaurants. Glenrose isn't exactly a haven for culinary hotspots."

"If you insist."

"And I do."

"Okay. But let me help at least."

"Why don't you try calling Rose again? Tell her to join us for dinner."

"Sounds good."

Leah tried Rose's phone number once more but still there was no answer.

"I guess Meemaw's still on the phone," Leah said, returning the receiver to its cradle.

"You could just drive over and give her a personal invitation, if you like," Grammie suggested. "You know where she lives."

"Yeah. I could do that."

"Go ahead."

"Alright." Leah got her car keys and headed outside to her VW, parked alongside Grammie's Ford Escort in the driveway. She started the car and circled around the neighborhood where she remembered dropping Rose off the day before. There were no cars in the driveway. Leah tried to remember if there had been cars in the drive the day before. She couldn't recall.

She parked on the street and went to the front door. She rang the bell. Leah heard no sounds coming from inside the house. She wasn't even sure the doorbell had sounded. She knocked, waited a few seconds, then knocked again, louder.

"Can I help you?" someone asked.

Leah saw a neighbor standing in the next yard spraying a bed of flowers with a water hose.

"Oh, hello," Leah said. "I guess nobody's home."

"I think they're all gone at the moment. Who were you looking for?"

Nosey neighbor, Leah thought, still the woman wasn't being ugly or anything. Maybe she was just trying to be helpful.

"I was trying to get in touch with Rose," she said, retracing her steps away from the door and toward her car.

The woman's face showed puzzlement.

"You mean Rose Haggerty?"

"Is that her last name? I wasn't sure. I just met her yesterday."

"Yesterday? I'm surprised she didn't tell you. She hasn't lived here for a good while."

That's odd.

Maybe Rose had me drop her off here because she didn't want me to know where she really lives?

Very odd.

Leah started to mention the fact that she'd dropped the girl off here the day before but then decided not to waste her breath.

"She lives not far from here.," the woman said. "Cute little house made of petrified wood." The woman offered the address.

Grammie's address.

Leah said nothing more. She went to her car.

"You're welcome!" the woman called after her, obviously thinking Leah was rude for not thanking her.

On her way back to Grammie's, Leah almost forgot where she was going. She was understandably distressed. It seemed she drove around in circles for a while, taking too much time to go just a few blocks. When the house came into view a calm settled over her.

It was just about sunset when she pulled her VW into the steep driveway in front of Grammie's place. The golden glow of the setting sun brought out millions of tiny sparkles, crystals embedded in the petrified wood.

There was a memory.

The house.

The petrified wood.

Leah hadn't brought much with her, a backpack with a few changes of clothes and some toiletries and, in a separate case, her laptop. Shouldering both, she approached the front door. The screen door was closed but the door behind it was standing open. Leah could hear kitchen noises, water running, the clink of utensils on ceramic. She glanced over her shoulder at the setting sun. The amber light through the dense foliage was dreamlike, familiar. For a moment she believed she was in a dream.

What a strange thought.

She knocked lightly on the doorframe.

"Come on in," a voice called from the kitchen. Whose voice? It was a young female, obviously not Grammie.

There was a sort of pop in her mind. The bursting of a mental bubble, like waking up.

Why am I knocking?

That's weird.

Why didn't I just walk in?

The living room was different. The family photos she remembered from her childhood were gone. There had once been a painting of a waterfall hanging on the wall near the doorway into the kitchen. The sofa looked the same, minus the crocheted throw Grammie used to keep draped over the back.

A wave of confusion washed over Leah. She was certain the living room had looked different when she'd left for Rose's house. Was that true?

Leah peeked her head into the kitchen.

A woman about Leah's age was standing at the stove, stirring something in a pot. She held a young child on her hip as she prepared whatever she was cooking. It smelled like oatmeal, possibly. The woman's hair was long and black. Her clothes were black. When she turned to look toward Leah her expression, first surprised, quickly turned to one of smiling welcome.

"Hello," she said. Her baby looked at Leah, gurgled and stretched an arm in her direction.

"Uh, hi, I was looking for my grandmother."

Leah had the strange sensation of her mind occupying two separate spaces, two separate realities, at one time. One half of her thought this occurrence, meeting this young woman in Grammie's kitchen seemed perfectly normal. The other half of her mind said, no, something's wrong. It should be Grammie standing at the stove. Who is this stranger?

Surprise and then an aha moment flashed in the woman's eyes. "Are you Leah?"

"Yes."

"Come in. Have a seat."

"Is Ila around?"

Why was she asking that question? Of course her grandmother was there somewhere in the house. Leah had left her there just a short while before.

Hadn't she?

"This one is," the woman said, looking at her child. "Please, have a seat."

Leah lowered her bags onto the floor and seated herself at the kitchen table. Only then did she notice that she was carrying her bags. How could that be? She had not taken them with her when she went to check on Rose.

"Can I get you a coke or a bottle of water?"

"No, thank you," Leah said. "Is Grammie around?"

"She said you'd show up. She didn't know when but she told me to expect you. She always made a point of saying you'd arrive right at sunset when you did finally show up. She was right. But then, Ila was pretty much always right. Wasn't she?"

A question was forming in Leah's mind but she was afraid to ask it.

"Ila died almost a year ago." The woman took the seat across from Leah at the table. Her child reached eagerly for Leah and cooed some preverbal message of greeting.

Suddenly, Leah knew who this woman was. "Are you Rose?"

A smile appeared on the woman's face. The baby laughed. Maybe it was a laugh.

"Yeah. That's me. I didn't know Ila had told you about me."

"You dyed your hair black."

"I've been coloring my hair a long time now." Rose seemed puzzled.

Certainly no more puzzled than Leah.

"You don't remember me, do you?" Leah said.

"Have we met?"

What should she say to that? Leah thought for a moment. She could remember her day spent with Rose in vivid detail. But how could she convince this young mother without sounding like a lunatic?

Leah reached into her purse. It probably would not work. She couldn't count on it. But was it any stranger than everything else she had experienced in the past 48 hours?

No, she decided. It was not.

She opened her phone and selected the photo app, holding her breath, not wanting to be hopelessly insane. It worked. There it was. Leah tapped the screen on her phone and handed it to Rose.

Rose accepted the phone into her hand and had to do some maneuvering to keep the baby from taking it away from her. Rose looked at the photo. It was a photo of herself as a teen and this prodigal granddaughter of Ila's clowning in front of the dinosaur statues at Dinosaur Valley State Park. Confusion seized control of Rose's face.

"That looks like me."

"It is you, Rose."

"And you. But you look the same. I'm like maybe fifteen."

"Fourteen. The day I took that picture you told me you were fourteen."

"I did? I don't remember that at all."

"You should. It happened yesterday."

They talked for hours. Leah learned that Grammie had left the house to Rose.

"Do you mind?" Rose asked with a pained expression. "I mean I'm not even a blood relative. In those last days before she passed I kept hoping you'd show up. She always said you would."

"Grammie loved you. That I know for sure. And you certainly deserve the house. I don't want it. I'm a tattoo artist in Austin. The last thing I need is a house in Glenrose. Property taxes and all that. Yuck."

"Really?"

"Really. Grammie would be so happy that you named your little girl after her."

"I really loved Ila. The world needs more women like her. She always made me feel like anything was possible. And some impossible things did seem to happen when I was with her."

"Same here."

"All we see and all we seem…"

"Is but a dream within a dream."

"Right."

The two women laughed and the baby joined in.

After Leah had told Rose everything; all about her mother, all about her insecurities and grasping for answers, all about Ramona and her advice to return to Glenrose, and every detail of each insane episode Leah had experienced in the time since she had returned, after all that, Rose invited her to spend the night.

"What about your husband?" Leah nodded toward little Ila. "I'm assuming you're married."

"I am. My husband, Tommy's a Navy pilot. He's on an aircraft carrier somewhere in the South Pacific."

Shades of Leah's own childhood.

"You must miss him."

"I do. He'll be home on leave next month. Tommy will be so surprised when I tell him about you. I've told him a lot about Ila. I don't think he believes everything I told him."

"Thanks for the invitation but I can't stay."

"We've got the spare bedroom. You're welcome to it."

"Not tonight. You can understand I'm not ready to sleep there again yet."

"You can have the sofa."

"Not quite ready for that yet, either."

"What are you going to do?"

"I'll go ahead and drive back to Austin."

"Tonight? Think that's safe? It's kind of late."

"I wouldn't be able to sleep anyway. I'm wired. I can stop for coffee somewhere on the way if I need to. But can I take a raincheck? It would really mean a lot to me if I could come visit sometime."

"Of course. Please do. I have a feeling we still have a lot to talk about."

They exchanged phone numbers and Leah went out to her VW. Rose and little Ila watched from the porch as she drove away into the night, waving goodbye until she was out of sight.

Someone was pounding at the door.

"Oh, for God's sake," Ramona said, waking from a deep sleep. She rose from her bed, wrapping a robe around her as she went to the door. "Who is it?"

"It's me, Leah."

Ramona glanced at the clock. It was 2:59 am.

"Leah, what are you doing here?" she said, opening the door. "I thought you were going to visit your grandmother in Glenrose."

"I did," Leah said, stepping inside.

"You turned around and came straight back? What happened?"

"I was there for two days and I've got a lot to tell you."

"Are you drunk? Or high?" Ramona asked.

"Fair questions. The answer's no to both. I just didn't want to be alone tonight. Can I sleep on your sofa?"

"Of course you can. Since when have you not wanted to be alone? Usually that's your preference. Weirdness." Ramona said, following behind Leah as her friend dropped onto the sofa.

"Everything I have to tell you is weirdness to the extreme. I'll tell you everything tomorrow. Right now I just want to sleep and know I'm close to my best friend."

"Okay." Ramona smiled. "I'll be all ears when you're ready to talk."

"You know anything about changing your name? Legally I mean?"

"Not a thing. You want to change your name?"

"I think so. I don't like Leah anymore. It means weary. I'm tired of being weary."

"Alright. What's your new name?"

"Not sure. Something full of life. Something vibrant."

"Tomorrow we'll search for names. Could be fun."

"Thanks. Goodnight."

"Night."

SF

Steven Purselley

I remember clearly the first time I met SF. I remember it so well because it was also the first day I ever ate an onion and mustard sandwich and the first day I ever saw a porno film. It was summertime. School was out. Dad was in Vietnam and Mom still had to work her job at Jones Realty so I spent most of those summer days at my grandmother's house over on Bomar Street near where Meadowbrook connects with Beach.

The neighborhood was different than the one where I lived with my mom. It seemed poorer, a little seedier, rougher around the edges. In my grandmother's neighborhood you were more likely to see kids wearing clothes that didn't quite fit them or frail old women struggling up the steps to their houses carrying heavy loads and no one to help them or old men with goiters or missing limbs or faces with scars where cancer had been removed. It seemed to me there weren't as many good things in

Grandma's neighborhood. Maybe it was just older, just different.

The ice cream truck still drove by blaring its amplified jingle bell music. The same popular tunes were played on the radio. There were some pretty girls here and there if you knew where to look for them. But the girls all seemed a little underfed and no matter how pretty they were I couldn't help but feel like they were flowers in a vase and soon, too soon, they'd be wilting. I guess I knew this because I saw them standing next to their own mothers and grandmothers. All the married women, the ones who had kids looked like all the life had been kicked out of them long ago. If someone said, Sadie looks just like her mother, it was hard to believe them because Sadie was young and cute and full of life while her mom was stooped and colorless with a cigarette hanging out of the corner of her wrinkled mouth.

Staying at Gran's house was an education for me.

Maybe things were just as grim on Crenshaw Street where I lived with Mom. Maybe it was all just a matter of perception. On Bomar Street nobody was trying to put on any airs. What you saw is what you got. In some ways I liked it better. For instance the boys all cussed and made no bones about it. In my neighborhood some of the kids were committed to a cuss-free vocabulary because they'd accepted Jesus and they didn't want any of their church friends to hear them using vulgar words.

Mom would let me out in front of Gran's every morning on her way to work. She'd tell me to be good and I'd promise her I would be. Then I'd go up the steps and let myself into Gran's house. She'd be flitting around with this or that. Sometimes if she'd already done too much flitting she would be sitting in her favorite chair, sipping iced tea, listening to gospel music or reading the Saturday Evening Post. It was always shady in Gran's house and usually pretty cool even on the hottest days of summer. The house was surrounded by trees and she had a couple of swamp coolers.

"Mornin' Billykins," she would always say. Instead of calling me Billy like everyone else she had to call me Billykins. She thought it was cute or something. I told her I didn't like iit but she never stopped. "Want some breakfast?"

She asked me every morning if I wanted some breakfast even though every day I told her I'd already eaten.

"I had a bowl of cereal."

"That's not much for a growing boy. I could make you some eggs and bacon, some toast."

"I'm not hungry, Gran. Thanks."

"Well, if you're sure."

Maybe she thought I'd always be hungry because a great many of the kids in her neighborhood usually were. She made a lot of cookies and she was generous with them. Neighborhood kids would stop by just to say hi, meaning they were hoping for a cookie, Usually oatmeal but sometimes sugar cookies. It made my grandmother happy to feed people.

"What are you going to do today?" she asked me.

"I think I'll walk down to the park and see if any of the guys are there." There was a small city park five blocks away from Gran's house. There was a backstop there and sometimes spontaneous games of baseball would arise. Other times guys would just hang out and write graffiti in the old shelter house. That's what I liked most. The graffiti.

I had a Marks-A-Lot permanent marker in my pocket for that very purpose. Something called bubble lettering was popular among kids my age and it was considered cool to write words like peace and love in bubble lettering. My friends had older brothers who were being drafted and sent off to Vietnam so there was also a lot of anti-war graffiti. The other boys would sit around smoking their cigarettes and I'd doodle with my marker. Sometimes they'd tell me what I'd written or drawn was cool. It was that appreciation from my peers that motivated me most.

I'd recently begun drawing a pattern I called the flaming sword. It was a curved sword like you'd see in an old movie about Arabs and flying carpets surrounded by curling tongues of flame. I'd read about it in a book about the Muslim invasion of southern Europe. It was a popular design and other kids asked me to draw it for them. It was especially nice when I had colored markers so I could make the flames yellow and red but it still looked okay in black and white.

Gran told me to behave myself and to come back for lunch around noon or oneish. I always said I would but it was no big deal when I didn't. Lunch was always just a sandwich she put together on the spot so there was never any food going to waste if I didn't show up. I'd just prowl the neighborhood and let the day unfold on its own terms. That was the whole point of summers to my way of thinking. Why plan? Planning was for the other nine months of the year when every damn minute of your day was planned by someone. And that someone was rarely you.

When I got to the park the morning coolness hadn't quite burned off but I could tell it was going to be a hot one. I went into the shelter house and searched for vacant spots where I could plant some graffiti. I'd already posted a lot of peace signs, bubble lettered words and a few flaming swords. I wanted to come up with something fresh. I toyed with the idea of drawing a naked woman with her legs spread. But I hadn't practiced much on human forms. A naked girl would go over well with the kids in the neighborhood whether it was drawn well or not, still I wanted to do it right, especially if it would adorn a public venue like the shelter house. I decided to hold off until I'd practiced in private a few times. Also, I'd have to bring along a pink marker to highlight the opening between the girl's legs. That would go over for sure.

I was up high in a corner drawing a big peace sign when I heard somebody behind me.

"Drawing a peace sign?"

It was Johnny Battles. I recognized the voice even before I turned around. I'd hung out with Johnny lots of times. He wasn't the sharpest tool in the shed but he was easy going, not mean like a lot of the other boys in this part of town.

"Yeah. How's it look from down there?"

"Looks okay."

Johnny sat down on the picnic table and stared up as I finished. I'd made it a little nicer than usual with a bold drop shadow around it. When I was done I hopped down and joined him on the picnic table to see my work from distance. It wasn't bad.

"What you been doing?" I asked.

Johnny shrugged. "Looking for cans."

It was only then I noticed the plastic bag at his feet. It wasn't stuffed but it had a pretty good collection of aluminum cans in it. He must've set it down real careful because I hadn't heard the cans rattle before he spoke. But Johnny was just sort of that way. Quiet. Intentionally so. Maybe it had something to do with the fact that there were nine kids in his family and they all lived in a little three bedroom house on the far west end of Bomar.

"How many you got in there?"

"I don't know. Maybe fifty."

"How far'd you have to go for them?"

"I walked along the railroad tracks to Ayers then came back along Lancaster."

"Wow! You've done all that already this morning?"

He didn't exactly smile but a fleeting glint of appreciation flashed across his face. "Yeah. I got up early."

"What you going to do with the cans?"

"When we get enough my dad takes them to the recycler. They pay ten cents a pound."

"You get to keep the money?"

"Naw. Dad and Mom use it for groceries and stuff." I'm just helping out.

That made sense. With nine kids every little bit helped. John's folks were from Massachusetts and still spoke with that kind of accent but all of the kids sounded like normal Texas kids. Sometimes they'd say a phrase that seemed foreign like 'cheese on crow' or 'that takes moxie' but otherwise you'd never know they came from a Yankee family. They were catholic. Mom said that was why they had so many kids. Mom said some of the kids had died at birth so it would've been even more. Johnny's dad worked with marble. Countertops and such. I'm sure he worked his ass off to keep food on the table.

"I guess that makes you a good son," I said.

Again I saw that flash of appreciation. Compliments were few and far between in my house and there was only one of me. I wondered what it would be like in a house with nine kids. Of course they weren't all kids. The oldest was Jackie. He was eighteen. The youngest was Raymond and he was five. Like me, Johnny was twelve.

"I'm heading back to my house," he said, standing and picking up the bag of cans. "Want to come along?"

"Sure."

Though Johnny lived on the same street as Gran you had to make a big detour to get there. When they widened Beach to accommodate access to I-30 they cut off the lower end of Bomar. On Johnny's end of the street there weren't many houses. There were businesses of various kinds including a wrecking yard. There were a couple of dive bars. A diner and a fairly recent addition was Jerry's Finne Arts Theater. It was a porno house in a brick building that had previously been a distribution center for electronic parts. I'd heard Gran talking about it with her friends. They thought it was a disgrace. The church going folks in Gran's neighborhood were mighty angry with the city for allowing that kind of trash. New York was one thing but down here in our town, that was another thing entirely. They pronounced it 'fine' just like 'that's a fine apple pie you made' but the marquis sign out front had that extra 'n' – Jerry's Finne Arts. I figured that unusual way of spelling the word was code so people who were in the know wouldn't mistake it for anything other than what it was, a place that showed dirty movies.

So me and Johnny walked the long way around, up the access road to Lancaster, down toward town a couple blocks then we cut through to Bomar where it ran behind Jerry's Finne Arts. Like I said, the building had been some electronics outfit before so there was a loading dock big enough for two trucks on the back side.

When we passed the loading dock I got my first sight of SF. Of course I didn't know he was SF then. I had no idea what he was called. SF was skinny with a bony face. I would've guessed he was about the same age as me and Johnny. But he looked like something was wrong with him. And I can't say exactly what that wrong thing was. Something was just wrong about the way he looked. His head seemed a bit too small. His eyes were beady and reminded me of a rat. The bones in his face were prominent in a way you don't normally see on the faces of kids. He stood sort of like one of his legs was shorter than the other. He was dressed up in a button shirt and a jacket and what my mom called slacks. Mens pants, you know. He wasn't wearing the usual T-shirt and jeans like every other boy on the east side of town.

Plus he was smoking a cigarette. Not hiding it one bit. Lots of the boys I knew smoked but they didn't stand out in the open dressed like little men french inhaling for all the world to see.

"Hey," I said, giving him the low wave like we all did in those days.

"Hey," he said back to me, waving with the hand that held his cigarette.

"Hey," Johnny said. No wave. He was holding his bag of cans with both hands because he'd slung the bag over his shoulder. I sensed Johnny was a little wary of the kid.

We walked on. Johnny's house was about a hundred yards on down the road on the opposite side of the street. I looked back over my shoulder after a bit and I saw the kid was still watching us, silvery blue smoke drifting out of his face.

On that end of Bomar the street was mostly dirt. It had been paved at one time but with all the wear and tear from industrial vehicles the pavement had broken up and was completely missing in places. Consequently me and Johnny ate a lot of dust on that last part of the walk to his house. When we got to the front porch of his house we were both coated with a fine layer of beige dust. We laughed and swatted it off one another before we went inside.

Johnny's mama was standing in the kitchen doing something but you could see her from the front door. No offense, but his mom had the biggest butt I'd ever seen on a white woman. Maybe it was having all those kids? What the hell did I know? I was only twelve but I'd never seen a butt like Mrs. Battles' except on the black women that worked in our school cafeteria. Her shoulders and head didn't look fat at all. Just average. But her hiney was extra-large.

"Hey, boys. Hey Billy," she said, smiling and drying her hands off. She always acted like she liked me. I think it was because my grandmother had been nice to her and her family. Gran was hardcore Baptist and most of them are kind of prejudiced against Catholics. At least the ones in our part of town were. But Gran was a real Christian and believed in helping folks whenever she could. Lots of times she took the Battles family good used clothes or a big pot of stew or chili. "Find a lot of cans?" she asked.

"About half a bag," Johnny said, holding it up for her to see.

"Put those out on the back porch."

We headed out the back door and she gave me a little pat on the shoulder. I smiled at her and she smiled back. That woman had been through hell, probably was pretty much going through hell every day of her life, that's the way my mama would've called it, but she had a sweet smile. There was a sincere look in her eyes I couldn't help but notice.

"I'm going to feed you kids some lunch in a little while so don't go too far."

"We won't," Johnny said.

He dropped his load on the back porch where there was a collection of maybe fifteen bags stuffed with aluminum cans.

"Come on," he said, swinging his head toward the back fence.

I didn't ask where we were going. I knew he wanted to go exploring through the Triple A Wrecking Yard. We climbed the cyclone fence, which wasn't much of a chore because the thing was sagging and about useless. A couple of stray cats took note of us and one of them tried to act friendly, you know rubbing up against Johnny's ankles. He pushed it away with his foot, saying, "Scat." He didn't kick the scrawny cat. He was gentle but he let the cat know he didn't have time for it.

We could hear Danny Abernathy talking to somebody in that loud voice of his. Danny was the guy that pretty much ran the wrecking yard. He always wore grease-stained gray clothes. His hair was black and greasy. I don't know if he took a bath at night when he went home but I never saw the guy that he wasn't 'filthy as a Biblical beggar.' That was a phrase my Gran was fond of using. You always knew right off where Danny was because he had the loudest voice I ever heard. He didn't shout exactly but whatever he did it gave his voice an extra punch so it carried a long way. He also had the biggest Adam's apple I ever saw.

We rounded some junk cars and came across Danny at an old pickup truck. The hood was raised and we could see he'd been working on it. There were greasy red rags and tools scattered around.

"Hey, Danny," Johnny said.

"Hey, Johnny." He looked at me and probably didn't remember my name so he just nodded and said, "Hey."

"What you doing?" Johnny asked.

"Trying to get this damn Ford started," Danny said.

"Need any help?"

Johnny and his brothers were always trying to help out Danny and some of the other local businesses. Sometimes they'd get a little spare change for their efforts. Sometimes they'd receive a few cigarettes or a bottle of soda. Whatever they got, they were glad to get it because sometimes what they got was nothing.

"If you could shoo them cats away I'd appreciate it."

There were dozens of cats in the wrecking yard. And more being born all the time. They got all up under foot and hid out in the salvage cars.

Johnny picked up a couple of pieces of metal and began banging them together. I followed suit and we banged and clanged and tried to shoo all the cats away from the truck

Danny was working on. But I'm sure you've heard what they say about herding cats. We lunged and dodged but every cat had a mind of its own and wasn't about to let us tell it where to go. One cat hissed at us and scrambled up under the truck right at the moment Danny turned the key in the ignition.

That's the fourth thing I remember about that day. The thing I didn't recall before. I saw a cat die and it left a deep impression.

Good news for Danny was that the truck started right up. Bad news for the cat was it was in a bad place at the wrong time. The belts and moving parts just tore that cat up. It screamed and a terrible shiver went right up my spine. For a second I thought I would vomit but the feeling passed. It didn't seem to disturb Johnny as much as it did me but I already knew that was because he'd led a harder life even though we were the same age.

"Damn cats!" Danny said when he climbed out of the cab and came back around to take a look under the hood with the motor running. "Stupid cats! I'll have to hose this engine off now. At least she's running. Corky Purcell's gonna buy this truck from me today. Well, one less damn cat is probably good news, too."

Johnny had told me the cats kept the rodent population under control in the neighborhood. Said he saw cats eating rats all the time. Still there didn't seem to be enough rodents to go around. None of the cats looked well-fed. You could count ribs on all of them. Now they were all scattered out and watching us from a distance. Suspicious, like they thought we'd killed the other cat on purpose. I felt guilty even though it was an accident.

Danny shut off the engine and began gathering up his tools and rags.

"Sorry we couldn't keep that cat out of the motor," Johnny said.

"No sweat." Danny grinned and ruffled Johnny's hair. "You did your best. Hell, if every damn cat on this lot died today I wouldn't miss 'em one bit. At least until the rats started taking over. And they would, too."

Danny eyed us both for a moment. He fished in his pocket and pulled out a pack of Chesterfields. He took one out and lit it then gave the rest of the pack, maybe five cigarettes, to Johnny. "Here," he said, "give these to your old man."

"Thanks," Johnny said. He put the cigs in his own shirt pocket. "Anything else we can do for you?"

"No. Thank you though. Check back tomorrow. I may have some little chore for you."

"Okay." Johnny nodded. "Mind if we look around?"

"Help yourself. Don't break anything!" Danny said that real loud and then he bellowed with laughter. I guess he thought that was a big joke because everything in that big lot was broken, busted up, twisted or mangled. His adam's apple bobbed up and down like a gerbil trying to escape from his throat.

"We won't." Johnny didn't laugh. He turned and headed for the part of the lot that almost touched the river. I knew where he was going.

Johnny had a favorite car back there. It was a 1957 Chevy Bel Air. He loved that car, said he wanted one when he was old enough to drive and making enough money to afford one. Lots of cars had come off the assembly lines since 1957 but Johnny swore the best car ever made was the '57 Chevy. I was partial to the '67 Corvette myself but I had little hope of ever being able to own one. I could look though, couldn't I? And maybe some rich guy might give me a ride in a Corvette.

Johnny sat in the driver's seat for a few minutes and imagined himself driving that thing down a city street. I liked that about Johnny. That he knew what he wanted and he wasn't ashamed for anyone else to know. I would never have pretended to be driving a junk car. I thought I was too old for that kid stuff. I wouldn't do it but I admired Johnny for doing it just as natural as you please, like there was no question that it was the most appropriate thing to do.

After a while he got out of the driver's seat and climbed up on top of the Chevy. I climbed up there too. The sun had heated the metal to where it was uncomfortably warm already. Johnny didn't seem to notice and I wanted to be as tough as he was so I just let the roof of that car burn my ass through the seat of my pants without saying a word.

From on top of the car I could see the loading dock behind Jerry's Finne Arts. That reminded me of the strange kid we'd see earlier. "Who was that kid?"

Johnny picked the top off a long weed and stuck it in his mouth the way farmer's do in cartoons on TV. "What kid?"

"The one we saw behind the Finne Arts smoking and all dressed up."

"I don't know his name."

"What do you think he was doing there?"

Johnny said, "I think he lives there." Then he gave me kind of a funny look.

"He can't live there. It's a place they show X-rated movies."

"I know. I know he's not supposed to live there. But I think he lives there anyway."

That was about the strangest idea I'd ever heard. A kid about my age living in a porno theater. As I thought about it I got an uneasy feeling in my stomach and a weird confusing feeling at the base of my skull. The feeling was new to me so I had no idea what it meant which made it even eerier.

Right about that time Johnny's mom stepped out on the back porch and hollered "Lunch time!"

Battles kids came running from all directions. I hadn't seen any of Johnny's brothers or sisters up til then but they came dashing out from the woods by the river and the other end of the junk yard and god only knows from where else.

"Let's go eat." Johnny hopped down and I followed him.

The inside of the Battles' kitchen was crammed full of kids and Mrs. Battles was dispensing Dixie cups of Kool-Aid and making sure nobody took more than one sandwich at a time from the tray where she'd stacked. "If you finish your first sandwich and you're still hungry come back and I'll give you another one."

At my house and at my Gran's adults were always making a fuss about washing your hands before you eat. There was no mention of that in the Battles' home. I did the math. Washing eleven pairs of hands before every meal was not in the budget. The water bill would've been too high for them to pay it. I knew my hands were dirty but I figured not washing them this once wouldn't kill me. Might even boost my immune system. I'd heard that sort of talk somewhere.

"What kind of sandwiches?" I asked Johnny's brother, Chuckie, as he pushed past us with his lunch and went out to sit under the Mulberry tree in the backyard.

"Mustard and onion," he said, taking a big bite and showing that he thought it was fine eating.

"Really?" I'd never heard of such a thing.

"Really," Johnny nodded. "They're good."

I could tell he was for real. Maybe onion and mustard sandwiches were a treat in this house.

I took my drink and sandwich from Mrs. Battles and thanked her. I followed Johnny out to his place under the Mulberry tree. Everybody was chowing down. Soon some were headed back for seconds. I took my first bite. In all fairness I had to admit it wasn't bad. The bread, onion and mustard had the familiarity of a hamburger with none of the meat. I wondered how much it cost to make that big batch of mustard and onion sandwiches. Not much. I wondered how often the Battles kids had these for lunch. Pretty often I figured. And they clearly liked it.

I finished mine and drained my cup of Kool-Aid. I was about to crush the cup and toss it but Johnny reached for it and I saw that all the kids were stacking their cups. They took them into the house and gave them to Mrs. Battles to rinse and use again the next day.

"Thank you for lunch." I said to Johnny's mom.

"You're welcome. Want another sandwich?"

"No thank you, ma'am. I'm full." I knew I'd be hungry as a bear by the time dinner rolled around.

Johnny pulled the cigarettes out of his shirt pocket and handed them to his mom. "Danny sent these over for Dad."

Without saying anything Mrs. Battles took the smokes and put them in a drawer next to the oven. There were several cigarette packages in the drawer, all different brands and all nearly empty.

We went back outside to sit in the shade. Chuckie came over and leaned toward us in a conspiratorial manner. "You guys want to watch some fuck movies?" he whispered.

Johnny shrugged.

"What do you mean?" I asked.

"Come on." Chuckie got up and went in the garage. We followed.

Up high on the shelf at the back of the garage was a brown paper bag. Chuckie climbed up on the tool bench and reached it down. He handed it to me. Inside was a tangle of film. It looked like the kind of film my great uncle Chester would show us on his projector at Christmas and at special occasions like family reunions.

"What's all this?"

Chuckie reached into the bag and pulled out a piece of film about a foot and a half long. He held it up to the light coming through a window in the wall of the garage. "See here. This is a guy fucking a woman."

"Let me see that!" I set the bag down and reached for the film clip. It was small and hard to make out but sure enough it was two naked bodies engaged in intercourse. "Where'd you get this?"

Chuckie grinned. "In the dumpster behind Jerry's Finne Arts."

"Wow! You got a magnifying glass?"

"I got better than that."

"What?"

"My friend Mark Cordell said if we brought 'em over he'd splice 'em together and show 'em for us on his Dad's movie projector."

"Really?" This day was turning into a much more interesting adventure than I had imagined.

"Want to come along?" Chuckie asked, taking the film from my hand and dropping it back in the bag. "We gotta hurry cause we gotta be done and outta there before Mark's folks get home from work."

I looked at Johnny.

"You wanna go?" he asked me.

I nodded.

"All right. Let's get a move on." Chuckie rumpled the top of the bag and folded it down like an oversized sack lunch. We left the garage and headed down the driveway.

Rachael and Hannah, two of the younger Battles girls, were playing hopscotch in the driveway. "What's in the bag?" Rachael asked in mid hop.

"None of your business," Chuckie answered.

"Tell us," Hannah insisted.

"If you really have to know, it's Easter eggs. We're taking 'em back to the Easter Bunny." Chuckie said.

"I wanna see! I wanna see!" The girls both chanted.

"It's not Easter eggs," Johnny said seriously, always kinder than his brother Chuckie.

"Mom!" Hannah shrieked. "Chuckie won't let us see his Easter eggs!"

By that time we were out of the driveway and headed up the street. It was getting pretty hot by then. There was a solid wave of heat rising up off the road wherever there was still some asphalt left. I avoided the pavement. Walking on dirt or grass was cooler, besides the melting tar from the asphalt clung to your shoes and I knew Gran would give me hell about it.

When we got to the loading dock behind Jerry's Finne Arts, Chuckie dropped the bag on the ground and scrambled into the dumpster. I knew what he was up to.

"Any more film in there?"

"I'm lookin'."

I could hear him scraping and bumping around in the dumpster. I wondered what kind of trash you'd find in a porno theater's dumpster. I couldn't think of anything I'd want to touch, much less swim around in the way Chuckie was doing. Still, I wanted to see those little film strips projected on a screen. The prospect was pretty exciting.

I looked over at Johnny. He was taking all this in stride. No big deal. Like I said, he'd had a very different sort of upbringing than I had and not much ruffled his feathers.

"Whatcha lookin' for?"

I turned and saw the weird, overdressed kid had come back out onto the dock again. He was lighting a cigarette. The way he stood there in his jacket, leaning on one leg, he just seemed like an adult trapped in a kid's body.

Johnny said nothing. His default position was to speak only when necessary.

"We're getting some of the old film clips," I said. "Is that okay?"

The kid laughed. "You like fuck movies, huh?"

I shrugged. "I don't know. I've never seen one."

He nodded and blew a lot of smoke. "Yeah, you'll like it. It'll make your pecker hard. You got a pecker don't you?"

That embarrassed me. Nobody'd ever talked to me that way. I looked at Johnny. Johnny was just looking up the street at nothing in particular. I got the feeling he didn't want to engage with the strange kid. Like it would hurt him somehow just to talk to the boy or acknowledge his presence.

"Yeah, I got a pecker," I said.

"I figured you did."

Chuckie climbed up out of the dumpster. "I couldn't find anymore," he said before he noticed the kid up on the loading dock. When he did notice, he said, "Hey."

The kid took another deep drag of his smoke. "If you boys like fuck movies I'll be sure to throw some in the dumpster when I can. Check back later. I'll try to give you some of the really good stuff."

Chuckie was surprised and grateful. "Really? Thanks."

"No sweat," the kid said.

Just then a little dark-skinned man came out on the dock. "Sick f…" he started to say, then he saw we were out there on the street. After he stared at us a second, he looked back at the kid. "S.F. you ain't supposed to be out here this early, you know that."

The guy was dressed in pretty nice clothes. His shirt was open and there was a big gold medallion resting on his hairy chest. He was short and shaped like a pickle. I don't know why I thought that. Just the way his back curved, the way he had a head too big for his body and a thick neck. He looked like a pickle with arms and legs, shiny shoes and a lot of slicked back black hair. The way he talked you knew right off he was from some place like Chicago maybe. Gran would've called him a greasy Yankee. I'd heard her say that about Mr. Delano the guy who sprayed her house for roaches.

"It's summertime," the kid said. "No problems here."

The dark-skinned guy looked at us then up and down the street. "What are you doing?"

"I'm talking to my friends." There was a defiant tone to the kid. He blew smoke.

The pickle forced a real insincere smile and said, "Oh, how nice you got some friends. Now come back inside like a good boy."

"No." The kid stared at the pickle. He was standing his ground but I could tell he was scared of the guy. I think I saw his hand tremble.

"Okay," the pickle said. He smiled real big and real fake and I knew right away that was a dangerous smile. "You just talk with your friends. I'll see you inside later."

I looked at Chuckie and Johnny. They were both uncomfortable as hell, almost squirming.

The pickle turned and started back inside. I heard the distinct clap of his expensive shoes on the cement surface of the loading dock. Then he whirled around like a tiger springing on an antelope. He grabbed the kid by the hair and dragged him toward the door. "You talk like that to me? You lost your fuckin' mind?" Without looking back at us the pickle said, "You kids get the hell out of here!"

We didn't hesitate. Right away we were moving at a fast walk away from the loading dock. I could hear the pickle shouting and the kid screaming. It was serious screaming, like he was being hurt pretty bad.

"Who is that guy?" I asked.

"I think he runs that place." Chuckie said. He tucked the bag of film up under his arm and glanced back over his shoulder.

"Is he Jerry?"

"I don't know."

"Is that kid his son?"

"I don't know," Chuckie said again. "Maybe."

"What do you think he's doing to him?"

"Beating the shit out of him," Chuckie said grimly.

It took us a good long while to get to Mark Cordell's house. I guess you could say it was roughly in the same neighborhood at Gran's but not really. You could tell the homes were newer and so were the cars parked along the street. All the houses on Gran's block were different. There'd be a clapboard house next to a brick house next to a house covered in asbestos shingles. Some were two stories tall and some were spread out filling up the lot they were situated on. Some were so tiny they made you wonder who had built them and why. The houses in Mark's neighborhood were all more alike than they were different.

I was hot and tired by the time Chuckie was ringing Mark's doorbell. Mark answered pretty quick. He looked us over a second then told us to come in. There was real air conditioning in Mark's house. It felt great.

"Let's see what you got," Mark said, reaching for Chuckie's bag. He kind of stirred around in the bag as he led us into a room he called the den.

There was a card table set up and there were some gadgets laid out on it. I'd seen this kind of home movie gear before. One was a viewer, a little thing with a screen like a tiny TV and arms going out to each side to hold film reels.

The other was a splicer. It had a folding top with a blade built into it that you used to cut film. There was a bag of splice tapes next to the splicer, Mark sat down at the card table.

"This'll take a little while," he said. "Make yourselves comfortable but don't mess anything up. If you do, I'll get my ass beat."

When he said that I thought of the cigarette smoking kid and the pickle. I was willing to bet that Mark had never in his life received a beating like the one I imagined the kid had received a short time ago.

"Can we watch TV?" Chuckie asked.

TV was a pretty big deal to the Battles kids because they didn't have a television in their house.

"Sure," Mark said. "Don't turn it up too loud, though. I gotta concentrate on what I'm doing here."

"Okay," Chuckie switched on the set and perched himself on the edge of the Naugahyde sofa. The show that came up was Let's Make A Deal. If it was me I would've searched all the channels looking for something better but, I suppose, if you never watch TV at home pretty much anything will be of interest.

"You guys can get a coke if you want one," Mark said. "But you gotta take the cans with you when you go. My mom counts the cans in the trash to check up on how many cokes I'm drinking."

Chuckie got up and went to the fridge. Johnny and I stayed where we were. I watched Mark splicing the clips together and rolling them up onto a metal film reel. He looked like he'd done this before, displaying a degree of proficiency.

"Have you spliced a lot of films?" I asked.

He glanced up at me and nodded. "Yeah. I like to make movies. I'm gonna make real movies when I grow up."

That was about the coolest thing I'd ever heard. "Really? Like in Hollywood?"

I could tell he liked the way I was interested. "Maybe. Maybe I'll do it right here. There are guys that make movies right here in Texas."

"There are?"

"Yeah. Larry Buchanan's one of them. He's made a lot of movies in Dallas. Ever heard of Bullet for Pretty Boy?"

I had heard of it. The Bonnie and Clyde movie had been a big hit and after that a lot of gangster movies came out. I remembered seeing the ads for the Pretty Boy movie on TV. Fabian played Pretty Boy Floyd. "Yeah, I wanted to see that but my mom wouldn't let me."

"I haven't seen it either. Not yet anyway. But Larry Buchanan made that movie."

"How do you know so much about movie stuff?" I asked.

"I read. Magazines and newspapers. It's what I want to do, you know? Some kids know everything about football. I couldn't care less about sports. I like movies so I read about them every chance I get."

Chuckie came back into the room with three cans of coke.

"Please, please, please don't spill anything," Mark said. "My mom will kill me if you do and I won't be able to let you guys come over anymore."

"We'll be careful," Chuckie said, handing me and Johnny our cokes.

I knew Mark was exaggerating about his mom killing him. Even so, I felt like I had a pretty good idea of what kind of woman she was. She probably dressed real nice and went to the beauty parlor regularly. She was probably a pillar of the church and active in the PTA. Maybe she looked like the mom on that old TV show Leave it to Beaver. You know what I mean, dressed perfectly and very confident but not actually pretty. I could tell by looking around the place that she dusted and vacuumed on a regular basis. The place was nice. Almost too nice to actually live in.

"I wish I could get on a show like this," Chuckie said, enthralled with the shenanigans happening on the game show.

"Maybe you can someday," I said, popping the top on my can of coke and sipping. It was a real nice burn in my throat. I remember thinking it was odd the way the flavor and the acid on my dry throat created a weird mixture of pleasure and pain.

"I doubt that," Chuckie said.

"It's possible. Once you're grown and making your own decisions. It's possible. Right, Johnny?"

Johnny gave a noncommittal nod of his head. "Yeah. Maybe."

We watched the rest of Let's Make a Deal. I was very intrigued by Mark's talk about movies and it sort of energized me to think I might know somebody who was going to be a real filmmaker one day. But I kept quiet because I wanted him to finish his task, I wanted to see my first fuck movie.

After a while Mark said. "Okay, let's turn off the TV and see what we've got here. I honestly think it's gonna freak you out."

I was thinking, I can handle it, bring it on. But as it turned out, Mark was right.

Mark set up a movie screen in front of the television set and threaded the reel of film into a projector. "Hit those lights," he said, pointing to a wall switch. I hastened over and flipped the switch which made the room a lot darker.

He had put all the clips in the bag together. It was just a tangle of spaghetti in the brown bag but now it was all lined up straight on a reel and proceeding into the projector in orderly fashion. Each clip was only a couple of seconds long and they were all pretty much from different movies. They went by quick but they left a powerful impression.

The first thing up was a young dark-haired woman straddling a man with a large dick. The second shot was two women sort of mutually fucking one another with a double-headed dildo. I'd heard the older guys talking about such things, about dildos and lesbos but hearing about it and seeing is two entirely different things. The third clip showed a skinny woman masturbating with her fingers. Then the same woman licking whipped cream from her fingers. I wondered what that was all about. It was the last two clips that threw me for a loop. There was a woman with long hair on a shaggy carpet. She was jacking off a German shepherd dog. Then as the final clip rolled through the projector, for just a second, we saw her sucking the dog's dick.

We had all been sort of giggling and making noises while the film played. When that final shot came up, Chuckie exclaimed, "What the fuck?"

Mark shut off the projector.

"Why the hell would she do that?" Chuckie asked.

"Turn on the lights," Mark said. I did and he began to rewind the film.

"Why would she do that?" Chuckie repeated.

"She's probably a junkie." Mark made the comment like it was a common fact of life, like something everybody automatically understood.

I'd heard of junkies, drug addicts, I'd been warned against drugs, but the thought had never entered into my head that drugs could somehow make you think it was a good idea to suck a dog's penis. The idea made my stomach do flips and a shiver went down my spine. I found myself wishing I had not seen that image. Even now, after all these years, that image is burned into my memory. Why couldn't the clips have just been plain old sex between a man and a woman? Something everyone could relate to. Then I wondered about the people who made movies like that. Adult men and women made a business out of such things? How could that be? It went against everything I'd been led to believe in school, much less church.

"Wanna watch it again?" Mark asked.

"So you think they gave her drugs to get her to do that?" Chuckie asked.

I looked at Johnny. He just seemed his same old imperturbable self. He looked at me and gave a little shrug. People said Johnny wasn't smart but I admired him right then. No matter what life threw at him, it seemed he just went 'oh, okay, what's next?' I thought that was something. I was disturbed and I wished I wasn't. Clearly Chuckie was bothered as well.

"Want to watch it again?" Mark repeated.

"I've seen enough," I said.

"Want to take this film with you?" Mark asked.

Chuckie thought about it. "If you got a safe place to hide it, you keep it," he said. "If my dad found it he'd whip me with the belt."

"Okay, I'll keep it," Mark said, putting the reel of film in a case. "Let me know if you ever want it back. And bring more clips if you find some. I can splice them onto the end of this reel."

"Okay," Chuckie said.

"Don't forget to take your cans with you," Mark said. "I don't mean to be rude but I kind of need you guys to clear out. I gotta put all this gear away or my mom will be interrogating me. I gotta straighten everything up so it looks like nobody was here."

We thanked him for the cokes and shuffled out the door. After we'd walked a while, Chuckie said, "That was sick."

"Yeah. I wish I hadn't seen it. The part with the dog," I said.

Johnny said nothing.

After a while we came back to the park. I showed Chuckie the peace sign I'd drawn that morning. I remembered the idea I'd had of drawing a naked woman but that film we'd seen at Mark's house had wrecked my appetite for anything to do with sex.

They needed to head home and I was close to Gran's place so I told them I'd see them later.

Soon as I walked in Gran's door she said, "Heavens, son, smells like you need a bath."

I did need a bath, from head to toe. Felt like I needed to scrub my eyeballs, too. I'd heard the phrase 'brain washing' and it made me wonder if there was a way to erase memories from a person's brain. I would've done it. If it wasn't too expensive.

The next morning Mom dropped me off at Gran's, same as the day before. Gran quizzed me about whether or not I wanted some breakfast. She said there was a story in the Saturday Evening Post she thought I might like. It was called Invasion of the Body Snatchers. She knew I went in for that weird stuff.

"It's hot outside. Why don't you spend some time reading today? Good for your brain. It's cool on the sofa. You can lay down and read and I'll fix up some pink lemonade."

I agreed. Mainly because I'd stayed gone all the day before. I knew she liked having me around and talking and stuff. And I like talking with her, too. Invasion of the Body Snatchers sounded like something good to read. So I kicked off my shoes and stretched out on the sofa and started reading. By lunch time I'd read the installment of the Body Snatchers and was disappointed to realize it was serialized and I'd have to wait for the next chapters.

"That's okay," Gran said, "It'll give you something to look forward to."

She made me a grilled cheese sandwich and a bowl of tomato soup for lunch. When we ate I told her about the onion and mustard sandwich.

"Those poor people. I don't know how they afford to feed those kids. Such a shame they're Catholic."

"What do you mean?" I asked.

"That's why they have so many children. They can't practice birth control."

After she said the words 'birth control' she turned a little red and I figured she was thinking I was too young to be discussing such things.

"It's okay, Gran," I said, "I know about birth control. Why are the Catholics against it?"

"I don't know. But I do know nobody needs that many kids. Poor Mrs. Battles. I'd lose my mind if I had to keep up with nine children."

After lunch Gran wanted to watch General Hospital so I told her I was going for a walk.

"You sure? It's awful hot out there."

"Yeah, but I won't be out there too long. I gotta stretch my legs. I can't just lay around all day."

"Yes, a boy your age needs his exercise."

First I walked down to the park. No one else was there. I thought about drawing something in the shelter house with my marker but I couldn't come up with any ideas good enough to follow through on. I noticed there were some new bits of graffiti. Nothing special, just cuss words. Someone had written them in big bold letters with a purple marker. I guessed it was the Owens boys. I'd seen Ted carrying around a purple marker in his shirt pocket a couple of times that summer.

I was bored and not ready to go back to Gran's so I decided to walk over to the Battles house and see what Johnny was up to. When I got there I found out Mr. Battles had taken all the older boys with him to help move stones for a job he was doing. I turned around and headed back up Bomar street and saw the weird kid out there on the loading dock smoking a cigarette.

I started to just walk on by without saying anything but that didn't seem right. I felt sorry for the kid. There was something wrong there. I didn't know what, if anything, could be done to help the kid. I did know it didn't seem right to shun the guy.

"Hey," I said as I approached the loading dock.

"Hey," he answered.

His left eye was black, a real shiner. It was swollen up, almost closed.

"Your dad beat you?" I didn't know what else to say.

"Tony's not my dad."

"He's not?" I paused at the edge of the loading dock, squinting up at him with the sun in my eyes.

"Come on up in the shade if you want to."

I climbed up and stood with him there on the dock.

"Is your…I mean Tony, is he gonna be mad I'm up here?"

"Fuck Tony!" he said quietly but full of venom. "I hate that little greaseball."

"How come he beat you?"

"He beats me all the time. That's just what him and his friends do."

"What about your folks? How come they let him?"

"I got no folks."

"Oh, man, I'm sorry."

"Not your fault. What's your name?"

"Billy. What's yours?"

"I'm S.F.. Want a smoke, Billy?"

"No. I don't like 'em. They make me cough."

"Yeah. They're no good for you."

"So, its none of my business but why you here with that guy that beats you?"

"Tony says my mom made him my godfather before she died."

"That true?"

"I don't know. I can't really remember my mom."

"She's been gone a long time?"

"Yeah. Maybe I was three when she died. That was back in Chicago."

"I thought he sounded like he was from there."

"We came down here when Jerry opened up this place. He's got one downtown, too."

I'd seen the other Finne Arts Theater downtown on Commerce Street when I took the bus downtown once to spend some of my birthday money at the Joke Shop on Main Street. I told him I'd seen it. I told him my folks said the city should shut those places down. "They're church folks, you understand," I added.

"Yeah, well, the church folks can't do nothing about Jerry's theaters. He pays the cops and the mayor too much money."

"For real?"

"Yep. Officer Tommy Howard comes around every week to collect a bag of money."

"Really?" That didn't seem right to me, though I wasn't certain why. I was at an age when a whole lot of what adults did just felt wrong. They paid a lot of lip service to doing the right thing but nobody ever actually did the right thing. The church people didn't act the way Jesus told them to. That much I knew for sure. The adults in Gran's neighborhood knew Jesse Hernandez beat his son all the time, beat him bad, but nobody did anything about it. Like they thought Joey Hernandez was Jesse's property and he could do anything he wanted with his kid.

"Jerry's theaters make a ton of dough. Plenty of horny men wanting to see what we have in here. Tony calls it a virgin market because it's only been legal here for a little while."

"Does Tony pay you? You work here?"

S. F. scoffed. "I work but he doesn't pay me a red cent. Think I'd still be hanging around here if there was any cash in my pocket?"

There was a lull in the conversation for a moment.

Not knowing what else to say, I said, "Where do you go to school?"

He thought that was funny. "I never been in no damn school," he snorted.

"I thought kids had to go to school. I thought it was a law or something."

"We pay the law to do whatever we want inside these walls." He spit and I saw one of his front teeth had been chipped leaving a gap through which he squirted his saliva. It was an impressive thing to see. Must've gone ten feet or so. "The law's just a racket like everything else. You only get whatever law you pay for. Jerry pays real good so he does whatever he wants in this town."

"So you've never been to school?"

He shook his head.

"Can you read?"

"A little. I can sign my name and all."

Tony came out suddenly onto the dock.

"So your little friend's back? How nice. What do you think of Sickie's eye?" he asked me.

I said nothing.

"Ice cream man's coming for a private party," Tony said.

I didn't know why but what Tony said made S.F. look kind of sick.

"You're a good-lookin' kid," Tony said to me. "You like ice cream?"

"No! He don't like ice cream!" S.F. said.

"Sure he does," Tony looked at me, grinning in a way that made my skin crawl.

"Leave him alone."

"Leave him alone? He don't want to be left alone. He keeps coming around. I think he wants to see what goes on inside. Come on kid, you're invited to the party."

I started to say something like I had to be going. The look in Tony's eyes was damn scary. No words came out of my mouth. I went to jump off the dock but Tony grabbed me by the hair and dragged me inside. S.F. rushed over and started beating on Tony and cussing him but he was no match for a grown man. Like I said before he was kind of spindly and unhealthy looking.

It was dark inside and my eyes took a while to adjust.

Tony shouted, "Lance! Come grab Sick Fuck!"

A big goon with no hair and really thick glasses that were held on his head by a black strap came in and grabbed S.F. around the chest and carried him inside. S.F. kept shouting. I tried to break away from Tony but he had a big handful of my hair and when I struggled he slapped me hard enough to make me see stars.

It was real dark in there. The walls were painted black. There were a few black lights burning up high and white things like light switches glowed under that kind of light.

The guy called Lance opened a door and just tossed S.F. inside. Tony swung me through the door by my hair. They slammed the door and I heard it lock.

I was scared. More scared than I'd ever been in my life.

"What's going on?" I said, trying my best not to start bawling.

"That mother fucker! I swear I'm gonna kill him! I swear it!"

"How do we get out of here?" I asked.

S.F. looked at me real sad like. "Are you my friend?" he said.

"Yeah. I guess so."

He nodded like what I'd said was very important to him. "Let's shake on it." He stuck his bony hand out. I took it and shook hands with him. Afterwards he said, "I swear I'll do everything I can to get us out of here. You gotta just play along, do whatever I say for a while. If they think you want to be here they'll relax. Then I'll be able to fix things."

"Fix things how?"

"I know where Tony keeps his gun."

I felt like flipping out but I didn't. Something inside me knew that my best odds of coming out of this okay was to play along. At least until they unlocked that door.

"Why am I here? What do they want from me?"

"There's this guy called the Ice Cream Man. He likes boys."

"You mean likes them to have sex?"

"Yeah. He likes to put ice cream on his, you know, and have someone lick it off."

"And you do that?"

"Yeah. That's not nearly as bad as some of the things they make me do around here."

I felt sick. I gagged but nothing came up, just some bitter acid in my throat. I wished like hell I'd just walked by and never stopped. I could be at Gran's reading or watching TV. But here I was locked up in a place like I never even imagined could be.

"What are we gonna do?"

"Just play along with what I say. Do it and you'll be okay. It's scary. I know. But you gotta trust me. We're friends now."

"Okay," I said.

S.F. went to the door and knocked. He had to knock a few times before the Lance guy shouted, "What?"

"Open up a minute. I need to talk to Tony."

A couple minutes later the door opened and Tony stood in the doorway. "What?"

"I been telling Billy about the Ice Cream Man and he thinks it sounds fun."

A look of surprise came on Tony's face. "That right?" He looked at me.

I nodded, trying not to look like I wanted to bust out crying.

S.F. leaned in and whispered something to Tony. Tony laughed. "For real? Looks like we got another little sick fuck. That's just fine."

S.F. whispered again.

"Sure. Go on." He patted S.F. on the shoulder and let him pass out through the door. To me he said, "Well, Billy, looks like this may be the start of a whole new life for you."

He turned to leave but stopped and turned back around. "S.F. says you like ice cream. That right?"

I nodded.

"Good. That's fine. So you want to party with the ice cream man?"

Again I nodded.

"Fine. Afterwards I'll buy you boys a pizza. You like pizza don't you?"

I mustered all the false bravado I could and said, "Yeah. It's my favorite."

Tony nodded and as he left I heard him say, "Lance I don't think you gotta lock the door. Just keep an eye on the boys till Ice Cream gets here."

"Right," Lance said.

I sat down on the edge of a black vinyl sofa and waited. In a little while S.F. came back in holding a black plastic tray, the kind waitresses use. On the tray were some bottles of oil and some things that I didn't even want to think about. Maybe you'd call them sex toys. Whatever you call them, they were just gross and frightening. He set the tray down on a small table by the sofa.

"Ice Cream Man just showed up," he whispered. "He'll be in here in a minute. Just act friendly. I won't let him hurt you. Okay?"

I nodded.

Just to show me he was serious, he raised his jacket a little and I saw a gun tucked into his pants.

I heard loud voices outside the room, then a big man came in. He was wearing a mask like the Lone Ranger. "Hey boys!" he almost yelled, "The Ice Cream Man's here!"

S.F. clapped his hands and acted like an excited kid. "Goody!" he said in a high-pitched voice.

"Two boys today? How nice! You like ice cream don't you?"

"You bet," said S.F..

"Yes, sir," I said.

"Don't call me sir," he said. "Call me Ice Cream Man or Icey if you like."

"Okay, Icey," I answered. It was then that I knew for sure who that man was. His real name was Sargent Montaigne. He owned a lot of businesses on the east side and he went to Gran's church. He was one of the deacons there. Gran had been in high school with him. All the women her age thought he was just the greatest guy ever. He was always giving money to the church and helping with the athletic teams in the neighborhood.

I guess at the same time I recognized him, he recognized me, or thought he did. "Do I know you, boy? You look familiar."

"No sir. No Icey," I said.

"Well we know each other now. And we're going to be great pals. Isn't that right, Sickie?"

"You bet!" S.F. said, reaching around the big man's waist and giving him a hug.

"Ready for some ice cream?"

"You know it!"

S.F. started unbuckling the man's belt.

"You boys friends?"

"Yes. He's my friend," S.F. said very seriously.

"Good. That's good."

S.F. slid the man's pants down and he stepped out of them. S.F. folded the pants semi-carefully and placed them on the end of the sofa.

"You know how he came to be called Sick Fuck?" Icey asked me.

"No."

"When he was really young Tony and the boys went to a party and forgot about him. They got so high they didn't come back for a few days. When they did what do you think they found? This boy was trying to eat his own shit." Icey laughed real hard at that and S.F. winced. He was pulling the guy's underwear off now. "Tony sees that and says we got us one sick fuck!"

Icey laughed again. He sat down on the sofa and spread his legs.

"What's your favorite flavor?" he asked. His dick was getting hard.

"Chocolate," I answered, nervous as hell.

"We know what your favorite flavor is, don't we?" he said to S.F. "Unfortunately I don't think they sell shit flavored ice cream."

"I only did that because they starved me, you sorry bastard."

Then I saw the gun in S.F.'s hand. I think I saw it before the Ice Cream Man did. The smile was just leaving his face when S.F. squeezed the trigger. The first bullet hit him right between the legs. The guy screamed and S.F. shot him again in the head. He was quiet then but I could hear Tony and Lance outside running for the door.

S.F. grabbed my wrist and pulled me into the corner behind the door.

I don't know what Tony and Lance were thinking. They must have heard the gunshots. Even so, they came racing through the door. Before they spotted us in the corner, S.F. fired a bullet into Lance's head. The big guy's glasses flew off and landed on the floor. He came down hard on the table scattering the things from the tray all over the place.

I heard a sound and smelled a smell and, by god, I knew Tony had shit his pants.

"Sick f…S.F. put that gun away."

"Go ahead and say it Tony. Call me Sick Fuck. Billy don't care, do you?"

I said nothing. Did nothing.

"You think it's funny that you starved a little kid until he was willing to eat shit? That's funny. Now reach in your pants and eat some of your own shit. I know it's there. I can smell it."

S.F. stepped closer to Tony. Tony whined and waved his hands.

"Eat shit, Tony."

Tony just shook his head. S.F. shot him in the leg just above the knee. Tony screamed and fell on the floor holding his bloody leg.

"Get some shit out of your pants and eat it."

Tony was smart enough to know he was already dead no matter what he did. "Fuck you!" he screamed, drooling and whimpering.

"My godfather." S.F. walked up real close to Tony. "You're a shitty godfather, Tony."

Tony looked like a wild man, his eyes wide and rolling around. "Your mama didn't die!" he screamed. "She was a fucking junkie hooker. She sold you to me for fifty bucks."

S.F. winced. Then he fired a shot into Tony's other leg.

"Fucking hell!" Tony screamed. He was bleeding all over the place.

S.F. looked at me. "Come here, Billy," he said.

I wanted to run but I did what he said.

"You're gonna finish him off," S.F. said. "Put a bullet in this greasy motherfucker's head."

"Me?"

"Don't do it Billy! Don't you fuckin' do it!" Tony was crying now and gasping. I know he was in a world of pain."

"Why me?" I asked.

"You have to. We're friends now. If I do all the killing then it's all on me. I go to jail and you walk away. Friends don't do that. Kill him." He put the gun in my hand.

"Don't listen to him. He's crazy."

"Kill him," S.F. said quietly. "After all you seen here don't you think he deserves to die?"

"Yeah. He deserves to die, but…"

Tony was sobbing and crying out in pain.

"He owns the cops. If you don't kill him, they'll probably kill us."

I didn't really want to kill Tony. But what S.F. was saying made sense. He'd never been to school but he was smart enough.

"Just put one in his brain," he said.

So I did.

We went out on the loading dock. As far as we could tell no one had heard anything.

"Wait here a minute," S.F. said. "I'll be right back."

I waited and it was probably no more than two minutes but it seemed like a long time. I found myself wishing I could wake up in my bed and find out this was all a dream. It was a nightmare but it was real. S.F. came back out.

"Okay. Let's go." He started climbing down from the dock.

I followed him.

"What did you do?" I asked.

"I locked the front door. I got the cash out of the register and more bullets for the gun."

"Damn!" I was impressed. We'd just killed some guys and he was acting and thinking like a cool-headed guy checking off items on a to-do list. "I don't know how you can think so clear right now."

"I been thinking about this all my life," he said.

We walked along Bomar toward Beach. He couldn't walk very fast because of his limp.

"What happened to your leg?" I asked.

"Tony broke. A long time ago. I guess he didn't want me to be able to run."

"Where are we going?"

"You decide," he said. "Someplace in the woods maybe. Someplace with no people around."

I thought a second. "Yeah. I know a spot."

I took him down on the other side of the river where there was a stretch of property that was really overgrown. I'd gone there before a couple of times. There was part of an old house up under the trees. Somebody's farm a long time ago. Maybe still part of somebody's farm, because on the north end, away from the river there was a big field with corn growing in it.

When we got to the spot under the trees and so overgrown you'd think you were out in the country if it wasn't for the sound of the cars in the distance, S.F. said, "Yeah. This is perfect."

"What're you gonna do now?" I sat down on a rock and he sat on a fallen tree.

"I don't know. I'm gonna think for a while. I can sleep here tonight and maybe do something different tomorrow."

"S.F."

"Yeah?"

"You said you'd been thinking about killing Tony for a long time."

He nodded.

"Why didn't you do it before now?"

"I was waiting til I had a friend. I couldn't do much without a friend to help me. You're my first friend."

I nodded. I understood what he was saying.

"What do you want me to do?"

"Tomorrow can you bring me some food and some clothes. I can't really walk around wearing this stuff. People notice how different I look and they'll remember me. I want to look like you and the other guys."

"Jeans and a T-shirt?"

"That's right."

He was about my size, maybe a little smaller, which was good.

"I'll bring you some of my old stuff. I've got an old pair of tennis shoes too. I'll bring those."

"Thanks. You want some money for them?"

"No. I can't take money from a friend for my old clothes."

He liked that. He smiled and nodded.

"What kind of food you want?"

"Anything but ice cream," he said.

I looked at him kind of shocked that he'd said that. I guess the expression on my face made him laugh. Once he was laughing, I couldn't help but laugh, too.

Before I left him there that day we went for a swim in the river. Gran says the river's polluted and I should never go in that water but it wasn't the first time I'd broken that rule. Besides S.F. wanted to swim and I didn't want to make him do it alone. For all I knew this would be the first time he'd ever gone swimming in his whole life.

When we stripped down to our underwear to swim I saw lots of scars all over his body. He saw me looking and guessed I was wondering about them. "Cigarette burns," he said.

"Why?"

"A lot of sick fucks get off on hurting kids," he said. "They called me Sick Fuck but every last one of those motherfuckers was sicker than me. I hope they all go to hell."

"Think there really is a hell?" I asked him.

"How would I know? All I know is they deserve it."

"Yeah. That's true." I knew Gran believed in hell. Maybe my mom did, too. Would they think I should go to hell now that I'd shot a man in the head? Even a really bad man like Tony?

While we were swimming around I told S.F. about how I'd thought Tony looked like a pickle. He got a big laugh out of that.

"Yeah," he said, "a big fat ugly pickle. A pickle with a bullet in him, now."

Finally, I told him I had to go home or they'd be looking for me.

"You gonna be alright here by yourself?"

"Are you kidding? This is like heaven compared to where I've been."

I stuck out my hand to shake. He took it and squeezed it real hard.

"Thanks for being my friend."

"Thanks for saving my life," I said.

As I was walking away, I called, "I'll be back around 8:30 tomorrow morning. So don't wander off too far."

"Okay," he said. Then I left him in the woods.

For the next few days I got asked a whole lot if I was okay. Mom asked, Gran asked, a few of my friends. I kept saying I was fine but I guess there was no hiding the burden on my mind. I never told anyone what was eating at me but they kept asking what was up. Finally I guess they got tired of asking. I wasn't sick. Didn't need to go to a doctor. I made a point of eating. Not a lot but still I ate something at every meal.

The next day after we'd killed Tony I brought a bag with some old clothes, a pair of shoes and a couple cans of ravioli. I had a little pocketknife with a can opener built into it and I threw that in the bag, too. I told Mom and Gran I was gonna give the old clothes to the Battles family. They acted like that made me a saint or something. I was about as far from being a saint as a twelve-year-old kid can be.

When I showed up in the woods down by the river I could hear S.F. talking with someone. Then I saw there was a tall skinny Mexican kid with him.

"Hey," I said.

They got up from where they were sitting and came toward me.

Turns out the other guy was a runaway named Joe Gonzalez. Joe had been living at the orphan's home out on East Lancaster. The night before he'd run away and just happened to end up in the same spot where S.F. was hiding.

"This ain't the first time I run away," Joe said. "Last year I took off and stayed gone for eight weeks."

"Where'd you go?" I asked him.

"Got a job washing dishes at a Mexican restaurant on the north side. They came in checking everybody's IDs one day. Took them a while but they figured out I was the kid that ran away from the orphanage."

"What are you gonna do now?"

"Find another job. Maybe we'll go to some other town. I'm thinking we head east."

"Bring me some clothes?" S.F. asked.

I gave him the bag.

"Thanks," he said. He took his clothes off and changed right away. "Now I look like a regular kid."

"Yeah, you do," I said.

"Food! I'm hungry." He took the two cans of ravioli out and tossed one to Joe.

"I couldn't bring any forks or spoons," I said. "My mom would've missed them."

"No sweat," he said. "I can just drink it right out of the can." And that's what the two of them did.

When he went to hand me back my pocket knife I told him to keep it.

"You're a good friend, Billy. Joe's a good friend, too. I got two friends now. I feel lucky."

"Are you going with Joe to find work somewhere?"

"Yeah. I think that's best, don't you?"

"I guess."

"He'll be my friend. He'll help me out. You gotta stay with your family, you know. It's not like you could run away. Unless you wanted to." The way he said that last part I think he was hoping maybe I did want to run away. I told him I couldn't.

After they ate, Joe went off in the woods to find a place to crap.

I whispered to S.F., "How much does he know?"

"I didn't tell him anything except I ran away from some mean people."

"Does he know about the money? Does he know about the gun?"

"I'll tell him about the money when I need to. If we're going to be partners I gotta share with him till we get jobs. The gun I threw in the river last night. Nobody'll ever find it and I won't tell anyone about it. Ever."

"What about the bullets?"

"In the river."

When Joe came back he said they needed to get moving, maybe they'd find a place to work that night.

"I hope you guys find a job real quick," I said.

"Billy says he don't mind sucking a few dicks if he has to," Joe said, grinning. "We'll be alright."

"Billy?" I was confused.

"Yeah. That's me now. Hope you don't mind me borrowing your name. I don't want to be Sick Fuck anymore. I don't want to be S.F.. I just want a regular name like Billy."

"Good," I said. "That's good."

So they stood there looking at me for a while.

"Goodbye, Billy," S.F. said.

"Goodbye, Billy," I said back at him.

"Thanks."

They headed north through the woods. I noticed S.F.'s discarded clothes on the ground. I picked them up and tossed them inside what was left of the old farmhouse where I thought nobody would ever find them. Then I headed east along the river toward Beach Street.

Later Johnny and Chuckie told me some people had been killed at Jerry's Finne Arts Theater. The place was shut down of course and stood empty for a long time before someone turned it into a carpet outlet. Gran talked a lot about the place and said to whoever would listen that those were the wages of sin. The church and the whole east side was pretty disturbed when they heard Sargent Montaigne had been shot in a place like that. Even worse that it was said his pants were off when he was killed.

A lot of times over the years I thought about S.F., the new Billy. I'd be in a crowd of people somewhere and I'd look around expecting to see his face. I never saw him again, never heard anything about him on TV or in the newspaper. I never will see him again but his face haunts my mind.

Whether he's still alive or not he's a ghost that haunts me. I don't suppose I'll ever be free of that.

The Last Ray of Summer
Anthony Ferguson

"Goddamit, boy. I asked you a question."

Ray swivels around from where he has been sweeping dirt along the floor of the family store to fix his pa with what he hopes passes for an apologetic look. He glances across to where momma sits on her stool behind the cash register, polishing her nails.

"Well, don't stand there dreaming about getting your pecker wet. I told you half an hour ago to re-stock that soda fridge. It's touchin' on ninety out there. Now why ain'tcha done it?"

Ray looks from pa to the diminished stack of cans in the fridge, and swallows.

"I'm sorry pa. I restocked the smokes and the grass-feed, like you asked. I meant to do the soda. I just forgot is all."

Jerry Corbin exhales, and Ray sees his father's eyes turn waxy black, fixing him with a death stare.

"What was that? Speak up, boy. I can't hear you."

Ray clears his throat and starts over. "I said I forgot."

"Louder boy. Goddammit. Are you a man or not?"

"Yes sir…" Ray stammers, turning a shade of beetroot.

"The Hell is wrong with you? Did I raise some kind of…"

"Jerry!" Momma mercifully cuts him short. "He's just a kid. Don't be so hard on him."

"Goddammit Brandi, he's fifteen…"

Ray takes the opportunity to turn and flee out of his father's sight, out of range of his father's hateful voice. He hurries to the big walk-in cooler and starts hauling out the trays of soda. Stacks them on the two-wheeler and edges back into the shop, where he starts re-stocking the drinks cabinet, making sure to rotate the older cans to the front, like pa showed him.

He can feel his father's eyes boring into the back of his neck without turning around. The bell above the store door tinkles and someone breezes through the tacky faded streamers adorning the doorway. Ray catches a glimpse of summer skirt and a whiff of perfume. He hears the tone of pa's voice change completely as he ushers the young woman to the perfume shelf. From the corner of his eye he sees his father's silhouette loom above the petite woman, as he leans in to speak in hushed tones to her. Ray hears the girl's soft laugh. Sees Momma look on with veiled contempt. She runs her lacquered fingers through her peroxide tresses.

Later, after dusk when the last customer has gone, and Pa's truck has screeched off down the road to the nearest bar, Momma fixes them both a plate to eat. They sit a while on the couch watching repeats on the old black and white box. Momma pulls him in for a hug and strokes his coal black hair.

"Your daddy don't really mean them nasty things he says," she tries to reassure him. "He loves you really. Loves us both. He's just been a bit troubled since…" Brandi pauses. Hesitant to bring up the touchy subject of the conflict in Vietnam. Ray finishes the thought for her.

"He's changed," he whispers into her shoulder, careful not to lean too deeply into the already fading purple-yellow blotch near her arm. A gentle but persistent scratching at the door turns their heads.

"I think someone loves you almost as much as I do," momma smiles. Ray peels himself from her embrace and goes to the door. Opens it and a small, brown and white mottled fox terrier trots in, tail bobbing proudly.

"Hey, Buddy."

The dog circles his feet and yips a greeting. Ray picks the pup up and lets its tongue lash his face.

"Night, Ma."

Ray carries Buddy upstairs to his room, where he has a bowl of cool water sitting inside the door. After the dog laps his fill. Ray hunkers down on the faded rug to muss the dog's head and romp. When Buddy is sated, he flops on his side and breathes gentle and relaxed. Ray mirrors the dog and curls himself around it, holding a tiny paw in his hand.

"At least I got you, Buddy. You're my best pal in the world… you're my only pal."

Ray watches the old faded yellow school bus approach, kicking up a storm of dirt. He boards, exchanging a terse greeting with Mr. Stimson, the old driver. Shuffling down the aisle past a swathe of baleful faces, he is forced to take the only vacant seat, next to a pale blonde tousle-haired girl he recognizes from one of his classes. She gives him a mournful glance then scooches across the bench seat as if to get as far away from him as possible, clutching her books to her thin chest. Ray racks his brain and tries to recall her name from assembly. He thinks it might be Kim. He steals a glance on the off chance she might make conversation so he can drop her name in, but she refuses to meet his eyes, stares dead ahead.

He drifts through the day in his regular state of obliviousness. At lunch he sits alone on a bench, chewing a sandwich, pensively staring over at the more successful kids, whooping, hollering, and showboating, enjoying each other's company. For Ray, adolescence seemed to come on too suddenly, edging out the joy of childhood and elementary school. It's as if his mind hasn't caught up with his spurting limbs yet. He looks with yearning at the girls, especially the popular ones, enjoying the blossoming of their youth and the attention of the boys.

After school, loitering out back of the store, Ray checks his reflection in a thin mirror hanging on the wall and grimaces as he applies a thick white cream to his latest crop of acne, shuddering as his fingers brush against the flaring red mounds with their snow-white caps. Pa's stern voice calls him into the shop to serve, and Ray quivers as he spies Shauna, the best-looking girl in school, waiting at the counter.

Ray hesitates like a scolded pup and tentatively approaches, blushing as red as the zits on his chin as she greets him with a sardonic smile. Ray fetches down the pack of cigarillos she requests and hands back her change. Shauna's red-lacquered fingers linger on his, a tad longer than they should, and she gives him a teasing grin before she skips out of the store, unfurling the plastic wrapping of her prize.

Ray turns to find his father's coalescent eyes boring into him.

"Dammit, boy. You some sort of pansy?"

"Huh?" Ray is grateful that the small avalanche of customers has left the premises.

"That piece of tail is screaming for it… Do you even *like* girls?"

Ray stammers. He knows what's coming. The lecture on biology is all too familiar. He is grateful Momma isn't in the store to hear it.

"Jeezus, when I was your age boy, I was drowning in pussy. I was fighting them off. How do you ever expect to get laid, way you mope around with your tail between your legs."

Ray doesn't stop to consider his father's words. It seems impossible that a fifteen-year-old could gain that much experience, with his hormones raging. He always found himself tongue tied in the mere presence of a female. Instead of experiencing the sport sex his father talks about, Ray sits alone in his room, wondering if indeed he might be a homo. Never mind the fact that he has no interest in boys, with their chest beating self-aggrandizement and their false bravado. Ray's head is constantly filled with images of the girls in his class, short skirts and pony-tails. Late at night in his single bed, Ray thinks of Shauna and her pretty mouth and painted nails as he touches himself, and whimpers in shame after he achieves orgasm. Buddy stirs and stretches at his feet.

On the rare occasions Pa sits him down and attempts a man to man, Ray is left more confused than when they started. Pa's breath often reeks of booze, and the talk usually segues back to his experiences in the war. He doesn't realize that his father simply has no one else to listen to his stories. The only understanding that gets through to Ray's fuddled, hormone-riddled brain, is that this strange foreign country that messed up his pa must be a really horrible place.

"The Cong were bastards," Jerry's eyes get all misty as he revisits his wartime nightmares, staring dead ahead as if Ray isn't even in the room. In his head, Jerry Corbin is back in the steaming jungle. "They used to set traps for us, in the ground."

Ray meets his father's gaze. "Traps? Like the ones you set for rabbits in the woods? Them's pretty cruel traps, Pa."

Jerry lets out a savage laugh. "Much worse than them pussy rabbit traps, boy. Out in 'nam, the Gooks had this thing they called a punji. You'd be on patrol, sweat dripping down your neck cos it's so damn humid, and there'd be a scream. Some asshole treads on the camouflage over the hole, and his foot goes through, right onto a goddamn spike."

"Gee!' Ray let's out a breath and, sensing a rare glimpse of camaraderie and paternal bonding, he leans in close, encouraging his pa to go on.

"Sometimes even worse. Two traps, one atop the other. Mug's boot goes through the first one to the second, and there's like a bear trap 'neath that one, snaps shut on his lower leg."

Pa makes a clapping sound with his big hands to emphasize, causing Ray to flinch.

"Then just for a kicker, sometimes the devious assholes would lace the jaws of the trap with poison or leave a snake down in the hole. Nasty way to lose a goddamn leg."

Sometimes, Ray sneaks up on his Pa in the shed out back, when the old man thinks he's alone, and catches him talking to himself, or at least, to someone who just ain't there. Ray knows who it is. His old man has mentioned the name sometimes in his war recollections. An older guy he looked up to, his NCO he called him, feller by the name of Billy Kane.

Ray recognizes the name when his pa speaks aloud to the empty air of the shed. Surrounded by rusting tools and the smell of grease. Even if he doesn't comprehend the nature of the discussion. "I know I done bad things, Billy. I can't help it." Ray figures Pa must be referring to the bruises on momma's face and arms, or maybe stuff that happened in that war, but sometimes he wonders if there's something else he doesn't understand.

The ghost, or whatever Billy Kane is, must be answering, cos Pa always carries on the one-sided conversation by replying to unspoken questions.

"I can't do it." Pa shakes his head. "I can't ask the good Lord for forgiveness, not for this. Not in his house." Ray sees his pa's shoulders start to shake, and when he starts weeping, Ray runs back to the sanctity of his room.

Ray pictures Momma and him on their knees in the stark wooden church sat atop the hill on the edge of town. The one she forces him to attend every Sunday. The one his father has refused to enter since his army service. Though Ray would much rather be out in the woods that run off the back of the house, chasing rabbits with Buddy.

Ray doesn't like the traps his pa sets on the lip of the woods for rabbits. Kids at school say the law says you got to use State approved padded jaw traps. But the traps Pa uses don't have pads. They have thin steel jaws in them. Ray seen him making them himself in the shed before Pa chased him away.

Pa made him come out early one Saturday morning, showed him how to fix the trap, how to dig a hole just the right depth, how to anchor it to a fixed object like a log or sturdy birch. How to set the spring and anchor chain just right, to give it some drag so the rabbit can wear itself out trying to pull away. How to camouflage the area around the trap with leaves and grass, but always leaving a small, cleared area about the plate. "So you don't step on the damn thing yourself," Pa explained.

The last time Pa took Ray out hunting, they came across a snow-colored rabbit caught in one of the traps, the fur around its leg was bloody and torn. It thrashed and tried to tear itself free, even at the risk of amputating its own limb.

Pa made him watch as he grabbed the rabbit and pried the jaws open. Then he picked the twitching bunny up, and giving a slow and deliberate narration, he turned it upside down by the legs in one firm hand, and with the other he took its neck between his thumb and index finger, pushed down so its head tilted backwards. Ray could see its nose twitching, until his pa stretched its head out and he heard a soft but audible snap as its neck broke. Ray flinched as the rabbit set out in a series of violent kicks, but pa assured him that was just the death throes. Sure enough, the rabbit soon lay still.

Ray saw that rabbit in his dreams for weeks after. In other dreams though, ones that made him blush with shame, he saw himself out in the woods setting bigger traps, warm, soft, furry traps in which Ray hoped to catch much prettier prey.

Two things catch Ray's eye on his walk from school to where the bus picks up the kids from out of town. The first is the poster glued to a lamp post. It's about a girl who has gone missing. Ray doesn't recognize the girl's name, but he heard all the kids talking about her during class. She had once been a student there, not so long ago. Ray heard tell she wasn't the first to disappear, and he makes a mental note to keep an eye out for more of these posters in future.

That's when he sees a familiar figure up ahead in front of him, shuffling along. Ray recognizes the cheap, rough cut of Kim's blonde hair and slows down instinctively. He had sat beside her on the bus a half dozen times since that first occasion, and not a word had passed between them.

Ray is intent on keeping it that way when a strange thing happens. If he was a little more perceptive, he might have called it serendipity. Kim drops the books she is hanging onto, and papers scatter in the afternoon breeze. Before he can even think to stop himself, Ray is scampering to collect the papers blowing back his way.

"Here, lemme," he says as they both stoop and crawl around on the ground, gathering her things, to the point they almost bump heads. Ray smooths out the papers, stacks them neatly and hands them back to her, his face blushing.

They sit in the dirt, gathering their breath, and Kim looks at him for the first time. He notices she has sparkling emerald eyes.

"Thank you. That's real kind," she blurts out, and then looks like she wants to swallow the words down again.

Ray feels a bead of sweat running down his spine. "Momma always taught me to be polite," he says. Then as an afterthought. "I'm Ray."

This time she does smile. "I know who you are, Raymond."

When Ray finally bites the bullet and lets Kim come over to his place, it elicits the response he most fears from his father.

"Well, lookit this, our dipshit kid finally grew a set. Cute little blonde piece too."

"Hush now, Jerry," his mother has the good grace to drag her husband aside. "Leave them be. I think it's adorable."

Ray had tried his best to keep Kim away from his embarrassing family, despite the fact he had been to her place a dozen times and had been doted on by her mother. Kim had no father, at least no visible father. Since Kim and her mother made no reference to a father or what had become of him, Ray did not ask questions. Kim kept showing up at the store, even though she had no money, until his momma realized what was going on and invited her back to the house.

Mostly they sit in Ray's room doing their homework and gossiping about school, while buddy scampers around them, soliciting affection. It's all pretty innocent to start with.

Ray's arm accidentally brushes against Kim's and they both redden, later they share a clumsy kiss. Things don't progress much past the holding hand stage, but never in public, and definitely not in the schoolyard.

Sometimes, after she closes the store, Momma makes them come sit at her feet on the porch to watch the sunset, as she stirs her home-made martinis and smokes her cigarettes. She regales them with stories about how happy she was when she was their age, and they listen quietly, surreptitiously holding hands. Most times Pa has taken the truck to whatever bar holds his fickle fancy in town, and Ray can sense it is as much a relief to Momma as it is to him. He wonders if she has heard Pa talking to his invisible friend, but isn't brave enough to ask her.

"Your daddy was so sweet when he started courting me," Brandi says, staring off toward the horizon. "So gentle, like you are, Ray."

Dinner is always a time to fear in the house, and Ray is silently grateful it's not an event that Kim has been asked to partake in. Instead, he and momma sit poised over their plates and holding their breath, hoping Pa will take a liking to what she has served up, and not throw it against the wall like he sometimes does. Jerry makes them say grace as usual, and something in Ray's lizard brain senses the absurdity of the gesture.

"You say somethin', boy?" Pa asks through his steepled fingers.

"Nothin' Pa." Ray flinches in anticipation of the blow, but it doesn't come this time.

Later, Pa makes him sit in the front room watching the television. Another pageant celebrating the Bicentennial. Jerry rages about something Ray doesn't quite comprehend, about how the government abandoned the likes of him after they served their country. Ray just wishes the old man had ponied up for one of them color TVs. The flags and ribbons don't look so good on the old black and white. He chews his lip and wishes he could light over to Kim's house. Her momma has a nice color set with a bigger screen, and she doesn't scream and yell.

After, Pa forbids him to go see his girlfriend, out of spite Ray reckons, by the sneer on his face, and orders him to go check the shelves in the store for the morning.

Ray rages internally at the injustice, and when he hears the old man's truck fire up, he does something he never dared do before. He pulls his bike out from beside the shed and heads out in pursuit.

Pedaling like a fury down the bumpy road, Ray manages to keep Pa's old truck in his sights. He doesn't fear the old man spying him, on account of the darkness and the fact he has no lights. He just hopes nothing big comes out of a side street and takes him out. Though an accident is unlikely in their little Podunk town, with its big blocks and large gaps between the few houses. Still it pays to keep your wits about you.

He spies Pa's truck pull into the half full lot of a roadside bar and waits back on the side of the road until Jerry goes inside. He dismounts and pushes his bike up to the front window. There is a gaudy neon sign on the frontispiece of the building. Ray stores his bike in the shadows and edges toward the door. That's when he notices the huge figure standing atop the steps, blocking the way in. He recognizes Jimmy Blaine's father a second too late, as the big man locks eyes on him.

"Ray Corbin, that you down there?"

Ray tries to retreat, but he is too slow. Blaine reaches out and grabs a hold of his collar before he can escape.

"Dang it boy. You shouldn't be hangin' around a place like this, not at your tender age, but I can guess what you're about. Your old man is in here. Hold on."

Ray squirms but Blaine's grip is secure. He fixes Ray with a wicked grin and shoves the door open, hauling Ray inside.

"Hey, Jer. Look what the cat dragged in. Your kid's looking for ya."

Ray watches in terror as his Pa's head swivels to look his way, along with everyone else in the bar. Before Jerry rises from his stool, Ray notices the scantily dressed girl hanging off his father's arm. She is like something out of a magazine, with her rouged face, flickering lashes, painted nails, and fancy high heeled shoes. Jerry shoves the girl off and stalks toward him, accompanied by the sound of raucous laughter that almost drowns out the music from the jukebox.

"Goddammit boy, what the hell are doing here?"

Jerry doesn't wait for an answer as he shoves Ray out the open door. Ray goes tumbling down the steps to land in a heap in the dirt. His pa follows and the door closes behind them, shutting out the light and muffling the music and the laughter.

Before Ray can scramble to his feet, Pa has a hold of him and lifts him roughly off the ground. "Following me, is that it?"

"No, Pa…"

Jerry isn't interested in his excuses.

"I'll teach ya to spy on me!"

Before Ray can duck, the old man catches him with a backhander across the face, sending him flying.

Ray rolls and leaps to his feet and runs for his bike before Pa can get to him. The old man gives chase for a moment before he thinks better of it.

Ray hears Pa's angry voice over his shoulder. "I'll kill you, boy. I catch you followin' me again!" He pauses at a safe distance and turns to see his father retreating back into the warmth of the neon lit bar.

He pedals off into the night, back toward home, biting his lip and trying to hold back the tears.

To his relief, Pa doesn't mention the incident again, and Jerry seems content to call a truce when he realizes Ray hasn't spilled the beans to his momma. He tells Kim instead, and she opines that his Pa is a creep, and that Ray should move out of home as soon as he is old enough.

"Can I come live with you, Kim, you and your momma? That would be sweet."

On the weekend, when Pa is out picking up supplies for the store, Ray heads out to the old man's shed, Buddy in pursuit. He doesn't know what he's looking for exactly, but Ray has the type of curiosity common in teenagers who begin to sense that adults have a whole secret world hidden from them.

He finds his answer buried beneath a swathe of papers in a drawer in the old workbench. Ray pulls out a pile of glossy magazines. He feels a stirring in his loins when he looks at the cover of the first one. In a full body shot, a bare-naked lady squats on the ground gazing into the camera lens with a look of wide-eyed fear. There's a gag around her mouth, with a big red ball wedged in between her teeth. Her arms and legs are tightly bound, and it looks sure like she can't move or even stand.

Ray flicks through the magazine to find a whole range of similar images, most in black and white, a few in color. He puts it aside and tries the next one, the same. There is a whole collection of similar bondage magazines, but when he gets halfway through, Ray sees something slide out from between the pages and fall to the greasy floor.

He reaches down and picks it up, sees its not one thing, but a bunch of stacked photographs. Ray looks through them one by one. They are the same as the magazines, showing a woman trussed and gagged and looking into the camera lens like a deer caught in the headlights. The difference is these are personal images, taken by someone with their own camera. It can only have been Pa, and the subject is the same in every photo. With the dyed blonde hair and the big doe eyes, Ray blanches as he stares into the face of his own mother.

On the school bus the next day he takes his seat next to Kim.

"Penny for your thoughts, Raymond?"

He elects not to share his turbulent thoughts with her.

On reaching the school grounds, an even more unwelcome distraction awaits. Hushed voices spread the word along the grapevine. "Did you hear? Shauna Mitchell disappeared."

"She snuck out to meet some older guys. She never came home."

The shock and grief among the missing girl's friends are laced with schadenfreude from those not so enamored of her. "I knew she'd come to no good."

"Serves her right."

They go to Kim's house after school and her momma sits them down for a chat about Shauna and the importance of being careful of your surroundings. She fixes them a nice meal. After dark, Ray engages in some necking and light petting with Kim, kisses her good night and rides home on his bike, being sure to stick to the middle of the road but staying well out of the way of any passing vehicles.

It's dark when he gets home. He feeds Buddy and they retreat to his room. Drowsing in bed, he hears his folks arguing in their bedroom. There's the sound of fist on flesh, his mother crying, and then, the definite sound of noisy sex. Unable to resist, Ray touches himself as he listens to it, the dog stirring at his feet. He assuages his guilt by thinking about Kim.

The next night, slipping out of the house to the outdoor bathroom near the storefront, Ray hears a muffled litany amidst the chirping of crickets. Intrigued, he edges closer to the shed and peaks inside the crack of the door. He sees Pa on his knees, shirtless, before a big cross he has nailed to the wall, but it isn't Jesus the old man is praying to.

"God forgive me, Billy, I know I sinned. Oh, Lord! In my head, I'm still in that God forsaken jungle. I left that hell hole, but it never left me. It lives inside me, Billy…"

A sudden gust of wind blows across the shed from nowhere, showering his father in dust. In the midst of it, Ray sees a fleeting shape, then it is gone. He gasps, and Jerry turns, but Ray ducks out of sight.

Later, he hears quiet footsteps outside his bedroom door, and cowers beneath the covers. Buddy growls, low and guttural, and the steps retreat. Ray shivers, replaying the scene over in his head, but what puzzles him most are the deep red welts he saw on his pa's back.

"Your old man weirds me out," Kim says when they sit in his room doing homework later in the week. "Talking to folks who aren't there."

"It's his commanding officer in Vietnam, like I said. I've seen him in pictures."

Kim excuses herself to go to the toilet. Ten minutes pass, and Ray gets concerned. She is nowhere to be seen. He checks every room in the house, even though he knows it is futile. She would have come straight back to his room. His folks are still in the store, and he goes to them.

"Have you guys seen Kim?" he asks.

They shake their heads.

"No, she didn't come through here," Momma replies. Pa shakes his head and looks away.

Worried, Ray checks the side gate. It is closed but the padlock is off. Not unusual, Pa often leaves it unlocked until after sundown. He pushes it open and looks forlorn down the empty street. Nothing stirs beneath the dim streetlights. Momma eases up beside him.

"It's not like her to just disappear like that, without a word," he tells her.

"Maybe something urgent came up?" Brandi says without conviction.

"I always give her a ride home," he says. "She knows it ain't safe out there in the dark. Especially with..." Ray leaves the rest unsaid. *Shauna never came home.* Momma squeezes his shoulder.

Ray turns and rushes to his bicycle.

"Ray, wait."

He's already pushing away, calling over his shoulder. "I got to find her, momma. At least check and make sure she's home safe."

"Be careful," he hears her yell at his back, and lifts an arm in acknowledgement.

Ray dumps his bike by the side of Kim's house, and strides toward the door. The porch light is on, and he can hear the television inside. He stops and has second thoughts. If Kim is in her room. He might not need to alarm her mother.

He sneaks around the house to her bedroom window and is relieved to see a light within. Then Ray does something he never would have contemplated just a month or so earlier. Seeing the window ajar and wind billowing through the soft curtains, Ray grabs purchase on the sill and lifts himself into Kim's room in one steady movement. He knows there is nothing on the other side to hinder his entrance.

He lands on the floor with a dull thud. Kim sits scrunched on her single bed, back against the wall. She looks at him in shock.

"Ray… you shouldn't be here."

Ray dusts himself off and tries to move toward her, but she raises a hand to ward him off and shrinks further back.

"Well, what did you expect me to do, Kim, when you just disappeared like that. I was worried about you."

Kim chews her bottom lip and looks away.

"Kim? What's wrong?"

She swallows and finally meets his gaze.

"When I came out of the bathroom at your house, your pa was waiting there. He asked me to help him get some stuff out of the cool room. I went in and he pointed to a box of ice cream. He was behind me…"

Ray felt his whole-body tense.

"When I turned around, he had his thing out, and he was playing with it."

"My god…"

"He looked at me and he said, *You see this girl. This is what you gonna be gettin' soon.* I managed to get past him and he just laughed at me."

"Kim I… don't know what to say. He's such an asshole."

"I didn't know what to do, so I just ran, all the way back here." Kim hugged her arms into her torso, shivering.

"I won't let him come between us."

She shook her head sadly. "I think it would be better if we didn't see each other. I'm sorry, Ray, I just can't."

"No, don't say that."

"Just go please, Ray."

Ray stands clenching his fists by his side, shaking his head.

"Ray, please go." He sees tears welling in her eyes and wants so desperately to hold her. He wants the floor to open up and swallow him. Wants to punch a hole in the wall. Most of all he wants to run to her and pull her into his arms, tell her he will make it right again.

Ray does none of these things. Kim starts to cry. He starts to cry, then he turns and climbs back out of her window.

His anger mounts as he pedals furiously in the direction of home, tears and snot running down his face in the cold night air. By the time he throws his bike into the weed strewn yard, Ray is ready to explode.

He slams the door open. His parents are in the sitting room. Pa is just cracking the lid on a beer when Ray screams and jumps him.

"What the f…?"

Ray intersperses the haymakers he is throwing with shouted accusations and foul language. By the time his tone grows hysterical, Jerry has shrugged him off and knocked him flying. Now Momma is screaming.

Jerry pounces on Ray and starts dragging him along the floor. Brandi leaps on his back and claws at his eyes. "Get offa him, you son-of-a-bitch!"

The three of them crash through the fly screen door and across the porch onto the lawn. Jerry grabs his wife by the hair and swings her around, throws her into the porch railing. This further enrages Ray. He throws himself at his pa again, but by the time he has punched himself out, to no advantage, he realizes he is outmatched. Jerry picks him up and forces him onto his hands and knees, tearing off his plaid shirt with a pop of buttons. Ray hears the unmistakable sound of Pa pulling his big buckled belt out of his pants.

"This is gonna hurt you more than it does me, boy."

The last thing Ray hears before suffering the beating and curling into a fetal ball is his mother sobbing. He cries and dozes there until he feels Buddy licking his face. He hugs the dog to his chest as he weeps bitter tears.

Ray swallows down his misery, but what hurts even more than the beating is that despite missing a week of school until the bruising is mostly gone, Kim doesn't even ask him where he's been. She keeps her distance from him.

Pa stops him one morning as he pushes his bike through the gate in the direction of school. The bus is no longer an option now that Kim is giving him the cold shoulder.

"I see you moping about over that girl, Ray. Lemme give you some advice."

Embarrassed, humiliated, Ray tries to pull away, but Pa keeps a firm grip on the rim of the bike.

"Son, she ain't the only girl in the world. I know it might feel that way right now, but trust me, when you git older, you'll find that one woman just ain't enough."

"What about Momma?" Ray yanks the bike out of his father's grasp.

"In a manner of speaking…"

"Who's Billy Kane, Pa?"

"Whut?"

Ray pauses, weighing up the next words. "Who's the dead guy I heard you talking to and what are you seeking penance for?"

Ray sees his pa's face change. He starts to run, dragging the bike along and mounting it.

"You little …"

He hits the pedals with fury and shoots off down the road. He hears the old man yelling.

"I'll see you later, boy!"

Ray senses something amiss the minute he gets home that afternoon. His mother meets him at the gate. Her eyes red raw. Ray tenses up immediately.

"What is it, Momma? What's wrong?"

He rounds the corner of the back yard to see his father standing in the middle of the patchy lawn. Then he sees the small still figure lying at the old man's feet.

Ray drops the bike and screams.

"NOOO! Buddy!"

He runs at his pa and pummels his chest, but Jerry grabs his arms and holds him at bay.

"What did you do to him, you bastard?!"

"Easy boy! I didn't do nuthin'. Damn fool dog got hit by a car is all. Nuthin' we can do."

Jerry lets him go and Ray sinks to his knees. He picks up Buddy's still form and cradles the dog in his arms. Jerry backs away as Ray starts sobbing.

"I'm sorry, boy."

Ray spits words over his shoulder. "Oh, I bet you are." He hugs the dog, feels its neck roll uselessly on its shoulders. His pa's words cut deep into his soul.

"Man up now. Go bury your dog out in the woods, but don't go in too deep, boy. Ya hear?"

Ray hears his father's footsteps retreat. He lays Buddy down gently and curls his body around the dog, and whispers in his ear. "You're my best friend, Buddy, always. You're my one true friend."

Not long before sundown, Ray takes a shovel and carries Buddy down through the back yard into the woods.

He finds a nice spot, a shady tree lined glade where he and Buddy often used to play. He lays his little companion down on the ground and begins to dig. Bitter tears fall from his cheeks and his mind rages.

There was no car!

As he pauses for breath, Ray feels a gentle hand on his shoulder, and a gruff voice whispers in his ear.

"That's a damn shame, son. Man's best friend in the world."

Ray spins around and falls back on his ass when he sees nobody there.

"Easy, boy."

"Who said that?" Ray looks around desperately, wielding the shovel like a weapon.

"You can't see me, kid. But my name is Billy Kane."

Ray lowers the shovel and looks at Buddy's glazed eye. "I'm losing my mind now. I'm losing everything."

"Hush now, boy." The barely audible voice comes again. Unlike his pa's voice, it has a gentleness to it. "Your pa is a bad man. I know. I served with him. I tried to help him, but some folks just can't be helped."

Calmer now. Ray sits back and listens. "Pa came back different from that war."

"The war just made him worse, but your pa was always bad."

Ray feels the soft touch on his shoulder again.

"Just bury your little buddy there."

Ray does just that. After it is done, he stands and whispers a quiet prayer.

"You still there… Billy?" Ray sniffs and wipes his nose on his sleeve.

"I need you to walk a little deeper into these woods."

Ray looks at the thick, overgrown trees beyond the small opening. "Pa told me never to go out there."

"There's something you need to see."

Wiping his tears away, Ray pushes his way further into the thickening trees.

After several minutes of slogging and dry branches catching on his shirt, the voice comes again. "That's far enough. Look down."

Ray looks down around his feet. At first, he sees nothing, and then a hint of color catches his eye in the undergrowth. He reaches down and extracts the object, holds it up for closer inspection. A woman's shoe, not the type of footwear you would wear on a hike into the woods.

Ray runs his hands over the shoe. "I don't understand."

"Take it home with you. Don't show it to anyone yet. Hide it somewhere good."

The sense of being with an unseen companion vanishes. As he walks home Ray wonders if he has inherited some sick mental illness from his pa.

By the time he reaches the house, Ray puts the strange encounter, if that's what it was, down to emotional distress. Still, he feels a strange sensation, like something coursing through his veins, giving him strength. He feels a change coming on and not just a physical one.

He mostly stays in his room, maintaining a distance and an uneasy truce with his father. One evening, venturing out to where the old man sits watching the glowing TV screen in the sitting room, he sees a news item about the missing girls from surrounding counties. Pa shifts in his chair, sucks on a beer and growls.

"They ain't never gonna find them bitches. They gone."

Understanding dawns on Ray. Lying in bed that night, he slips into a fitful sleep, until a faint voice wakes him.

"Get up, Ray. We got work to do."

Ray sits up. His eyes adjusting to the half-light reveal nothing.

"Billy?"

"Yep."

Ray shuffles over to the window. He rubs sleep from his eyes and looks down over the yard.

"How do I get down there? I can't risk sneaking downstairs. Pa sometimes sleeps in his chair in the sitting room."

"The window."

"But it's so far down."

"Just do it."

Ray pries the window open and tentatively climbs over the jam. He balances on the precipice. To his left sits a mass of dark vine attached to a trellis running all the way down the side of the house. He reaches out and tests if it will take his weight. He looks down and swallows. Billy's voice whispers in his head.

"You got this, son.."

Once his feet hit the dirt below, Ray follows the instructions he hears, grabbing a shovel, and the old man's war knife, a Ka-Bar, sticking it in his backpack with a couple of other items from the shed.

He makes his way to a shallow clearing a little in the woods, near where he found the shoe. Seeing a stand of cane, Ray knows he needs to cut a half dozen shafts. He knows he needs to sharpen the shafts. "Are we making a trap?" he asks wordlessly.

"Just dig."

Hours later, Ray sits atop the wide hole his labors have created in the earth. The bottom of the pit is lined with the sharpened bamboo stakes, then leafy branches sprinkled with dead leaves camouflage the pit. He wipes dirt and sweat from his brow and rubs at a blister forming on his grubby palm. "Am I done?"

"Yep."

"So… Billy… are you a ghost?"

There is a pause, so long that Ray thinks Kane has gone.

"I'm whatever you choose to call me, Ray."

His mind racing, Ray probes deeper.

"How did you die? Why does Pa talk to you?"

"Who says I'm dead? You know we gotta stop him. Don't you, Ray?"

"Shit! Yeah, I guess we do."

"You. You do."

Ray hears his folks arguing in their room. He sits on his bed, listening intently to the exchange of their harsh words, half-hoping to hear the calming voice of Billy in his ear. It never comes. Was it ever really there? Crazy! Ray slams an impotent fist into his pillow.

Then, setting his jaw, Ray retrieves the item hidden in a box at the back of his dresser. He strides toward his parents' bedroom and shoves the door open. Momma breaks off from an accusation about where Pa has been spending his evenings. They both turn to look at Ray and the object in his hands. His father speaks first.

"Goddammit boy! What do you want?"

"You should answer Momma. What do you get up to on them long nights outta the house, pa?" Ray holds the woman's shoe out before him and twirls it around in his hands.

Pa's face goes dark, his eyes narrow. "Where the Hell did you get that?"

"I found it out deep in the woods. Now what else do you suppose might be out there?"

His father's eyes widen. With what? Fear? He recognizes the item and Ray's implication.

Momma, oblivious but hackles raised, begins yelling anew.

"What the hell is he talking about, Jerry? Whose damn shoe is that?"

Jerry lurches toward Ray.

"Damn you boy. I told you to keep out of them woods. Gimme that!"

Ray turns sharply and runs.

Momma pulls at her husband's sleeve, giving Ray the chance to get out the back door.

"Get off me, woman!"

Ray hears a crash of furniture and his mother's scream. Then he's across the yard and into the lip of the woods.

"You get back here, boy!"

Ray runs into the setting sun, the sound of frogs accompanying the pounding of his feet through brush and grass. The only other sound is the breathless rasp of his pa's voice, hot in pursuit but not gaining. Twenty years age difference gives Ray the advantage. Maybe Ray was foolish to fear him for so long.

Ray's feet hammer in league with his heartbeat as he nears the spot where he dug the trap before. His head begins to fill with self-doubt, he remembers pa from his infancy, boosting him up on his knee and telling him stories, before that damn war took him away, and spewed him back out as what he now is. Sick? Killer? Psycho? What the hell is his pa? He remembers his momma, beaten down, and Shauna, and what could have happened to Kim, and worst of all, Buddy, lying in the yard with his neck broke.

That steadies him, though he wishes he could hear Billy's voice. *Where the hell is he? Did he imagine the whole thing?* Ray almost forgets himself and manages to stop a second before he blunders into the pit. Jerry, following rapidly and blinded by rage, fails to register the movements of his son as the boy heads closer and closer to the point where he had found that damn shoe.

A loud crack silences the croaking of the frogs, followed immediately by an ear-piercing scream.

Ray sees Pa stagger with his leg caught in a rabbit trap. He gasps as he realizes, he must have run straight over it by a stroke of luck. Good luck for Ray. Bad luck for Pa. Pa falls on his backside and raises his right leg off the ground. The jaws of the trap are firmly locked around his ankle.

Jerry fixes Ray with a look of fury. He grits his teeth and spits words through the pain.

"You little motherfucker! Look what you did to your own pa."

Ray stands chest heaving. "It's your own trap, I didn't set it. You were gonna hurt me Pa. Like you hurt Buddy… like you hurt all them girls."

His father's face changes, his dark eyes flash like burning embers. Ray finds him almost unrecognizable.

"Damn you to hell, boy!"

Jerry winces and grabs the jaws of the trap in both meaty fists. He sets his jaw and pulls the cruel steel mechanical mouth open.

Ray swallows and watches, transfixed, as his groaning pa extricates his wounded foot and tosses the trap aside.

"Ah !" Jerry slowly climbs upright and tests his weight on his damaged foot. He yells in pain as he takes a step, then fixes his eyes on Ray again.

"You better run, boy. I don't know what I'll do if I get my hands on you. For god's sake, run!"

Ray hesitates. He looks and sees the marker he had laid for the pit.

He takes a step back and his heart sinks. After all his efforts, he falters as he looks down at the camouflaged pit, and back at his father, who watches him quizzically.

"What's the matter boy, cat got your tongue?" Jerry begins to limp closer, dragging his wounded foot behind him. He stops a few paces in front of Ray, both breathe heavily.

"I didn't mean it to come to this, Ray. Really, I didn't." Jerry shakes his head slowly. "But them girls. You know they got what they deserved. Prettying themselves up like that. Acting like whores. You don't understand what they do to a man, son. But one day you will."

Ray shakes his head, tears forming in the corners of his eyes. "You're evil, Pa."

"I know, boy. But nobody needs to know. I'll change. We can put it behind us, you and me, and your momma. We can be together again, like it used to be."

Ray moans. "You can't blame the war for what you done, Pa. I know that now. You can't change, neither. What you did is in your nature. Billy Kane told me. Billy says the war didn't change you. It just made you worse."

Jerry emits a low cold guttural laugh.

"That right, boy? I suppose Billy showed you how to dig that pit just behind you there too."

Ray lets out his breath and holds his tongue.

"Yeah, I see it. You don't think I know how to camouflage a trap, son? I taught you everything you know. You don't need any damn ghost to show you."

"Pa…"

"I'm sorry it has to be this way, boy."

Jerry lets out a yelp of pain and runs toward Ray, who stands frozen to the spot.

"Pa… no!"

Jerry raises his arms, tears running down his face. He lets out a primal roar.

Behind him in the faltering light, Ray sees the air itself start to shimmer, and a shape start to take form. A half-formed blurred figure in military khakis.

Shocked and open mouthed, his survival instincts kick in. Ray hunches down low, seizing his pa by his muscular forearms, then dropping to the ground with a mighty tug, using his pa's own momentum against him. Jerry flies headlong. Pa's scream is cut short as he pitches into the mouth of the pit and is impaled on the pointed stakes below.

Ray sits on his backside, rocking back and forth, sobbing as he listens to his father's low agonized moans and wet sputtering breaths. The stars come out in full overhead. His pa's anguished sounds fade away and the frogs start up their chorus again. A gentle hand touches his shoulder, and a calm voice speaks inside his head.

"I killed him, Billy. I killed my pa."

"No, your pa died a long time ago."

"They'll blame me though. They'll put me in prison or whatever they do to kids who done wrong."

There is a pause before the voice speaks again. "Go comfort your momma. Tell her something bad happened. Then they'll see. The truth will all come out."

Huge sobs rack Ray's body. He sputters out his words. "I'm a killer, like my pa. I'm just like him."

"No, son. You're nothing like him."

He hears his mother's frightened voice in the distance, calling his name. She has never ventured out in the woods before. He stands and looks in the direction of her pathetic cries.

Steeling himself, Ray knows what needs to be done. He moves forward through the brush, to cut his mother off before she gets near enough to see.

Ray sits in the front row of the tiny chapel, averting his eyes from the coffin, or at least trying to. Every time he lifts his gaze, a wave of nausea threatens. He tunes out the minister's drone. He feels uncomfortable with his teenage frame squeezed into the suit borrowed off a younger cousin, absent-mindedly drumming his fingers on his knee, until Momma stops him, gripping his fingers in her manicured hand.

"Quit it!" she hisses, dabbing at her eyes with a lace kerchief.

Ray hesitates when she pulls him to his feet and drags him toward the open coffin. Aunt Belle is with them. He is handed a rose and told to lay it on his pa's chest. Ray tries to avert his gaze but cannot avoid his dead father's face. He winces, seeing how well the parlor stitched Pa up, covering his puncture wounds, covering most of him in his old army uniform.

Momma squeezes his hand a little too hard and whispers, "Say a few words to your pa," and for one awful moment Ray feels like he's going to throw up into the casket. When he turns to toward his pew, he catches a glimpse of Kim sitting alone in the back row. She lifts her hand and gives him a quick wave.

Back home at the wake, Aunt Belle corners Ray and, mistaking his somber mood for grief, tries to offer words of comfort. "Your daddy meant well, Ray. He tried." The words sound hollow, and Belle's face belies her own discomfort at trying to pass off her lies as truth. Ray remembers his father pulling Belle forcibly onto his lap in front of the fire last Christmas. Wrapping his arms tight around her waist so she couldn't wriggle free.

He is glad when the wake is over and the last drunk relative has stumbled off into the night. Aunt Belle pulls his momma close for one last sisterly hug. "If you need anything, Brandi, just call."

Ray helps momma clean up. The house and store are all packed up ready for them to leave, fleeing the county on account of what Pa did. When he sees her shoulders sag and heave, he wraps his arms around her. She leads him into her room, and he lays with her on top of the bedspread for a while, her head on his shoulder.

"I know it ain't been easy these past few months," she forces the words out. "Your pa weren't the same after he came back from that godawful war. God knows what they did to his mind out there."

Ray bites his tongue, murmurs something unintelligible deep in his throat. His mind stuck on something he overheard at the wake earlier. A veiled conversation in a corner of the room.

"I knew it would end like this. Such a terrible thing. I warned Jerry to stay out of them woods."

The autumn wind whips through the curtains in Momma's upper story window, bringing the first hint of rain, and Ray stares out over her yellow-blonde head into the dark starless night. He can smell the woods from here.

Cherry Boy
Che Trujillo

Jaime woke to the sound of his phone vibrating on the top of his nightstand. He was dreaming of making pancakes and the sound of the mixer in his dream was the buzz of his phone vibrating around the cluttered top of the nightstand. The phone pushed slowly, like an ice bound ship, through a loose pile of coins and set them tinkling against an empty beer bottle under the lamp. His eyes opened and took in the window where an evening breeze was stirring the dirty blue curtains. There were traffic noises from the street below. Somewhere a man shouted, "Move it!" A car honked its horn and tires squealed on pavement.

The phone kept buzzing.

Jaime was disappointed to find that he was not actually about to eat pancakes. He was ravenous. His stomach growled. His mouth was dry and he was hungover from the drinking in the wee hours of the morning. He grabbed the phone.

"Yeah?"

"You awake, chulo?" It was Jaime's blood brother, Nathan.

"I am now."

"Jaime, it's 6:30, man."

"I didn't get to bed until around four, pendejo. Why you waking me up?"

"It ain't 6:30 in the morning, fool. It's 6:30 at night. You done slept all day. We supposed to be at Raul's at 7:30."

"Oh, shit."

"Shit's right. Now who's the pendejo? I'll be at your house in five minutes."

"It's gonna take me longer than that. I gotta have a shower."

"Make it ten minutes. I'll be out front. After that I start honking."

"Don't be an ass."

"You want to explain why we're late? To Raul?"

"No."

"Then don't make us late."

Nathan ended the call.

Jaime swung his legs off the bed and groaned. His head hurt.

In the bathroom, he took aspirin from the medicine cabinet and chewed four of them, wincing as they hit his stomach. His reflection was not a pleasing sight. Jaime's eyes were red and there were bags under his eyes. His hair looked like a tossed salad made of licorice. He squirted Visine in each eye and rolled the orbs around in the moist broth under his eyelids. It burned. For a moment. Then it felt better.

He climbed into the shower. The hot water worked wonders. By the time he finished, Jaime felt almost human.

Why did he drink so much last night? He knew today was a big day. The first day of the rest of his life. The day he was to lose his cherry and become a full member of Los Gatos Negros. Jaime had thought ahead a couple days before, making sure he had clean clothes for the occasion. Now, he slipped them off the hanger from his closet, dressed and checked himself in the mirror. Not bad. He went downstairs.

Mama was cooking dinner. Her hair wilted around her face as she divided her attention between a collection of pots on the stove top.

"So, his royal highness decides to join the world of the living?" she says.

"Please, Mama, don't start?"

"You off today? Don't you normally start at four?"

Jaime worked in the kitchen at La Playa Azul.

"I'm off."

"What's the special occasion?"

"I traded hours with Manuel. He wants this Saturday off."

"You gave up your Saturday off? That doesn't sound right." Mama turned and faced his, her expression interrogative, her arms folded in front of her and the ladle in her hand a little like a judge's gavel ready to whack and pronounce sentence.

"He asked, so I said yeah. No big thing. Mama, I am so hungry."

"It'll be ready soon."

"Can I just grab a couple of those tortillas? I gotta rush."

"Rush where? You're off."

"I told Nathan I'd hang with him."

"I don't like the way Nathan's turning out, Jaime. I know you boys have been friends forever…"

"Best friends."

"Right. But I think he's heading for prison. You want to hang with your bestie in prison? Is that the plan?"

"Mama! You're too serious."

Jaime moved toward his mother, leaned in and kissed her cheek.

The unmistakable sound of Nathan's horn blared in through the open window above the sink.

"That'll be Nathan. I gotta go."

"So he can't even knock on the door anymore like a normal person?"

"I don't know, Mama. Maybe he's in a hurry. I'll tell him to come in next time."

"Do that."

Jaime grabbed two corn tortillas, kissed his mother a second time and headed for the door. His two younger brothers, Ricardo and Frankie, were watching TV in the front room. Stranger Things. His brothers liked those nerdy kids and the monster from another reality. Kid stuff.

"Hey, Jaime! Where you going?" Frankie asked.

"Out with Nathan."

"Man you slept all day long!" Ricardo cried, his words half chastisement, half admiration.

"Yeah. Once you start working, you'll understand."

"You don't ever watch TV with us anymore," Frankie whined. It was a fake whine intended to make his older brother feel guilty.

"I can't handle it," Jaime said, grinning. "That monster from the underworld gives me nightmares."

There was another solid, prolonged blast from Nathan's horn.

"Tell that idiot to stop blasting his horn!" Mama shouted from the kitchen. "That's noise pollution! We already got plenty of that!"

"I'll tell him."

Then Jaime was out of the house into the breezy spring evening. The sun was low and the shadows were long. Smells of cooking emanated from all the houses. Mr. Carrillo was grilling chicken on his front porch on a cheap little charcoal grill from the dollar store.

"Smells good, Mr. C!"

"It is good!" Mr. Carrillo grinned and waved with his spatula. "If you're good, maybe I'll give you a wing, eh?"

"No thanks. I gotta dash. Next time."

The grin faded from Mr. Carrillo's face. His eyes went to the shiny blue 1972 Impala rumbling at the curb. Carrillo shook his head, returning his gaze to the sizzling, smoking grill.

As Jaime got into Nathan's car he saw his mother's face in the kitchen window. The blue curtains fluttered around her like a pair of angel wings. Her mouth was moving. A prayer, no doubt. She crossed herself. Jaime knew she was afraid. She had good reason to be. Jaime himself was scared shitless. He crammed one of the tortillas into his mouth, quickly chewed and swallowed, hoping that food in his stomach would ease the acid burn he had been experiencing all week.

Nathan's car pulled away from the house and eased into the stream of traffic on Magnolia Street.

Jaime stared straight ahead seeing nothing. He stuffed the second tortilla into his mouth.

"Whoa, bro, you look like a chipmunk stuffing its pouches." Nathan grinned.

"I'm really hungry. I drank too much last night and I haven't eaten anything since lunch yesterday."

"Let's go to the drive-thru. What you want? Burger or tacos?"

"Cheeseburger."

"You got it."

After the burger, fries and a soda, Jaime was beginning to feel something like normal. He was still chewing the last bite of the burger when Nathan's Impala came to an easy stop in front of a prefab building with a large bay door.

"What's this?"

"Headquarters. Raul's waiting for us inside."

"I thought his place on Vine Street was the headquarters."

"Naw, that's his house, man. That's the front for nonmembers. This is the real deal."

Jaime had thought of himself as an insider. He hadn't earned his tattoo yet, but he had been hanging with Los Gatos Negros for the netter part of a year. He must have had a concerned expression on his face because Nathan punched him in the shoulder and grinned.

"Take it easy, Jaime. Tonight we bust your cherry. After that you're a full member. Come on."

Nathan climbed out of the car and Jaime followed his example.

Above the big bay door there was a faded sign that read Gutierrez Auto Body. The sign was so weathered the letters were barely visible and partially obscured by rust. To the left of the bay door was a regular door with a small glass window. Nathan rapped on the door. A dirty towel had been hung over the window in the door blocking the view into the building. A minute passed and as hand shifted the towel out of the way. Half a face appeared in the window. It was not a friendly face. There was a deep scar under the one visible eye. The face retreated and Jaime heard the sound of the door as it was unlocked. Three separate locks.

The door swung open and Nathan and Jaime stepped inside. They found themselves in a small office. Random furniture was strewn about. Everything was covered in dust and the place looked like it had been vacant for years. The scarred face they had seen in the window belonged to an enormous guy that looked to weigh upwards of three hundred pounds. The big guy reset the three locks on the front door.

"Julio, this is Jaime," Nathan said, exchanging a knuckle bump with the big man.

Julio stared at Jaime for a long time. No expression, just hard assessment. Finally, he nodded and gestured with a head movement toward a second door. Nathan gave Jaime a reassuring slap on the shoulder and stepped through the door. Jaime followed. Julio went in after them. Jaime could not help but notice that Julio locked the second door as well. No quick exits or entries from this place.

In stark contrast to the outer office, this inner area was at least 1200 square feet in size. It was well lit and looked like what Jaime imagined a gang's clubhouse should look like. There were sofas and chairs strewn about. There was a makeshift bar made from 55-gallon drums and 2 x 12 planks. Next to the bar was a big screen TV. Behind the bar were shelves stocked with every kind of booze. Parked near the big bay door was a black SUV. It looked to be a ten year old Chevy Equinox.

At the back of the large space there were a couple of offices with glass windows. Jaime could see into one of the offices but the other had curtains in the window.

"Where's Raul?" Nathan asked.

Julio said nothing but gestured with his chin toward the office with the curtains. The big man turned and went to a pinball machine to the left of the bar, On the machine was a can of beer and an ashtray with a smoking cigarette in it. Julio stuck the cig in his mouth and shot a ball into the machine. Bells rang and lights flashed.

Jaime looked at Nathan.

"Relax," Nathan said. "Have a seat." He gestured toward one of the sofas, a black vinyl thing with a few holes in the upholstery. "Want a beer?"

"No, man. The way I feel right now I don't want to ever drink again."

"This too shall pass."

As Jaime sat on the sofa, Nathan went behind the bar and grabbed two cans of beer from a cooler. He popped the top on both cans and took them to the sofa. In front of the black sofa was a battered coffee table covered with girly magazines and empty cans and bottles. Nathan sat down and placed one of the beers in front of Jaime.

"I said I didn't…"

Nathan whispered, "It looks better this way. You don't have to drink it but we don't want Raul thinking you're nervous. Understand?"

Jaime nodded. He looked over his shoulder at the giant playing the pinball machine.

"Relax, bro. After tonight you're one of us."

Again Jaime nodded. He picked up the can in front of him and wet his lips with the beer.

Nathan offered an approving nod.

The first words out of Julio's mouth were, "Aw, fuck!" when the pinball game didn't go exactly to his liking. The loud exclamation gave Jaime a start. Nathan said nothing but touched his shoulder.

Then the door to the office with the curtains opened and a skinny woman covered with tatts came out laughing, She noticed Nathan and Jaime but said nothing. She went to a small glass table and quickly did a small line of coke. A moment later, Raul came out of the office, tucking his shirt into his pants. His eyes fell on Nathan and Jaime. The look of greeting came to his face but it was slow in arriving.

Nathan stood and Jaime followed suit.

Raul took Nathan's hand. As he shook it his eyes were on Jaime.

"Ready for this?"

Jaime nodded self-consciously.

"Hell yeah he's ready," Nathan said loudly.

"What are you? His mama? I was talking to Jaime. What about it, Jaimito? Ready to lose your cherry? Ready to join Los Gatos Negros?"

"Yes, Raul." Jaime was tired of all this talk of losing his cherry. It was starting to get under his skin. He held eye contact with Raul. It wasn't an easy thing to do. There was a tangible darkness emanating from the man. Raul was a good ten years older than any of the other gang members. He had done time at San Quentin. The man had been through the shit and he was hard as a granite gravestone.

A big grin burst onto Raul's face. "I believe you!" He placed a hand on each of Jaime's shoulders and gave him a little shake like an uncle might do to a favorite nephew.

The skinny woman was unpacking a bag and placing the contents on a table next to an old barber chair. Jaime saw that the gear from the bag was hoses and needles and everything else a tattoo artist might use.

"Lucinda, say hello to our latest candidate. His name is Jaime."

Lucinda glanced up from her instruments and gave Jaime a brief and sardonic smile. "Greetings Jaimito."

Jaime nodded. He didn't like this scrawny woman calling him Jaimito. He had to put up with it from Raul but after tonight he would set Lucinda straight if she ever called him that again.

"I see you have cerveza," Raul said. "Want anything else? A little bump?" Raul brought his thumb up to his nostril.

"No, thanks. I want to be clear-headed," Jaime said.

"Good. Real courage is the best kind, better than the courage you snort up your nose."

Nathan grinned and nodded.

All of them looked toward the front door when they heard the sound of a key in the lock. Two men came in. They were both dressed in black. Unlike Julio these men weighed somewhere around 180 pounds. Both looked hard as a rock. They approached Raul, Nathan and Jaime.

"Dos hermanos," Raul said. One of the men nodded at Raul. Both of them eyed Nathan and Jaime with expressions betraying no hint of emotion.

"Hey, I'm Jaime." Jaime offered his hand to one of the men but the stranger did not take it.

"We save the introductions for later, Jaimito," Raul said. "After you do your thing, then we give these two names. Understand?"

"Yeah. Sure."

Raul reached into his pocket and took out keys. He offered the keys to Nathan. "Nathan, you drive. Jaime you ride shotgun. Your tios will ride in the back. Time to go. When you get back you get your colors Jaime and we all party."

Nathan took the keys and headed toward the Chevy SUV. Jaime followed.

Julio raised the bay door. As Nathan backed the stolen SUV out of the building Jaime saw Raul and Lucinda exchanging words and laughing. They were looking at him. Were they laughing at Jaime? Or was he just being paranoid?

The SUV paused in the parking lot next to Nathan's Impala.

"Choose your turf, Jaime," said one of the unnamed passengers in the back seat.

"Hmmm?" Jaime turned to look at the man.

"Pick a destination. What part of town you want to do you first kill in?"

Jaime drew a deep breath. He looked at Nathan. His friend shrugged.

"It's up to you, bro. Just pick one."

"Okay." Jaime thought for a moment. "Ridgewood."

Both of the passengers in the back seat laughed. Nathan smiled.

"Something funny?" Jaime asked.

"It's all good." One of the passengers patted his shoulder. "We all want to kill some white motherfucker, don't we?"

Nathan drove the SUV out of the parking lot and through the surrounding neighborhood to the Hammond Street on-ramp heading west on the freeway.

Jaime had always imagined that if he ever had to kill someone it would be personal. He would kill someone he knew, someone he believed deserved it. Now he was on a journey to locate a perfect stranger and extinguish that stranger's life. Jaime's stomach tightened. Every muscle in his body seemed to tense. His mind raced in a way it never had before. Connections between all the events of his life rose in his consciousness and presented themselves for evaluation. Everything he had ever done, everything that had ever happened to him seemed to have irrevocably led to this moment.

Why had he picked Ridgewood? The only connection he had with that part of town was one of his aunts lived there with her white husband. Together they ran a dry-cleaning company. One summer when Jaime was nine, he and his mother had lived with Tia Rebecca and Tio Larry. That was right after his father had been sent to prison for armed robbery. Jaime and his mother had no place else to go. Rebecca and Larry had been good to him, hadn't they? Yes, as far as he recalled they had. They fed him well, let him eat lots of ice cream and watch all the TV he wanted. They had paid for him to attend the local YMCA day camp. So why had Jaime picked Ridgewood? He had no reason to kill anyone in that suburban neighborhood. Did he?

"Here you go, homes," said one of the tios in the back seat. He pushed a red bandana forward against Jaime's shoulder.

The bandana was hard, filled with a rigid hunk of metal. Jaime took it and unfolded the bandana on his lap. It was an automatic pistol. Maybe a nine-millimeter.

"It's loaded. Nine in the clip. Nothing in the chamber til you put it there," said the man in the backseat.

"Is it clean?" Jaime asked. He wanted to know if this gun had ever been used in a crime that could possibly be linked to him at a later date.

"Clean as it gets," the other guy in the back said. "I got it from a friend in Philadelphia. He buys the parts and assembles the guns himself. No serial numbers. Nothing to trace. After you use it tonight we'll put it somewhere nobody will ever find it."

"Right," said Jaime.

"Pretty slick, eh, bro?" Nathan said beaming. "These Hermanos know their shit."

All sorts of possibilities raced through Jaime's mind. What if he killed everyone in the car and just drove off into the unknown? Where would he go? He had no money. The car was stolen. It was only a matter of time before the cops and Los Gatos would be tracking him down. Besides he couldn't kill Nathan. Nathan was his best friend. So why had he even had the thought? No time to answer that question because his mind was already racing on to other thoughts, other fantasies, other anxiety-ridden possibilities.

Soon, too soon, the SUV was easing off the freeway onto the Gaston Street exit. Gaston formed the north boundary of the Ridgewood area. Gaston led to Fitzhugh where there were a lot of businesses. Nathan automatically wheeled the car in that direction.

Jaime remembered that summer when he had stayed with Rebecca and Larry. It was all good memories. Or was it? Something was digging its way out of the shallow grave where it had been buried in his unconscious mind.

Jimmy. He remembered Jimmy. They had become friends at the YMCA day camp. Jaime had slept over at Jimmy's house. Jimmy's family attended the Assembly of God Church on Belton Avenue. They had invited Jaime to go on a camping retreat at the State Park Labor Day weekend. A guy named Chandler Trent was the youth minister. Jaime saw the man's toothy grin rising up out of the murky past. He could smell the man's heavy cologne. He remembered seeing Chandler whip some of the boys with a belt for minor infractions during the retreat. He had invited Jaime to sleep in his tent. Chandler had called him Cherry Boy.

This was beyond strange. Jaime had buried these memories for years. Had he even thought about what happened any time after the fact? Now, in a split second, everything about that sordid retreat had burst open like a sunbaked bag of meat scraps and the stinking details were laid out in full view of his mind's eye. He wondered why he had buried that shit so deeply, so completely. Why he had felt the burden of guilt when he had done nothing wrong. Why had he never told his mother or his aunt and uncle?

This explosion of memory had taken less than ten seconds to unfold.

"Put on in the chamber," said a voice from the back seat.

The other voice said, "There's a supermarket up ahead. Want to swing through the parking lot and just pick someone?"

"No," said Jaime. "Go to Belton Avenue."

"He says go to Belton. You ain't planning something personal are you, Jaimito?"

"Killing somebody you know is a good way to get caught."

"No it's not that," Jaime heard himself saying. "I remember a church over there."

"Oooh a church!" One of the guy's in the back seat laughed.

"Good place to surprise someone, Jaimito. I like the way you think."

Nathan turned off of Fitzhugh onto Belton. The church was four blocks ahead on the right. The street was pretty much empty. Jaime could see a van driving away about six blocks ahead.

When they arrived at the church, Jaime said, "This is the place."

"I don't see nobody, homes," said one of the guys in back.

"You ain't gonna walk up inside that bitch and start shooting, are you?" The tios laughed.

"Go around the block," Jaime said.

As the SUV turned right, just before his view of the parking lot was obscured by the yellow brick church building, Jaime saw a man sitting in a white Escalade talking on his cell phone. He was older. His hair was gray but it was still combed in that retro looking swept back style that TV preachers always favored. That was Chandler Trent.

Jaime's heart felt like it was about to explode as the SUV circled the block. He had not even thought of this man for years. Now he needed to kill a man and he had remembered somebody who deserved killing. How had this happened? Had God helped him? No, God doesn't assist with murders. Or does he? Jaime's chest was tight. He was having trouble breathing.

"So what you gonna do, killer?"

"Want us to pull up in the parking lot?"

"No. I saw a guy sitting in his car. Just pull up to the curb."

"Where at the curb?" Nathan looked confused. This wasn't the way things usually went down in Los Gatos initiations. Usually the car remained in motion and passed within ten feet of the target. Usually the crew disappeared down the road before the body hit the ground.

"Just drive, Nathan." Jaime chambered a bullet. "Come on!"

They circled the block and came back to the parking lot.

"Where's the guy?" Nathan sounded anxious.

"There. In the Escalade. Just pull up to the curb and stop."

From the backseat, a tio said, "He's too far away."

The Escalade was parked in a space a good fifty feet away from the curb.

"Just pull over!"

"I'm saying you can't hit him from…"

But Jaime opened his door and walked quickly toward the man in the parking lot.

"Motherfucker!" one of the tios exclaimed.

"Get ready to split," the other one said quietly to Nathan.

Nathan felt sweat oozing out of his palms onto the steering wheel.

The man was speaking quickly into his phone and did not notice Jaime until he was three steps away. He looked up, grinned, and began lowering his window.

Jaime raised the gun and fired three quick rounds into the man's face. One hit the left eye, one struck the forehead and the third entered the man's mouth, cutting a path through those big white teeth. Almost instantly, Jaime was turning back toward the SUV but not before noting that in a strange way, Chandler Trent still seemed to be grinning. He walked briskly back to his crew, forcing himself not to run. He did not see Chandler's body fall over inside the car. But all three of his Los Gatos brothers saw it.

Jaime got in the car.

Nathan punched it and they were gone.

"Not to fast. Don't draw attention," a tio said.

"Motherfucker you have some cast iron balls on you!" A hand clapped Jaime on the shoulder. "You just walked right up and shot the motherfucker not once but three times!"

Nathan looked at Jaime with awe, maybe even fear.

Jaime fought the urge to vomit.

"Give me the piece." A hand slapped Jaime's shoulder. He wrapped the gun in the red bandana and passed it into the back seat.

"Los Gatos Negros just got themselves a natural born killer! We gonna celebrate tonight!"

Jaime breathed deeply pushing the nausea down with all his willpower. Flashes of his grandfather danced in his mind. He had died when Jaime was six. Jaime had few memories of the man but now his grizzled face loomed large in Jaime's internal vision. His grandfather was in a wheelchair, crippled by cops trying to end a fruit pickers protest in 1969. In his mind, Jaime heard his grandfather saying, "Justice doesn't wear a robe, you won't find justice in a courtroom. Son, if you ever need justice you will have to take it with your own hands."

Nathan drove carefully back to the warehouse.

Jaime withdrew into place deep within himself. What the hell was happening here? Why had he suddenly remembered all the dark details of his abuse at the hands of Chandler Trent? How did he know exactly how to get to the Assembly of God Church after all these years? And what were the odds that perv would be parked right out front where Jaime could fire three rounds into his face? And the memories of his grandfather, as if Abuelo was talking to him here and now, saying things Jaime didn't really remember. Shooting Trent had legitimized what would have otherwise been a dark and difficult task. This was like some brujo story where the spirits help the warrior, the kind of story his grandmother used to tell.

"… hear me? Jaime!"

Jaime popped back into the here and now, realizing Nathan had been talking to him. The tios were out of the car already. "Yeah!"

"Man are you alright?"

"Yeah. Just making peace with killing, Nathan."

Nathan's eyes communicated surprise. Jaime's words made perfect sense but they were calmer and more thoughtful than what he had expected to hear. "Yeah. I get it."

"Guess we better go inside."

"Right. Tonight's your night, bro. You're all the way in now. Lucinda's gonna give you your tatt and everybody's gonna party til they drop."

"Well, I guess we better get on with it then."

All eyes were on Jaime as he and Nathan entered the room. Music was playing, people were dancing and eating, drinking and snorting. The tios had already begun spreading the word about Jaime's pair of iron huevos. People smiled and nodded, they hoisted their drinks.

"Go on over to the chair," Nathan said, "I'll get you a cerveza."

Jaime nodded and went to the barber chair. Lucinda eyed him intently and stood as he approached. She took a small white towel and whipped it over one shoulder. "Let's put some ink on you, Jaimito," she said.

"Don't call me that," he said, seating himself in the chair.

"Ooh, touchy." Lucinda smirked.

Jaime took hold of her wrist. "Listen, bitch, I just killed a man. That's worthy of a little respect. Right?"

Lucinda's became nervous. "Right."

"Now, give me the fucking tattoo. And it better be perfect."

"I only do good work." Lucinda pulled her arm loose.

"Good. Me too."

Lucinda swabbed his shoulder with alcohol. "You're not a hemophiliac or anything are you? A free bleeder?"

"No."

"Okay. I just gotta ask."

Nathan approached and handed him a beer. Jaime took a sip. It tasted good.

"Man, you're already a hero in here. I mean everyone gets respect for doing the kill but our tios are telling it like you're the next John Dillinger."

"Who wants to be some old white gangster. Didn't he get shot down in an alley coming out of a movie?"

"Okay. Don't be touchy. Who should I have said?"

"Nobody. I don't want to be nobody but myself."

"I hear you."

Across the room Jaime saw the tios talking with Raul. Those two senior gang members had undergone a transformation. They each had a beer in their hands and they were no longer the somber men they had been at the beginning of the evening. They grinned and talked quickly using lots of gestures. One of them was clearly acting out Jaime's actions, showing the cool manner in which he had stepped up to the car and fired three rounds into the target's face. Raul nodded appreciatively and looked over at Jaime. They made eye contact. Raul nodded. He was impressed. But there was something else there. Raul was accustomed to being the big shot. It was clear to Jaime that the tios were laying it on too think. Raul would not warm to being eclipsed by a newbie.

Jaime would need to watch his step. He would be a good soldier and do as he was told. Then at some as yet unknown date in the future he would have to kill Raul. Jaime was certain that someday when his hate was full grown he would point his weapon at Raul's face and squeeze the trigger.

Crepuscular

Bret McCormick

I was in pretty bad shape when I came back to stay in Fort Worth at my Mom's house. My arm, the left one, was broken and I guess I looked a lot worse than I really was with all the bruises on my face. The family treated me the way you treat an elderly person with dementia, sort of overly conciliatory, never offering open opposition verbally about what I claimed had happened, but not really bothering to conceal the fact that they thought I'd gone round the bend. I could see it in their eyes and they'd be like super nice to me, as if they were really worried about my welfare. Like I might fall and break a hip or descend into a state of detachment. Hell, I can't blame them. How would I feel if I was in their shoes?

To make my Mom feel better I agreed to some counseling at a clinic that lets you pay on a sliding scale, based on how much you make. Since I'm not making anything right now, the price is damn cheap. Not free, but cheap enough. This doctor I've seen a few times, Joel Henshaw, suggested that I journal about it. I would've done that anyway. I like to write. That's probably part of the problem with my family.

I was always the *creative one*. The one who dreamed up fantastic stories. The stork dropped me in the wrong nest. If any of them ever had a creative impulse, maybe they'd be a bit closer to understanding. They're all good Christians and they believe all manner of mystical and miraculous stuff if it's in the Bible, but anything like that happens to a living person, especially someone they know, and every last one of them is a doubting Thomas.

Yeah, I see the anger in the words I'm writing. I suppose that's normal, too. Back to the point; this journal about my unbelievable experience is supposed to help me work through my feelings and come to grips with all of it. Maybe it's supposed to make me realize none of it ever happened. At least that's what my family's probably thinking. Who knows? Maybe someday I'll decide it's better to pretend it didn't happen. Maybe I'll pretend to snap out of it one morning and return to my senses. That'd make everyone a lot more comfortable with me. And I may do that.

But, I know what happened.

The town is called Fodice. It's located in the southern part of Houston County. Some of the locals say the name is a corruption of the phrase "four dice." Another version of the story says that most of the town's founding members were from a plantation in Fordyce, Arkansas and that they gave their new home in east Texas a name familiar to them. All agree that the town was a freed man community. In other words, it was comprised of former slaves who had left the site of their slavery in search of new opportunity and a new identity. I've lived in Texas most of my life. Even so, I'd never heard of Fodice until I was well into my forties.

I'd been leasing a great old three-story house that was built in 1889 on Galveston Island when Hurricane Ike came along and displaced me. My book business came to an end when forty thousand dollars' worth of uninsured inventory was destroyed in the flood. For a time, after that, I made a modest living selling used merchandise of every description at pseudo-garage sales. I call them that because I'd set up in various friends' driveways and sell all sorts of stuff I'd acquired at Salvation Army auctions and at other garage sales. There was a motel in South Houston owned by an Indian family and they'd let me hold a sale in their parking lot once a month in exchange for ten per cent of my gross sales. It wasn't a booming business, but it helped me keep my head above water while I searched for a better, more permanent solution to my financial situation. I rented a storage unit to house the merch and I slept in my minivan in the parking lot of whatever Wal-Mart was nearby. Sometimes I slept at the homes of friends when it didn't feel like I was imposing.

In March of 2009 I did a sale in my cousin Michael's driveway in the Houston neighborhood known as "the Heights." Mike's got a lot of friends in the arts community, painters and sculptors, and some of them came to my sale looking for junk they could turn into art. That's how I met Sean and Julie. Sean was a thirty-something, good-looking guy from a wealthy family who pretty much dabbled in whatever struck his fancy. His wife, Julie, was a knock-out from a middle-class family in Waco. They were both artists and had met while attending the University of Texas at Austin.

I talked with them the better part of an hour as they foraged through the glassware, framed art by amateurs (from the Salvation Army), toys and kitchen utensils. I learned that they'd recently purchased an abandoned school building in Fodice, Texas. They intended to turn it into an art studio and gallery of sorts as a weekend destination for curious Houstonians. Really tired of sleeping at Wal-Mart, I went out on a limb and mentioned that I had a lot of experience as a handyman and if they ever needed an on-site caretaker for the place, I'd sure be interested. I told them I'd done repairs for lots of folks over the years and could provide them with references. For the next couple of months, every time I ran into Sean and/or Julie, I'd bring it up. About the time I realized I was probably being a pain-in-the-ass and determined never to mention it again, they called and asked me when I could move in. Turns out someone had broken some windows and vandalized the place and they'd decided it might be good to have someone living there to keep an eye on the place.

I liquidated as much of my pseudo-garage sale merch as I could. What I couldn't sell I returned to the Salvation Army. It made me wonder how many times some of those things had been through that place. The second Saturday of May I moved into the empty school building. I replaced all the broken glass in the first few days I was there and began cleaning up the interior. There was a room with a sink and some counters and cabinets which I imagined had been the school's kitchen. I used this room as my bedroom because it was the easiest to put into a livable order, plus it kept my stuff concentrated in that area and out of the way as I worked on the larger rooms.

The first couple of nights I slept there I had dark dreams. Nothing real solid or linear, just dark shapes swimming through the atmosphere and me in a disembodied state, but feeling a bit like a small, wounded fish surrounded by sharks.

For the first couple of months I stayed busy cleaning, building shelves and a few partitions, patching old plumbing and landscaping the grounds. When I say landscaping what I really mean is mowing, eliminating unwanted trees and putting in a small vegetable garden. Sean and Julie had lots of ideas for improving the property and they had the money to pay for it. They set up a bank account for building supplies and such and gave me a debit card to use. In addition to money for materials, they gave me a modest stipend for food and other necessities. It was a win-win. They were getting the improvements they wanted at a bargain rate and my presence discouraged any further vandalism. I was glad to be out of the pseudo-garage sale business. I enjoyed working with my hands and I had plenty of time to work on my novel. Well into middle-age I was still fantasizing about earning my living as a writer. I felt a bit like Henry David Thoreau, sometimes going three or four days without speaking to another human. Does that sound funny? Human? Well, that's just the way I meant it. I did plenty of talking; to myself, the trees, the small animals, to my hammer when it hit my thumb. I just didn't talk to other people much.

There was a platform outside the back door to the place, just under the window over the sink in the kitchen where I was sleeping. It had been built of sturdy wood. The supports were mostly good, but I had to replace a lot of the decking. When I got it in reasonably good shape I bought a cheap charcoal grill and started cooking out there. The place had no A/C, not even electricity really, just what I got from the small generator Sean had supplied. Long-term plan was to install solar panels, but that was still a ways down the road. So, around sunset I'd sit out there and grill a piece of meat and listen to the crickets, cicadas and birds. It was pleasant after a strenuous day. I'd usually have a little cooler with some iced down bottles of water and beer.

I've often wondered if everything would have still happened if I hadn't decided to kill a couple of squirrels for dinner one night. There were plenty of squirrels around and I'd heard my grandfather talk about growing up eating mostly squirrel meat. I'd never tasted any and I just thought I'd try to grill a couple. I had a pellet rifle I'd been trying to sell at the pseudo-garage sales. When I saw the condition of the old place and the raccoon droppings everywhere, I'd decided to hang onto the gun to discourage small animals that might make it into my new home. Anyway, the pellet gun was perfect for hunting squirrels. I made a marinade out of oil and red wine and soaked the squirrel carcasses in there a while, then rolled them in a southwestern rub before throwing them on the grill. They smelled great.

While the squirrels were cooking I noticed the place got real quiet. No cicada or cricket noises. No birds. The sun was sinking low and I thought I saw people moving around the trees on the east property line, but there was nothing there. No people anyway. I remember musing for a while about cleaning the meat; removing the head and feet, gutting the torso, peeling the skin back. Most people would be put off by the task. In fact, I'm pretty sure most modern Americans would give up eating meat if they had to kill and butcher everything they ate. Or maybe they'd just eat a lot less of it. I was realizing that life and the way it is sustained is really not a very pretty state of affairs.

I dug a hole and deposited the cast off parts of the squirrel into it. I don't know why, but something made me decide to keep the tails. I tied a string to each one and hung them from the eaves of the roof above the kitchen window. If I'd hung them somewhere else or if I'd never killed those little animals, maybe things would've been different.

After I washed up, I sat on the platform in the growing darkness and drank beer. When the squirrel meat smelled done, I took it from the grill, let it cool a bit, then tasted it. I liked it. I didn't feel so bad about my poor granddaddy growing up with nothing to eat but squirrel. It tasted fine. Granddaddy probably never had it marinated and rubbed, but that wasn't my fault. Gradually, the natural sounds of the place returned and I remember feeling satisfied as I sipped my beer, my stomach full of squirrel meat.

After I was certain the fire was out and the ashes cool, I went inside and stretched out on my cot. I had one of the beers with me and I was just nursing it along. I pulled out one of the spiral notebooks that I use for writing first drafts and I may have written three or four paragraphs, but my heart wasn't in it, so I closed it back up and slid it under my mattress. For a couple of days before sleep I'd been reading ***The Three Stigmata of Palmer Eldritch*** by Phillip K. Dick. It was a battered paperback I'd picked up the summer before. Dick's one of my favorites. Twice, as I read the pages of the musty-smelling book, I could've sworn I heard sounds like a crowd of people talking, but distant, faint, the words unintelligible. The second time it happened I actually got up and went out onto the platform to take a look. Even as I made the effort, I knew I wouldn't find anything. I was far away from any parks or churches or any other place where people might congregate this time of night. But, there was a breeze stirring and a rain smell in the air. I saw a flash of lightning to the south. I just stood there a minute, taking it in, appreciating it. Rain would cool the summer night and make it easier to sleep. Going back inside after a bit, I don't think I read anymore that night. I finished my beer and fell asleep.

Now, I distinctly remember the dream I had that night. I was wandering through an old building, really old, maybe even a castle. It was dark and dusty and I was searching for something. I noticed a tapestry stirring on one of the walls and as I neared it, I was taken by the colors and the quality of its execution. I thought to myself, *Wow, I didn't know they could do tapestries of this quality back then.* Although, I wasn't even sure when *back then* was. I reached out and was about to touch the thing when it suddenly came to life. In an instant it was like an animated movie. The key figure in the tapestry was a large horse. The horse began to gallop and as it went along, it was gobbling up everything in its path; first vegetation, then small animals, then larger animals, other horses and people even. Finally, it came upon a dragon and the dragon tried to fight it, but the horse ate that thing, too. Still, it galloped along; seemingly no less hungry than when it started. I muttered to myself, "What the hell is this?" As if in response, my mind was filled with a message, not in language, but emphatically and clear as a bell as an idea just forced into my head. The message was, *Everything is eating everything else. This is the first rule of life.*

When I woke up it was pouring rain outside. Lightning flashed and thunder shook the walls. I looked through the window above the sink and saw the squirrel tails whipped around by the wind. I stared at the tree line along the east end of the property. My eyes kept going to the big oak tree that stands about midway along that boundary and I just had this anticipation of seeing something or someone. No one would be out in a storm like that, still I watched for a long time, certain that I would see something. *Something that shouldn't be there.* Of course, there was nothing. Then, just as I was turning to go back to my bed I thought I saw a pair of hands trying to grab the squirrel tails. They were little hands and dark, like a small black child was on the platform, jumping up in an effort to reach the tails and pull them down. The hallucination or vision was so convincing that I went back to the window and stood on my tip toes so I could look down onto the platform below the window. There was no child.

I lay on my cot a long time, listening to the storm. I even drank another beer thinking that would help me get back to sleep, but I really felt creepy. like there was something wrong, but it was something I did not understand and could do nothing about. That's not a good feeling. Most of the time I believe whatever the problem is you can take steps to fix it. Maybe small steps, but positive steps nonetheless that lead to progress, a solution to the problem. Lying on that cot I felt like a man drifting on the open ocean in a life raft without even a paddle. The worst part was that I didn't even know why.

The following morning I got a visit from Sean and Julie. I'd allowed myself to sleep in because of the weirdness of the night before and the heavy rainfall. Most of the work I had planned was on the exterior of the building and I needed to let things dry out a bit. So, I was still drinking coffee and reading my paperback book when I heard the approach of their car. At first I wondered who it was, then I heard Sean cursing about the mud as he climbed out of the vehicle. I met them at the platform. Sean was growling and looking down at his expensive boots as he made his way through the standing water. Julie was bright as ever, smiling and carrying a brown paper bag that I knew contained food or some other gift for me. They came into the kitchen area, Sean shaking my hand and Julie giving me a friendly hug.

"Damn, you got some serious rain," Sean said.

I pointed to some rags piled near the end of the counter. "You can clean your boots with those," I suggested and right away he took my suggestion, leaning on the counter top with one hand and using the other to carefully wipe the mess from his lizard skin boots.

"The place is looking great," Julie beamed and placed the bag on the counter next to Sean. "I brought you some goodies."

"And it's not even my birthday," I said.

Julie liked to be playful. "It's not? Damn, I got my dates confused. I'll have to take this home and bring it back on your birthday."

"On second thought, it is my birthday," I said. "What'd you bring me?"

"No big deal." She waved a hand in the air and wandered away from the kitchen to check out my progress. "Just some snacks and stuff."

When she left the room, I joined Sean at the counter and peered down into the bag. It contained a six pack of beer, some corn chips, dry-roasted peanuts and some tins of sardines. All things I enjoy. "Thanks for the food. How's everything going?"

Sean dropped the dirty rag on the floor. "Everything's okay. We're on our way to the airport, wanted to let you know. We'll be out of the country until mid to late September."

This was a surprise to me. "Really? Where you headed?"

"Italy. My uncle has a place on the Mediterranean that he's offered to us for the summer. It was too good a deal to pass up. Julie's got a couple of art dealers in Europe interested in her stuff, so we'll try to do a little business, too."

"Great, man." I was genuinely happy for them. Plus, the better things went for them, the likelier I was to continue to have the run of the school.

"Here," he said, pushing a wad of money toward me.

"What's this?"

"We appreciate everything you're doing here," he said, and though Sean wasn't big on handing out compliments, I could tell from the look in his eyes that he meant what he was saying. "Call this a bonus. We want you to have a good summer."

"Thanks." I slid the roll of bills into my jeans pocket.

"I've put enough money into the special account to keep you going until we return. Here's an email address you can use to let us know if anything comes up. I can always have Mom put some extra cash in the bank for you."

"I'm sure everything will be fine," I said.

"I love this place," Julie called from the area I'd come to refer to as the grand gallery. "Sean, come see."

I'd incorporated some found objects into one of the walls I'd erected. Julie was impressed, as I'd hoped she would be.

They spent an hour or so with me before heading on to the airport, complimenting me on my work, suggesting things they'd recently thought about adding. They were happy and so was I. The more work I did, the more ideas they got and the more work I had ahead of me. None of us had talked about what would happen once the place was finished and opened up to artists and art collectors. There'd be time enough to think of that later. I hated to see them go, knowing I wouldn't see them again until the fall. But, I also imagined the fun they'd have in Europe and in a way felt like I was a part of that.

"Take care of yourself," Julie said, giving me a goodbye squeeze.

"You, too," I answered.

Sean took my hand. "Great job, man. We're glad the place is in good hands."

"Thanks, Sean. I appreciate that. Here," I said, handing him a few of the rags from the counter, "use these to keep from getting mud in your car."

He smiled and nodded and followed Julie to the car. He honked the horn before pulling away, Julie waving rapidly through the windshield like a kid. I laughed and waved back, then they were gone.

I felt a little depressed, so I popped the top on one of the beers they'd brought me and sat down on the platform. I don't mind being alone; quite the opposite, really. Most of the time I enjoy my solitude. It's always been that way. Maybe I just needed to make some friends in the local community. Someone with whom I could play an occasional game of cards. As a last resort, I could attend a church. There would be social interaction there, but not really the kind I wanted. There would be potluck dinners. Those were good. I tabled that internal discussion and looked out at the old oak tree on the edge of the property.

A couple of beers later, the sun was setting and I was still sitting on the platform, doing nothing but vegetating. I didn't feel like reading or much of anything else. I considered for a minute or two what I should do about dinner, but then determined I'd just eat some of the snacks Julie had given me.

I'd set up a compost bin not far from the platform near a cluster of shrubs and a family of field mice had adopted it as their own personal cafeteria, enjoying the scraps I tossed on there almost daily. As the sun sank lower, the rodent family ventured out onto the compost heap, sniffing about for tasty morsels. They watched me, but not with fear. I really think they'd come to accept me as a sort of benefactor. I'd never frightened or harmed them and I left a lot of stuff for them to eat. They probably felt toward me a bit like I felt about Julie with her bag of beer and snack foods. When I mention field mice, most folks think I'm talking about the little gray things they've seen. But, when most Americans lay eyes on a field mouse for the first time, they usually exclaim something like, "My god, look at the size of that rat!" They're almost as big as bunnies, some of them. To me they're cute, but I know most folks don't think of any rodents as cute. Smiling as I mused about the field mice, I heard a scuffle nearby and turned to see a couple of children near the edge of the platform, to my right.

The sight of the boy and girl confused me at first. I couldn't imagine how they'd gotten so close to me without my hearing their approach. "Hello," I said.

"Hi," the girl said softly. The boy beside her just waved his hand in a noncommittal arc. The girl looked as if she wanted to smile at me, but hadn't yet. The boy, a year or so older than her, just studied me with a blank expression.

"I'm Richard," I said. "What's your name?"

The girl twisted her body in an expression of self-consciousness and replied in a voice that was barely audible, "Anna Mae."

"Anna Mae?" I asked making sure I'd heard correctly. She grabbed at the hem of her dress and nodded. "That's a nice name. I like it." Anna Mae smiled a real smile, now. The boy still stared expressionlessly. "How about you? What's your name?"

The girl looked at him to see if he was going to speak and at first it seemed like he wouldn't.

"It's okay," I said. "I don't bite."

Anna Mae smiled big at this, almost laughing. The boy smiled in a tentative way, almost a smirk. "I'm Calvin."

"Calvin. That's a good name, too." Anna Mae looked up at him smiling. "Are you Anna Mae's brother?" The two of them nodded. "I thought so," I said.

There was a noise to my left and I looked over to see a couple of the field mice fussing with one another, probably fighting over a choice nibble.

"What's those?" Anna Mae asked, pointing at the compost bin.

"Oh, they're just field mice." I said. "They won't hurt you."

"They big," said Calvin.

"Yeah, they're fat from eating my scraps." I said. Then a word popped into my head and I thought I'd share it with the kids, the way my grandmother and my mother had done with me when I was young. "They're crepuscular. Know what that means?" I'd picked the word up from a college biology professor I'd met when I was working for an organic restaurant in Arlington, Texas.

"Cruh…" Calvin started, crinkling his nose with the effort. "Cruh…"

"Crepuscular," I repeated. It means animals that like to come out at sunset to feed and water themselves. The kids said nothing. I looked at them and actually noticed for the first time how they were dressed. Anna Mae was in a shapeless brown dress, probably something her mother had sewn. Calvin was wearing overalls that were too small for him, pant legs only reaching halfway down his calves and a single gallous draped over his left shoulder. *These kids must be poor*, I thought to myself, *and maybe hungry*. "Would you like some corn chips?" I asked.

Anna Mae looked up at her brother, then they both stared at me as if they were uncertain how to respond. Maybe they'd never had corn chips? I supposed it was possible.

"They're good," I said, standing up. "Wait here and I'll get you some." I stepped toward the door.

"Are you a good white man?" Anna Mae asked. *Not a good man, but a good white man.* I turned back and looked at both of the children with as much benevolence as I could muster.

"I like to think so," I said. "One thing's for sure. I'd never hurt you or your brother."

They stared at me and I hadn't a clue what they were thinking.

"I'll be right back. I'm going to get you some chips." I went into the kitchen and opened the bag of chips. Then, realizing the salty chips would make the kids thirsty, I got a couple bottles of water. Through the window over the sink I heard them laughing.

"Crepulsive!" Calvin exclaimed. "You're crepulsive."

"I'm not crepulsive. You're crepulsive." Anna Mae giggled.

I couldn't help, but laugh myself. "It's not crepulsive," I called through the window. "It's crepuscular. Rhymes with muscular." The rhyming thing was a trick my folks had used to help me remember words way back when. The kids fell silent and I wondered what they were up to as I gathered up their snack and headed back out to the platform.

Outside, I was surprised to see that they were no longer beside the platform. I looked about, then I saw them almost to the oak tree. It seemed impossible to me that they could have gone so far, so quickly. They were laughing loudly to themselves. As I watched, Anna Mae turned and looked back at me, just for an instant. I saw something like a black shoelace dangling from her mouth. Then they were gone in the trees.

Well, I thought, maybe their folks had taught them not to take food from strangers. That was good advice, but the kids sure looked underfed. I wondered where they lived and why I'd never seen them before. Returning to the kitchen, I put the bottled water away and grabbed a beer. I resumed my perch at the edge of the platform and ate the chips I'd intended to give to Anna Mae and Calvin.

There's a store called Howard's Gas 'n' Go about five or six miles from the school. They sell some grocery items, the usual convenience store fare, but they also sell some damn good barbecue that Howard himself cooks in an old smoker on the back patio. The day after I'd first seen the kids I got a hankering for Howard's ribs and around one in the afternoon, I headed that way for lunch. Howard's brother-in-law Grady has a business salvaging building materials from old houses and there's a fenced yard beside the store where Howard sells some of the used lumber and old hardware like doorknobs for Grady. I thought I'd have lunch and look through the stuff to see if there was anything I could use.

I grabbed a beer from the cooler and went up to the counter. After a couple moments Howard came from the back, wiping his hands on a rag that he kept hanging from his belt.

"Hey," he says, smiling and pointing his chin at me.

"I'm hungry for some ribs," I said.

"Aw, man, I'm sorry. Just sold the last of the ribs little while ago."

"Got any brisket?"

"Oh, yeah. Plenty of brisket."

"In that case I'll take a brisket sandwich, bag of chips and this beer."

He rang it up, told me the total and as I dug the money out of my jeans pocket, he said, "How's things going out to the school?"

"It's shaping up pretty good. You should stop by and take a look sometime."

"Maybe I'll do that. I'm glad somebody's doing something with that old place. Any of the locals nosing around in your business out there?"

"No, hardly anybody comes around. This week the only people I've seen were the owner and his wife." Then it occurred to me to add, "Oh, Anna Mae and Calvin were playing around the old loading dock." I figured he'd know who the two children were. Everybody in Fodice seemed to know everybody else in town. Hell, in the county for that matter.

Howard just stared at me over the tops of his glasses as I handed him the money. "Yeah, right," he said.

"Mind if I take a look at your building materials?"

He gave me my change and said, "Help yourself."

"I'll take a look and be back for my sandwich in a minute," I said, heading for the door. Howard went into the back to put my sandwich together.

Out in the fenced-in salvage yard there was everything a carpenter might need; studs and siding, bins of hinges and all sorts of hardware. I took the notepad out of the hip pocket of my pants and jotted down a few reminders for future reference. A lot of the stuff I could use later, but I wasn't ready to buy it then and there. The prices were a handyman's dream. It beat the hell out of driving twenty five miles to one of the big superstores. After poking around, I went back inside to pick up my lunch.

The bag was sitting on the counter by the register, grease stains already darkening the brown paper. I didn't see Howard, so I grabbed my food and called out, "Thanks Howard. I'll see you later."

"Hey," he said softly, rising up from where he'd been bent over pricing merchandise on an aisle to my left. He actually scared me because I'd had no idea he was there.

"Whoa, brother," I said, jerking the paper bag to my chest. "You scared the crap out of me."

"Were you serious before?" His eyes were solemn, almost mournful, peering over his glasses.

"Hmmm?" I did not have the slightest clue what he was talking about.

"Anna Mae and Calvin." He stared at me. *Stared hard.* "Who told you about them?"

I was confused. "Who told me? Nobody *told* me anything. Like I said, they were playing around by the dock. I talked to them a bit, then I tried to give them some chips and water, but they took off." The way Howard just stood there staring made me uneasy as hell. It went on for so long, I finally felt obligated to say something. "Is there something wrong? I don't understand."

Then, it was like he just snapped out of it and he was good old friendly Howard again. "Naw, naw, nothing wrong. You enjoy your brisket. See you soon." Stooping down he began clicking the price gun in his hand, sticking little white labels on the cans in front of him.

Outside, I climbed into the van, popped the top on the beer and unwrapped my sandwich. I just sat there in the gravel parking lot, satisfying my hunger and puzzling over Howard. The sandwich was good as usual and when I'd finished eating and sipping the last of my beer, I wadded my trash up in the bag and tossed it into the floorboard. I started the van and headed back to the school, but I couldn't stop thinking about the two children and how weird Howard had acted.

Late in the day I was out on the platform assembling a little wooden cabinet when I heard the scuffing sound of shoes on the gravel behind me. I turned and had just enough time to see a big black man in a dirty t-shirt before he hit me. It wasn't exactly a punch in the face and it wasn't a slap. It was a smack from the back of his huge fist that connected real good with my right cheek bone. That smack carried enough power to send me to my knees. While I was down on all fours, trying to clear my vision, the man talked. He had a deep, rumbly sort of voice.

"You don't talk about Anna Mae and Calvin, white man. I hear you mention 'em again and I'll mess you up. Who the hell you think you are?"

He took an angry step toward me and I raised an open palm to ward him off. "Listen, man," I said. "I didn't do anything to hurt those kids. What's the problem?" I looked up at him and saw the same expression on his face that I'd seen on Howard's earlier that day. It was faraway and mournful, frustrated and panicked in a wordless, quiet way. The man's pain was tangible. I could feel it. He looked to be about my age, big and brawny; a man accustomed to hard work. His cheeks were flecked with little dark spots, his eyes red and puffy. I'd never before seen anybody look both pathetic and terrifying at the same time, but he did.

The man shook his head violently, let out an anguished, angry sound something like a dog coughing, then he just turned and walked away quickly. He disappeared behind the corner of the building and I heard a car start and move away. I wondered how I hadn't heard the car arrive in the first place. I'd been busy with the little cabinet I was building, distracted and preoccupied. It wasn't so strange. It wasn't strange by itself, that is, but everything that had been happening was starting to add up to one big ball of weirdness. *What the fuck?*

I stood up and touched my sore cheek. He'd walloped me for sure. Pissed off and not in the mood to do any more work, I went into kitchen and got a beer. I held the cold bottle against my face. In the bathroom, I checked my reflection in the mirror and saw a red, swollen lump that made my face look lopsided. Yeah, I knew that would be one massive bruise in the morning.

I spent the rest of the afternoon drinking beer and reading a bit in my science fiction novel. Leaning against the building, seated on the old loading dock, I was on my fourth beer when the sun began to set. It had the usual soothing effect on me. I decided a philosophical approach was best. Somehow, sometime I'd figure this mess out. The man was obviously disturbed, maybe with good reason. I'd seen torment in his eyes. I was in the process of breathing deeply and releasing my negative emotions when I heard the sound of laughter. Children's laughter.

The laughter came from the bushes near the compost bin. It was the two kids, I knew it. Now, a lot of shit ran through my mind, like was the man who hit me their dad? Had they run away from him? Was he on his way over to kick my ass? All of this and more in the matter of a couple seconds.

"Calvin? Anna Mae? Is that you?" I called. "I don't think you're supposed to be here."

The only response was more laughter.

"Hey! What are you two doing over there?"

What I saw is something I can't forget, but I wish I could. Little Anna Mae stepped out from behind the bushes. She eyed me with a sort of taunting expression. In her hands was one of the big fat field mice, squirming and trying to get free. The little girl wasn't at all frightened by the wriggling rodent. When I realized that, it just sent a chill through my spine. She grasped the animal firmly by the tail and held it up, looking from the mouse to me, measuring my reaction. Now, what happened next sounds completely impossible. I *know* that. Still, I know it happened. She just opened her mouth. I mean really big and wide, like a boa constrictor getting ready to swallow a pig and she dropped the fat mouse, almost as big as a bunny, into her face. Anna Mae closed her mouth and grinned at me, the rodent's tail between her lips whipping about with the futile expression of the desire to stay alive.

Calvin stepped out from the cover of the bushes and stood behind his sister. There was a frantic mouse in each of his hands. The children just stared at me. They said nothing, but I knew their intent was to frighten me. They wanted me scared. I got the distinct impression that they'd feed on my fear as much as they were feeding on the rodents. Then, they turned to go and another seemingly impossible thing happened. They were there by the compost bin, then instantly they were out by the old oak tree. Then it was black as night and there were three bodies hanging from the tree; one big one and two small ones. I heard a crowd of people shouting. I saw a little white girl standing in front of me, sort of leering and gloating. And then it was all gone. The sun was setting and I was sitting alone with a beer in my hand.

When I say I was goddamned scared there's no way you can know the depth of terror that took over me right then. And if Calvin and Anna Mae and whoever the little white girl was, if they all wanted to feed on my fear, then by God they were having a feast.

Next thing I know, I'm in the van driving. Don't know if I locked up the school before I left. I just can't remember. I drove to the interstate and went to the first motel I could find. I used some of the cash Sean had given me to pay. There was no way I could sleep in the school that night. I barely even slept in the motel. I tossed and turned, sometimes wide awake, other times half asleep but tormented by flashes of nightmare imagery. My logical mind kept trying to make sense of it all. Maybe I'd fallen asleep on the platform and dreamed it. Maybe the blow to my face had given me a concussion. Maybe I had a brain tumor. Maybe I'd ingested some hallucinogenic substance without knowing it. All that kind of garbage running through my mind all night long.

But, deep down, in my heart of hearts I knew the truth. Everything had happened just the way I described it. Something dark owned that schoolyard…owns that schoolyard. Something humans don't know or maybe they know it and just don't like to think about it. That something has a hold of that place. It's got a grip on that little spot and it's hanging on, trying to drag itself more completely into our world.

I woke up when a maid barged into the room to clean up. I told her to give me a minute. So, at least I'd slept. I felt nominally better. The sun was high and the terror I'd known the night before seemed distant. I got in my van and drove back to the school.

It looked normal when I arrived. It was just an old building. Hell, it was my home. Had been for many weeks now. I went into my room and got my Bible. Holding it in my hand, I walked the perimeter of the property, praying and saying whatever popped into my mind that might disperse the dark energy I believed was living there. When I passed under the oak tree it was like my right arm suffered a spasm and the Bible fell out of my hand. I picked it back up and held it close to my heart. I said something like, "You may think you own this place, but you don't. There's a higher power that owns this place and everything else. There's nothing here for you. There's only light in this place."

I waited to see what might happen next, but nothing did. I went back inside.

It wasn't long before I heard a car pull up. *Great,* I thought, *just what I need is for that big guy to come back and kick my ass some more.* The only weapon I had was the pellet gun, so I picked it up and carried it with me out onto the old dock. I was relieved to see it was Howard. It was only then that I realized it was Sunday and his store was closed. I leaned the pellet gun against the wall and stepped down off the platform.

"Thought I'd take you up on your offer to see the old place," he called as he closed his car door. Howard walked toward me grinning, but the grin disappeared when he got a good look at my bruised face. After sighing, he said, "That's a hell of a shiner."

"Yeah," I said, offering my hand.

He shook my hand and said, "Listen, man, I feel like that's my fault. See, I told Luke you saw Anna Mae and Calvin."

"You did?"

He nodded solemnly.

"Come on in and sit down," I said. He was my first real guest since I'd been living there. "Want a beer?"

"No. Thank you, though. I don't drink beer on Sundays."

"How about a bottle of water?"

"Okay."

We went into the kitchen area and I fished a bottle of water out of the cooler for him. It was fairly cool, though all the ice had melted. He took it, screwed the top off and took a good, long drink. Then, he stared at me a long time. His face twitched and he seemed to feel genuinely guilty about my bruised face.

"I shouldn't have said nothing to Luke. He's touchy. You had no way of knowing. I saw you were telling the truth. Nobody around here'd have any reason to tell you the old stories. Would they?"

"Stories?"

"Yeah. Lots of folks have seen Anna Mae and Calvin. That's why there's plenty of locals think this place should be tore down."

"Really?" This was news to me.

"Yeah. See, Luke's granddaddy was Silas Dowdell. He was Anna Mae's and Calvin's little brother. Silas and his mama was hiding under that sink there the night them KKK boys lynched his daddy and the other two kids." Howard gestured with the water bottle toward the sink.

"My God," I said.

"You can see why he's upset. He wants to believe his grandfather's brother and sister can rest in peace. It hurts his heart to think a little murdered boy and girl are trapped here outside heaven. You know?"

"I understand." Even as I said this, I was thinking, *That's not them. It's something that uses their images to generate fear.*

"Nobody knows for sure what got the white boys over in Alvin all riled up. But a bunch of them come out here and made a night's entertainment out of it. Brought their families with them. Hell it was like a picnic. They was some sick bastards."

I said nothing. I couldn't think of anything to say that would be appropriate in this situation. I guess you could say I was stunned.

"Miss Hattie said tell you to come on over this afternoon if you want to."

"Miss Hattie?"

"Miss Hattie Tanner. She's an old lady lives nearby. Never married. Used to teach school. She's sort of a historian for the town. She wants to talk to you."

"Think I should go?" I asked. "I don't want to make things worse."

He nodded. "I think you should go. Come on. I'll go with you."

We both got into Howard's old Chevy. It smelled of motor oil, perspiration and barbecue smoke. He drove and we spoke sparingly for the ten minutes or so that it took to reach Miss Hattie's house. Under different circumstances I might have laughed when I saw the place. Unlike the other houses in that part of Houston County, it was freshly painted. There was a picket fence, also freshly painted, and a variety of yard decorations like birdbaths and a wisteria arbor. The place was full of flowers and fruit-bearing trees. Miss Hattie had spent a lot of time making the little frame house attractive. We moved up the walk and onto the porch, the steps creaking a bit under Howard's weight. There was a nice porch swing with a cushion. On the swing lay a copy of the Saturday Evening Post. This place seemed like a monument to the simpler, gentler and more beautiful aspirations of a bygone era.

Howard rapped at the doorframe. A sweet, high-pitched voice responded.

"Yes? Who is it?"

"It's me, Miss Hattie. Howard."

"I'm on my way," the old woman called from the interior of the storybook house. It was a few moments before the door finally swung open to reveal the slight form of Miss Hattie. She was dressed in her church clothes, complete with a hat that had a flower made from cloth attached to one side. She smiled big. Her eyes were bright and welcoming. "I'm so glad you came. Come inside. I have a fan and its cooler in here. I just made some lemonade."

Howard introduced me and held the screen door while I stepped into the house. It was a good deal cooler inside. Cooler than I'd expected. I remember thinking the place must've been really well-insulated. Miss Hattie indicated that I should sit on the sofa. The room was packed with furniture and I carefully maneuvered my way. The paths between chairs and the coffee table were an appropriate size for a little woman like Miss Hattie, but a challenge for most full-grown men. Howard accidentally let the screen door slam shut and Miss Hattie stared at him sternly over her spectacles.

"Howard," she said, simply. In that moment she looked like everyone's idea of an elementary school teacher.

"Sorry, Miss Hattie, it slipped out of my hand," Howard answered quickly, reverting to his eight-year-old self for a moment. It was hard not to laugh, seeing that hulk of a man staring uncomfortably at the little woman.

"Make yourselves at home. I'll be right back." Miss Hattie went into the kitchen. I sat on the sofa and Howard perched uneasily on a rocker like he was afraid he'd break it. Miss Hattie returned with a tray containing a pitcher of lemonade and three plastic tumblers. I would've expected glassware, but I suppose her expectations of Howard leaned toward breakage. I had never thought of Howard as clumsy or self-conscious, but in the presence of Miss Hattie I saw he was both. She seated herself on the sofa beside me and after she had poured each of us a serving of lemonade, she scrutinized me for a time. Not harshly, but with a benevolent half-smile. "You know, I was worried about you moving into the old school. I knew the bad things that happened there had not yet exhausted themselves," she said, at last. I found her choice of words interesting.

"Miss Hattie," I said, "all I know about what happened there is what Howard told me today."

She nodded with pursed lips and gave my knee a reassuring pat with her small, bony hand. "You walked into something you couldn't possibly understand." In silence, I agreed. "Howard says you're a good man. I can see for myself that's true. I hope you won't hold a grudge against Luke. He's still full of pain and hate over what happened even though it happened before he was born."

I don't remember everything Miss Hattie said that day, but a lot of it had metaphysical overtones. She spoke of "energies" and "resonances" and when she said it's up to those of us who will, to hold the light on this planet and not let the darkness rule, there was a power to her presence that seemed very real to me. As I sat there listening to her talk, I felt that I'd rediscovered the true nature of humankind, that Miss Hattie was what all of us had come here with the intention of being. At one point, she pulled a large photo album out from under the sofa, scooted closer to me and opened it up across both our laps. It was filled with amazing old black and white photos of early members of the Fodice community. She quickly passed over those until she came to a horrifying photo that, although I'd never seen it, was all too familiar to me. In the photo Model A and Model T Fords were gathered around the old oak tree. There was a bonfire and torches scattered throughout the scene. Three bodies hung from the tree. One big, two small. There were people sitting on blankets, eating and drinking like it was a church picnic. A tiny little blond girl was nibbling at a chicken leg and staring directly into the camera. It was the little girl I'd seen.

"My God," I muttered. The photo sent a chill down my spine.

Miss Hattie sighed heavily. "I don't know why they felt like they had to kill the children. Normally, they would've made them watch, just to terrify them into toeing the line for the rest of their lives. I've prayed over that place many times and I know in my heart that evil will gradually dissipate…sort of like the lingering radiation after an atomic bomb, this evil has a half-life. A real long half-life."

"Miss Hattie, you're a remarkable woman," I said.

She smiled. "And you're a remarkable man. I never would've thought anyone could live in that place. Not yet.

And least of all a white man." She covered her mouth in a gesture of embarrassment. "I meant no offense."

"None taken." I pointed to the little girl in the picture. "Who's that little girl? I've seen her at the school."

Miss Hattie drew in a quick breath and turned her head sideways. She shot a look at Howard, who grimly nodded. With lips squeezed tightly together, she shook her head slowly. "Mmm mmm mmm…well, it doesn't surprise me that you saw her, but you're the first one who has, that I know of anyway."

"Who is she?" I asked again.

"That's Phoebe Warner. Her daddy was the head of the Klan back then. Folks say she's as dark-hearted as they come. Pretty little thing. Evil often comes in attractive packages."

I couldn't help but notice Miss Hattie used the present tense when she referred to Phoebe Warner as dark-hearted. "You mean she's still alive?"

"Barely, but yes. She's in a nursing home over in Alvin. Hanging onto life very tenaciously. Maybe she's not too eager to go wherever she's headed when she leaves here."

"How old is she?"

"I don't know for certain, but I've heard she's close to a hundred. Might even be a hundred by now."

The three of us were quiet for a time. I was the one who broke the silence. "Miss Hattie, you wanted to see me. Well, I came. What now? What am I supposed to do?"

She traced the line of her jaw with a thin index finger, then wagged the same finger at me. "That's a good question. Are you a religious man?"

"No," I admitted.

"Didn't think so. Do you have faith in a higher power?"

"You mean God?"

"Doesn't matter what you call it, him or her. Have you ever experienced the intervention of a higher consciousness in your life? Have you ever had faith in something or someone you could not see, but you knew was there all the same?"

"Yeah," I said. "I'm not sure it's what you or anyone else would call God, but I know there's something watching over me."

"Good." She clapped her skeletal hands together. "That's faith, the knowledge of things unseen. That's your protection."

Without saying anything about it, I recalled how I'd grabbed my Bible as if it was a charm when things got crazy at the school house. I didn't really believe the book could protect me, but that it somehow represented a connection to something that might.

"All I can do for you is pray," Miss Hattie said. "But, I know from experience how powerful a tool prayer can be."

"Amen," Howard muttered.

"I'll call my prayer circle and have them all pray for a circle of divine protection around you. Howard and his family will be praying for you, too."

"That's right," he agreed.

"We're done here." Miss Hattie smiled at me and patted my knee again. As I rose from the sofa I thanked her for the lemonade. "You are so welcome. And you are welcome to come back and visit anytime." As we moved toward the door she added, "Howard, I know you are not going to let my screen door slam."

"No ma'am," he answered.

Neither Howard nor I knew what to say, so we rode in silence back to the school. When he showed no intention of getting out, I thanked him for checking on me and introducing me to Miss Hattie.

"Least I could do," he answered, offering me his big, hard hand. "You're a brave man."

"Brave?"

"Well, yeah, I think so. You're gonna spend the night in this place aren't you?"

I nodded.

"In my book that makes you brave. Don't think I could do it. And we will be praying for you. I'll talk with Luke again and make sure he doesn't bother you anymore."

"Thanks."

I climbed out of the car and he drove away, honking and waving as he left the property and turned out onto the county road.

Time passed slowly. I was restless. I placed the Bible over my heart and lay on the bed. Again and again I tried to read my science fiction novel, but I was easily distracted. Every little sound drew my attention. Finally, I set the paperback aside and just lay there. After a while it began to rain. The sound of the rain on the roof was somewhat comforting. There were a few flashes of lightning, not many, and the thunder rumbled out many miles to the east. Sometime after the rain began I fell asleep.

There was laughter. High, shrill giggling. It was the mischievous titter of a little girl. I was pretty sure I knew who was laughing. I woke with a start, but was afraid to move. My hand went to the Bible and pressed it to my chest.

"Hello…" the little girl's voice called from out there in the rain.

I sensed that I was at a crossroads. My life situation and mindset, coupled with the history of that place, had created an opportunity for something from somewhere else to get a foot in the door of our world. I thought about Miss Hattie. Knowing that she and the others were praying for me, helped ease the tension a bit. I realized the little girl I heard laughing was not a little girl at all; just something dark, malevolent trying to frighten me. It was using the forms of Phoebe Warner and Anna Mae and Calvin because the contrast between its own evil and the innocence of children was bone-chilling, deliberately grotesque and confusing to the human mind. What was it? Had it ever been a living thing or was it always a parasitic something that latched onto unsuspecting people and made them do things like lynching the two children and their father? Thinking again of Miss Hattie and her prayer circle gave me a bit of courage. Still holding the Bible, I sat up on the bed. As I write this I realize it sounds like I was mulling it over the way one might consider a bit of information from a magazine or textbook. It takes longer to write it than it took to experience. Though these insights flashed through my mind as quickly as the lightning flashed in the rainy night outside, mostly I was just plain terrified. The dread that had hold of my mind was not to be shaken off by a rational inquiry.

I heard the sound of something, tossed by the wind, bumping against the glass of the window above the sink. Not wanting to, but knowing I had to; I turned my eyes in the direction of the repetitive thump. There, where I'd seen the squirrel tails dancing in the wind before, I saw two little black hands, one slightly larger than the other, tied by string and hanging in front of the glass.

Something pounded on the door that led to the dock. I heard the little girl's tittering laughter.

"Let's plaaayay…" she called. "I won't hurt you…" She laughed louder than before and I knew she meant exactly the opposite of what she'd said.

The bolt snapped in the door and it creaked open until it was far enough out for the wind to catch it and it slammed against the outside wall. Lightning illuminated the yard and I saw the little blond girl peering over the edge of the dock. She smiled playfully and laughed, covering her mouth as she did. I stood and moved toward the open door. At that moment I wanted nothing more than to bolt it and shut the thing out. I stepped cautiously toward the opening. There was a stirring at my feet. My head automatically jerked downward to see what had brushed against me. It was a large rodent. I guess it had come into the school to escape the storm. But, now it ran like an insane thing straight for the little girl. Phoebe opened her mouth really wide. Her mouth just got bigger and bigger and the rat rushed right in. She chewed with satisfaction, her eyes never leaving mine, savoring my disgust and fear.

She swallowed and wiped her mouth with her little forearm. "Hungry?" she called. "Let's have a snack."

The lightning flashed again and I saw the three bodies hanging in the oak tree. Phoebe noticed me noticing them. "They're my friends. Do you want to be my friend?"

Water swept into the kitchen through the open door. Already there was a large puddle at my feet. Again I felt movement. I looked down to see a large snake weaving between my legs, headed for the girl. It slithered onto the dock and, like the rat, willingly rushed into her mouth. "Mmmm," she moaned as the snake slowly disappeared between her lips.

I sort of lost it then. Like a frantic animal trapped in a cage, I rushed to grab the door and pull it closed. I could clearly imagine being the next snack to disappear into Phoebe's mouth. Seizing the door handle, I pulled against the wind. When I looked down at Phoebe I saw, not a little girl, but a hideous old hag clad in a worn and filthy night gown. The snake was still slowly making its way into her mouth. My feet slipped on the wet linoleum and I went down. A burst of pain shot through my back. The wind shifted and flung the heavy door in my direction. I tried to move, but I was too late. The door slammed on my arm. I heard the snap of the bone over the sound of the storm. Then the pain in my arm made the pain in my back seem like nothing.

The old woman was up on the platform now, crawling toward me in the pouring rain. From her mouth, the snake's tail hung, writhing and slapping against her face. For an instant it seemed like I heard the sound of many voices, speaking in unison, though I couldn't make out what they were saying. Then a hellacious bright light and a bolt of lightning came down smack dab on the old woman. The sound of the atmosphere being ripped by thunder was deafening.

That's all I remember about that night.

I woke up in the county hospital. For what seemed like the longest time I was alone in the room, but it was clean and dry and represented a reality with which I was familiar. I could hear voices in the hallway and on the intercom. Tell the truth, I wasn't sure I was still alive. Maybe I was in some sort of waiting room for heaven or a purgatory or something? I really didn't care. I felt safe.

Later I learned that Howard had come by in the morning and found me on the dock. He's the one who called the ambulance. That evening after he closed the store, he and Miss Hattie came to see me.

"Sorry I couldn't be here when you woke up," Howard said, "but my profit margin at the store doesn't allow for unscheduled days off."

I told him not to worry about it and thanked him for checking on me. Miss Hattie quizzed me about everything that had happened. I told her everything she wanted to know. Then she told me something every bit as strange as what I'd told her. Seems her niece or great niece is a supervisor at the nursing home where Phoebe Warner had been living for years. The night before, during the storm, the staff heard a shriek coming from the old woman's room. Two or three of them rushed to her bed immediately. What they found was a scorched sheet and part of a hand lying on the floor beside the bed. There was no trace of the rest of her body. It wasn't going to be in the papers. Why? Because people don't like to talk about or read about what they don't understand. Miss

Hattie said, with some indignation, that her niece had told her the primary concern of the nursing home's administrators was how the incident might affect their bottom line.

Okay, so now I'm at my mom's place. When I've healed enough I'll look for a job. Maybe I'll go back to the school and finish what I started. I don't know. I haven't told Sean and Julie everything that happened, just that I had a bad accident and I'm recuperating in Fort Worth. They're understanding and supportive. I wonder if I'll ever be able to tell them the truth.

I spend my days reading a lot and watching a little TV. Mom's always been the suspicious type. She hasn't come out and said it, but she's hinted at the idea that maybe I got crosswise with some drug dealers or thugs of some other stripe. Other than her suspicions, she's been real good to me.

I've had plenty of time to think about what happened and the larger implications of the whole good versus evil thing. One thing that occurs to me is this; most people never get a good close look at evil. Maybe that's one reason that our world is as sane as it is. It's like once you notice evil and it has your full attention, then it's able to slip into this world through even the smallest crack. With all the thinking I've done about evil, I've come to the conclusion that there are four types. First, there's evil with a lower case "e." That's the way we think of mean bosses or people who cheat us in a business deal of some sort. Then, there's B-movie evil. That's largely a literary construct used to educate children. The guys in black hats in an old western movie, or Ming the Merciless, or maybe a murderer from an episode of Perry Mason; these are examples of the B-movie evil. They illustrate evil in an entertaining and understandable way, but keep it out there at arms length. It's always someone else and it's not a part of us. The third kind is what I call the King-Lynch kind of evil. Stephen King and David Lynch.

This evil is informed by an understanding of what it is to be evil. The evils these guys present in their work is disturbing to lots of people because it clearly points out that evil's not a foreign entity, but a part of us. We don't want to believe that it's hiding down deep somewhere, waiting to get out or that maybe it's the bulk of the iceberg and the tip, or what we normally think of as ourselves, is just the smallest, but most visible part of what we are. Last there's true evil. That's what the Allied forces must've felt when they liberated the Nazi concentration camps. It's the damning realization that our attempts at civilization are fragile at best. At any moment, the sum total of our collective good as a race can be swept away and replaced by our worst nightmares.

Those forces that we identify as evil are allowed in when a human soul is in twilight. I'm not a religious man at all, but I think I understand good. It's the light. Its clarity and a sense of community. We're social creatures because we need the company of others to help us stave off the darkness. I don't know what would've happened to me if Howard and Miss Hattie hadn't intervened. So, if you're not focused on the light, you can drift like I did into a twilight region where evil can step up and shake your hand. I guess you could say evil is crepuscular. It lives in the darkness, but it feeds in the twilight.

Well, my hand is cramped and tired from writing. I'm hungry. Think I'll grab a sandwich and see if there's anything good on the tube. Maybe I'll write more later.

The Interlopers
Saki
(H.H. Munro)

In a forest of mixed growth somewhere on the eastern spurs of the Carpathians, a man stood one winter night watching and listening, as though he waited for some beast of the woods to come within the range of his vision, and, later, of his rifle. But the game for whose presence he kept so keen an outlook was none that figured in the sportsman's calendar as lawful and proper for the chase; Ulrich von Gradwitz patrolled the dark forest in quest of a human enemy. The forest lands of Gradwitz were of wide extent and well stocked with game; the narrow strip of precipitous woodland that lay on its outskirt was not remarkable for the game it harbored or the shooting it afforded, but it was the most jealously guarded of all its owner's territorial possessions.

A famous lawsuit, in the days of his grandfather, had wrested it from the illegal possession of a neighboring family of petty landowners; the dispossessed party had never acquiesced in the judgment of the Courts, and a long series of poaching affrays and similar scandals had embittered the relationships between the families for three generations. The neighbor feud had grown into a personal one since Ulrich had come to be head of his family; if there was a man in the world whom he detested and wished ill to it was Georg Znaeym, the inheritor of the quarrel and the tireless game-snatcher and raider of the disputed border-forest.

The feud might, perhaps, have died down or been compromised if the personal ill-will of the two men had not stood in the way; as boys they had thirsted for one another's blood, as men each prayed that misfortune might fall on the other, and this wind-scourged winter night Ulrich had banded together his foresters to watch the dark forest, not in quest of four-footed quarry, but to keep a look-out for the prowling thieves whom he suspected of being afoot from across the land boundary.

The roebuck, which usually kept in the sheltered hollows during a storm-wind, were running like driven things to-night, and there was movement and unrest among the creatures that were wont to sleep through the dark hours. Assuredly there was a disturbing element in the forest, and Ulrich could guess the quarter from whence it came. He strayed away by himself from the watchers whom he had placed in ambush on the crest of the hill and wandered far down the steep slopes amid the wild tangle of undergrowth, peering through the tree trunks and listening through the whistling and skirling of the wind and the restless beating of the branches for sight and sound of the marauders.

If only on this wild night, in this dark, lone spot, he might come across Georg Znaeym, man to man, with none to witness – that was the wish that was uppermost in his thoughts. And as he stepped round the trunk of a huge beech he came face to face with the man he sought.

The two enemies stood glaring at one another for a long silent moment. Each had a rifle in his hand, each had hate in his heart and murder uppermost in his mind. The chance had come to give full play to the passions of a lifetime. But a man who has been brought up under the code of a restraining civilization cannot easily nerve himself to shoot down his neighbor in cold blood and without word spoken, except for an offence against his hearth and honor. And before the moment of hesitation had given way to action, a deed of Nature's own violence overwhelmed them both.

A fierce shriek of the storm had been answered by a splitting crash over their heads, and ere they could leap aside a mass of falling beech tree had thundered down on them. Ulrich von Gradwitz found himself stretched on the ground, one arm numb beneath him and the other held almost as helplessly in a tight tangle of forked branches, while both legs were pinned beneath the fallen mass. His heavy shootingboots had saved his feet from being crushed to pieces, but if his fractures were not as serious as they might have been, at least it was evident that he could not move from his present position till someone came to release him. The descending twig had slashed the skin of his face, and he had to wink away some drops of blood from his eyelashes before he could take in a general view of the disaster.

At his side, so near that under ordinary circumstances he could almost have touched him, lay Georg Znaeym, alive and struggling, but obviously as helplessly pinioned down as himself. All round them lay a thick-strewn wreckage of splintered branches and broken twigs. Relief at being alive and exasperation at his captive plight brought a strange medley of pious thank-offerings and sharp curses to Ulrich's lips.

Georg, who was early blinded with the blood which trickled across his eyes, stopped his struggling for a moment to listen, and then gave a short, snarling laugh. "So you're not killed, as you ought to be, but you're caught, anyway," he cried; "caught fast. Ho, what a jest, Ulrich von Gradwitz snared in his stolen forest. There's real justice for you!" And he laughed again, mockingly and savagely.

"I'm caught in my own forestland," retorted Ulrich. "When my men come to release us you will wish, perhaps, that you were in a better plight than caught poaching on a neighbor's land, shame on you."

Georg was silent for a moment; then he answered quietly: "Are you sure that your men will find much to release? I have men, too, in the forest to-night, close behind me, and THEY will be here first and do the releasing. When they drag me out from under these damned branches it won't need much clumsiness on their part to roll this mass of trunk right over on the top of you. Your men will find you dead under a fallen beech tree. For form's sake I shall send my condolences to your family."

"It is a useful hint," said Ulrich fiercely. "My men had orders to follow in ten minutes time, seven of which must have gone by already, and when they get me out – I will remember the hint. Only as you will have met your death poaching on my lands I don't think I can decently send any message of condolence to your family."

"Good," snarled Georg, "good. We fight this quarrel out to the death, you and I and our foresters, with no cursed interlopers to come between us. Death and damnation to you, Ulrich von Gradwitz."

"The same to you, Georg Znaeym, forest-thief, game-snatcher."

Both men spoke with the bitterness of possible defeat before them, for each knew that it might be long before his men would seek him out or find him; it was a bare matter of chance which party would arrive first on the scene. Both had now given up the useless struggle to free themselves from the mass of wood that held them down; Ulrich limited his endeavors to an effort to bring his one partially free arm near enough to his outer coat-pocket to draw out his wine-flask.

Even when he had accomplished that operation it was long before he could manage the unscrewing of the stopper or get any of the liquid down his throat. But what a Heaven-sent draught it seemed!

It was an open winter, and little snow had fallen as yet, hence the captives suffered less from the cold than might have been the case at that season of the year; nevertheless, the wine was warming and reviving to the wounded man, and he looked across with something like a throb of pity to where his enemy lay, just keeping the groans of pain and weariness from crossing his lips.

"Could you reach this flask if I threw it over to you?" asked Ulrich suddenly; "there is good wine in it, and one may as well be as comfortable as one can. Let us drink, even if tonight one of us dies."

"No, I can scarcely see anything; there is so much blood caked round my eyes," said Georg, "and in any case I don't drink wine with an enemy."

Ulrich was silent for a few minutes, and lay listening to the weary screeching of the wind. An idea was slowly forming and growing in his brain, an idea that gained strength every time that he looked across at the man who was fighting so grimly against pain and exhaustion. In the pain and languor that Ulrich himself was feeling the old fierce hatred seemed to be dying down.

"Neighbor," he said presently, "do as you please if your men come first. It was a fair compact. But as for me, I've changed my mind. If my men are the first to come you shall be the first to be helped, as though you were my guest. We have quarreled like devils all our lives over this stupid strip of forest, where the trees can't even stand upright in a breath of wind. Lying here tonight thinking I've come to think we've been rather fools; there are better things in life than getting the better of a boundary dispute. Neighbor, if you will help me to bury the old quarrel I – I will ask you to be my friend."

Georg Znaeym was silent for so long that Ulrich thought, perhaps, he had fainted with the pain of his injuries. Then he spoke slowly and in jerks. "How the whole region would stare and gabble if we rode into the market square together. No one living can remember seeing a Znaeym and a von Gradwitz talking to one another in friendship. And what peace there would be among the forester folk if we ended our feud tonight. And if we choose to make peace among our people there is none other to interfere, no interlopers from outside … You would come and keep the Sylvester night beneath my roof, and I would come and feast on some high day at your castle … I would never fire a shot on your land, save when you invited me as a guest; and you should come and shoot with me down in the marshes where the wildfowl are. In all the countryside there are none that could hinder if we willed to make peace. I never thought to have wanted to do other than hate you all my life, but I think I have changed my mind about things too, this last half-hour. And you offered me your wine flask … Ulrich von Gradwitz, I will be your friend."

For a space both men were silent, turning over in their minds the wonderful changes that this dramatic reconciliation would bring about. In the cold, gloomy forest, with the wind tearing in fitful gusts through the naked branches and whistling round the tree-trunks, they lay and waited for the help that would now bring release and succor to both parties. And each prayed a private prayer that his men might be the first to arrive, so that he might be the first to show honourable attention to the enemy that had become a friend. Presently, as the wind dropped for a moment, Ulrich broke silence.

"Let's shout for help," he said; "in this lull our voices may carry a little way."

"They won't carry far through the trees and undergrowth," said Georg, "but we can try. Together, then."

The two raised their voices in a prolonged hunting call.

"Together again," said Ulrich a few minutes later, after listening in vain for an answering halloo.

"I heard nothing but the pestilential wind," said Georg hoarsely.

There was silence again for some minutes, and then Ulrich gave a joyful cry. "I can see figures coming through the wood. They are following in the way I came down the hillside."

Both men raised their voices in as loud a shout as they could muster.

"They hear us! They've stopped. Now they see us. They're running down the hill towards us," cried Ulrich.

"How many of them are there?" asked Georg.

"I can't see distinctly," said Ulrich; "nine or ten,"

"Then they are yours," said Georg; "I had only seven out with me."

"They are making all the speed they can, brave lads," said Ulrich gladly.

"Are they your men?" asked Georg. "Are they your men?" he repeated impatiently as Ulrich did not answer.

"No," said Ulrich with a laugh, the idiotic chattering laugh of a man unstrung with hideous fear.

"Who are they?" asked Georg quickly, straining his eyes to see what the other would gladly not have seen.

"Wolves."

About Bret McCormick

By all accounts, Bret McCormick seems to have been born with a natural fondness for all things strange, sinister and outré'. Poe, Lovecraft, Bierce, Bradbury, Bloch and Matheson all found their way into his welcoming library during his pre-teen years. Karloff, Lugosi, Chaney, Lee, Cushing and the films they populated were loving fixations for this horror geek from Fort Worth, Texas. McCormick was experimenting with his own horror tales and films by the time he was a teenager. At age thirteen he began submitting stories for publication and acquired an impressive stack of rejection slips before making his first sale in 1981.

McCormick studied Motion Picture Production at Brooks Institute in Santa Barbara, California.

From 1984 to 1996 Bret McCormick was the most prolific feature film producer/director in Texas. Capitalizing on the emerging home video market, he created a variety of low budget action, horror and science fiction movies for international distribution. McCormick's ultra-cheapie-gorefest, **The Abomination** (1986) has a small, but rabid, cult following worldwide and continues to be the subject of articles and interviews in print and online publications. Roger Corman was a major influence on McCormick's approach to filmmaking. His childhood dream of making films for Corman came true with the production of **Rumble in the Streets** (1995) and **The Protector** (1996).

McCormick left the film industry in 1996 and today writes and paints from his home in Bedford, Texas. He is employed part-time by the Bedford Public Library and volunteers weekly at Central Arts of Hurst and True Worth Place.

In 2016, McCormick and E. R. Bills began editing a recurring anthology of homegrown horror tales known as **Road Kill**. The series features terrifying stories penned by the best horror writers the Lone Star State has to offer. The latest installment of the series, **Road Kill Vol. 4** will be available from HellBound Books in October 2019.

In 2018, HellBound Books published an anthology of horror inspired by 1980s schlock cinema, compiled by Bret McCormick, **Schlock! Horror!** This weighty tome featured the fiction of some of the hottest up-and-coming talent in the genre from all over the world.

HellBound Books released a bathroom reader of short horror edited by McCormick in 2019 – **The Toilet Zone.** These 32 tales are certain to chill, terrify and linger hauntingly in the reader's mind for months to come.

Skin Dreams (Poor White Trash Part 3) is McCormick's latest novel, in which a young 'Texas white trash gal', Sadie Richards, runs afoul of a widespread cult of politicians, businessmen and clergy who kidnap, enslave and sacrifice young women and children to dark forces from beyond this dimension. Purchase **Skin Dreams** from HellBound Books beginning in October 2019.

McCormick's nonfiction book, **Texas Schlock**, examines B-Movie Sci-Fi and Horror produced in Texas from the late 1950s up to the present day. The films and careers of such cinematic trailblazers as Larry Buchanan, S.F. Brownrigg, Tom Moore, Edgar G. Ulmer, Robert A. Burns, Glen Coburn and McCormick, himself, are explored from a fun and appreciative perspective.

A partial list of McCormick's film production credits can be found on the IMDB page:

https://www.imdb.com/name/nm0566506/?ref_=fn_al_nm_1

For more information on McCormick's film career, or to order limited edition DVDs of his work, visit collectorsreleases.com.

Visit Bret McCormick's Amazon Author Page at https://www.amazon.com/-/e/B01F2Z2Q90

To see Bret McCormick's artwork, visit the Facebook page Bret McCormick's Paintings and More @BretMcCormickArt

Other HellBound Books Titles
Available at: www.hellboundbookspublishing.com

The Toilet Zone
RESTROOM READING AT ITS MOST
FRIGHTENING!

Compiled and edited by the grand master of 80's schlock horror, Bret McCormick, each one of this collection of 32 terrifying tales is just the perfect length for a visit to the smallest room....

At the very boundaries of human imagination dwells one single, solitary place of solitude, of peace and quiet, a place in which your regular human being spends, on average, 10 to 15 minutes - at least once every single day of their lives.

Now, consider a typical, everyday reading speed of 200 to 250 words per minute - that means your average visitor has the time to read between 2,500 to 4,000 words, which makes each and every one of these 32 tales of terror - from some of the best contemporary independent authors - within this anthology of horror the perfect, meticulously calculated length. Dare you take a walk to the small room from where inky shadows creep out to smother the light and solitude's siren call beckons you?

Dare you take a quiet, lonely walk into… The Toilet Zone

ROAD KILL: TEXAS HORROR BY TEXAS WRITERS - VOL 3

Everything is bigger in Texas - including the horror!

A Piney woods meth dealer clones Adolph Hitler. A nightmare exorcist meets an inexorable fined. An eyeball collector gets collected. The apparition of a lynching victim tracks down his executioners. A Texas lawman is undone by shades of his past. A Baphomet recruits converts as a local summer camp. The tales of the baker's dozen who appear in this anthology demonstrate why everything is scarier in Texas…

Including tales of terror from

Jeremy Hepler

Madison Estes

Bret McCormick

James H Longmore

ER Bills

Shawna Borman

And many more...

Crime Pays

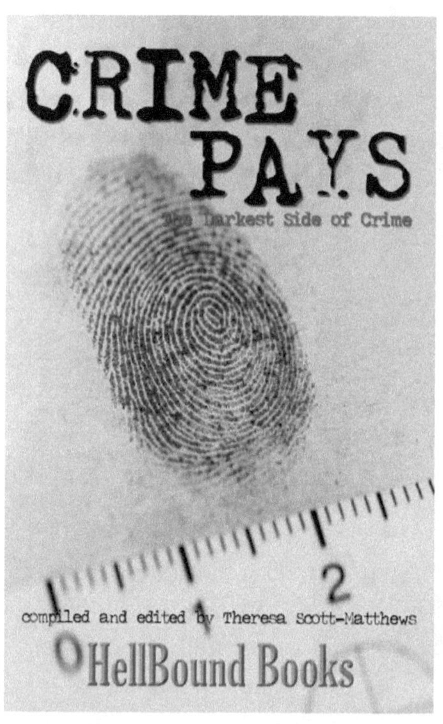

In the murky, muddied waters where crime meets horror, we are introduced to some of the most heinous monsters of them all – the human variety.

It would seem all bets are off when it comes to criminal matters - so expect to stumble into nefarious wrong-doing, crosses, double crosses, violence, and murder with the pages of this exceptional anthology, and all mixed in with an insight into the darkened souls of some of the most hardened criminals with whom you would never wish to cross paths.

All in all, Crime Pays is a baker's dozen of exceptional dark crime stories from the likes of: Matthew Wilson, Matthew McKiernan, Steve Stark, Roger Lime, Nick Swain, Bill Davidson, Tim Mendees, Sergio 'ente per ente' Palumbo, Alexander Marais,
June Trop, Victoria Greenaway, and Marcus Cook.

Skin Dreams

These men were a part of a conspiracy that reached far back into ancient times.

If this was taking place in a Podunk town like Draper, where else might there be branches of the cult? Were they everywhere? Did ancient relics, impregnated with dark energy, line the basements of buildings in Washington, D.C.?

How could I fight an organized effort as potentially huge as this one? If I escaped, how could I evade others of their group? Were they controlling everything? Was my hope of freedom just a cruel joke?

"Consuela, what will I do once I'm out of here? Who can I go to for help?" She laughed a harsh laugh. It was the kind of laugh people use to mock one another. "If you get out of here. If! You will have to rely on your inner sight. If that fails you, you will die."

Meet Sadie Richards. Maybe she's just a little white trash girl from Texas, but she ain't about to let no pussy-grabbin' politician tell her what to do!

A HellBound Books LLC
Publication

www.hellboundbookspublishing.com